THE AMBER PHOTOGRAPH

THE AMBER PHOTOGRAPH

A NOVEL

Penelope J. Stokes

WORD PUBLISHING
NASHVILLE
A Thomas Nelson Company

THE AMBER PHOTOGRAPH
Copyright © 2001 Penelope J. Stokes.

Published by Word Publishing, a division of Thomas Nelson, Inc.,
P.O. Box 141000, Nashville, Tennessee 37214.

Library of Congress Cataloging-in-Publication Data

Stokes, Penelope J.
    The amber photograph : a novel / Penelope Stokes.
      p. cm.
    ISBN 0-8499-3722-1 (alk. paper)
    I. Title.
PS3569.T6219 A79 2001
813'.54—dc21   2001017799

ISBN 0-8499-4283-7 (hardcover)
ISBN 0-8499-3722-1 (trade paper)

Printed in the United States of America
01 02 03 04 05 06 PHX 9 8 7 6 5 4 3 2 1

Prologue

"Twirl me around, Sissy!"

Recklessly they twirled, the two of them, hands linked together. "Spin me faster! Faster!" The older girl, nearly grown, threw her head back and laughed in childlike abandonment as the young one lifted her feet from the earth and began to soar.

"We're flying, Sissy! We're flying!"

And fly they did, until it seemed as if all movement suspended and only the world around them kept whirling.

At last, exhausted and breathless, they flung themselves to the ground and lay silent on the soft summer grass, watching the sky circle above them. The great blue dome, split into wedges by tree branches overhead, reeled down to stillness like the big prize wheel at the county fair. Slower, slower, until the universe ground to a halt and righted itself . . .

She jerked awake, her breathing heavy and labored. Without the briefest moment of internal prodding, she recalled every vivid detail of the dream. She knew it by heart, had dreamed it a thousand times in the past twenty years. Even in daylight, the image hovered at the edges her mind, a misplaced photograph in sepia and amber tones, urging her to turn the page of some unseen album and remember it all.

But she could not remember.

And none of it made sense. This vision was no nightmare—it was a benign likeness of two happy youngsters, a joyful image—perhaps even a benediction. Still, something about it gnawed at her, tore at her soul. She always awoke in tears, vaguely aware of a nameless emptiness, a black void, a vast yawning chasm that threatened to swallow her whole.

She could not let it go. Despite the pain, she clutched the dream with the determination of a child, drawing it close the way she held her pillow for comfort, weeping until the dream itself grew damp and cold against her cheek.

It was all she had left of her sister.

Part 1

~⌒~

The Spinning Dream

Dreams, like faith,
arise from deep within and far beyond us.
We hold to them
no firmer than we grasp the dawn
or anchor ourselves to wind.
Dreams, like faith, escape us,
and yet the gift,
hidden where only the heart can find it,
still remains.

I

The Intruder

HEARTSPRING, NORTH CAROLINA
APRIL 1995

Cecilia McAlister held her breath against the agonizing stab that shot through her. She shifted in the velvet chaise and tried to sit upright. When the pain subsided, she straightened the afghan and lay back on the pillows, breathing heavily. The slightest movement was a monumental effort now; just getting from the bed to the chaise could sap her energy for half a day.

Still, she was determined not to give in. The hospital bed—that hideous metal monster with its electronic controls, brought into this room eight months ago and installed in the corner—was her coffin. If she stayed there, she would die; she was certain of it. As long as she could get up and move to the chaise, have Vesta fix her hair and put on a little makeup, wear a nice bed jacket, hold a book on her lap, she might fend off the Intruder for a little while longer. It was a futile deception, but at least for the time being she might fool Death into believing he still had a fight on his hands.

Her breath came a little easier, and Cecilia looked around what once had been the music room of the massive house. What echoes this room held, with its grand piano and big bay windows looking over the garden. Memories of singing and laughter and voices calling her name. When she sat like this, with her back to the hospital bed, she could almost believe things were now as they once had been. She could see flowers blooming beyond the patio and watch spring storms building over the mountain vistas beyond. From the very beginning, this one room had been her refuge, her sanctuary, the single corner of the world where she felt alive and whole and—

She could barely think the word: *normal.* Nothing had been normal for years. And now, facing the inevitable repossession of her soul, Cecilia was forced to consider what might have been, if only she had claimed the power, years ago, to say "no" to her husband. No to his grandiose dreams, his ambition. No to his vision of what their life should be. No to—well, to a lot of things.

But no one—not even a wife—said "no" to Duncan McAlister. When he had built this house thirty years ago, he had claimed he was doing it for *her*—a doting husband giving the wife he loved a grand home.

But she knew the truth then as she knew it now—this house had never been built for *her*. It was Duncan McAlister's giant billboard, a huge, hulking "I-told-you-so" to all the people in his past who had called him a nobody, the good-for-nothing son of an alcoholic and abusive father.

Well, he had done it. He was rich. He was Somebody. A real estate mogul. Mayor of one of the Top Ten Small Towns in America. An icon. An idol. There was even talk of erecting a statue in his honor on the neatly trimmed town square.

Her husband had proved himself, Cecilia mused. But what had become of the man she had married, the gentle, wounded, compassionate boy who haunted her memories? Had he ever really existed, or had he only been a product of fantasy and imagination and wishful thinking?

She willed the question away. She didn't have enough years left—or enough energy—to answer all of life's dilemmas. You couldn't pull every loose thread, or the whole thing would unravel.

Death had a way of bringing life into focus, of distilling out peripheral concerns and leaving you with pure, undiluted, pristine truth. A truth that had to be spoken—now, quickly, while there was still time.

A line from Keats wandered through her drug-fogged mind: *Truth is beauty; beauty, truth . . .*

Cecilia shook her head. It sounded high and noble, such poetry, but until you had everything stripped away and were left with nothing but your last gasping breaths and a world centered in pain, you couldn't begin to imagine how infernally ugly reality could be.

The truth might set you free, but first it would drag you through hell and back.

2

The Dreamer

A narrow shaft of sunlight pierced the slit between the closed curtains and invaded Diedre McAlister's left eye. Groaning, she threw one arm over her face, but there was no escaping it. The shaft of light pierced through until she could see the road map of blood-red vessels silhouetted against the thin flesh of her eyelids.

She rolled toward the wall and pulled the covers up higher. It was no use. Sleep might offer a few blessed hours of respite, of welcome oblivion, but morning always came again, bringing with it pain. Duty. Worry. Responsibility. A mother dying by inches from the ravages of cancer. Ubiquitous reminders of the fact that Diedre was losing, one tortured breath at a time, the person she loved most in the universe.

It was too much for a twenty-four-year-old to bear.

Then she remembered. Today was her birthday. She was twenty-five. Twenty-five going on seventy, if the weariness in her body were any indication.

She heard the creak of hinges as the bedroom door opened, the scrabbling of toenails against the hardwood floor. A leap, a thump, and then a series of joyous canine grunts. Diedre caught a whiff of dog breath and felt a warm tongue licking her cheek and ear.

She groaned again, opened her eyes, and struggled to a sitting position. "All right, Sugarbear; take it easy, girl. I'm getting up."

The dog pawed playfully at the covers and thrust her muzzle under Diedre's hand, and Diedre felt a rush of warmth well up in her. A shelter pup, primarily a mix of cocker and Lhasa, Sugarbear was the original dumb blonde—not the brightest bulb in the chandelier, but intensely loving and loyal. And despite the abuse and neglect heaped upon her by her previous owners, the beast was blessed with a disposition that made Pollyanna look like a curmudgeon. She had been with them for ten years, and no matter what Diedre's emotional state, she could always count on Sugarbear to make her smile. Prozac with paws.

The bedroom door opened a little farther, and a seamed and wrinkled brown face peered around the doorjamb. "You awake, honey?"

"I am now." Diedre propped the pillows against the headboard, moved Sugarbear to one side, and motioned Vesta Shelby to enter the room. Vesta had been with the McAlisters for ages, and Diedre adored her. To a little girl who had grown up as an only child, Vesta represented an eternal, apparently inexhaustible source of unconditional love and uncritical acceptance.

The stooped old woman pushed her way into the room bearing a tray loaded with scrambled eggs, bacon, and—Diedre's favorite—French toast made from cinnamon challah bread.

"What's all this?"

"It's your birthday breakfast, of course." Vesta set the tray on Diedre's lap and eased into a small chair that sat next to the bed. "Surely you didn't think your old Vesta would forget your birthday."

"To tell the truth, I wish people *would* forget. I don't exactly feel like celebrating."

"You don't mean that, honey. Just 'cause your mama's sick don't mean you stop livin'."

"How is Mama this morning?"

"'Bout the same, I reckon. Eat your breakfast, now, before it gets cold."

"Maybe I should—" Diedre pushed back the quilt and started to get up.

"You can't make her well by worryin'," Vesta said firmly. "I took her medicine to her an hour ago. She'll sleep for a while yet. Now, eat."

Diedre relented, transferring half the eggs onto the French toast plate and rearranging the breakfast to accommodate two. "You *are* going to help me eat all this, aren't you?"

Vesta pulled the chair in closer and accepted the plate Diedre held out in her direction. "I can't hardly believe my baby is twenty-five years old."

"I haven't been a baby for some time, Vesta."

The old woman smiled and winked at her. "You'll always be *my* baby. You should know that by now." She raised a warning finger toward the dog. "Get off the bed, Sugarbear," she commanded in her sternest voice. "You can't have people food."

In response, Sugarbear edged closer and held very still, gazing up at Diedre with soulful eyes. "Just one little piece," Diedre said, breaking a slice of bacon in half. The dog wagged all over.

"It ain't good for her."

"It's not good for me, either, if you want to get technical. But I'm going to eat it anyway."

Vesta laughed, and Sugarbear, aware that she had won this round of the ongoing begging controversy, gulped down the bacon before Vesta had a chance to protest again.

When the meal was finished, Diedre laid the tray aside and let Sugarbear lap up the remains from the china plates.

"You know your Daddy don't like her doing that."

Diedre shrugged. "What Daddy doesn't know won't kill him. Besides, it saves *you* time. Now you won't have to rinse everything before it goes in the dishwasher." She took a sip of coffee, leaned back, and sighed. Sugarbear settled on top of the blanket, as close to her human as she could possibly get. Absently Diedre stroked the dog's head. "You need a grooming, girl," she murmured. "Just look at that mustache, poking out in all directions."

"She's going to Dapper Dogs for a bath and trim tomorrow morning," Vesta answered. "And if you ask me, you could do with a little sprucing up, too."

"I haven't had time."

"You haven't *taken* time, you mean." Vesta reached out a shaky hand and fondled a wayward curl behind Diedre's ear. "You ain't been out of this house in who knows how long. Miss Celia won't mind you takin' a little time to yourself."

In exactly the same way Sugarbear nuzzled in to be petted, Diedre found herself leaning in to Vesta's touch on her neck. For a moment, just a heartbeat, she became a little girl again, recalling what it felt like to be safe and comforted, free of the anxieties of adult life. Then she sat up and ran a hand through her unruly hair. "You don't like my hairdo?"

Vesta chuckled and tugged on the curl. "I think you could use a new cut." Her smile faded, and her dark eyes went sad. "I can take care of your mama, honey. You don't have to be here twenty-four hours a day. Why don't you go down to Asheville, buy a birthday present for yourself, maybe have lunch with your little friend Carlene?"

Diedre smiled inwardly at Vesta's description of Carlene as "her little friend." Nothing about Carlene Donovan could justifiably be described as "little." A large, exuberant woman given to wearing purple and red and fuchsia, Carlene was the flamboyant, extroverted yang to Diedre's subdued yin. She had been Diedre's best friend since undergraduate school, and they had remained close even while Diedre was at Duke pursuing her master's. For the past five years Carlene had taken it as her personal mission in life to teach Diedre how to dream big. She had almost succeeded.

Carlene's most recent dream—and, by extension, Diedre's—was to open a shop in Biltmore Village. A boutique called Mountain Arts, dedicated to featuring the work of local painters and sculptors. Now that

Diedre had completed her education, she and Carlene were ready to begin the process of opening the shop. Their plan was to be equal partners in the venture—Carlene would run the shop and do most of the buying, while Diedre, who had put up most of the money for the place, would pursue freelance photography and display and sell her prints. It would be an instant success, Diedre was certain—if for no other reason than the compelling force of Carlene's personality.

They had gone as far as making an offer to purchase a storefront a block down from Holy Trinity Cathedral, and during her last semester of grad school, Diedre had begun to do Internet searches for a house of her own. But when Mama's cancer had returned, Diedre had put the dream on hold and come home to Heartspring, leaving Carlene to do the legwork in Asheville.

For a minute or two Diedre let herself revel in the idea of spending the day in Asheville. It was a beautiful spring morning, and she desperately longed to get away—to sit with Carlene on the terrace at La Paz, their favorite Mexican restaurant, soaking in the sunshine and the ambiance of Biltmore Village. But she couldn't. Given her mother's condition, it was out of the question.

"Why don't you call Carlene and make a day of it?" Vesta prompted.

"You know I hate shopping," Diedre hedged. It was the truth, but only part of the truth. How could she say to Vesta what she could barely admit to herself? Mama was still sick. Diedre's life was still in limbo. The burden of responsibility still circled over her like a vulture waiting for its prey to drop. A shopping spree, a new haircut, or a lunch with Carlene wasn't going to change anything.

Coming home had been the right thing to do, Diedre was certain of that. But after four years of college and two years of grad school, living under her parents' roof again had engendered a kind of schizophrenic division in her, a languishing of soul she could neither overcome nor control. She could no longer be who she perceived herself to be—an independent woman of twenty-five, with two university degrees and a bright future ahead of her. Instead, she had by sheer force of will taken on the roles of both parent and child. Her mother now depended upon her, and once again her father's overbearing protectiveness threatened to smother her.

She was trapped—locked in a gilded cage, perhaps, but imprisoned nevertheless. And even though love had compelled Diedre to volunteer for the duty, she still felt shell-shocked, captive to a war that seemed to have no end.

She changed the subject. "Is Daddy home?"

"Mr. Mayor? He hightailed it outta here about seven-thirty this morning. Said something about a breakfast meeting with a bunch of those real estate investors." Vesta frowned. "He needs to be here, with his wife, where he belongs."

Her eyes widened suddenly, as if she had shocked herself with this outburst. Diedre, however, was not surprised. This might be the first time she had ever heard Vesta speak an unguarded word about her employer, but with Vesta, words weren't always necessary to convey her innermost thoughts.

"Give him a break, Vesta," Diedre said softly. "He's hurting, too; he just doesn't know how to show it. It's hard for him, watching her like—like this."

Still, Diedre had to admit that she felt the same way about Daddy sometimes. He was loving and concerned, even to the point of smothering her. She had spent years trying to convince him that she was an adult, capable of taking care of herself. But occasionally, she caught a glimpse of something in him that held back. Something hidden, as if he nursed some secret wound that rendered him incapable of giving himself fully. He had been this way with Mama of late. Apparently watching her waste away was simply too much for him to bear, and so his only choice was to withdraw, to take his pain to work and bury it there.

"You look tired, honey," Vesta said, interrupting Diedre's thoughts.

"I didn't get much sleep."

"Worrying about your Mama?"

"Yes." Diedre paused. "And the dream."

"You been having that dream a lot since you came back home."

Diedre nodded. It made sense, she supposed, that returning to the house of her childhood would resurrect what she had always called the Spinning Dream. In the vision, she was young, maybe three or four years old. The other girl, she was pretty sure, was the older sister she had never known.

For years the dream had haunted her. But no one ever wanted to talk about it. It made Mama cry and made Daddy sullen and silent. At last she had given up with everybody except Vesta.

"Tell me about Sissy."

Vesta shook her head. "It don't do no good, resurrecting the dead." Although the words were harsh, the tone was kind, compassionate. Almost wistful.

"But I need to know, Vesta. She was my *sister*."

Vesta gathered up the breakfast tray and got to her feet. "Why don't you get cleaned up and go see your Mama? She'll be awake by now."

She paused at the door and turned back toward Diedre, her ancient eyes watering. "You need to let it go, child," she declared. "It don't have to mean nothing. Sometimes a dream is just a dream."

3

The Photograph

Diedre paused outside the music room and listened at the door. If Mama was sleeping, she would come back later. But she didn't hear the shallow, rasping snore that had grown steadily worse as her mother's lung capacity had declined. All was silent.

She pushed the door open a crack and peered in. Mama lay on the chaise with her eyes closed and a book turned upside down on her lap. Diedre felt a jolt in her chest, as if her heart had stopped beating for a second or two. Every time she entered this room she held her breath, hoping that her mother wouldn't just slip away without a chance to say good-bye.

Protracted dying wore on everybody in different ways. Daddy was in denial, going about his business as if his wife of more than forty years had merely holed herself up in the music room to finish reading a compelling book or to decide on a new wallpaper pattern. Vesta—always there, always faithful and loving—had steadfastly refused to take part in any discussion of what would happen when "Miss Celia" finally passed over. And Diedre found herself vacillating between the two—longing to flee, wishing she could take refuge in denial—but able to do neither with any degree of success.

Six months earlier, before the pain medication had been increased, Diedre and her mother had talked about dying. "Don't let them put me on any machines," Mama had made her promise. "No more surgery, no more chemo. I've had enough. Just keep me comfortable and let me go."

The cancer had first appeared three years ago in the right breast, but Mama adamantly refused to allow Diedre to leave college during the last semester of her senior year. After a double mastectomy, the doctors seemed to think she might be able to beat it—she was not yet sixty, and a prime candidate for survival. But then the tumors began to appear—in the lungs, in the liver, in the pancreas. It was like fighting mildew in a shower stall, Mama said—you scrub and scrub, but when you come back a day later, there it is again. Different corner, same mess.

And so Diedre had put her own dreams on hold and returned to Heartspring. Mama had held on for nine months, but she was beginning to lose the battle. Diedre could see it in her mother's eyes, hear it in every labored breath, feel it in the paper-dry touch of those trembling fingers. Even smell it in the odor of antiseptic and decay that lingered in the corners of the room.

Well-meaning friends said Diedre was lucky—or blessed, depending upon their religious beliefs and philosophies. Here she was given the opportunity to spend time with Mama, to express all those unsaid feelings, to say a proper farewell.

But despite months of grieving the inevitable loss, Diedre knew she wasn't really prepared for that moment. She would never be prepared. How do you steel your heart to let go of someone you love?

"Mama? Are you awake?" As Diedre pushed the door open a little farther, Sugarbear shoved past her and launched herself onto the chaise lounge where her mother lay. "Bad dog!" Diedre hissed. "Get down!"

"Let her be, sweetie."

Mama's eyes didn't open, but one hand reached out slowly to pet the dog's silky ears. Almost as if she understood the situation, Sugarbear settled herself on the edge of the chaise, careful not to crowd her mistress. Her tongue reached up and kissed the hand that stroked her.

"Miss Barrett will receive you now," Mama said wryly, her voice little more than a whisper against the morning.

Diedre smiled. Ever since Mama had been moved to the music room, she had likened herself to Elizabeth Barrett Browning—the elegant invalid, couched with her faithful spaniel Flush upon a velvet chaise, welcoming visitors in proper Victorian majesty.

"How are you feeling this morning?" Diedre pulled a chair up close to the chaise and took her mother's hand.

"Like Death, not quite warmed over." Mama's eyes fluttered open. "Happy birthday, sweetheart."

Tears stung Diedre's eyes. "Let's not talk about my birthday."

Mama frowned. "Why not? It's not every day you turn twenty-five. This is a big day. I have a present for you—the last one I'll ever be able to give you." She pointed toward the bay window. A brightly wrapped box sat on top of the grand piano.

"Mama, how—?"

"Vesta helped me. As always." Diedre's mother struggled to sit upright, and a fit of coughing overtook her so that she couldn't continue for a moment. "My last gift, and my best."

Diedre went over and retrieved the package, then came back to her chair. "Do you want me to open it now, or wait until tonight when Daddy comes home?"

A shadow passed across the woman's face. "Everything is now," she insisted. Her brow furrowed as she summoned the strength to wave a hand. "Open it."

Carefully, Diedre removed the wrapping and opened the package. Inside, in a nest of pale blue tissue paper, lay a scarred wooden cigar box. Nothing more. It had finally happened—in the last throes of the disease, her mother's mind had gone completely. "It's . . . nice, Mama," she stammered.

A flash of fire briefly illuminated Cecilia McAlister's expression. "Not the *box*, Diedre." She rolled her eyes heavenward. "What's *inside* the box. That's your gift. It's what you've always wanted, what I've never been able to give you . . . until now."

Diedre started to lift the lid, but her mother reached out and stopped her.

"Sweetheart, I need to explain something to you . . ."

Diedre stared down at the hand that gripped her own. A claw. A skeleton with skin. Not her mother's hand. She inhaled sharply.

"Yes, Mama? What is it?"

"I should have told you a long time ago. Things . . . aren't what they seem to be."

More than the words, it was the tone of Mama's voice that sent a shock coursing through Diedre, as though someone had shot ice water into her veins.

"What do you mean, Mama?" Against her will, she tried to extract her hand from her mother's grasp.

"Just—" She pointed a trembling finger in the direction of the box. "Open it."

Diedre obeyed. There, in the box, lay an old photograph, yellowed with age and worn around the edges—a black-and-white picture of a small child. An image trapped in amber.

The girl, perhaps four or five years old, sat perched on a man's lap. He leaned back in a ragged, overstuffed chair, and behind them Diedre could make out a dingy living room scene: a sparse Christmas tree and a cardboard fireplace with three stockings pinned to the fake mantle. The girl had dark curly hair and scuffed black shoes with bows on the tops. But it was the face that made Diedre's skin crawl—a round little face with huge brown eyes, white, even baby teeth, and one deep dimple in her left cheek.

Diedre's face.

"It's a difficult thing to lose a parent, Diedre," Mama was saying. "But it's even more terrible to lose a child . . ."

Diedre focused on the photo again. It *could* have been her face, but it *wasn't*. The clothes were all wrong. The room was totally foreign to her. The man, however, seemed familiar. He was smiling broadly, his arms wrapped around the child in an attitude of pure joy.

Then the significance of the picture struck her like a physical blow.

"It's Sissy," she breathed. "My sister! With Daddy!"

"Gone," her mother wheezed, her breath more labored now. "Gone forever." Alarmed, Diedre leaned forward. "Mama, are you all right?"

"I will be . . . now." With monumental effort she reached her hand in the direction of the photograph. "Find yourself," she whispered. "Find your truth." She sagged back against the pillows. "Just don't expect it to be what you thought it would be."

4

The Visitation

Diedre sat on the chaise lounge in the music room and absently fingered the soft cream-colored afghan Mama had made for her more than twenty years ago. In recent months Mama had kept it close, as if holding it and feeling its warmth might chase the chill of death away.

But it hadn't worked. Cecilia McAlister had died in her daughter's arms, here in this very room, and Diedre had been able to do nothing except hold her and watch as the light faded from her eyes.

"I love you, Mama," she whispered to the empty room, just as she had whispered to her mother in those last moments. Diedre had been expecting the moment, waiting for it, fearing it, yet when it came, it left her numb and disbelieving.

The one thing Diedre wanted was the very thing that money couldn't buy, that wishing couldn't retrieve, that even God denied her. Time. Time to say *I love you* again. Time to see her mother's smile and hear her laughter. Time to ask the thousand questions that crowded into her mind.

But there was no time. No time for explanations. No time for grief. The ambulance had finally pulled out of the driveway, taking her mother's lifeless body away, and now Diedre braced herself to be thrust into a frenzy of activity. Decisions had to be made, a funeral planned. Mama might be resting in peace, but the rest of the household was moving into overdrive.

Tired. She was so, so tired.

Heartspring was a small town, but even the largest parlor at Dower and Gray Funeral Home wasn't nearly big enough to accommodate the hundreds of people who would come to pay their last respects. After much discussion with Mr. Dower, Diedre and her father reluctantly decided to give in and hold the visitation at the McAlister home.

That meant food. Caterers. Hiring extra help. Removing Mama's hospital bed from the music room. Getting ready for an onslaught of guests.

The expansive rooms of the big stone mansion might have been more spacious than the Serenity Parlor at Dower and Gray, but the effect was still a little like stuffing sumo wrestlers into a Volkswagen Beetle. It seemed that every one of Heartspring's 3,159 citizens had decided to show up—all at once. Diedre had trouble just negotiating her way from one side of the room to the other. The place was packed with wall-to-wall mourners—at least that was what they were called, according to tradition. A good many of them, as far as Diedre could tell, had apparently come for other reasons than to grieve the passing of Cecilia McAlister from this world into the next.

At first she hadn't noticed it so much. She had been caught up in the daughterly duties of arranging flower sprays, shaking hands, receiving hugs, and trying to suppress fresh tears as she listened to everyone who came through the door tell her what a wonderful, sainted woman her mother had been.

It was true, of course. But every kind word about Mama became a knife-thrust into Diedre's wounded heart, and soon the emotional involvement became too intense to bear. If she caved in now, she'd be in shambles within the hour. Better to disengage, to withdraw a little. The real grieving, no doubt, would come later. For now she simply had to get through this any way she could.

But distancing herself from the pain had its drawbacks. Her attention started to wander, and other concerns began imposing themselves upon her consciousness. She wasn't accustomed to wearing high heels, and her feet ached. Her lower back was beginning to spasm. She needed a break, desperately wanted to get away for a while. Where was Daddy?

She let her gaze wander around the room and finally found him, surrounded three-deep by men in dark business suits, each one jockeying for the honor of standing beside the mayor in his hour of grief. It looked more like a cocktail party or an election fund-raiser than a wake. The women, like elegantly clad Stepford Wives, all seemed to be wearing the same Perfect Little Black Dress and sporting identical strands of pearls at their necklines. Some of the guests were clamoring for Duncan McAlister's attention. Some were huddled together in little clusters, gossiping. Others seemed to be posing for photo ops as a few reporters from the local paper milled about snapping pictures.

Diedre pressed a hand to her temple and closed her eyes for a moment. When she opened them, she found herself staring into the eager, watery eyes of Oliver Ferrell.

He gripped her fingers in a moist, earnest handshake. "Miss McAlister," he said breathlessly, "I am just so, so sorry. Such a loss, such a loss, a terrible, terrible loss. Your dear, dear mother was such a lovely, lovely woman, such a fabulous, fabulous asset to your father's career."

Diedre fought to suppress the grin that tugged at the corners of her mouth. She didn't know Ferrell well, but she had heard Mama and Daddy talk about him often enough. He had been on the City Council for years—the loyal swing vote who made sure that every program Duncan McAlister proposed would be approved without question. Her father had often regaled them with stories about Ferrell, imitating the man's annoying habit of repeating every adverb and adjective at least twice, sometimes three or four times. By the time Daddy was done with one of his Ollie Ferrell impersonations, Diedre and her mother would be doubled over the dinner table, laughing so hard they had to wipe away tears.

Now the memory came flooding back, and Diedre felt herself trying to muffle a snicker. But it was too late. It overtook her before she could stop it—the kind of uncontrollable hysteria that makes you disrupt a church service or blow milk out your nose. She jerked her hand from Ollie's grasp, thrust her face into her handkerchief, and stood there with her shoulders shaking, unable to restrain the convulsions of laugher.

Fortunately, Ollie took her reaction for a fresh outpouring of grief. He patted her awkwardly on the arm and tried to console her. "Oh my, oh my, oh my," he murmured. "There, there, Miss McAlister. We will all miss your wonderful, wonderful mother so very, very much. Her passing, her untimely passing, her terrible untimely passing leaves such a void, such a vast, vast void, in our little community."

He paused, apparently waiting for some response, but Diedre was laughing so hard that no sound came out, just a series of high-pitched, breathless little squeals.

"We all share your pain, your deep, deep pain," Ollie tried.

"Th-thank you," Diedre managed, her face still buried in the hand-kerchief.

"Excuse me," a deep voice interrupted. "I think Miss McAlister needs to be alone for a few minutes."

A firm hand steered Diedre away from the crowd and into the library across the hall. When the door shut behind them, Diedre looked up to see Jackson Underwood grinning down at her.

"Uncle Jack!" she exploded in relief. "Thanks for . . . rescuing me." She put a hand to her chest, fighting for air.

He folded his arms. "Ollie Ferrell's quite a piece of work, isn't he?"

"I couldn't help myself, Uncle Jack. He was just there, spouting out all those adjectives, and I—" She dissolved into laughter again and sank into a leather armchair.

"Why don't we just sit in here for a few minutes until you regain your sense of decorum?"

Diedre sighed. "I think that's an excellent idea. Could I get something to drink, do you suppose?"

"There's punch and coffee in the dining room. Which do you want?"

"Something cold, please. I'd rather have a Diet Pepsi if you can find one, but otherwise punch will be fine."

"I'll be right back."

He opened the door, and a wave of noise rolled toward her, indistinguishable voices that from this distance sounded like the chattering of geese on a riverbank. When the door closed again, silence washed over her like healing waters. Good old Uncle Jack. Always dependable. Always around when you needed him.

Jackson Underwood wasn't her real uncle, but he had been a friend of the family since before Diedre was born. As Daddy's attorney, business associate, closest confidant, and sometime campaign manager, Jack had been present for every McAlister family celebration, fund-raiser, election banquet, and funeral for more than twenty-five years. He had three ex-wives but no children and had become Diedre's unofficial "bachelor uncle" so long ago that he might as well be kin. And he always treated her as if she were the most important person in his world.

It was rumored around Heartspring that Jack Underwood was something of a womanizer. Diedre didn't know that for sure, but given his trim physique, quick wit, and charismatic personality, she wouldn't be surprised if women threw themselves at him. He had a way about him, a kind of effortless charm that made people instantly comfortable in his presence. Maybe it was that brilliant smile of his. He laughed readily, and although he had to be close to Daddy's age, he seemed ten years younger.

Yes, she guessed, he would undoubtedly be considered quite a catch. But no one had caught him since his last divorce, which had been more than fifteen years ago.

The library door opened, and Uncle Jack entered the room balancing two crystal punch cups and a small plate heaped with finger sandwiches and cake. "I thought you might be hungry." He sat in the chair opposite hers and extended the plate.

Diedre waved the food away. "I couldn't eat. But thanks for the punch." She sipped at the pink liquid, a combination of lemonade and grape juice which tasted vaguely like the SweetTarts candy she used to love as a child.

She looked at Jack and tried to consider him objectively, as if she hadn't known him all her life. He was handsome, she concluded with surprise. She had never really noticed that before—

"Is something wrong?" He ran a hand through his hair. "You're staring."

"No, I—" Diedre shrugged. "Sorry."

"I know, this is all so difficult." He grinned and winked at her. "So very, very, terribly, terribly difficult."

Jack's imitation of Ollie Ferrell wasn't as good as Daddy's, but Diedre chuckled nevertheless.

He took her hand and squeezed it. "So, how are you doing, kiddo?"

"All right, I guess." She let out a sigh. "For a while I was running on adrenaline, I think, but my supply is used up. I'm exhausted."

"The funeral's tomorrow. Then things will get back to normal."

Back to normal. The words echoed in her head like a foreign language, elusive sounds she should be able to understand but couldn't get her mind to comprehend. It had been so long since anything had seemed normal—with her mother's illness and then coming home to help with her care—that Diedre couldn't remember what that felt like. And now *without* Mama, she couldn't imagine life ever being normal again.

A light knock sounded on the door, and it opened to reveal a long-legged, attractive blonde in the requisite black dress and pearls—but with significantly more makeup than the other Stepfords. "There you are." She sidled in Jack's direction, casting a desultory glance at Diedre. "Busy, Jack?"

"Does it look like I'm busy?"

The blonde arched one immaculately tweezed eyebrow. "It looks like you've cornered someone half your age. Really, Jack!"

He set his punch on the table and took a step in the woman's direction. "This is Diedre McAlister," he said, speaking slowly and deliberately, as if to a very stupid child. "Mayor McAlister's daughter."

A confused look came over the woman's face. "Oh. Sorry."

Uncle Jack rolled his eyes. "Diedre, this is Pamela Langley, my new secretary."

"Legal assistant," Pamela corrected with a vacant smile. She shook Diedre's outstretched hand with the tips of her manicured fingers. "A pleasure to make your acquaintance. Nice party." She turned her attention back to Jack and lowered her eyelids to half-mast. "Isn't it about time we were leaving?"

Jack frowned and cut a glance in Diedre's direction. "Not now, Pamela—"

Diedre waved a hand. "Never mind, Uncle Jack. Go on. I'm sure you've got work to do. It's all right."

"You'll be OK?" he asked.

"Of course. I need to get back to our guests, anyway."

Diedre stood to see them out, but before they could make their exit, a large, familiar figure blocked the doorway of the library.

"Carlene!" Diedre reached out a hand toward her best friend. "Come in!"

Carlene Donovan shouldered past Pamela Langley and Jack and drew Diedre into an exuberant hug. "Sorry it took me so long. I got here as soon as I could."

Diedre held onto her for a minute or two, then stepped back to look at her. She was decked out in a flowing tunic and pants of peacock blue and actual miniature peacock feathers dangled at her earlobes. With her round face, pixie haircut, and bright silk outfit, she provided a striking contrast to—and relief from—the thin, blonde, black-clad Pamela.

"I'm so glad to see you!" Diedre said, gripping both of Carlene's hands. "You weren't there when I called; I wasn't sure you'd get the message."

"I got it, all right. I came as fast as I could."

The legal assistant raked cold eyes up and down Carlene's ample form, making no attempt to camouflage her blatant assessment—and obvious disapproval. If she had spoken aloud, her opinion could not have been more clear: a woman of size and substance, especially one who had the audacity to wear bright colors and carry herself with confidence—had no right to exist in the svelte Miss Langley's world. "Can we leave now?" she whined in Jack's direction without taking her measuring gaze off Carlene.

He cleared his throat. "You go on without me."

The woman's face took on a pinched expression, as if she had just caught a whiff of something distasteful. "If you insist." She straightened his tie and pushed a cocktail napkin into the pocket of his suit coat. "I'm not going back to the office. Here's my new cell phone number. Call me later."

Jack hustled her out the door and turned back toward Diedre. "Sorry." He lifted his shoulders in a shrug, then offered his hand to Carlene. "I don't believe we've met. I'm Jack Underwood."

"This is Carlene Donovan, my best friend from Asheville," Diedre said. "Carlene, this is my Uncle Jack."

"Your *uncle?*"

"In name only, I'm sorry to say," Jack responded smoothly. "I'm Diedre's father's attorney, and an old friend of the family. You'll be here for a few days, Miss Donovan?"

Carlene nodded. "At least for the funeral."

"Then I'll look forward to seeing you again." He leaned over and kissed Diedre on the forehead. "Bye, honey. I'm going to talk to your dad for a few minutes, and then take off. I'll see you tomorrow."

Diedre watched him go. When she turned back, Carlene was lounging in the leather library chair, shaking all over with laughter.

"What's so funny?"

"Your dashing Uncle Jack and his anorexic model. What a pair."

"They're not a *pair*, Carlene. She's his *secretary*."

"Right. And I'm Cindy Crawford."

"You think they're *together?* I don't believe it."

"Believe what you like." Carlene chuckled. "But they *are* a couple—of some kind, anyway. And from what I just saw, they probably deserve each other."

"That's not a very nice thing to say about my Uncle Jack. He's a very compassionate and generous man."

"If I were a woman anywhere within thirty years of him, I'd watch out." Carlene insisted. "Easy on the eyes, hard on the heart."

5

Daddy's Girl

Diedre lay in the dark and listened. The house was silent. The last of the mourners had drifted back to their respective homes, leaving the refrigerator and freezer stuffed with enough food to feed a small army for the next month and a half. Carlene had returned to Asheville. Vesta had finally gone to bed, and Daddy was no doubt sequestered in his study.

The events of the past few days swirled in her mind. Everything was moving too fast, and with all the chaos—the ambulance, the funeral home, the service and interment, the constant reminders of Mama's absence—Diedre had almost forgotten her birthday gift.

She sat up in bed and turned on the light. The wooden cigar box lay in the drawer of her bedside table. She pulled it out and opened the lid. With one glimpse of the faded, browned photograph of her long-dead sister, images of the Spinning Dream filled her mind, and a sense of loss and loneliness overwhelmed her. She was twenty-five years old, yet she felt like an orphan, a tiny child abandoned and terrified in a threatening and uncertain world.

Her eyes burned with unshed tears, mocking her, tormenting her with the promise of release. But when she tried to let herself cry, no tears would come. She missed her mama. She wanted her daddy. She longed for the sister she had never known.

But Mama was dead, and Daddy was locked up with a private grief she could not share. She clutched the photograph to her chest and held it there, but it brought little comfort.

All her life, Diedre had longed to be close to her father. She was, at heart, a Daddy's girl—or at least she wanted to be. And she couldn't deny that he loved her. He had always doted on her, protected her. But something was missing, something she couldn't quite grasp.

She fingered the amber-toned photograph. No wonder she hadn't recognized the man in the picture right away. He was smiling. Laughing. Maybe even tickling the little girl on his lap. But it wasn't just any little girl. It was Sissy. Her big sister. And the two of them together looked like the perfect portrait of father and daughter.

This was what she had missed all her life, without any words to express it. The abandonment. The joy. The freedom of loving and being loved without reservation. Diedre had never seen *that* look on her father's face. With her, there had always been a split second of hesitation, the tiniest fraction of holding back.

At last long-overdue tears welled up in Diedre's eyes and ran down her cheeks. She cried for a long time—sometimes sobbing like a child, sometimes weeping silently. Sugarbear jumped onto the bed and lay beside her, whimpering softly.

Things are not what they seem to be.

Mama's words came back to her, an echo in her mind, and as Diedre considered the photograph, she wondered what Mama had meant. Was it possible that Daddy had once been open and loving, a true father? Had the loss of his firstborn child driven him inward, so that he could not give himself completely to loving his younger daughter? Was it too much of a risk for him, such wholehearted love?

With the death of Mama a fresh wound in her heart, Diedre could almost understand such reticence. Loving deeply opened you to being deeply hurt. And although time, she was told, would ease the immediacy of the pain, it would never erase the scars completely. They stayed forever—reminders, warnings, of what could happen when you gave your heart away.

Mama was gone. Sissy was gone. But Daddy was still here. He was all she had left. Perhaps, deep down, there was still a spark—even a small glimmer—of the Daddy who smiled back at her from this old photograph. Some tender place that could dare to reveal itself now that they only had each other. Maybe they could find a way to be a family.

Diedre couldn't bring back her mother or her sister. But she had to take the chance that she might be able to bring back her father.

What did she have to lose?

Tomorrow, she thought as she set the cigar box aside and settled down to sleep. *I'll talk to him tomorrow.*

6

Sugarbear's Treasure

Diedre awoke to a snuffling sound and a movement on the bed. The illuminated numbers on the clock said 6:55. Outside the window, night was beginning to give way to gray dawn.

"Settle down, you beast," she muttered, reaching a hand to rub Sugarbear's head. "It's too early. Go back to sleep."

The snuffling continued.

She sat up and peered through the half-light at Sugarbear, who was pawing and rooting her nose at something. Diedre flipped on the bed-side lamp. "Sugarbear, no!"

She had gone to sleep with the cigar box next to her on the bed. Now the dog had her snout in the box and was pushing it toward the edge of the mattress. In the instant before it fell, Diedre grabbed it.

"What on earth is the matter with you?" she reprimanded. "Look what you've done—slimy nose prints all over my sister's picture." She wiped the photograph on the blanket, held it to the light, and scrutinized it again. Her sister, looking remarkably like herself in her own baby pictures. Her father, much younger, so loving and attentive that it made Diedre's heart squeeze with unwelcome envy.

She had to stop torturing herself like this. *Just put it back in the box and go to sleep*, she thought. Then her eye fixed on something she hadn't seen before. "What in the world—?"

Sugarbear positioned her furry little face over the box and looked. Beneath the picture, a rectangle of cardboard lay in the cigar box—just about the same size and color of the box itself. Sugarbear's investigation had pushed the cardboard down in one corner. Now Diedre lifted it up and saw that it made a neat little false bottom to the box. And underneath lay a folded paper and a couple of envelopes.

With trembling fingers she unfolded the sheet of heavy-stock paper. At the top, in elaborately scrolled letters, it said:

State of North Carolina
Certificate of Live Birth

Diedre's eyes scanned the document

Child's name: Diedre Chaney McAlister
Gender: Female
DOB: April 3, 1970

It was her birth certificate. But why would there be a copy, and why would Mama keep it in this box, hidden away?

The original was in Diedre's own desk, along with a passport she'd never had a chance to use, a copy of the life insurance policy Daddy had taken out on her when she was six months old, and the telephone numbers of Daddy's insurance agents and stockbrokers.

Then she looked more closely.

Mother's name: Cecilia A. McAlister
Father's name: Unknown

The document blurred in front of her eyes. Diedre blinked. *Unknown?*

Mama's words echoed in her mind: *Things are not what they seem to be . . .*

Diedre knew she ought to slow down, to think through this situation logically. There had to be some rational explanation. But the accelerator on her brain seemed to be stuck; her mind lurched ahead, leaving reason idling at the caution light.

Like a slide show on fast-forward, images began to click into place in her mind: Daddy's faltering attempts to demonstrate his affection. His reserve with her, compared to the love and joy that emanated from the picture of him with Sissy. He had provided for Diedre, lavished her with material gifts, taught her discipline, nearly smothered her with his insistent overprotectiveness. But he couldn't give Diedre the kind of love and warmth he had given her sister, because—

Because he was not her father.

Her breath came in shallow gasps, as if she were drowning. Was it possible that Daddy was not her daddy? That Mama had cheated on him, and Diedre was the fruit of that infidelity?

No wonder she felt like an orphan. If she was not who she believed herself to be—not Diedre McAlister, daughter of Duncan and Cecilia McAlister—then who was she?

And what else had they kept from her?

Diedre laid the birth certificate aside and reached into the cigar box gingerly, as if it contained a mousetrap, or something alive that might bite. She lifted out the envelopes and looked at them—letters, addressed not to "Mr. and Mrs. Duncan McAlister," or even to "Mrs. Duncan McAlister," but to "Cecilia McAlister"—her mother alone, as if she were a single woman.

Were these letters from her birth father, a man her mother loved? The envelopes bore no address, just the name. And they were folded oddly, as if they had been inserted into a second envelope. Her mind raced, jumped to conclusions. A go-between, perhaps. Someone who would keep her mother's dark secret. Maybe even Vesta.

Diedre's hand shook as she stared at the letters, reason grappling with emotion for supremacy. She wanted to know. She didn't want to know. But she *had* to know. She straightened the blanket around her legs and propped a pillow against the headboard of the bed. Mama had given her these documents for a reason.

Was this the truth she wanted Diedre to find? Had Mama been looking for forgiveness, a way to expiate her sins before she met her Maker? The image of Mama with someone else assaulted Diedre's senses, bringing with it a wave of nausea and a chilling sweat. She shivered and pushed the thought away.

Gathering all the nerve she possessed, she opened the first letter and began to read. But if she thought she had met her quota of bombshells for one morning, Diedre realized from the first sentence that there were land mines she hadn't even begun to uncover.

November 1974

Dear Mama,

I'm sending this letter through Vesta so you'll be sure to get it. Forgive me, but I don't trust Daddy not to burn it or keep it for his own purposes.

I'm sorry for the upheaval I caused by coming home again. I didn't mean to hurt anyone, least of all you. At least I got to see little Diedre, and that was almost worth the price I've paid. She is a beautiful child. She can't possibly understand all this, can she?

I'm sure you must be hurting, and probably feeling guilty, too. But, as my doctor keeps telling me, you have to let it go and learn to forgive yourself. Please try—for my sake, and your own.

By the time she finished reading, Diedre was shaking all over. The letter wasn't signed, but it had to be from her sister—the one she had longed for, dreamed about all these years. And apparently she knew all about the circumstances of her little sister's birth! It seemed impossible. Yet here it was, in black and white.

Mama was right. This wasn't the truth she expected to find. And it was almost too much to take. Diedre's father was not her father. Her mother had been unfaithful to him and had borne a child out of that adulterous affair. Her sister had known all about it—and, if the letter was any indication, had not condemned her mother for what she had done.

What else?

She closed her eyes and sent up a silent prayer for strength, then drummed up the nerve to open the second letter.

April 1979

Dear Mama,

This will probably be my last letter from Raleigh. My doctor seems very happy with my progress and is recommending that I be given early release in the next few weeks. Five years is a long time to be hospitalized, and the world outside will probably seem very foreign to me. I hope I'm ready.

I don't think it's a good idea for me to come home when I get out. A friend of mine has offered me a place to live and work, a place where I won't be bothered. I'll change my name and start over, hoping this time will be different. God knows I'm different.

Try not to worry about me, and give D a hug and a kiss. Wish I could be with her—maybe someday. I'll try to keep in touch.

Diedre sat back on the bed, stunned, and her eyes focused on selected phrases from the letter: *my doctor . . . hospitalized . . . released in a few weeks*. Daddy had led her to believe that Sissy was dead; even Mama, at the end, had said she was *gone forever*. But here it was, clear as day—her sister had been in a hospital. For five years.

Was it possible she had died after her release? Was that why Diedre's parents had been reluctant to talk about her, to give Diedre any details about her sister's life and death? Yet in the letter, she didn't sound sick. She seemed perfectly well and in control. She appeared to be resigned to her past and determined to make the future better. And she had loved the little sister she barely knew. *Give D a hug and a kiss. Wish I could be with her—maybe someday . . .*

Tears stung at her eyes; Diedre blinked them away and bit her lip. *Someday* had never come. She had never had a chance to know her sister.

The sister who knew the truth about Mama, and about the circumstances surrounding Diedre's birth.

Only the two letters; no more. Precious little information about one whose presence had invaded Diedre's dreams for twenty years. Once she got over the initial shock, it was disappointing, really. She had hoped that when she finally did learn something about her long-dead sister, it would bring her more comfort and closure than this. But all it brought was more questions.

She stared at the letter again. There was something wrong, something about—

The date.

1979?

In 1979, Diedre had been nine years old. But from what little her parents had told her about Sissy, the girl had died when Diedre was very small. Diedre's only memory of her sister had been immortalized in the Spinning Dream, in which she was three or four and Sissy was a teenager, perhaps. But at the time of this letter—she did a quick mental calculation—her sister would have been twenty-four, nearly as old as Diedre was now. A grown woman, not a confused young girl on the brink of adulthood.

Suddenly everything crystallized, like the colors of a kaleidoscope falling into place. The pattern fit, and hope descended upon Diedre in a breathtaking rush.

Her sister was still alive.

7

Truth in the Inward Parts

"Daddy, are you in here?"

Diedre stood at the door of her father's Inner Sanctum and knocked on the half-open door.

"Come on in, honey."

Diedre entered, and her heart constricted with anguish when she caught a glimpse of the man behind the desk—the man she had called "Daddy" for the last quarter-century. His eyes, usually bright with mirth, were now deeply shadowed and rimmed with red. His thick, gray hair needed washing. He looked as if he hadn't slept in a week. Bereavement was taking a heavy toll on him—a grief he apparently could not let his daughter share.

Then she remembered: she was not his daughter.

"I—I need to talk to you," she faltered.

She watched as her father's gaze cut to the corner of the room, and suddenly Diedre realized they were not alone. She turned.

"Uncle Jack!"

"Good morning, Diedre." Jack Underwood came to her and enveloped her in a massive hug. "You doing all right, sweetie?"

"I—I guess so. I didn't realize anyone was here."

"Your father and I had some business to discuss. I can leave if you'd prefer to—"

Out of the corner of her eye, Diedre caught a movement, a quick jerk of her father's chin, as if to tell Uncle Jack, *No, stay.*

She shook her head. "That won't be necessary. As close as you've been to our family all these years, you probably know all about this anyway."

Jack paled visibly, but he managed a smile. "All about what, Diedre?"

Diedre went over to her father's desk and laid the cigar box down. "Mama gave this to me right before she died. Sort of a parting gift of truth, I suppose. I guess she figured it was time I knew."

Her father—Duncan, she corrected herself—opened the box and flipped through the contents.

"Yes. A little going-away present, it seems." His voice shattered over her nerves like falling icicles. "I wish she hadn't done that."

"Daddy—" Diedre's voice choked on the word. "Why didn't you tell me? How could you keep this quiet all these years?"

"Your mother and I had . . . an agreement."

"An agreement?"

"Yes. We—" He groped for words. "We thought it would be best if you didn't know. We wanted you to have a . . . a normal life."

"A normal life?" Adrenaline shot through Diedre's veins, and her voice jumped an octave. "A life based on a lie? I don't know who I am anymore! I feel like the earth has opened up under my feet, and I have no firm place to stand. I need to know the truth, Daddy—all of it."

Uncle Jack stepped to Diedre's side and put an arm around her. "Duncan, I think the girl deserves to have her questions answered. Why don't we have a seat and talk about this calmly?"

"That's a good idea, Jack." Daddy motioned to the two leather chairs in front of his desk. "Let's all sit down."

While Diedre and Jack settled themselves, Duncan went to the sideboard and poured coffee. He handed Diedre a cup. When she took it, her hands were shaking.

He sat behind his desk. "Now, Diedre," he said softly, his eyes meeting hers, "why don't you tell us what this is all about?"

"I think you both know what it is about." She leaned across the desk and took a folded sheet of paper from the cigar box and handed it to Jack. "Here, you're the lawyer. Is this or is it not my birth certificate?"

Jack scanned the paper and passed it on to Daddy. "It appears to be."

"Then this man—" Diedre pointed at Duncan, "is not my real father."

Daddy looked at the certificate, then back to Diedre. He glanced at Jack, who raised one eyebrow quizzically.

"Honey," he said finally, looking into her eyes, "it was not our intention—your mother's or mine—to deliberately deceive you." He spread his hands, palms up, a gesture of contrition. "At the end, I'm afraid Cecilia wasn't thinking clearly, else she would not have burdened you with this. But since it's out in the open now—" he leaned forward entreatingly, "ask anything you want, and I'll answer it."

Ask anything. The words reverberated in Diedre's head and she felt herself relax a little. Finally, she was going to get some answers. But there was so much she needed to know, so many gaps to fill in. She wasn't quite sure where to begin—or how.

She took a deep breath. "All right, let's start with the birth certificate. It says *Mother: Cecilia McAlister. Father: Unknown.* I assume that to mean you, Daddy, are not my real father. That Mama had—" she balked at the word, then summoned her strength to finish, "an affair. That you decided to raise me as your child, and that you, Uncle Jack, complied in the deception so that no one would ever find out the truth."

Neither man said a word, but an inscrutable expression passed between them.

"I suppose I should thank you," Diedre continued, conscious of the need to remain calm, to keep her voice down. "You had no real responsibility to support me, but you did it anyway. My upbringing, my education. Why did you do it?"

Duncan shifted in his chair. "As I said, your mother and I came to an agreement. We wanted to protect you, to do what was right for you, and we thought it was in your best interests to keep the past in the past."

An odd sense of detachment came over Diedre, as if she were looking down on the scene from a great height. "But you are Sissy's real father."

Duncan nodded. "Yes."

"I should have realized," she said, trying to keep her voice from trembling. "It's so obvious in the picture, how much you loved her. And you loved me, too, I know that, but I always suspected something wasn't quite right—I felt it, instinctively. Mama was so loving and nurturing, but you—you were always a little—I don't know. Tentative."

"I—I just—" He stopped abruptly and ran a hand over his eyes.

Diedre stared at him. Was he . . . *crying?* Clearly, he had cherished his elder daughter, and something—something terrible—had happened. And then, at age forty, he had taken on responsibility for a child who wasn't even his.

"I know this is difficult, Daddy—" She stumbled over the word, uncertain whether she should use it any longer. But she pressed on. "It's hard for me, too, finding out after all this time that my family has lived a lie for the past twenty-five years. Sissy knew the truth about the, ah, circumstances of my conception."

"Is that what you think?"

"I think she knew who my real father was. And I think you do, too."

A shadow passed over his weary countenance. "Don't do this, Diedre. Please. Don't smear your mother's memory. Don't exhume old skeletons. Leave the past buried, where it belongs."

"I can't, Daddy. Don't you see that I *have* to know?"

Uncle Jack fingered the letters that lay in the pile on Duncan's desk. "What do these letters say?"

Diedre turned in his direction. "That Sissy didn't die when I was a very young child, as I have been told. That she was still alive—at least in 1979. That she spent time in a hospital in Raleigh." She swiveled around to confront her father. "Is she alive, Daddy? What happened to her? Tell me the truth."

Her father shrugged. "I honestly don't know. It's been years—"

"But you *loved* her! You adored her. I know you did. I can see it in your eyes!" She picked up the photograph and waved it in his direction. "What could she possibly have done to cause you to turn your back on her—your own flesh and blood?"

"Yes, I loved her." Duncan sighed heavily. "But tell me, Diedre—if you were a parent, and one of your children was, well, troubled, would you want your other children—especially an impressionable young girl who idolized her big sister—to be exposed to that kind of influence? Is that the kind of role model you'd want for your own daughter?"

Diedre closed her eyes and took in a ragged breath. "She was—unstable? And that's why you'd never talk about her—why you let me believe she was dead? You wanted to keep me from finding her—from discovering the truth—even after I was old enough to handle it?"

"I had no choice."

"Of course you had a choice!" she choked out, fighting the tears. "Did you think I was unaware of those hushed conversations that were cut off midsentence as soon as I entered the room? Didn't you listen when I told you about the dreams, the vague memories of a sister who had just vanished into the shadows? How am I supposed to decide now what to believe?"

"You adored her, Diedre. Even as a baby, you worshiped her. We had to protect you. We couldn't take the chance that you might—"

"Might grow up to be like her? Might find out what secrets she held about Mama and my real father?"

He shook his head. "Might disappear and never be seen again."

An icy finger ran up Diedre's spine. "What did she do, Daddy? Besides knowing the truth about my birth, I mean?" She braced herself for the answer, not sure if she really wanted to hear it.

He rose from behind the desk and came over to where Diedre sat.

Kneeling down beside her, he took her hand and stroked it gently. "She snapped, honey. Just went over the edge."

Diedre frowned at him, her heart a lump of lead in her chest. "If she was mentally unstable, Daddy, she needed help, not condemnation. Why did you send her away? Did she threaten to expose Mama's infidelity? To ruin your reputation?"

He leveled a chilling gaze on her.

"She tried to kidnap you."

❦

Vesta held on tight and prayed for the Good Lord's wisdom. "Honey, you got to stop this. You're gonna make yourself sick."

Still weeping, the poor girl shifted on Vesta's bed and allowed Vesta to cradle her like a little child. Vesta rocked back and forth, singing under her breath. "Calm yourself, now," she murmured. "Everything's gonna be all right."

"Vesta, you've got to tell me what you know," Diedre sobbed.

"All right, baby." She stroked the girl's back and kissed the top of her head. "Reckon it won't hurt anything now that your mama's gone."

"What was she like?"

"Your big sister? She was God's own sweet child."

"Was she very ill? Crazy? Violent?"

The old woman pulled away and frowned at Diedre. "What do you mean?"

"Daddy said she snapped. Went over the edge. She was in some sort of hospital for years. Was she—you know, not all right?"

Vesta shook her head sadly, hesitating. The memory gnawed an empty hole in her stomach, and she pressed one hand to her belly. "Till she was 'bout twelve, thirteen, she was a regular angel. Loved everybody. Had a laugh like heavenly chimes. Then something happened—I ain't quite sure what. She changed."

"Changed how?"

"She got sullen. Withdrawn. Almost never smiled. Started sneaking out at night, disobeying. Your mama and daddy couldn't deal with her anymore."

"But what about you, Vesta? Couldn't you help her? *You* loved her."

"I did love her, child. But I wasn't here."

Diedre swiped at her eyes and stared at Vesta. "But I thought you had worked for Mama and Daddy since long before I was born."

"That's right. After your daddy built this fine house, when your sister was just a little bit—maybe eight or nine—I come to work for your folks. By the time she was gettin' on toward a teenager, though, I wasn't needed so much anymore, and my own mama was sick with the cancer and needed tending. But I couldn't rightly afford to quit. That's when Mr. Duncan gave me a leave of abstinence."

"You mean leave of *absence?*"

"That's it. He told me to go on home and nurse my mama, and he'd keep on paying my wages, long as I agreed to come back if they needed me again. I felt kinda funny about it, like it was charity or something, but Mr. Duncan, he's a generous man. He made me feel like I was doing him a favor. I was gone nigh onto a year, and he paid my salary every month, just like clockwork."

"So you weren't here when she was sent away."

Vesta shook her head. "I heard about it, though, and I was real sad. Then, after my mama went on to heaven, your daddy called and asked could I come work again. I'd heard that your mama nearbout died of sorrow when that little girl went away—kept to herself for months on end. Then the Good Lord gave them another little baby to take that poor child's place. That was you, honey—kind of a late-life surprise, I guess. And Miss Celia, she needed help. So I come back."

Vesta paused. There were some things she couldn't tell—like how Miss Celia didn't seem too happy about the baby, how she just cried and cried. For a while Vesta had thought it was just what Mr. Duncan called "post-partial depression"—the blues a woman sometimes gets after a baby is born. But it went on so long, and Miss Celia cried so much. Just like her heart was breaking, or like she had some big old sin weighing her down—something she could never get forgiveness for.

"And when you returned, my sister was gone," Diedre prompted.

"Yes, bless her heart. They sent her down to Charlotte, Miss Celia told me, to stay with your Aunt Edith and go to some clinic there. She stayed gone a long time. Then, when you were about three or four, I guess, she showed up again—just appeared at the door, out of the blue." Vesta stroked Diedre's hair. "She adored you. And you took to her like a baby duck to a puddle."

Diedre closed her eyes and felt herself relaxing, just a little. "I took to her," she murmured.

Vesta leaned back and held the girl at arm's length. "But then she was gone again—and everyone was all angry and scared—your Mama, your Daddy. Scared she'd hurt you, maybe. I don't even know what happened, sweetie. I just know she never came back. Your daddy said she snapped. Maybe. I don't know."

Vesta exhaled a deep sigh. For the better part of twenty-five years she had done her best to protect this child from the danger and ugliness of the world. But it hadn't worked. Not money or privilege or love or even faith could shield the soul from truth.

Diedre flexed her shoulders and took a deep breath. "Vesta, in that box was my real birth certificate. Everything seems the same except that it doesn't say who my real father is. It says, 'unknown.'"

"Your *real father?*" Vesta felt a shock run up her spine, just like the time she touched a frayed light cord that was still plugged into the wall.

Diedre nodded. "When Mama told me, right before she died—or at least gave me the box—she wanted me to know. Daddy's not my real father. You didn't know?"

"I never heard a word breathed about it."

"Sissy knew. She knew everything. But she's either dead, or so far gone I'll never see her again."

Vesta got up from the bed and went to the dresser. With her back turned to Diedre, she blinked back her tears and screwed up her courage.

For a minute or two she rummaged in the top drawer, then found what she was looking for and handed it to Diedre. "Maybe she's not as far gone as you think."

❧

Diedre stared at the picture postcard.

Her hand trembled so violently that she could barely read the words: *Vesta—Settled and happy—or at least content. Thanks for believing in me when I couldn't believe for myself. Merry Christmas.*

"It's from her? You're sure? There's no name."

Vesta nodded.

Diedre looked at the picture. The front of the postcard showed a parade of boats on the water, illuminated with holiday lights, and a caption that read, *Christmas on Puget Sound.*

"Seattle?"

Vesta stroked her hair. "That's right, hon. Seattle."

Diedre turned to the other side of the postcard and squinted at the faded postmark. December 12, 1989. Her heart hammered painfully. "Six years ago?"

"She's a long ways away," Vesta said. "But she ain't dead. I can feel it in my bones. She's alive."

Part 2

༄

Soul's Journey

A voice calls us out,
beyond the well-lit path
into the darkness.
We follow, trembling,
or trembling stay behind.
But whether we heed the call
and launch into the dim unknown
or cling to the familiar,
we are changed.

8

The Artist

Amber Chaney lay in the darkness, waiting. What she was waiting for, she couldn't have articulated to save her life. Awareness, perhaps. Some flashing lightning bolt of insight that would finally make all the pieces of the puzzle fall into place. Some word from On High interpreting her emotions, sorting things out. Putting a name at last to the emptiness and longing that opened up in her without warning, a worm hole sweeping her soul into another dimension, a different time.

Sleep was out of the question now. She got up, pulled on a sweatshirt and jeans, and moved silently along the worn footpath from the house to the old barn. Even in total darkness, she knew the way well enough that she could have negotiated the path without stumbling, but tonight she walked by nature's lamplight. Except for a few wispy clouds, the sky was clear. A full moon hung over the Olympic Mountains and painted the snowy caps with a whitewashed blue.

A perfect color for a pottery glaze, Amber thought idly. Her imagination

49

drifted toward the idea, and she could see in her mind's eye a zigzag pattern on a dinner plate, mimicking the jagged peaks of the familiar mountains that rose up behind the Hood Canal.

With a sigh she sank into one of the Adirondack chairs in front of the barn and stretched her legs out in front of her.

Nature was putting on quite a show tonight. The setting moon, a perfect circle of silver, had paused in its descent to admire itself in the calm waters. A reflection of reflected light, she mused, twice removed from the source. Down the ragged slopes of Mount Constance, over the lower hills of the Toandos Peninsula, and across the silent depths of the Hood Canal to the shoreline, moonlight flowed like melted asphalt.

Amber sighed and raked her hands through her hair. When she had first come to Washington State, she had let herself believe that a continent would be sufficient to distance her from her pain. The move did prove to be a turning point for her, Amber had to admit. The misty serenity of the Northwest's woods and waters had wrapped like cotton wool around her soul. Old razor-sharp barbs of outrage and anguish ceased to tear at the wound. Daily torment softened to a muffled, persistent ache.

For a while, she thought she had forgotten. And then the dreams had returned, jolting her awake with heaving breath and a racing pulse. The black hole had opened up again.

Amber Chaney knew a thing or two about dreams—how certain dreams raised messages from the subconscious, an attempt to release something buried or hidden, something she had tried unsuccessfully to contain or deny. That in order to free yourself from a dream, you had to find a way to bring that reality to the surface. That healing could only begin when a wound was exposed to the light.

Amber assented to this, and more. She also believed that a dream could be a gentle nudge, a hint of direction or guidance—an assurance that, whatever dark reality lay hidden in the deep recesses of her soul, she was probably strong enough to face it and deal with it.

It was not strength she lacked or faith or even imagination. It was courage.

She knew what she ought to do. She needed to let the truth come out and have its say. She needed to mold it into reality—to cast in clay, in the strong light of day, the images that haunted her by night. A creative outlet, that's what she needed—dancing or writing or painting—a way to put into movement or words or visual forms the feelings and memories that emerged.

But Amber was no dancer. And her attempts at keeping a journal turned out flat and superficial. She had discovered, instead—using popsicle sticks and children's colored modeling clay—that she had a gift for sculpting.

Earth and water, blended and shaped into something useful, something beautiful. The primal elements submitting to the skills and gifts she possessed. From the first moment her hands touched clay, Amber knew she had unearthed something totally unexpected. Not only did sculpting lead to understanding and healing, but it also sustained and nurtured her soul. It filled some of the empty spaces inside, as if she had been waiting for it her whole life.

It wasn't always comfortable, this process of uncovering the truth that lay buried in the clay. But it was her calling. Her gift. Her destiny.

And maybe, God willing, her way out of darkness into light.

9

Blindness and Sight

When Amber began working on a new sculpture, she was never quite certain where she would end up. It was like taking a journey blindfolded, feeling your way along one step at a time without the benefit of visual clues. You only knew what your destination was once you had arrived.

She closed her eyes and ran her hands over the damp clay figure that lay on the sculpting table in front of her. For some reason she had never quite ascertained, she could always "see" a sculpture better with her hands than with her eyes. She had learned to read the form with her fingers—the fluidity of a body in motion, the graceful turn of muscle and bone, the fine detail of facial structure and proportion and balance.

Once, long ago, she had read an arresting story about a man born blind, who had his eyesight miraculously restored through experimental surgery. Everyone told him how blessed he was to be able to see for the first time, but in private moments he would shut his eyes and feel objects around him, as if shutting out the distractions of sight enabled him once more to "see" in a way that made sense to him.

Amber had never been blind, but she could almost understand. In the past, the ability to withdraw into herself had been a welcome and necessary escape—a safe, sightless cocoon. And darkness certainly had its benefits. But these days she found herself less and less adept at shutting herself off from the truth, with its blinding lights and shocking verities, its inexorable pull toward reality.

Emotional health, Amber thought wryly, *is vastly overrated.*

She sighed, opened her eyes, and looked around at the barn that housed her sculpting studio and served as a storehouse for her work. Dawn had broken more than an hour ago. Beyond the open door, she could see an expanse of blue sky, studded with a scattering of clouds; and below, in mirror image, the blue reflected in Hood Canal, with small choppy whitecaps stirred by the wind. In the distance, on the other side of the canal, the Olympic Mountains caught the early sun and cast back colors of pink and gold and lavender. Amber paused for a moment to let her gaze absorb the ever-changing beauty of the view. Her soul might be in turmoil, but the mountains stood firm. Solid. Immovable.

Inhaling fresh resolve on the cool morning air, Amber swiveled back to the sculpting table, narrowing her eyes at the image that lay before her. With these two small figures, no more than ten inches high, she was casting a new light on her dream. The forms were coming along—the flow of the skirt, the arch of the little one's neck as she raised her face toward the sky. She had almost captured the ecstasy of a child's abandonment, but the expression wasn't quite right yet.

"Nice," a voice murmured behind her. "I like the smaller one's laughing eyes." A square brown hand reached over her shoulder and set down a steaming mug of coffee. "Someone you know?"

"I'm busy, TwoJoe." Amber realized too late how curt her response sounded, but she swallowed down an apology and threw a damp rag over the sculpture to hide it from his scrutiny. She and TwoJoe had been friends for almost a year, but his presence—especially when she was working on a new project—made her feel exposed and a little vulnerable.

"Not much sleep last night, huh?" He chuckled. "Maybe the coffee will help." He patted her amiably on the shoulder. "Don't mind me, but you've got another visitor."

Amber turned and found herself looking into the soft, liquid gaze of an enormous chamois-colored male llama. "Lloser!" she reprimanded gently. "What are you doing in my studio?"

"He thinks it's *his* studio," TwoJoe chuckled. "Poor fella prefers your company, it seems, to ladies of his own kind. He keeps wandering up here. Be nice to him, now. I think he's in love with you. Not that it would do him any good."

In spite of her initial irritation at TwoJoe's interruption, Amber laughed and reached out to stroke the llama's velvety face. "Don't listen to him, you darling big old baby," she cooed at him. "Mean old TwoJoe thinks you're good for nothing if you can't produce a whole herd of little Llosers. But you're still the best pack llama in the bunch, and the sweetest-tempered, too."

"He does have a sweet nature," TwoJoe said. "I just wish he had turned out to be the stud he was reputed to be when I bought him. He eats more than Llarry and Lloyd put together—if he could reproduce himself, it would at least help to pay the feed bills. And we could use a couple more big packers like him."

Amber pointed. "He may not be anybody's father, but Llittle Bit has certainly taken to him *as if* he's her daddy."

Llittle Bit, the herd's newest cria, had followed Lloser into the barn and now ambled up to the sculpting table and dangled her snow-white muzzle over Amber's coffee mug.

"Get your whiskers out of that," TwoJoe scolded. "You're too young to drink coffee." Gently, he prodded the two llamas toward the door. "I'll take them out to the pasture and make sure the gate is latched so Lloser can't open it again. Be back in a minute to pack up your order for the Baxters."

Five minutes later TwoJoe returned as promised, whistling under his breath. He assembled a cardboard box from the stash under the loft steps and began to load it with the plates, cups, and saucers Amber had completed the day before.

"So, are you going to tell me about this latest sculpture?" he asked over his shoulder.

"No."

"You're a hardhearted woman, Amber Chaney." He laughed lightly and went on working. "This is a nice glaze," he commented, holding up a dinner plate. "I like the mix of blue and purple."

Amber said nothing, but watched him as he carefully nested the plates in shredded paper. TwoJoe Elkhorn, half Suquamish, was a gentle, quiet man whose bronzed skin, high cheekbones, and animated dark eyes made him look younger than he was. A year or two older than Amber, TwoJoe had returned to his childhood home on the Kitsap Peninsula a year ago to arrange his mother's funeral and had simply stayed.

His grandfather, the original Joseph Elkhorn, had been something of a legend back in the thirties—the famed Jump-Off Joe, after whom a local creek was named. According to popular myth, old Joe had stationed himself in the creek bed and refused to move until local authorities refused a building permit to a small industry that threatened the purity of the water. But TwoJoe had told Amber the real story.

Once, in the early years of their marriage, Joe and his Norwegian wife, Simi Lundvig, had gotten into a terrible argument. When she threatened to go home to her mother, Joe got drunk, fell into the creek, and was still lying there, half-frozen and hung over, when the sheriff arrived to escort him home. Simi took him back on the condition that he never touch another drop of liquor as long as he drew breath, and evidently Joe kept that promise. He and Simi lived together for fifty-nine years, producing four children, nine grandchildren, and dozens of great-grands. In Amber's opinion the best of the bunch were Joseph Elkhorn II, the eldest grandson—called TwoJoe since infancy—and his sister Meg.

Amid marriages and divorces and financial catastrophes and people moving away, much of the Elkhorn-Lundvig property had been sold off over the years. TwoJoe himself had left Kitsap County to get his education and had stayed away almost twenty years. But now he was back, for good. And he held the last forty-acre section of Elkhorn land.

Real estate developers from all over the county and across the Sound in Seattle had long been badgering TwoJoe to sell. The Elkhorn place wasn't a lot in terms of sheer acreage, but it stretched in a wide pie shape all the way from the Hood Canal to Clear Creek Road, a prime waterfront development site, with half-million dollar homes going up all around them. As Seattle's ferry commuters moved onto the Peninsula in droves, property values skyrocketed. Even the most dilapidated property was worth a fortune, if it was on the water. TwoJoe Elkhorn was sitting on a gold mine. Just sign on the dotted line, and he would be a rich man.

But even though making ends meet was often difficult, TwoJoe wasn't interested in being a rich man. He had already made his choice, leaving a lucrative accounting business behind him when he moved back from California. He had abandoned the fast track for the more placid pace of life here in Washington, and he refused even to consider their everescalating offers. Instead, he had renovated the log farmhouse, handcrafted from second-growth Douglas firs a hundred years ago. Adding on a little apartment for himself, he turned the rest of the house over to Amber and his sister Meg, made some necessary repairs on the old barn, which Amber had taken for a studio, and purchased half a dozen llamas to breed as pack animals and wool producers.

Content to raise his llamas and serve as accountant and general manager of their little cottage enterprise, TwoJoe Elkhorn was a man at peace with himself. Between tending the stock and keeping the books, he worked day and night to hold the place together and keep them all warm and dry and well fed. Amber could barely remember how they had survived before he came and she couldn't begin to imagine what they would do without him now.

To Amber's way of thinking, they made a strange trio: TwoJoe, a dark-skinned, brown-eyed CPA from Berkeley who raised llamas; his sister Meg, a weaver of llama wool rugs who looked exactly like her blonde, blue-eyed Norwegian grandmother; and Amber, the displaced artist who had come to live with them. But nobody else in Kitsap County seemed to consider them the least bit odd. Amber supposed that over the last hundred years there had been so much intermarriage between the Norwegian loggers and the native tribes that no one thought twice about a brother and sister who looked as if they had come from different planets.

Amber had met Meg during the early days of her sojourn at the Women's Facility, and the two had instantly become friends. Behind barred windows and locked doors, you didn't often find a kindred spirit, but Meg was different. For one thing, she was innocent of the drug charges that had landed her in the recovery unit in the first place.

She had been convicted of possession with intent to distribute heroin. It was an open and shut case—an anonymous tip to the authorities about a stolen vehicle resulted in her being pulled over and searched at 11:30 one night. The state troopers found the drugs in the tire well of her trunk—a street value of nearly $70,000. The trial took two and a half days.

It was her "first" felony conviction, and even though the circumstantial evidence stacked up against her, the judge, Meg suspected, was not thoroughly convinced of her guilt. Besides, the prisons were already crowded past capacity. Meg was sentenced to a minimum of five years in the Women's Psychiatric Facility, ordered to undergo drug treatment, psychiatric evaluation, and reparative therapy.

Technically, the facility was a hospital, not a jail. But it might as well have been a prison, populated as it was by drug addicts, alcoholics, and a myriad of social misfits. All of them claiming they weren't junkies, weren't drunks, weren't crazy. The recovery rate was almost nil; recidivism was off the charts.

Even though everyone in lockup *said* they were innocent as newborn babes, in Meg's case it turned out to be true. Still, it took three years and a passionate ACLU lawyer to get her sentence overturned. Her abusive and vengeful ex-husband, Bart, it seemed, had planted the heroin in her trunk and ultimately proved to be the "reliable source" upon whom the prosecution had depended. When he finally confessed, he said he did it because he loved her and wanted her back. The unimpeachable logic of an addict.

Meg's three years at Raleigh, however, turned out to be a blessing in disguise—or if not exactly a blessing, at least not a total loss. She got a good deal of free therapy, dealt with the debilitating effects of Bart's abuse, and was emotionally healthy enough, by the time she left, to reclaim the Elkhorn name and sever all ties with him. When Meg was released, she shook the dust of North Carolina off her feet, and returned to Washington for good.

Amber was happy for her best friend, of course, but devastated for herself. All that kept her going during those last two years were Meg's encouraging letters, and the invitation to join her here, at the far western edge of the country, where she could start over and build a new life.

She just hadn't anticipated that the new life would eventually come to include Meg's older brother TwoJoe.

TwoJoe had made it abundantly clear that he would like to be a more intimate part of Amber's life. At forty-two, he had been married once before, and although the relationship had ended in a divorce initiated by his ex-wife, TwoJoe obviously still believed in forever.

And he was good marriage material, as Meg reminded Amber at every opportunity. "He doesn't drink; he's funny and sensitive and intelligent. And he's got all his own teeth," she would say. "He only needs a little encouragement—he's half in love with you already."

Amber was sure it was more than half. And the truth was, she liked TwoJoe. She respected his values. She thought he was a fine, gentle, compassionate, sensible man. But no matter how much she appreciated TwoJoe's good qualities, falling in love—with him or anyone else—was out of the question.

She had tried it once, a couple of years before TwoJoe came on the scene. Meg's mother was still alive, and the three of them were living in the enormous old log house together like spinster schoolteachers. Then Rick Knutson appeared in her life, with his "aw, shucks" down-home charm and his promise to love her forever.

It was a disaster. There were too many unwelcome memories, too much baggage. The first time Rick tried to touch her, it took her by surprise and she pulled away. He was gentle and understanding, but by the second time she knew she wasn't ready for anything physical. He was hurt and pouted for days. The third time, when she tried to explain, he flew into a rage, and although he never once struck her, the accusations he leveled at her left wounds she could not forget, no matter how hard she tried. In the end, he left her standing alone in the middle of the road while he roared away in a cloud of gravel dust.

Maybe Meg was right—maybe TwoJoe *was* different. But Amber was still the same.

She couldn't take that chance again—she wouldn't. Despite the loneliness, it was better just to close her eyes, to push down the memories, to block out the insistent voice in her head that told her she would never be good enough.

Sometimes blindness was safer than sight.

10

Sam Houston

TwoJoe forked hay into the central feeding trough and watched as the newest cria, Llittle Bit, came forward to investigate. Her mother, LlouEllen, leaned over Llittle Bit's head and pulled out a tuft of fresh hay. In the adjacent stall, Lloser, the disinterested stud, also came up to feed.

TwoJoe stepped back, admiring his handiwork. Llamas preferred open shelters to closed stables, and in general were congenial, sociable animals, but occasionally skirmishes broke out at feeding time. He had developed a system to deal with the problem, and it seemed to be working like a charm.

The key was to have each llama separated for feeding, but still free to roam. To that end, Joe had devised a series of adjoining two-sided stalls that came together in the middle to form a central feed trough. From above, with the roof lifted off, the structure looked like an enormous Greek cross—all of its arms the same length—with a large circle in the center. From the ground, each unit was comprised of four pie-shaped shelters with the feeding trough at the pointed end. The buildings provided shelter from the elements, open visibility, and separation at mealtimes.

Methodically, TwoJoe made his way around the north end of the pasture, distributing hay and talking to his llamas as he worked. As he often did in the company of these gentle beasts, he marveled at how different his life was now—not at all how he had envisioned his future when he left Kitsap County for Berkeley.

No doubt his CPA friends back in California would have a good laugh at his expense if they could see him now, getting drenched in the incessant spring drizzle and kicking manure off his boots after he got too close to the dung pile. Most of them, he knew, had built lucrative accounting firms and were raking in money hand over fist. They wore Armani suits and Italian leather loafers and conducted power lunches to seduce millionaire clients. His idea of a nice wardrobe was a new pair of jeans and a couple of shirts from L.L.Bean; going out for dinner meant grubbing on his own beach at low tide for a harvest of oysters and clams.

TwoJoe had actually run into one of his old Berkeley classmates on the Bainbridge Island Ferry not long ago—a snobbish, dull-witted bore named Reginald Something the Fourth. How the man had ever ended up at a state university like Berkeley would forever remain a mystery; it was a good school, but pretty far below Reggie's gold-plated standards. TwoJoe suspected that he hadn't been bright enough to get into the Ivy League on his own merits, and that his family, despite their aristocratic name, had not been influential enough or rich enough to buy his way in.

But he was rich enough now. TwoJoe had pulled his battered Dodge pickup onto the ferry right next to Reggie's silver twelve-cylinder Jaguar. They took the elevator to the upper deck, where Reggie ordered a double nonfat cappuccino while TwoJoe had plain old coffee, and in the course of a thirty-minute crossing, Reggie had taken five important calls on his cell phone, dropped Bill Gates's name six times, and made sure TwoJoe knew that he was meeting in Seattle with a major client, one of Microsoft's VPs.

"And what are you doing these days, Joe?" Reggie had finally asked after he had run out of breath singing his own praises.

TwoJoe had paused for a moment, relishing the reaction he knew he'd get. "Raising llamas."

"Ah, llamas?" Reggie had stammered. "Llamas. Right. How . . . interesting. I gather the CPA thing didn't work out for you." The rest remained unsaid, but the condescension in Reggie's voice left little to the imagination. An Indian, no matter how bright or ambitious, had no place among the high rollers of corporate accounting.

They had parted without another word, but as they drove off the ferry, TwoJoe couldn't resist gunning his engine. He eyed the rearview mirror with satisfaction as the silver Jag behind him was enveloped in a cloud of black oil smoke.

Now, recalling the contemptuous sneer on Reggie's face, TwoJoe stabbed his pitchfork viciously into the pile of hay. Sure, money like that would be nice. It would be a relief not to have to scratch and scrape for every dime just to feed the livestock and pay the taxes and put Hamburger Helper on the table. But he had been around long enough to know that there wasn't enough money in the world to buy what really mattered.

Belinda had taught him that. For her, everything had been about money. No matter how much they had, it was never enough to fill the bottomless spaces in her soul. She had always wanted more of every-thing—except him.

For years TwoJoe had tried to be the man Belinda wanted him to be. He had lived in the corporate world, played the game, given in to her lust for acquisition, and felt his spirit atrophy with every new demand. When he found her in bed with another man—an obscenely wealthy man, TwoJoe's biggest client—it was almost a relief. He didn't contest the divorce; he simply walked away. From her. From the job. From a life that weighed him down like a cast-iron trench coat.

No, financial stability wasn't worth selling your soul for. He'd had that carrot dangled in front of his nose often enough. If money were all that mattered, TwoJoe would have already sold this place to the highest bidder.

There was more to life than skimming a couple hundred thousand a year off the top of some Microsoft bigwig's fortune. He had what he wanted. Peace. Freedom. Serenity. A little corner of the most beautiful place in the world to call his own.

Everything except someone to share it with. Everything except Amber Chaney.

TwoJoe tried to put the thought out of his mind. She had made it perfectly clear that she didn't want a relationship with him—at least not *that* kind of relationship. She loved him like a brother. He was family.

Without revealing any details, Meg had let him know that Amber was dealing with some difficult personal issues right now, and that she wasn't in a position to consider a romantic relationship. But TwoJoe suspected that his sister was being generous, trying to spare his feelings. Though Meg had implied that Amber might come around, given enough time, TwoJoe's skin wasn't that thin. He knew that Amber might never grow to love him in the way he loved her. If she did, she did. He was patient. He could wait. If she didn't—well, he'd be a brother to her, if that's what she wanted. Either way, it didn't change his feelings about her.

TwoJoe wasn't some love-struck teenager or the hero of a romance novel, after all. With Belinda he had learned what a terrible mistake it was to give not just your heart but also your *soul* to another person. It had cost him too much—too many years of misery, too many nights of restless dreams and struggle and self-doubt.

TwoJoe believed in love, and he would continue to love Amber even if his love were never returned. But he also knew that he couldn't base his happiness and contentment on someone else—not even Amber Chaney.

This was the path he had chosen, and he was grateful for it. With or without Amber, he still had the farm. He still had his llamas. He and Lloser could grow old together like two venerable gray-haired bachelors, watching the sunsets over the Olympic Mountains.

When he had finished with the feeding and had refilled the common water trough, TwoJoe walked the fence line and checked the pasture, making sure there were no hidden hazards that might endanger the curious animals. Llamas were notorious for getting themselves into trouble—they would eat leftover baling twine, chew on lumber, entangle themselves in wire. They might be highly intelligent, intrepid explorers, but they weren't wise enough to leave things alone.

"Hey, mister!" a reedy voice called.

TwoJoe looked up. The rain had stopped, and at the fence line on Clear Creek Road stood a tow-headed boy who looked to be five or six years old. He had jumped the ditch and was pressing his body up against the fence, straining to reach out and touch Llittle Bit, who had drawn near to investigate. TwoJoe gave a wave and walked over.

"These are llamas, right, mister?" The boy didn't look at him; he had his eyes fastened on Llittle Bit's velvety face.

"Yep." TwoJoe nodded. "That one's called Llittle Bit. She's the newest cria."

"What's that?"

"A cria is what we call a baby llama. She's five months old." He peered at the boy. "What's your name?"

As if he had suddenly remembered his manners, the boy stood up straight and looked TwoJoe in the eye. He had a clear, guileless expression and a turned-up nose covered with freckles. "I'm Sam Houston. I'm from Texas," he drawled. "I'm visiting my grandpa. He lives down the road—" He pointed back toward Ahlswede Lane, where a row of million-dollar homes stood guard over Hood Canal.

TwoJoe regarded the child and suppressed a grin. He had heard rumors that some Fort Worth oil baron had built a vacation home in Kitsap County; but from what he remembered of his American history, he had expected the president of the Republic of Texas to be a little bigger. "Well, it's nice to meet you, Sam." He rubbed his hand across the front of his jeans and extended it over the fence to the boy. "My name is TwoJoe Elkhorn."

"You're an Injun, aren't you?" Sam blurted out. "Oh, sorry. I mean, uh, Native American."

"It's okay." TwoJoe shook the boy's hand solemnly. "I'm half Suquamish. Would you like to see the llamas?"

Sam held back. "Do they bite?"

"Not if you don't bite them first. They're very gentle."

"All right, then."

With TwoJoe's help, the boy scrambled over the fence and dropped into the pasture. He approached Llittle Bit quietly, with respect, and stroked her on the neck, murmuring to her.

"You're good with animals, Sam."

"Grandpa's got horses at his ranch in Texas. I've been around 'em since I was a little boy."

He turned, then took two quick steps backward, stumbled, and fell bottom first onto the ground. Lloser had ambled over to pay his respects, and the huge animal towered over Sam, gazing down at him with limpid eyes.

"This is Lloser," TwoJoe said with a laugh as he helped the boy up and brushed manure off his jeans. "He's our best and strongest packer."

"What's a packer? And why is his name Lloser?"

TwoJoe paused, wondering how he could delicately explain the problem of a stud llama who wasn't interested in the ladies. "He was supposed to be the Big Daddy for the herd and father a whole lot of strong sons," he began. "But he, ah . . . well, he—"

"Shoots blanks, huh?" Sam nodded knowingly. "Yeah, that happened to one of Grandpa's stallions once. Paid ten thousand for a stud who turned out to be a dud."

TwoJoe took off his hat and scratched his head in wonder. Apparently this child knew a great deal about the mysteries and misfortunes of breeding stock.

"You said he was a packer?" Sam took a step closer to Lloser. He had to reach very high to stroke the big llama's side, but he stood his ground.

TwoJoe pointed through the trees, to where the Olympic Mountains were visible beyond Hood Canal. "See those mountains? That's called the Olympic Wilderness. People go in there to explore and do mountain climbing and camp, but there aren't any roads. They use llamas to carry their gear. Llamas have soft feet, so they don't tear up the terrain like horses or mules do. They're very surefooted, easygoing. And they can forage for their own food, so you don't have to haul in feed for them. They can carry a hundred pounds or more. We rent them as pack animals for folks going into the mountains."

"Can you ride them, too?"

TwoJoe shook his head. "No. But they're versatile, useful animals. We shear them for their wool, the way you do sheep—my sister spins the wool and weaves rugs and blankets out of it. They can even serve as guards for other livestock, like sheep and cattle. They're extremely intelligent, and they make great pets. You can even take them out for walks."

"You mean I could get one of these and keep it, like a dog? Cool."

TwoJoe raised a warning finger. "Not one. You have to have at least two. Llamas are extremely social animals, and they don't do well alone."

"I like this one," Sam declared, tangling his fingers in Lloser's thick, tan wool. "He's very nice. I think he's a winner, not a loser."

"Apparently you're a winner in his book, too."

"You know what else I think?" Sam went on in a serious tone, as if he were a very wise old man instead of a six-year-old boy. "I think you're doing a very good thing here, raising llamas to carry people's burdens and keep them warm."

TwoJoe grinned. "Say, I was just about to go up to the barn and do some stuff. Want to come along?"

Sam squinted at the cloud-covered sky like an old-timer assessing the remaining hours of the day. "Thanks, mister, but I better get home. My grandma's probably wondering where I am." He climbed back over the fence and set off toward Ahlswede Lane.

"Sam!" TwoJoe called. The boy turned. "Why aren't you in school?"

"Teacher's strike," Sam yelled back. "I'll be here two weeks at least, maybe more. Is it all right if I come back and visit the llamas again?"

TwoJoe waved. "Any time."

"Thanks. See ya."

An unexpected stab of loss knifed through TwoJoe as he watched the diminutive Sam Houston head down the road, kicking rocks with his little boots—a sense of something missing, even though he loved his life.

Sam was right. It was a good thing TwoJoe was doing here—carrying burdens and keeping people warm. But who, he wondered, would do the same for him?

11

The Sculpture

"So, what's next? New York, Paris, or Rome?"

Amber raised her head at the sound of Meg's voice. "What do you mean?" She didn't turn around, nor did she cover her sculpture-in-progress the way she had when TwoJoe had appeared unexpectedly. Somehow she didn't feel quite as vulnerable or exposed when Meg looked at her unfinished work; Meg had already seen the rough places in Amber's life.

Most of them, anyway.

Meg pulled up a stool and sat down next to Amber. "Look at this," she said, pointing toward the small sculpture of the two figures. "The forms, the expressions. It's fabulous." She cuffed Amber playfully on the shoulder. "You're getting so *good!* Next thing we know, some art critic will discover you, and you'll be leaving us to hop a private jet for your first showing in the Big Apple." She grinned. "Remember us when you're rich and famous, okay? Your old friends the llama farmers and weavers of wool."

Amber let out a self-deprecating chuckle. "Don't hold your breath. I doubt I'll be going anywhere any time soon."

"Then you have no idea how talented you are," Meg countered. "This is a wonderful piece, Amber. It's so . . . so real. Where did the inspiration for this come from?" Meg asked. "I want to know all about it. Weavers don't often think about shape and form and dimension. I may not be an artist myself, but I love hearing about the creative processes."

"What do you mean, you're no artist?" Amber tried to divert the conversation, to quiet the churning in her stomach. She didn't want to talk about the sculpture, didn't want to confront the memories that had been eating at her ever since she had begun to work on this piece. "You weave the most beautiful rugs and wall hangings I've ever seen. Everybody says so."

Meg shrugged and carelessly pushed a lock of hair out of her eyes. She was only two years younger than Amber—closing in on forty—but she still looked like a college kid. She was small and slim, with a perfect heart-shaped face, high cheekbones, and the kind of lithe, athletic figure that seemed more at home in denim than in sequins. Clearly she favored the Norwegian side of the family—fair skin and blonde hair that arranged itself in disheveled layers without much more than a quick blow-drying. The kind of face and body Amber might have envied, if Meg hadn't been so completely oblivious to her own attractiveness.

"I really do think it's time for you to quit doing stoneware settings and vases for the tourists and start concentrating on your sculpture," Meg persisted. "This is amazing, Amber—trust me, it's really good. Now, come on, tell me more."

Amber hedged again. "There's not much to tell. It was just—I don't know—an image I had in my mind."

Not just *an* image. *The* image. The one that had haunted her dreams. The one captured in a faded photograph hidden in the bottom drawer of her dresser. The one she had tried to suppress, to rationalize. The image that would never let her rest.

"It's perfect," Meg said. "It has a dreamlike quality about it. The little one on the left seems filled with joy and totally at peace, trusting that the other one won't let go, won't let her fall." Amber felt a lurch in her gut, and she wheeled around to look at Meg. For a full minute she searched her friend's familiar countenance—those bright blue eyes, the crinkly laugh lines that shot upward from the corners of her mouth. Meg's expression held nothing but openness and candor. No sign that she was fishing for information. No indication that she knew she had struck a nerve.

Amber turned back to the sculpture, and all at once a fury rose up in her—a rage born of powerlessness. Meg's words reverberated in her mind: *totally at peace, trusting that the other one won't let go, won't let her fall.* But she *had* let go, hadn't she?

She snatched up a sculpting knife, and with one swift motion severed the soft clay connection between the two figures. The smaller figure fell sideways onto the table like a discarded rag doll with its hands cut off at the wrists, holding out empty arms.

"What are you doing?" Meg let out a strangled cry and grabbed for the hand that held the knife. "Amber, stop!"

"I can't . . . I just can't—" She flung the knife aside and put her hands to her face. Tears came unbidden, and she could not push them back. For a few minutes she sat there, sobbing, vaguely aware of Meg's hand stroking her back, attempting to soothe her, calm her.

"Amber?" Meg's whisper finally pushed into her consciousness, as if from far away. "That smaller figure holding on—that's your sister, isn't it? The one you told me about, back in Raleigh?"

Amber nodded and dragged a response to the surface. "Yes."

"And the one spinning her around is you." Meg pointed toward the larger figure, the older girl in the sculpture, still standing there with her hands outstretched, the grisly remains of the little one's fingers dangling in space.

"Yes."

Meg's arm slid around Amber's shoulders and squeezed. "You still miss her, don't you?"

"I try not to." Amber shrugged. "I guess I just need to give myself time to forget. It's only been—oh, twenty years, give or take a few." She attempted a weak smile.

"You never forget family," Meg murmured. "For better or worse, they're always with you."

"Mostly worse." Amber took a ragged breath and began to cry again.

❦

Meg sat very still, holding her friend while the tears came and subsided, then came again. She hated this feeling of helplessness, but all she could do for the moment was be there.

From the earliest days of their friendship, years ago in Raleigh, Amber had always held back. The two of them had connected from the beginning, but while Meg talked openly about her emotional struggles, her progress in therapy, her recovery from the devastating effects of her ex-husband's abuse, Amber had mostly listened, volunteering very little information about herself.

Meg knew the basics about Amber's life, of course. The background of financial security and entitlement. The powerful father and sweet, submissive mother. The little sister she had barely become acquainted with before she had been sent away. The pain of being cut off, isolated, swept aside.

But there was a great deal Amber hadn't told Meg, huge dark pieces of her story that still lay shrouded in shadow. What had happened to her to send her over the edge in the first place? How had this daughter of wealth and privilege fallen so far?

Meg had watched while Amber floundered through the early stages of her own recovery, sinking deeper into depression like a doe caught in quicksand. And then, with Meg on the sidelines cheering her on, Amber discovered her talent for making things out of clay. Her life turned around. She found purpose and direction and an outlet for her emotions.

Art had been Amber Chaney's salvation. At least for a while. By the time Amber was released from Raleigh, Meg had reestablished her life here in Kitsap County. TwoJoe was still living in California, and their mother, alone in the big log house, had encouraged Meg to move back home. It was the obvious choice: for one thing, it was nearly a continent removed from her ex-husband, Bart, whom she devoutly hoped never to see again. In addition, the tranquillity and beauty of the place stirred Meg's soul and brought her peace.

Inviting Amber to come and live with them was an easy decision, the natural outworking of their friendship. Amber needed somewhere to go, and the Elkhorn place had more than enough room. Perhaps the serenity Meg had found here would seep into Amber's soul and bring her some quietness of mind and heart as well. It was the one thing Meg could do to help her friend find healing.

For a while, it seemed to work. Amber loved being here; she would sit for hours on the deck, just gazing across the canal to the ever-changing play of light on Mount Constance and The Brothers, some of the highest peaks in the Olympic Mountain Range. She purchased a secondhand kiln and set up a studio in the barn, turning out the loveliest pottery anyone in Kitsap County had ever seen. She encouraged Meg to buy a loom and take up weaving, and within a year they began to show a profit. A minor profit, anyway. During tourist season in the nostalgic little town of Viking Junction, the shops that ran along the waterfront of Liberty Bay were filled with Amber's delicately colored stoneware and Meg's hand-woven llama wool rugs. They weren't rich, by any means, but at least they sold enough on consignment to sock away money for the rainy winter months.

They lived like sisters, sharing each other's lives, supporting each other's hopes and dreams. Amber forged a deep bond with Meg's mother, Beatrice, whom she affectionately called "Elkie." She began to loosen up, to laugh more. Meg began to believe that they had outrun the darkness.

Then, suddenly, a little more than a year ago, something happened. Meg didn't know if it was really Rick Knutson's fault that Amber ricocheted back into the past, but the timing indicated that, at the very least, her relationship with him had triggered some memory or opened an old wound. Rick wasn't the right kind of man for Amber anyway; he was a bad debt—self-centered, completely insensitive to anyone's needs except his own. He made promises he had no intention of keeping, and when he left, Amber began to sink.

She grew morose and irritable. She slept fitfully, often awakening with nightmares. Slowly, she began a downward spiral into a gray and empty place where Meg could not follow.

Nothing seemed to help. After Meg's mother died, months of grief compounded Amber's depression, and her inability to work resulted in the added stress of financial insecurity. TwoJoe's appearance on the scene seemed to ease Amber's burden a little, until it became obvious that Meg's brother harbored his own romantic feelings for Amber. He never pressured her, and he was always tender and compassionate, but the very fact of his presence seemed to make her agitated and uncomfortable.

And now this. The mutilated sculpture. Amber's uncontrollable weeping. Her ongoing depression. The palpable presence of some oppression in her, some secret she couldn't reveal, even to her closest friend.

Meg was no novice when it came to therapy. She had been around the block a few times herself, and she knew the signs. And as much as she resisted the idea, it was time for an intervention.

Meg waited for a few minutes more while Amber cried herself out. Her eyes were red-rimmed and swollen, and her breath still came in fitful gasps, but at least she was a little more composed.

"Can we talk now?"

Amber nodded.

"We've been friends for a long time," Meg began cautiously. "And we've gone through a lot together."

"Yeah."

"And we always promised we'd tell each other the truth."

Amber contorted her face in a cynical grin. "Just when did we make this promise? Remind me."

Meg smiled briefly. At least she was still able to joke about it; that was a positive sign. "You've been going downhill emotionally, Amber. Ever since . . . well, ever since Rick."

"Rick doesn't have anything to do with this."

"Maybe not. But his presence in your life—or his leaving—seems to have triggered this depression. I think—" She paused, summoning courage. "I think you need to see someone who can help you deal with this."

Amber lowered her head and stared at the ruined statue on the sculpting table. With one trembling finger she reached out and touched the severed hands. "I guess you're right. But—"

"But what?"

"Therapy is expensive, Meg. You know how it is. I can barely afford basic health insurance, and it sure doesn't cover ninety bucks an hour for counseling."

"I have a suggestion."

Amber looked up. "All right, let's hear it."

"Well, you know that TwoJoe and I attend All Saints' Episcopal most Sundays. Our rector has a Ph.D. in psychology and is a licensed counselor, so—"

"A *priest?*" Amber bristled. "Absolutely not. For one thing, there's no way I'm going to pour my guts out to a man. I've had it up to here with them—" She shook her head vehemently. "No. A man would never understand. Not in a million years."

Meg held up a hand. "This priest's name," she said quietly, "happens to be *Susan*. And she's good. Very good."

"A woman priest?" Amber stared at Meg. "Well, that's a switch. How do you know she's so good?"

"I've talked to her. She was married once—for seven years, as I recall."

"Great. Not just a priest. Not just a *woman* priest. A *divorced* woman priest."

"She finally left her husband after he beat her within an inch of her life."

Silence descended between them, and Meg could almost see the wheels turning in Amber's mind. She caught Amber's eyes and held them. "The abuse had been going on since their honeymoon," she continued quietly. "Susan understands. She's been there."

The skeptical expression on Amber's face softened a bit. "Is she going to try to convert me?"

Meg laughed, a welcome relief from the tension. "I doubt it."

Amber exhaled a sigh so heavy it sounded as if it were dredged up from the very depths of her soul. Meg followed her gaze as it drifted toward the table, where the crumpled clay figure of a little girl lay with her arms outstretched.

"I have to do something," she said at last. "Call her."

12

Father Susan

In the hallway outside the closed office door, Amber squirmed and shifted on the unforgiving chair. It wasn't a chair, actually, but a segment of old church pew, sawed to a width of about four feet and held upright by the bench ends glued back in place. Her artistic mind relished the aesthetics of the piece: its intricate grain, the living luster of the oak, buffed to a rich, dark sheen by the oil of thousands of human hands that had touched it on thousands of Sunday mornings. Her lower parts, however, found less to appreciate; the hard wood had put her butt to sleep ten minutes ago, and now a tingle, like a mild electric shock, traveled up and down her sciatic nerve.

She rose, stretched, and walked over to the door, peering at the nameplate: *Rev. Dr. Susan Quentin, Rector.*

What did you call a woman priest, anyway? Most Episcopalians referred to their clergy as *Father*, but that felt like more of a gender shift than Amber was comfortable with. *Mother*, perhaps? No, that was a designation for the head of a convent. *Sister* indicated a Catholic nun. *Reverend Doctor* seemed just a bit stilted and overblown. Maybe something simpler, more to the point, like *Your Excellency*.

She shouldn't have come. This was getting far too complicated, and she hadn't even met the woman yet. If she didn't know how to address Susan Quentin on their first meeting, how on earth did Amber expect to be able to—

The door swung open, and Amber found herself nose to nose with Father Susan.

"You must be Amber Chaney," she said, extending a hand. "Come on in."

Amber didn't know quite what she had expected, but Susan Quentin definitely wasn't it. She was a tiny, slender woman, about Meg's size, with reddish-blonde hair layered back from her face and eyes an unusual mingling of gray and blue. She wore stonewashed jeans, white leather tennis shoes, and a black clerical shirt under a cable-knit rag wool cardigan. How old was this woman? She didn't look more than twenty. Amber entertained a fleeting image of some pimply faced clerk asking her to show ID before she could buy communion wine.

"Please, have a seat," she said, motioning toward a small sofa and a pair of cushy leather chairs that looked as if they'd been around as long as the parish itself. "Can I get you anything? Coffee, a soft drink?"

"Bottled water would be great, if you have it." Amber chose one of the chairs and settled her numb posterior gratefully into the soft padding.

The woman went to a small refrigerator in the corner and returned with two bottles of water. She handed one to Amber, then set the other on the coffee table and adjusted the second chair at an angle before she sat down. "You have questions, I assume?"

The primary questions on Amber's mind were *Can I see your driver's license?* and *What the heck do I call you?* The first question seemed rude, so she opted for the second, somewhat censored. "I'm not sure how to address you," she admitted. "Father? Doctor? Reverend?"

"Ah, the age-old question. One of the many dilemmas caused by the ordination of women." The priest threw back her head and laughed—a mellow, musical sound that instantly put Amber more at ease. "How do you feel about *Susan?*"

Amber let out a pent-up breath. "Fine by me. You're a psychologist, Meg tells me—as well as a minister?"

Susan nodded toward the wall above the sofa. "Licensed by the State of Washington, ordained by the Episcopal church."

Amber's eyes drifted to the collection of framed credentials: Certificate of Ordination, License for the Practice of Clinical Psychology, Diplomas from Columbia University, Notre Dame, Yale Divinity School, University of Washington. "You've been around, I see."

"My former husband was a university professor, first at Columbia, then at Notre Dame. I received my bachelor's and master's degrees from the colleges where he was teaching at the time."

Amber frowned, trying to assimilate this bit of information. "A professor? But Meg said—" She stopped, unsure how to proceed.

"Meg told you my ex-husband was an abuser." She raised her eyebrows and shrugged. "He was. He was also head of his department at Notre Dame, a Rhodes Scholar, Outstanding Professor two years in a row, and a very accomplished liar." She gazed at Amber and waved one hand thoughtfully. "Abuse—physical, sexual, emotional, whatever—is not limited to one ethnic or social sector. It crosses all boundaries of race and class and wealth and status."

Amber looked into Susan Quentin's eyes, and suddenly she didn't seem so young and inexperienced anymore. Penetrating eyes, whose color deepened in intensity with increased concentration. Old eyes, that looked as if they had witnessed every terrible thing the world had to offer, and still survived.

"Well, enough about me, let's talk about you." Susan paused for just a heartbeat. "What do *you* think of me?"

Her timing was perfect, and Amber laughed out loud at the familiar Bette Midler punch line. Maybe this wasn't going to be so bad. Maybe Susan Quentin did have something to offer her—something besides the pat answers and meaningless jargon she expected from religious people.

Susan set a small tape recorder on the coffee table. "Do you mind if we tape our sessions? It's easier for me to focus if I don't have to take notes."

This was nothing new. All her therapy sessions in Raleigh had been taped, and after the first few times Amber hadn't even noticed. "Sure, I'm used to it."

"You've been in counseling before."

"In North Carolina. I was committed for five years," Amber answered bluntly. "That's where—" She caught herself before she said, *That's where I met Meg.* Would it be a violation of confidentiality if she divulged that bit of information?

"Where you met Meg Elkhorn." Susan completed the sentence as if she'd read Amber's mind. "It's all right; I know about that."

"What else do you know about me?"

"Not much. Only that you're a friend of Meg and TwoJoe's, and that you came here to start a new life after you were released." Susan smiled faintly. "Oh, and that Meg loves you like a sister."

Amber felt herself flinch, and she averted her eyes.

"Did I hit a nerve?"

"Well, yes, a little bit," Amber admitted.

"Do you want to tell me about it?"

Amber sighed. She might as well get into it, she supposed. That's why she came here, after all. It wouldn't do any good to postpone the inevitable. "Where do I start? My unhappy childhood?"

Susan chuckled. "Maybe something a bit less stereotypical. First I'd like to hear about your life now. You're an artist, is that right?"

"I do a little sculpture," Amber responded. "But I make my living as a potter. Vases, stoneware, that kind of thing."

"A potter. Then you already know a lot about the way God works in people's lives."

Amber felt herself recoil. *Here we go,* she thought. *The God speech.* She knew it would come to this eventually. This woman might be a psychologist, but she was also a priest. And a priest's job was to convert people, to bring them into the fold. "I'm afraid I don't respond very positively to the image of God as a potter, manhandling people, crushing them up and molding them into something other than what they are." She tried to keep her voice even, but the words came out curt and cynical.

Susan, however, didn't seem the least bit ruffled by her rudeness. "I was thinking more along the lines of God taking something that seems shapeless or common and creating a work of enduring beauty and usefulness."

For just a flicker of a moment, something in the image appealed to Amber. That was, after all, what she did every day of her life, and it was refreshing to think that a Divine Being might share that kind of creative passion. But she wasn't going to get sucked into that whirlpool again. She held her ground. "Do we have to talk about God?"

"Not if you don't want to."

"I don't believe in God." Amber let the words settle for a moment, then amended, "Actually, that's not technically correct. I do acknowledge the premise of a Higher Power. I can't help accepting that much, seeing the beauty of nature all around us. But I don't believe in a God who can be trusted."

"You don't accept God as a loving Father, for example?"

"A father?" Amber let out a derisive snort. "Not likely."

"Tell me about your father."

"My father was the one who had me committed."

Susan sat back and gazed placidly at Amber. "He betrayed you."

"My other choice was prison, seven to ten. The charge was kidnapping." Amber paused, taking a moment to assess the shock value of her words. The Reverend Doctor showed no sign of revulsion or outrage. "I tried to steal . . . my baby sister."

"To protect her from your father's betrayal?"

Amber braced herself against the rush of emotion that churned in her gut. "I believed in him. I thought he loved me. But he couldn't be trusted. He wasn't the man he seemed to be. He sent me away, and I never saw her again. I couldn't save her."

"So that's why you had the strong reaction when I said Meg loved you like a sister."

"A lot of things are causing strong reactions in me these days," Amber admitted.

"Like what?"

Amber swallowed down her apprehension and began to give Susan Quentin a thumbnail sketch of her life: her five years in Raleigh, the discovery of her artistic talents, the new life she had begun when she moved to Kitsap County, the disastrous relationship with Rick Knutson, and how she had begun to spiral into depression after he deserted her, and then this, the final straw—destroying her sculpture, the one she called the Two Sisters. "When I left Raleigh and came out here, I thought I had this licked," she finished. "The first few years, I did just fine. Then the dark place started to open up again. And when I cut up the sculpture I had worked so hard on, I realized I hadn't succeeded in getting well at all. I felt so much . . . I don't know. Pain. *Rage*. I couldn't seem to control it."

"Did mutilating the statue help?"

Amber shook her head. "I guess not. It was a stupid thing to do."

"Was it?"

Amber quit picking at a bit of clay lodged in her thumbnail and looked up at Susan. "What do you mean?"

"When I finally got away from my husband, it took a long time for me to understand my anger. I had healed—physically, anyway—and I had resigned myself to living with the scars." Susan gazed off into middle space. "But years later, when I thought I had finished with my recovery, suddenly I began to feel this irrational anger. Blind fury, like what you're describing. A depression so deep I felt as if I were drowning in it."

Amber nodded for her to continue. This was beginning to make sense.

"My own counselor helped me see that emotions can lie buried for a long time, especially powerful emotions like anger. And if we're accustomed to being powerless, we don't know how to deal with them in a constructive way, so we continue to suppress them until they explode inside us, like a psychological Mount Saint Helens."

"That's pretty much what happened to me."

"Emotional healing doesn't come all at once, Amber," Susan said quietly. "Sometimes it's like grief—we think we've gone through that long dark tunnel and come out on the other side, and then when we least expect it, the pain erupts again. It takes many forms—fear, depression, anger, denial. The important thing is not to shove it back down again. Let it come out. Face it. Work through it."

"How do I do that?"

"How have you done it in the past?"

"Through art, mostly. A lot of people use journaling, I know, but I'm just no good at writing. Instead I create images out of clay." She exhaled heavily. "Though I usually don't destroy them after I've made them."

A brief smile flitted over Susan's face. "It's okay to destroy them, if it will help. Let the images surface, and then deal with them as you need to. That's much more constructive than allowing the anger to fester, or taking it out on a human target."

"Makes sense." Amber glanced at her watch. "Looks like our time is up." She got to her feet. This hadn't been nearly as bad as she had expected. She actually liked the Reverend Doctor, even if she did talk about God now and then.

But this could get messy, an inner voice warned. *If you go down this road again, it's likely to get worse—a whole lot worse—before it gets better.*

13

Road Trip

"She ain't here, Mister Duncan. I done told you, she's gone."

"What do you mean, she's *gone?*" Duncan McAlister demanded. "*Think*, Vesta! What did she say?"

"She said she was leaving, Mister Duncan." Vesta fixed her gaze on the floral carpet at her feet. She watched out of the corner of her eye as he strode to Diedre's closet, opened the door, and stood there looking in.

"Some of her clothes are missing." He turned, surveying the room. "Her camera equipment. Her laptop."

"Yes, sir."

"So where did she go?" His voice went up higher, frantic. Vesta felt bad for him, but she had promised Diedre she wouldn't tell him, and she'd keep to her vow, even if Mister Duncan fired her over it. "Please tell me. When did she leave?" he asked. "And don't try to tell me you don't know—you've followed that girl's every movement since she was two months old." He lowered his voice. "Vesta, please. She's my daughter. I'm worried about her."

"She'd been mopin' around ever since her mama's funeral. Then yesterday she just come up here, packed her things, and skedaddled. Drove out of here like she was never coming back."

"And didn't say where she was going."

"Not directly." Vesta shook her head.

The man paced across the bedroom, raking his fingers through his thick white hair. "She's gone looking for her sister. Has to be. But where?" He ran a hand over his eyes and continued, talking to himself more than to Vesta. "I'll get Jack on it right away. He's got people who can track her down—"

He turned back to her. "She's only going to get herself hurt, you know. She's going to get everybody hurt." Suddenly a light came on in his eyes. "She drove, you say? Well, she won't be gone long. Her Camry needed new tires, and—"

Vesta hesitated. "Naw, sir. Not that car."

"She didn't take the Camry?" McAlister peered into her face. "What? She took her mother's new Lexus?" Vesta didn't answer, but he didn't need verbal confirmation. "All right, then, I'll have to think of something else."

He paced for a minute or two more, then smacked a fist against the opposite palm. "Her credit cards are billed to me," he declared. "One phone call—that's all it will take to get her back home where she belongs."

Vesta frowned and shook her head, but said nothing.

"Vesta, you can't possibly think it's a good idea for a girl her age to be on the road alone. I'm doing this for her own good. I'm only trying to protect her."

"She don't need protection," Vesta whispered to his back as he exited the room. "She needs the truth. And if I know my Diedre, she won't stop until she gets it."

Diedre awoke to the sound of water banging through pipes inside the wall. Someone, somewhere, had flushed a toilet. How anyone got any sleep in a place like this, she couldn't imagine. But only the low-end chain motels would accept dogs, so at midnight last night she had dragged herself and Sugarbear wearily through a maze of garishly painted two-story rectangles, located room 1115, and dropped into the sagging double bed.

She peered at the clock, then sat up, turned on the light, and rubbed her eyes. It was barely six, and Diedre felt as if she hadn't slept at all. Twelve hours of driving had brought her to some nameless suburb on the outskirts of Chicago—a strip of neon littered with fast food restaurants, cheap motels, and used-car dealerships. Through the crack between the curtains, she could see a bit of dark gray sky, a slice of parking lot, and a shabby sign across the street advertising *EATS*.

Diedre glanced at the foot of the bed, where Sugarbear still lay curled up amid the covers. The dog stirred, stretched, and reluctantly left her warm nest to come closer. Diedre stroked her upturned belly and gazed around the room.

Last night, too exhausted from the long drive to be particular about aesthetics, Diedre hadn't given the condition of the motel much thought. Now she saw how awful it really was—the matted shag carpet, the slippery turquoise polyester bedspreads and curtains, the dark veneered furniture, chipped on the corners and showing layers of fiberboard underneath the fake wood. On the wall next to the dresser hung a gaudy, amateurish print of rocks and seashore, its frame screwed to the wall as if the proprietor treasured it like one of the Old Masters and feared someone would steal it under cover of darkness.

"Not quite what we're accustomed to, is it, girl?"

Sugarbear grunted and snuggled closer.

Diedre welcomed the nearness and warmth, even if it was canine rather than human affection. She missed Vesta, missed her nice room at home, missed the prospect of a leisurely breakfast in the tastefully decorated dining room, or in the cozy bay window nook off the kitchen. She missed her mother—not the woman with the dark secret past, but the one who had loved and nurtured her since birth. And she missed her father, even though it seemed he wasn't really her father. But Daddy was probably still acting like a father—worrying about her, being his over-protective self. It was confusing, finding out the people you thought you knew weren't what you believed them to be.

But instead of being home where she belonged, she was stuck in a seedy motel on the outskirts of Chicago, on her way to . . . to what? To Seattle, certainly. But what would she find there? Answers, or simply more questions, more confusion, more heartache?

A surge of resentment rose up in her soul. Ever since the insidious disease had invaded her mother's body, it seemed that Diedre's life had been determined by forces beyond her control. First Mama's cancer, then the letters—the revelation that she had been deceived about her own birth and deceived about her sister.

She shouldn't have to do this. Shouldn't have to go on a wild-goose chase, searching for her missing sister, trying to discover the identity of her real father. If she were going to travel anywhere, she should be going to Asheville this morning, to meet Carlene and decide on furnishings and decorations, to make plans for the grand opening of Mountain Arts. She should be looking for a house of her own, or sorting through her photographs to decide which ones to feature. She should be having lunch on the terrace at La Paz.

A normal life. That's all Diedre wanted. She had endured the heart-break of watching her mother die. She had done everything that was expected of her. Wasn't it about time she got a chance to rebuild her life, get past all the pain, find the kind of life she wanted for herself?

Apparently God or fate or the forces of the universe didn't think so. For here she was, less than a month after her mother's funeral, seven hundred miles from home, on the first leg of a journey into the unknown. And even though it was a journey she had ostensibly chosen, Diedre had the odd feeling that she hadn't really had a voice in the matter. That she had been led, somehow—once again directed by a will other than her own.

By the time she had taken Sugarbear to the designated spot to do her doggy business and swung by the motel office for a Styrofoam cup of the world's worst coffee, Diedre had made a decision. She needed someone to talk to—someone objective, someone who could help her make sense of all this. She returned to the room, rooted out her calling card, and dialed Carlene's number in Asheville.

"Mmm-hmm?" a voice answered on the fourth ring.

"Carlene? It's Diedre. Did I wake you?"

"Late night," Carlene mumbled. "What time is it?"

Diedre glanced at the clock. "Quarter to seven. Central time. Almost eight your time."

"Central time?" Carlene's voice cleared. "Where are you?"

"Near Chicago somewhere, in a Super Dump Roach Motel. Can you wake up? We need to talk."

"Okay. Give me a second. I think I heard the coffee maker go on a few minutes ago. I'll get a cup and be right back."

After a couple minutes, Carlene came back on the line. "All right. I got my coffee. What's up?"

Diedre tried to formulate all the things she wanted to say to her friend. Everything had happened so fast; Carlene knew nothing of the developments that had taken place since the funeral. Where should she begin?

"Diedre? You there?"

"Yes, I'm here."

"Is something wrong? You sound . . . strange." Carlene paused, then let out a little laugh. "Stranger than usual, I mean."

Diedre chuckled. "You wouldn't believe it."

"Try me. For starters, what are you doing in Chicago?"

"It's a long story." Diedre took a deep breath and plunged in, telling Carlene everything—about Mama's birthday gift, the old photograph and birth certificate, the revelation that her sister might still be alive, the startling news that Duncan McAlister couldn't be Diedre's real father. "And so," she finished, "I left. Just packed up and drove away. I figured I'd head for Seattle, hoping to find Sissy. And if I do find her, that she might tell me about my birth father." She paused. "But now I'm having second thoughts about it. This is crazy. I mean, I left my father—or the man I thought was my father—I don't even know what to call him now. I tried to talk to him, but I didn't get anywhere, so I just left. He's got to be hurt by my leaving, but—oh, Carlene, am I nuts?"

"Of course you are, but that's not the point," Carlene said. "The point is, you're not looking for your sister. Or your father. You're looking for yourself."

Diedre's heart caught in her throat. She could always depend upon Carlene to hack through the jungle of tangled emotions and get to the heart of the matter, but that awareness didn't make the process any more comfortable. "Maybe you're right," she admitted reluctantly. "But I don't know where to find me. And I'm beginning to think I'm absolutely insane even to conceive of a plan like this."

"You could always come to Asheville and stay with me for a while," Carlene said. "But I've got a better idea. I'm going with you."

"Come again?"

"Listen, Diedre, we've run into a little setback at the shop. The seller has to bring the electrical system up to code before we can go to closing. The whole process will take about three weeks, and then another two weeks to finish up the paperwork. Meanwhile, I'm just down here twiddling my thumbs. How about if I fly to Chicago and meet you, and we'll drive out to Seattle together?"

Diedre had a sudden mental flash—of Carlene swooping through O'Hare like some great exotic bird, scattering bright purple feathers in her wake. She smiled to herself. "Can you do that?"

"I don't know why not. Mona next door can look after the kitties."

"So you really think I should pursue this?"

"I think you have to. For your own soul's sake." Carlene paused. "Give me your number there at the motel. I'll see if I can get a flight and call you back when I know something."

A wellspring of relief opened up somewhere in the depth of Diedre's heart. "Thank you," she whispered.

"For what?"

"For being such a good friend."

"Hey, it'll be fun. Like Thelma and Louise."

Diedre rolled her eyes. "I just hope it doesn't end like *Thelma and Louise*."

"You wouldn't drive into the Grand Canyon for me? I'm disappointed."

"Your geography is terrible. We're not going to the Grand Canyon."

Carlene gave a deep, throaty laugh. "With the two of us, you never know quite where we'll end up."

14

The Tackiest Place in America

"Where did you say we were going?" Diedre repeated for the third time as she headed the Lexus west along I-90. "Let me see that map."

"Accustomed to being in control, aren't you?" Carlene grinned, reached around to the backseat, and stroked Sugarbear under the chin. "I've got it all right here," she declared. She held up several pages of paper and waved them in Diedre's direction. "I ran across this when I was doing a Net search for maps. It's a great Web site—*The Tackiest Places in America*. And our route takes us right past several of them."

"This isn't a pleasure trip, you know."

Carlene turned her round, dimpled face in Diedre's direction and gave her a mocking scowl. "Maybe not, but there's no law that prohibits us from having a little fun along the way. Think of it this way: we've been given a great opportunity to see our nation's tackiness up close, in all its glory. We might not pass this way again."

Diedre shook her head. "You are a piece of work, you know that?"

"I am," Carlene assented proudly. "It's one of the things you love most about me." She shifted her ample form in the leather seat and grimaced. "And speaking of tacky, why are we driving this $50,000 car? I feel like a rich widow from St. Petersburg."

"The Camry needed new tires, and I didn't have time to get them. What's wrong with Mama's car?"

"Nothing's wrong with it—I'm just not very experienced at living like the overprivileged elite in the lap of luxury."

"Can we get back to the tacky list?" Diedre prompted.

"Oh, yeah. Well, here's the rundown—the most outstanding monuments to American ingenuity and bad taste." She flipped pages. "Carhenge, a reproduction of Stonehenge made from junked automobiles. The Roadkill Cafe. A black widow spider made from a Volkswagen Beetle."

"You don't actually expect me to stop at these places, do you?"

"Not those. They're not on our route. I was just giving you an appetizer."

Diedre laughed and realized with a little shock how good it felt. She hadn't laughed in a long time. And although the pall of her mother's death and the subsequent revelations still hung like a shroud at the perimeters of her mind, for now the curtain had been drawn back. This was a good idea, Carlene joining her on the trip. She knew what Carlene was doing, and she was grateful. Everybody should have such a friend.

"OK, I'll bite," she said at last. "What *is* on our route?"

"First stop, Blue Earth, Minnesota," Carlene proclaimed with a flourish. "A sixty-foot statue of the Jolly Green Giant."

"You're kidding."

"Nope. There's a picture, see? In fact, the Green Giant won the Web site award, if you can call it that, for *the* tackiest place in America. I'm afraid everything else will seem anticlimactic after this, but unless you're inclined to backtrack, it can't be helped. Blue Earth comes first." She pointed toward a road sign. "About ninety miles."

Diedre leaned over the steering wheel, trying to stretch the kinks out of her back. "Well, don't keep me in suspense. What else is on the agenda?"

Carlene scanned the papers. "Mitchell, South Dakota—the Corn Palace."

"What on earth is a Corn Palace?"

"Apparently it's a building elaborately decorated—like with mosaics, only made entirely with corn and corn husks."

Diedre swiveled her head and stared at Carlene. "Corn husks? Don't they rot?"

"Says here they change the displays regularly." She raised one eyebrow. "Welcome to the Midwest."

"Anything else?"

Carlene nodded. "A place called Wall Drug, slap in the middle of nowhere. Evidently it's the largest, tackiest tourist trap in the world. Sort of a way station en route to the Badlands, just in case you haven't had your daily fix of kitsch. They advertise free water."

"Gee, how can we pass up a bargain like that?" Diedre rubbed a hand over the back of her neck. "Let's stop at the next exit, and I'll let you drive the rest of the way to—what is it? Blue Dirt?"

"Blue Earth."

"Right. I just hope Blue Earth has a motel with indoor plumbing and clean sheets."

"Are you kidding? With an attraction like the Green Giant?" Carlene shoved the papers into the glove compartment and leaned back. "They probably have a twelve-story Hilton."

Diedre paused in the lobby and looked around. It wasn't a Hilton, exactly, but the tiny motel just off I-90 at the Blue Earth exit had other features to commend it. When they opened the door into the small lobby, the delicious scents of fresh coffee and warm cinnamon wafted over Diedre. Not a soul was in sight.

Carlene elbowed her in the ribs. "Looks like a Norwegian threw up in here."

Diedre let her eyes wander and wondered for a moment whether the owner would be flattered or insulted if she took out her camera to get a few shots. Nobody in North Carolina would believe this. Every available surface—the walls, the registration desk, even the backs of chairs—bore decorative flourishes, clearly hand-painted. "It's called tole painting," she said. "It's quite an art form, and I think it's nice. It gives the place— I don't know, a homey feeling. Not like most chain motels. Now be polite." She tapped the bell on the counter.

A pink-cheeked, middle-aged woman appeared from the office wearing a nametag that said: HEIDI. "Can I help you?"

"We'd like a room, please. A double. And—" She hesitated. "We have a dog—a small one, and very well behaved. Do you take pets?"

The woman's eyes crinkled up. "You betcha. But I'll have to charge you a little extra—company policy."

Here we go, Diedre thought. *The old shaft-the-tourist routine.* But she wasn't in any mood to argue. She was tired, and she simply wanted to get some dinner and go to bed. She pulled out her Visa card. "How much?"

Heidi slid a registration form and pen toward Diedre. "Thirty-seven dollars."

"Just for the *dog?*" Diedre reared back and braced herself for an argument. "That's highway robbery!"

Heidi's round face never lost its beaming smile. "For the *room*. That includes both of you, and your little puppy. And breakfast." She gave a self-deprecating laugh. "You don't want to miss out on breakfast. I make it myself—homemade cinnamon rolls and egg bake. Sometimes lefse, too. Fresh every morning, starting at 6:30, right here in the lobby."

Diedre hadn't the foggiest idea what "egg bake" or lefse was, but anything that would still the rumbling in her stomach sounded good. "We'll take it." She handed over the credit card and began to fill out the registration.

"Oh, and we've got coffee and cookies, too." Heidi pointed toward the table around the corner, where the coffee maker sat. "Chocolate chip and sugar cookies, and I think there might be some snicker doodles left. Help yourself, and feel free to take some with you to your room."

Diedre slanted a glance in Carlene's direction. Tole painting on the furniture, cinnamon rolls for breakfast and fresh-baked cookies at night, plus a room for $37.00? Blue Earth, Minnesota, might be a bit un-sophisticated, but if this was the way they treated visitors, she didn't mind it one bit.

"So, Heidi," Carlene said, leaning over the counter, "where will we find this sixty-foot statue of the Jolly Green Giant?"

"Why, he's right up the road, at the next intersection," the woman responded, her chest puffing out with civic pride. Obviously she had no clue that her little town had won the Tackiest Place in America award. "There's a little park, just across from Wal-Mart. You can see him from our parking lot out front, unless the floodlights have gone out again." She turned her full attention to Carlene. "There are steps to the base; you can walk up there and have your picture taken, if you like."

"That'll be the first thing on our agenda tomorrow morning." Carlene pasted on a broad grin. "After your egg bake, of course."

Heidi looked up; her smile had vanished. For a minute Diedre thought Carlene might have offended her, but then she shook her head as if she'd just received news of a fiery ten-car pileup on the Interstate. "I'm sorry, hon. Your card has been declined."

"Declined?" Diedre frowned. "What does that mean?"

"Could mean you're over your credit limit," Heidi volunteered. "Happens to the best of us. Or it could mean your account's been can-celed. They don't tell us the reason—just whether to accept the card or not."

"I can't believe this!" Diedre muttered. She turned to Carlene. "What could have happened? Daddy always pays the bill on time, so that couldn't be it." She paused, then felt an idea take shape in her mind. "Daddy! Do you suppose he—"

"What? Canceled your card?" Carlene put a hand on Diedre's shoulder. "Do you think he'd really do that?"

"What else could it be? He was pretty upset about the birthday present Mama gave me. And I'm not exactly sure he'd be thrilled that I took off without a word to him, especially in Mama's Lexus. You know him. This is probably his way of telling me I'm being foolish—that I should come home. He's never wanted to talk about my sister—and lately, not even about Mama. He'd want me to just let this go, let things stay buried. Maybe he's afraid I'll get hurt if I do find my sister."

"Or maybe he doesn't want you to find out who your real father is."

"Whatever his motives, he has to be the one behind this. I guess he figures if I don't have a credit card, I'll have to turn around and come home. What do you think? Can you figure out another explanation?"

During this interchange, Heidi had been staring slack-jawed at them both. Carlene pulled out her wallet and placed a gold MasterCard on the desk. "Put it on this one."

Diedre slapped her hand down over the card before Heidi had a chance to retrieve it. "Carlene, no! You've already sacrificed a lot to make this trip with me, and—"

"You're darn right I have," Carlene interrupted with a wink. "And don't you forget it. But if you think for one minute I'm sleeping in the Maison de Lexus, you've got another thing coming. Shoot, in a small town like this we could probably buy a *house* for the price of that car, but that still doesn't mean it makes for decent lodging."

Diedre let out a long breath. "All right. I guess I don't really have very much choice, do I?" She squeezed Carlene's arm and bit her lip. "But as soon as I get this straightened out—"

"So, do you want I should ring this up, or what?" Heidi looked from Diedre's face to Carlene's, then back again.

"Sure, go ahead." Carlene nodded. "We'll settle up later, don't worry," she told Diedre. "In the meantime, I intend to get a good night's sleep."

Heidi turned her back to them and ran the card through the scanner. "So, where are you girls headed?" she called over her shoulder.

"Ultimately, Seattle," Diedre answered. "Straight out I-90."

"There's lots to see out that way."

Carlene caught Diedre's eye and, behind Heidi's back, mouthed *Corn Palace and Wall Drug*. "What do you recommend?" she asked when the manager returned to the registration desk.

"You gotta see the Corn Palace in Mitchell," Heidi responded. "It's a real work of art. And Wall Drug—wouldn't want to miss that."

Carlene turned a wide smile in Heidi's direction. "Our plan exactly. But first, the Jolly Green Giant and your egg bake."

The next morning, by the time they had eaten breakfast and driven around a bit, Diedre noticed that even Carlene was ready to concede that Blue Earth did not deserve its title of the Tackiest Place in America.

For one thing, the motel, though not luxurious, was immaculate and comfortable, each room decorated with hand-painted wall murals that gave the place an old-world feel. They got a good deal more than their $37.00 worth, to Diedre's way of thinking. Heidi's egg bake turned out to be a melt-in-your-mouth quichelike concoction. Her cinnamon rolls, still warm from the oven and dripping with sugar frosting, were enough to make you quit your diet forever.

The Jolly Green Giant stood, just as Heidi had promised, on a swath of grass across the street from Wal-Mart. Diedre and Carlene dutifully climbed its base, stood between the giant's feet above the inscription that read, "Welcome to the Valley," and took pictures of each other. Diedre tried her best to get an artistic shot of the enormous statue, but situated as it was in an open grassy space with nothing to provide composition—or even interest—she settled for a closeup of Carlene reclining on one huge green bootie.

The outrageous sixty-foot statue was a bit overwhelming, Diedre had to agree, but one quick trip through the rest of Blue Earth made her want to run for a modem and rake the Web-master over the coals for his smug ridicule of this appealing little town.

"It really is beautiful here," Carlene admitted as they cruised the tree-lined streets with the windows down and listened to church chimes drifting on the chilly morning breeze. "So peaceful. Just listen to those bells. Makes you feel like you've gone back a hundred years."

In fact, Blue Earth reminded Diedre a little of Brigadoon, the mystical Scottish town that appeared out of the fog for one day every hundred years. A village caught in the past, but content with its blessings and not inclined to bemoan its shortcomings. Main Street boasted a stunning red stone courthouse and an enviable collection of well-kept Victorian homes. Except for the infamous Minnesota winters, it might well be the kind of community that entreated you to park yourself on the porch, have coffee, and stay forever.

"I'm a little sad to leave this place," Diedre murmured as Carlene put the Lexus in gear and headed for the highway. "It almost felt like home."

"Home?" Carlene gave a grim little chuckle. "Seems I remember somebody saying that 'home is where, when you go there, they have to take you in.'"

"Right," Diedre assented absently. Her mouth spoke the words, but her heart defiantly disagreed with Carlene's joking cynicism. *Home wasn't where they* had *to take you in; home was where they* wanted *to take you in. Home was where you always knew you were welcome, where their eyes lit up at the sight of you.*

But where was that for Diedre McAlister? Was there any place like that left for her, anyone whose days would be empty without her?

For a moment her mother's drawn face swam before her eyes, but she resolutely pushed the image back down. She couldn't let herself think of Mama's love, of that comforting, nurturing presence, or she would surely fall apart. Her heart, already so fragile, didn't dare confront those memories. Not now. Not until she was stronger. Diedre reached into her bag, pulled out the brown-toned photograph, and stuck it into the visor above her head. For a long time she sat in silence, staring at the smiling faces. This was all she had left of home.

A sister who was a stranger to her.

A father she couldn't call Daddy anymore.

15

Flat, Empty Spaces

Diedre gazed out the window as the prairie rolled by. Beyond her own ghostly reflection in the glass, ridged fields of dark earth stretched all the way to the horizon—furrowed, plowed under, awaiting the spring planting. An occasional white farmhouse dotted the landscape, and a barn or two. But except for these infrequent signs of human habitation, South Dakota could have been completely deserted. Empty. Flat. As flat and empty as the highway that stretched out before them like a straight line of railroad track.

Beside her, wedged into the storage spaces of the console, were Carlene's souvenirs from their stops along what they now called the Tackyville Highway—so far, a miniature Jolly Green Giant made of molded plastic and a triangular-shaped angel from the Corn Palace, woven entirely from corn husks. The angel had no face, and the twine around its neck, bearing a card that read *Handcrafted in Mitchell, South Dakota*, made the figure look as if it had just been lynched. If this was the kind of guardian angel she got, Diedre thought darkly, she was in big trouble.

They had stopped in Mitchell for lunch, toured the Corn Palace, and now began the two-hundred-mile stretch of nothingness, marked only by roadside signs luring them on to the uncontested Middle of Nowhere, to the infamous Wall Drug.

The monotonous landscape had a hypnotic effect, and Diedre's eyelids grew heavy. For lunch they had tried the Specialty of the House, what the locals called a "hot turkey sandwich"—white breast meat on white bread with white mashed potatoes smothered in white gravy—and the heavy meal lay like an undigested lump of paste in the pit of her stomach. She heard a soft snoring noise behind her and turned to see Sugarbear curled up in her bed, sound asleep.

"I think she's got the right idea," Carlene commented, briefly averting her eyes from the road. "You look tired; why don't you take a nap?"

"Are you all right to drive?"

"I'm wide awake. If I get sleepy, I'll let you know."

Diedre retrieved a small pillow from the backseat, leaned it against the window, and closed her eyes.

Carlene set the cruise control on seventy and pointed the Lexus down the unbending highway. One car passed going the opposite direction; the driver lifted one hand from the steering wheel and waved as he went by.

She had never driven west before. The two or three times she had traveled to California, she had been in the air at thirty thousand feet, skirting the flat prairie and vast deserts as if there were nothing of significance down below. The really important action was taking place on the coast, and everyone seemed to want to get there as quickly as possible.

This time she was getting a different perspective, a ground-level point of view. A lone bay horse, still in his winter coat, tossed his head and galloped in circles around his pasture, snorting in the chilly spring air. A flock of landlocked sea gulls picked languidly at the leftover seed in an unplowed cornfield. Far away, a thin column of smoke drifted toward the clouds.

The prairie held a different kind of beauty than the lush layers of the Blue Ridge Carlene called home, but it was beauty nevertheless. The sky was bigger, the air fresher, the pace of life slower. You could see for miles out here. You could let your mind drift, like that smoke on the breeze, and allow it to take you places you'd never been before.

She glanced over at Diedre, who sat with her feet tucked under her and her face pressed against the glass. *Where will her thoughts take her?* Carlene wondered. *And will she be willing to follow?*

The truth was, she was worried about Diedre. They had been best friends since college, and except for the recurring dreams about her sister, Diedre had seldom been faced with a major life crisis. Until now. If struggles made you strong, Diedre McAlister might end up winning a gold medal in weightlifting.

It wasn't that Diedre was shallow—in fact, she had always been re-markably insightful and steady for a girl who had every kind of security offered to her on a silver platter. But suddenly, without warning, she had been subjected to a blitzkrieg of pain and emotional upheaval. First the recurrence of her mother's cancer, then Cecilia's death, then the revela-tions that followed about her mother, her sister, her father.

And Carlene had been forced to stand by and watch, feeling helpless, while her closest friend shut down. Diedre hadn't really grieved the loss of her mother yet—she hadn't been still long enough. Almost immedi-ately, she had been swept up in a storm of confusion and frantic activity surrounding the visitation and funeral. And before that turmoil had even begun to settle, she had lit out on this trip like a missile launched from a slingshot, blindly catapulting toward—

Toward what?

Toward the truth, Diedre believed. Toward an unknown sister, a nameless father, an identity she couldn't begin to comprehend. And although Carlene valued the truth and understood the necessity of Diedre's search, she also knew that truth came at a high price: there was pain in breaking through to it.

Still, she reminded herself, a real friend didn't try to control another's actions or second-guess her decisions. Free advice was a bad bargain on both sides. Carlene's job as she saw it right now was to be with Diedre, to wait, to be present, to love, and—as much as possible, given her nature—to keep her mouth shut until she was invited to open it.

In the meantime, she would pray that when Diedre finally did discover the truth, she would also find the strength to bear it.

Through half-open eyes, Diedre watched the landscape pass in a narrow band, like a movie in letter-box format on a nine-inch television screen. Sleep had eluded her, although she kept her face averted and pretended to doze. Maybe, if she remained quiet long enough, her mind would be able to sort some of this out on its own.

Long-distance driving, she was beginning to discover, was not an occupation for the faint of heart. The rhythmic thump of wheel against pavement mesmerized the soul, sending Diedre back into memories she thought were lost forever.

Images clicked through her mind—a panorama of isolated pictures from the past. Her birthday party the year she was six, with a cake created around a beautiful Barbie, so that the doll stood upright in the center, and layers of chocolate cake with cream cheese frosting arched out from its waist like a enormous skirt. Her first dance recital, with her parents in the front row, beaming proudly. The state high-school tennis tournament, where she had come in second in mixed doubles and brought home a trophy to display on the mantel. The photo taken before her junior prom, in which she and her date—was his name really Ken?—posed stiffly together like a plastic wedding-cake bride and groom in front of the big fireplace in the parlor. The bright blue Mazda convertible Daddy gave her as a graduation present the year she turned eighteen.

Happy memories, memories of the Perfect Childhood.

And all of it had been a lie.

How could she have been both blind and deaf to all the signs? How could she not have known that something in the McAlister household was terribly, terribly wrong? There were clues; there had to have been. Had she simply closed her eyes and shut her ears, willing the truth to go away?

Another image surfaced in her mind, this one fuzzy and indistinct, like a jerky old home movie. She had been very small, no more than three or four—she must have been that young, because she could re-member wearing soft flannel pajamas with feet in them and dragging her teddy bear by the ear. A nightmare had awakened her, but she hadn't cried out. Instead, she had gotten out of bed and was tiptoeing down the hall toward her mother's bedroom.

Didn't most children call out to their parents when they were fright-ened? Didn't the parents come to them in the night, rather than the other way around? But Diedre had gone to her mother, quietly, secre-tively, as if she had something to hide.

And didn't most parents sleep together, in the same bedroom? Yet she recalled how shocked she had been to hear her father's voice coming from her mother's room. His bedroom was down the hall on the other side of Diedre's, at the opposite end of the house. He had always slept down there. Diedre had been eleven years old before she consciously realized that other children's parents shared not just a room, but also a bed. And even then she assumed it was because the McAlisters were wealthier than most other people and had a bigger house.

The video in her mind played on, until the child Diedre stood at the door of her mother's bedroom. She could hear the voices clearly now, her father's raised in anger or exasperation.

"It's for the best. And after what she's done, she should be grateful she's not facing prison. But she's not coming back into this house. Not ever."

Mama was crying, and when she spoke, her voice sounded choked and rough. "But Duncan, she's our daughter!" At the word *daughter*, a thrill of fear went up little Diedre's spine. Was he talking about *her*? About sending her away? He had to be; he only had one daughter. But maybe if she kept very quiet and was very, very good, he would change his mind.

She huddled in the shadows while her father stalked out of the room, slammed the door, and stomped down the hall. She couldn't go in to Mama now; she had to be good and not cause any trouble. And she was getting to be a big girl, after all; she could take care of herself.

Strangling on unshed tears, the child Diedre hugged her teddy bear to her chest and waited until the door to Daddy's bedroom shut with a bang. Then she dashed down the hall as fast as her stubby little legs could carry her, jumped into bed, and pulled the covers up over her head.

They had been talking about Sissy . . .

In the backseat, Sugarbear grunted, pawed at the corner of her bed, and settled down again with a sigh. Carlene was humming quietly to herself, tapping her fingers against the steering wheel in time to the music in her head. Diedre shut her eyes and tried to will herself to sleep as the tires made dull thudding noises across the expansion spaces in the highway. But the images kept coming, as if she had unwittingly opened a floodgate to the past and couldn't get it shut again.

All those hushed conversations that ended abruptly the moment she walked into a room. Her mother murmuring, "I have to go" into the telephone, then slamming down the receiver and acting nervous and agitated for an hour afterward. Unintelligible voices raised behind closed doors. Uncle Jack coming to the house at all hours of the day or night, explaining nothing, simply muttering that he "had business" with Daddy. Mama crying for no reason and stifling her tears if Diedre happened upon her without warning.

And "the look" Daddy sometimes gave her—that fleeting, panicked stare, as if he didn't know her at all.

Things aren't what they seem, Mama had warned her. And, *Don't expect the truth to be what you thought it would be.*

Well, Mama had spoken truthfully, at least that one time in her life, at the very end. But why had she done it—why had she been unfaithful to Daddy? People didn't just have an affair, bear a child, and then go back to their normal lives for the next twenty-five years as if nothing out of the ordinary had happened. Didn't she know an affair would eventually wreck everything, ruin not just her own life, but everyone else's as well? And then later, when the deed couldn't be undone, couldn't she have told the whole story, or none at all?

Keeping the secret all these years had been bad enough. But what kind of mother would dump the truth in her daughter's lap and leave her behind to clean up the mess?

Anger welled up in Diedre. Despair and abandonment, an adult's rage and a little child's fear, all combined into one enormous, suffocating sense of loss. The loss of her mother, her innocence, her identity.

For a moment Diedre saw herself again as that tiny child, cowering in the dark shadows of the hallway. Perhaps if she stood very still, her mama would come to her, explain everything, and kiss her fears away. Maybe if she were very quiet, and very, very good, this would all fade into nothingness, and she would awaken to find it had all been a bad dream.

But that wasn't going to happen, and the adult Diedre knew it. Mama was dead. Daddy wasn't Daddy anymore. The flat, empty spaces in her soul stretched out before her like a barren wilderness.

She laid her head against the cold glass of the window and began to cry.

16

Badlands and Black Hills

With her left hand on the wheel and her right hand gripping Diedre's, Carlene steered the Lexus down the straight line of highway. Outside the car, a bright afternoon sun shone in a chilly April-blue sky. Inside, the storm had finally broken, and torrential forces lashed at her best friend's soul. For a long time Diedre sobbed and muttered incoherently, and Carlene just sat there, holding her hand and murmuring over and over, "It's all right, let it out."

Sugarbear, instinctively aware that her human was distressed, became restless and began to whine and paw at the back of Diedre's seat. At last Carlene reached over and scooped her into the front of the car. There wasn't much room, given the console between the leather bucket seats, but the dog managed to wedge herself in, half on the seat and half in Diedre's lap, and began nuzzling at Diedre's arm.

After a moment Diedre stirred and lifted the dog to her shoulder. "It's okay, sweetie. I'm fine." A long wet tongue darted out and slobbered across her cheek, and Diedre relented and gave a halfhearted smile. "She can always make me feel better," she murmured, cutting a sidelong glance at Carlene. "I don't know why, but it never fails."

"It's unconditional love," Carlene responded. "Total selflessness. She's only interested in what makes you happy."

When Sugarbear had calmed down, Diedre returned her to her bed in the backseat. The dog sighed and propped her chin on the edge of the bed, her soulful brown eyes following Diedre's every move. Carlene watched her, too, wishing she would talk, but unwilling to intrude into her private grief. The time would come, sooner or later, and when it did, Carlene would be here.

For a long while Diedre said nothing, just sat staring out the window. Finally she turned back to Carlene. "Where are we?"

Carlene pointed to a sign on the right, a huge billboard bearing the likeness of a cowboy on a bucking horse. *Wall Drug, Next Exit.* "Tell you what," she said. "Let's stop for a few minutes, get some of that free water and something to eat, and see this wonder of the modern world. Then before the sun sets we'll drive on down and take the loop through the Badlands National Park."

"Badlands," Diedre repeated, shuddering a little. "I feel like that's where I've been living lately."

"From what I understand, it's barren, but beautiful."

Diedre grimaced. "Like I said—my life. The barren part, anyway."

Wall Drug turned out to be nearly as tacky as the Web site promised. Its claim to fame was its sheer size—acres, Diedre thought, maybe even square miles of rubber snakes and plastic squirt guns and acrylic deer with clocks in their bellies and cheap T-shirts, all plastered with the logo, *I ♥ Wall Drug.*

The place made Diedre feel claustrophobic and grimy, but she tried to be patient while Carlene bought a small red birdhouse with WALL

DRUG in block letters on the roof. They purchased sandwiches, chips, and soft drinks, a bottle of water and a small bag of doggy treats for Sugarbear. At Carlene's insistence, Diedre took a few pictures, but her heart wasn't in it. Within forty-five minutes they were back on the road again, heading into the loop that would take them through the Badlands.

It was still early in the season, and the park was almost deserted. On a hillside overlooking waving prairie grass flanked by the high buttes and sharply eroded spires that gave the Badlands its name, they stopped the car and ate their sandwiches.

After a few minutes of silence, broken only by the sounds of chewing, Diedre opened the door and got out.

Carlene grabbed her arm. "Where are you going?"

"Relax, I'm not going to jump off a cliff," Diedre said. "Pop the trunk, will you? I need my camera."

Carlene let go of her arm and rolled her eyes heavenward. "Atta girl."

"Don't make a big deal of it, will you?"

"OK. But the wind's cold out there. Put on your coat."

"Yes, Mother." The words were out of Diedre's mouth before they registered in her brain, and just as quickly, tears stung at her eyes.

Carlene's gaze never left her face. "Are you all right?"

"I'm fine. Or I will be. I just need to get some of this on film before the light changes."

She got out of the car, pulled a camera and two telephoto lenses from the trunk, and began walking, searching for just the right vantage point to make the best use of the remaining sunlight on the hills. The buttes were magnificent, splashed with late-afternoon sun that turned gray rock to gold. Behind her, Diedre could hear Carlene walking with Sugarbear in the grass, and before her, the vistas swam in her tear-filled eyes as if reflected in a shimmering pool.

She finished one roll of film and was beginning to load another when she realized that her fingers, now numb and clumsy, had taken on the color of pale putty. The sun had shifted, and the wind whipped through her hair and made her cheeks tingle with cold.

Carlene put down the driver's side window and called to her. "Got what you need?"

"Yeah. I'm coming." Diedre sprinted to the car and got in.

When she shut the door, the sudden silence descended around them, so profound that Diedre could hear the rush of her own blood pumping in her ears.

Finally Carlene spoke. "Do you want to talk about it?"

"Talk about what?"

"Your grief. Your confusion. The things you've been crying over for the last two hundred miles."

"No, I don't want to talk about it."

"Yes, you do."

Diedre looked up to find Carlene smiling faintly, gazing out over the vast pinnacles that loomed up from the prairie—gray and purple steeples of rock, tall and forbidding.

"It's amazing, isn't it?" Carlene pointed toward the vista beyond the car window. "All those miles of open land, so comfortable, so predictable. Then you round a bend, crest a hill, and face this." She waved a hand at the imposing stone monuments. "I can only imagine what those wagon train settlers felt when they caught their first glimpse of this. Nature can be unnerving, intimidating."

Diedre twisted up her face in a scowl. "All right, you don't have to hit me over the head with a metaphor. I get your point."

"I was just making conversation."

"Sure you were." Diedre paused for a moment and let out a soul-deep sigh. "You're right. I've had my comfortable world uprooted, and I wasn't prepared for it. But how do you get prepared to face truths that have been hidden for years?" She frowned and narrowed her eyes. "If you were in my position, how would you deal with it?"

"I'd be outraged," Carlene answered immediately. "I'd be furious at my mother, both for not telling me sooner—and for having an affair in the first place. I'd be angry at my father for all this pretense and manipulation; I'd probably even be mad at my sister for not coming back to find me."

"Yes," Diedre said. "Yes to all of it."

"And I'd be hurt," Carlene went on. "Hurt and confused and grieving, and not knowing how to express any of those feelings."

Diedre felt tears stinging her eyes, and she blinked hard and turned
toward the horizon. It looked like the jagged jawbone of a dinosaur,
gaping with enormous dark teeth, ready to chew her up and spit her out
again. A terrifying beauty. She shuddered.

"I want to grieve for Mama," she said after a while. "I loved her so
much, and I miss her. But every time I think of her now, I just get so
angry. And I keep having to remind myself that Daddy's not my real
father, that someone else—" She stopped, unable to continue.

Carlene stared at her. "Go on," she prompted.

"The issue that keeps eating at me," Diedre said at last, "is, *who?* If
Daddy's not my real father, who is? Was Mama in love with him—and
if not, what led her to be unfaithful to Daddy? It's this enormous question mark, this big black hill that blocks the sun and turns my heart
cold." She shook her head. "I have to get the answer to that question,
Carlene. I have to know."

Carlene stashed her sandwich wrapper in the trash bin and cranked
the engine. "Well, that's what we came for," she said as she eased the car
back onto the road. "We've got two more days until we get to Seattle.
Let's see if we can locate your sister, and maybe we'll find the truth."

17

An Image Trapped in Stone

Diedre put a new roll of film in her camera, replaced the wide-angle lens with a zoom, and took a few closeups of Crazy Horse. Instinctively, almost mechanically, her mind went on autopilot, taking into account issues such as light and composition and perspective.

Two more days to Seattle, Carlene had said. But two days was quickly turning into three, maybe even four. From the Badlands, they had driven into Rapid City for the night, then detoured down Highway 16 to spend three hours this morning at Mount Rushmore—including, at Carlene's insistence, the hideous strip of tourist traps at the foot of the monument—and finally to the unfinished granite sculpture honoring the Native American chief Crazy Horse. After they left here, they would continue to Custer State Park and have an afternoon of relaxation, culminating in a night at the Blue Bell Lodge, which offered individual log cabins right on the park grounds, amid deer and antelope and buffalo. Diedre could almost hear the strains of "Home on the Range" being sung around the campfire.

Maybe Carlene was right. She had protested that they simply couldn't drive six hundred miles a day for an entire week, that they needed to relax a little and take in the sights. But she had coerced Diedre into snapping pictures everywhere they went, and Diedre suspected an ulterior motive, some half-baked plan for turning those photos into a major exhibit. She could see it now: a touring road show called *Tackyville USA*. They'd make a bundle.

She had to admit, however, that the Crazy Horse monument was impressive. So far, only the front half of the carving had been blasted from the rock, but when the entire memorial was completed, it would be a sculpting feat to rival the Great Sphinx or the ancient pyramids of Egypt. The Chief's head alone was nine stories tall.

"Look at the details!" Carlene said in awe-struck tones. "The way the chief's hair blows back from his head, the arch of the horse's neck, the hand stretching out pointing east—"

"Is that east?"

"Well, east on the compass, anyway." Carlene moved away, murmuring, "It's fabulous."

And it was. But what affected Diedre the most was not the beauty of the sculpture or the sheer impossibility of its size, but the agony of it. The massive Chief Crazy Horse emerged from the mountain—his chest and shoulders thrust forward, his eyes on the horizon, his hand reaching out—as if striving to liberate himself from the grip of the granite behind him. Even his horse struggled and flailed against the rock, pawing the air with its hooves, lunging vainly toward freedom.

Diedre understood, at least partially. Something inside her, too, was being chiseled from its moorings, released from a lifetime of captivity. But she couldn't be sure whether the transformation was positive or negative, a blessing or a curse. Whether she should, like Crazy Horse, strain forward toward her liberty or shrink back into the comfortable imprisonment of the rock from which she was being hewn.

⟋

The drive through Custer State Park had unique gifts of nature to offer—up close views of a buffalo herd, a doe with a fawn barely two days old, and a mother fox with an adorable litter of playful, adventurous red kits. Shortly before sunset, they checked in at the Blue Bell Lodge and settled their gear in a tiny log cabin overlooking a clearing with several deer browsing in the dewy grass.

The quietness of the evening was broken only by the music of birds, the gentle whoosh of wind through the tree branches, and the faint rush of a waterfall somewhere in the distance. Sugarbear, overly energetic from being cooped up in the car, had been chasing the tennis ball Carlene threw for her, but apparently she had tired of the game, or perhaps been lulled by the peacefulness of the place, and now lay on the top step gazing out into the gathering dusk. With a sigh of contentment Diedre parked herself on the porch.

"I'll be right out," Carlene called from inside the cabin. "I'm just changing into something a little warmer." A couple minutes later she appeared, dressed in black leggings and a bright fuchsia sweatshirt that came nearly to her knees. She handed Diedre a Diet Pepsi and deposited a bag of Oreos on the table between their chairs.

For a while Diedre busied herself with the task of unscrewing Oreos and licking the cream filling off. Only after half a dozen cookies did she work up the nerve to broach the dilemma that had been weighing on her all day.

"Carlene, what do you believe about God?"

Carlene was leaning back in the deck chair with her tennis shoes propped on the porch rail, sipping her diet soda and watching as the sunset spangled the clouded sky with red and yellow and orange. At first she didn't move, didn't answer—didn't give any indication that she'd even heard the question. Then, slowly, she removed her feet from the rail and dropped them heavily onto the wide planks of the porch floor.

"What kind of question is that?" She turned to face Diedre.

"A legitimate one," Diedre countered. "I know you believe *in* God— that's not what I'm asking. I want to know what you believe *about* God."

"Do I believe in the *omni*s, you mean? That God is omnipotent, omniscient, omnipresent, and all the rest?" She scratched an eyebrow with one finger. "I suppose I do. I'm not always sure what that means, or how those qualities translate into God's relationships with people, but I do believe."

"So do I. At least, I've always believed that there is a Supreme Being, and that God is loving, compassionate, powerful, all-knowing. But that's not quite what I'm asking. I guess I'm looking for something more specific, more immediate."

Carlene took another sip of her drink. "Where is all this coming from?"

"I suppose it's coming out of my own need," Diedre admitted reluctantly. "All my adult life—an admittedly short time—I've regarded myself as a capable, resourceful, relatively intelligent person who could handle pretty much whatever came along."

"I'd say that's a fair assessment."

"When Mama got sick, I felt helpless, but I didn't feel angry with God. Cancer is just one of those things that happens to people. I prayed for her healing, of course, but I didn't blame God when she didn't get well. I accepted it as part of the natural course of life and death. But ever since her funeral—"

She paused and shrugged. Carlene waited, motioning for her to continue.

"Well, I feel as if I've been going around in circles," Diedre said after a minute. "Right before she died, Mama told me to search out my own truth, but not to expect it to be what I thought it would be. And that's what I'm trying to do, except that I've only got bits and pieces of it, like a jigsaw puzzle with whole chunks of the picture missing and no box cover to go on. I don't know where to find the missing pieces, don't even know what the finished picture is supposed to look like."

"And just how does your question about God play into this?" Carlene leaned forward and rested her elbows on the porch rail, gazing off into the distance.

"I need—I don't know, *something*. Insight. Wisdom. Direction. Hope, maybe. I need to feel as if I'm not alone in this, that Someone who knows more about it than I do is with me, watching over me, giving me guidance along the way. I've attended church most of my life, but I'm still not sure how God works, or even if God does get involved in people's lives. That's why I asked you what you believe about God. I'm not sure if I'd recognize divine guidance if it came up and bit me on the leg."

Carlene stifled a laugh. "Maybe you don't need to recognize it. Maybe you just need to listen to it."

"How do I do that?"

Carlene considered this question for a moment. Then she cocked her head to one side and said, "Follow your heart."

"That's it? That's your great offering of wisdom?"

"Hey, you asked me what I believe about God. Well, here it is: I believe God knows our hearts, knows the deepest desires and needs of our souls. I don't accept the idea that God bulldozes into our lives without being invited, but I also think we can be unaware that we've issued the invitation."

"How do you mean?"

Carlene thought for a minute. "I guess just that we don't always have to get on our knees and compose some intentional kind of prayer. God sees beyond the walls we erect around our souls, walls of self-protection or self-sufficiency."

"You mean that God hears when our hearts call out, even if the cry is too faint for human ears?" Diedre asked.

"Exactly," Carlene nodded. "It's the universal, quintessential prayer: *Help.*"

"I'm not very accustomed to asking for help."

"You've already asked. You've admitted you need it."

Diedre thought about that for a minute. "So what kind of response should I expect?"

"Who knows?" Carlene shrugged. "Maybe all the things you've enumerated: wisdom, direction, the missing puzzle pieces. Maybe just the strength to endure whatever the future holds." She ruffled a hand through her hair and looked into Diedre's eyes. "When we were in college, we pretty much thought we understood everything about everything, didn't we?"

Diedre laughed. "Did we? Well, we were wrong—in a big way."

"Yeah," Carlene said. "I guess we grew up and found out how little we can really be sure about. But of one thing I am very, very certain: you can't go back. You have to keep going forward. And for me, faith in God means that I don't have all my questions answered, and yet I still believe."

"Like Crazy Horse," Diedre mused.

"Crazy Horse?" Carlene repeated. "You mean the big guy in the rock?"

"Right. I had a very powerful response to being at the Crazy Horse monument today," Diedre said. "I felt like I was there in the mountain with him, half-trapped in the granite, straining forward, trying to escape the imprisonment of the rock, yet uncertain whether I really wanted to get out or not."

"Freedom is risky, that's for sure." Carlene frowned and bit her lower lip. "But honestly, what choice do you have? You've already been confronted with at least part of the truth. You can't go back to being Daddy's girl. I know you, Diedre; I can't imagine you'd want to go on being deluded. It's scary and it's costly and things are very confusing right now, but I can't help believing that when you get to the end of all this, the payoff will be worth the price."

"I guess you're right. Something inside me keeps pushing me on, insisting that I can't stay in the past, that I have to build the future on the truth rather than on a lie."

"Don't you think you'll be glad you did?"

Diedre heaved a sigh. "Maybe. But it sure felt safer inside the mountain."

18

The Shepherd and the Lamb

Kitsap County, Washington

Early May

In the past few weeks, ever since she had begun meeting with the Reverend Doctor Susan Quentin, Amber had vacillated between hope and despair. On her best days, she found herself looking forward to the challenge and progress that counseling could bring—and, of course, to some distant point in the unknown future when she would, once and for all, be free from the black cloud that cast a shadow over all her relationships, present and past. On her worst days, she doubted that the sun would ever shine again.

Prodded on by Meg's gentle encouragement, she had repaired the statue of the Two Sisters, and now it sat on a shelf next to her sculpting table. At the place where the girls' hands joined, you could still see a faint line in the clay, a hairline scar.

But nothing was ever perfect, was it? No matter how idyllic life seemed, there was always a dark underbelly, a hidden place, a secret. Something families didn't talk about in public—or even in private.

Amber had learned long ago that perfection was not an option. You could try to keep them quiet, but the skeletons in the closet insisted on rattling about and making their presence known. Most things got fractured in the end, and the only thing you could do about it was try to effect a competent repair job.

That's what she was endeavoring to do now, Amber mused—to repair her life, the same way she had put the pieces of the ruined statue back together again. The work was agonizing, and there would always be scars, evidences of the damage. But the only other option was to throw the whole thing away and forget about it.

Just as her father had attempted to do with her so long ago.

She shifted her gaze from the Two Sisters statue back to the current work in progress. This was the sculpture she would take with her to her next session with Father Susan, the one that revealed, at least in part, the source of the pain and anger that overwhelmed her.

She was almost finished, and she could barely stand to look at it. Whenever she touched the cool, pliable clay, she fought against the temptation to smash the figure into nothingness. Every time her eyes rested on that face, a flame rose up in her belly that felt as if it might consume her.

What doesn't kill you makes you strong, she reminded herself, and in truth, the fire of her rage seemed to be having a purifying, cleansing effect. In years gone by she had tried to forget, to run away, to put the past behind her. But it hadn't stayed back there; it never did. It kept following her, stalking her, waiting for her to let down her guard.

Just as in the dream that came again last night—the one where she was running, panting, falling, trying to escape. And following her, up the mountains and through the woods—what? A shrouded form, a figure whose face she could not make out.

And yet, instinctively, she knew the identity of her pursuer. Knew that if she stayed asleep long enough, one of these nights the beast that shadowed her would overtake her. She would hear its footsteps on her heels, feel its hot breath on her neck, and turn in terror to see—

Herself.

It was time to stop running and let the beast catch up.

◦⌒◦

Susan Quentin sat in her office, her chin propped on her fingers—preparing herself, praying, thinking. Thinking about Amber Chaney.

The woman had so much going for her. She was wise and witty, intelligent and intensely creative. Under different circumstances, exactly the kind of person Susan would choose as a friend and confidante.

But they couldn't be friends. At least not yet.

That was the problem with being a parish pastor—and a counselor. You had to keep a professional distance, to care and yet remain objective. She loved the work, loved the challenge of helping people sort through their problems and come to a resolution. Loved the intellectual and spiritual stimulation of opening people's minds to new ways of perceiving and relating to God. It was a calling that made her feel complete, at one with God and with herself.

But sometimes it could be isolating, too. Isolating and exhausting. Even when she wasn't technically working—meeting with clients or parishioners, preparing worship services, visiting hospitals and nursing homes, planning weddings and funerals—her mind and heart were never far away from the flock.

The flock. It was still an apt image, Susan thought, even if it was two thousand years removed from its social setting. In Jesus' day, a shepherd lived with the sheep, night and day. A shepherd stayed out in the fields, eating on the run, sleeping on the ground. Keeping watch for predators, leading the sheep to fresh water and good pasture, midwifing at lambing time and burying the bones of the old ones when they died.

And that was exactly what she did. She was a shepherd. A *pastor*.

Although *pastor* wasn't the preferred title among modern Episcopalians—it was too intimate, she suspected, too personal—she preferred it immeasurably to *priest*, and probably for the same reasons.

Referring to herself as *pastor* made her feel more connected, some-how. Still, she imagined that even those good shepherds Christ talked about, the ones who had lent their name to her present calling, were no doubt solitary, isolated individuals with few friends except among other shepherds.

Susan could just see it—all those filthy, smelly sheepherders from the hills of Judea congregating at the Nazareth Rotary Club once a month for the Shepherd's Association luncheon. Trekking to Jerusalem every year for the National Council of Shepherds Annual Meeting. And then going back to their respective lonely hillsides to carry on.

Things hadn't changed much in the past two millennia.

So here she was, the Reverend Doctor Susan Quentin, parish priest in a community where everyone recognized her face, greeted her by name on the street, and welcomed her with the place of honor when-ever she walked through the door. Everybody loved her, but nobody really *knew* her.

She had read once about an old Jewish rabbi, an acclaimed teacher with a large following of young and eager pupils. One of his students, overcome with wonder at his mentor's wisdom, cried out, "I love you, my master!"

The rabbi thought about this for a moment, and then responded, "How can you claim to love me if you do not know what makes me weep?"

None of Susan Quentin's flock knew that she rarely cried when she was sad, but couldn't hold back the tears when touched by some poignant sweetness. They weren't aware that she despised slapstick but loved satire. They had no idea that she planned her daily schedule around the airing of *Jeopardy*, or that she preferred her steak rare, or that she hated big parties but loved a cutthroat foursome of Trivial Pursuit.

Still, she found satisfaction in her work, even if it came with a dis-tance. And her work with Amber had been rewarding. Amber had done a lot of the hard work already. Most of her recovery had already been accomplished years ago, and despite her current depression and anger, she was much more emotionally healthy than she gave herself credit for. Remarkably healthy, considering what she had been through. They were just tying up loose ends now.

Susan was fairly certain she understood the secrets her client wasn't willing to talk about yet—at least not with her counselor. The recent setbacks were not a result of repressed memories, some hidden truth Amber did not know about herself. She knew, all right. She just needed to tell the story in her own time, in her own way. She needed to find forgiveness. Rest. A place of peace in her own soul.

And much to Susan's surprise, she was beginning to look for it. For all her protests against a God who could not be trusted, Amber had actually started coming to church with Meg and TwoJoe. She had admitted that parts of the worship service were becoming meaningful to her, that she might consider giving this faith thing another try.

After that first session, Susan hadn't talked to Amber again about God. But as had been her experience in the past, the Almighty seemed to be working in the background entirely without her help. When Amber finally did come to peace with herself, it wouldn't happen because some counselor-priest had coerced her into swallowing religion whole. It would be the result of her own search for truth, a combination of inner reconciliation and spiritual insight.

And it didn't matter one bit whether counseling or faith turned out to be the primary catalyst for Amber Chaney's emotional healing. Therapy and spirituality were both in God's hands.

All Susan Quentin could do was listen and pray.

On the edge of her desk lay a worn, dog-eared copy of *The Book of Common Prayer*, bound in burgundy leather. Susan picked it up and turned to the Order for Compline, prayers for the end of the day. This was her favorite of the daily offices, with its eloquent prayers for protection during the hours of the night. She had long been convinced that those words applied not just to physical darkness, but to the dark night of the soul as well.

Her eyes lingered on the evening Collect. She knew it by heart, but her gaze touched down lightly on the familiar, comforting supplication, and she smiled. As she had done so often in the past, she would pray again for all whose hearts languished in the darkness: for clients who labored uphill toward mental and emotional health, for parishioners who groped toward God. For all who found themselves enervated by the sheer effort of living.

Including herself.

Including, and especially, Amber Chaney.

"Be present, O merciful God, and protect us through the hours of this night, so that we who are wearied by the changes and chances of this life may rest in your eternal changelessness; through Jesus Christ our Lord. Amen."

At the appointed hour, Amber Chaney paused outside Susan's office. The door stood ajar a couple of inches, and Amber pushed it open with one shoulder and set her burden down on the desk. "Well, here it is, raw and unfired," she said, and with a little flourish removed the wet towel that covered the still-damp clay.

Susan sat for a few moments in silence, considering Amber's work. Clearly, the woman had taken seriously the exhortation to let her feelings come out in her sculpture, not to hold back. It was a magnificent piece, full of dark power and subtle emotional clues.

Rendered in a charcoal-colored clay, almost black, the sculpture depicted an enormous easy chair occupied by a man with a little girl in his lap. On the surface it looked as if this might be the loving embrace of an adoring father or a doting uncle, his arms wrapped around the girl in an attitude of devotion. But the smile on his face was devoid of any real compassion, his eyes seemed hollow and empty, and his hands, clasped around the child, knotted into fists at her waist. As if she were trying to break free from his grip, the girl's tiny fingernails dug into his forearms, her wiry little body taut and unyielding, tense and trapped.

Susan could feel Amber's eyes scrutinizing her as she surveyed the sculpture. "Interesting," she said at last.

"Interesting?" Amber let out a enormous laugh and dropped into the leather easy chair. "Come on, Reverend Doctor, you can do better than that. I opened a vein for this piece. I nearly destroyed it twice, and it just as nearly destroyed me. And all you can say is, 'Interesting'?"

Susan grinned, leaned back in her chair, and regarded Amber. "That's what a shrink is *supposed* to say. It's in all the books." She slipped a fresh cassette into the tape recorder and pushed the red button. "Shall we talk about it?"

"What's to talk about? It's all there." Amber edged forward. "What do you see?"

Susan watched Amber's face carefully as she spoke. "I see a representation of a grown man—a father, perhaps, or an uncle, someone close— and the child he supposedly adores. Everything seems fine and loving and normal, until you look harder, and then you see that the man has his little girl trapped against her will. He pretends to be holding her, but he actually has her captured by his superior strength. She's trying to get away from him, but she isn't powerful enough."

The grin faded, and a shadow passed over Amber's countenance. "Very good, Doctor," she whispered. "Meg was right. You *are* the best."

"You're doing the work here," Susan corrected. "I'm just sitting back and watching."

"So how come I'm paying you ninety bucks an hour?" Amber quipped. Then she shrugged. "Oh, that's right; I'm not paying you, am I?"

Susan laughed. "If you are, somebody else is getting our money." She let the silence settle between them and then said quietly, "Tell me about the men in your life."

"You know about my father; I've already told you. The great man, loved and honored by all who know him. The man who threw his daughter away like last week's garbage."

"Anyone else?"

"Yes. Uncle Jack. He wasn't really my uncle—he was my father's attorney, and a close friend of the family. He worshiped my mother; I always thought he was secretly in love with her. And he treated me like his own daughter." She grimaced. "Yes, exactly like his daughter. The same way Daddy treated me, at least in the end. He helped my father put me away."

"So he betrayed you, too."

Amber hesitated for a moment. "Everyone did."

"Your father and your Uncle Jack both claimed to love you. But neither of them was what he seemed to be."

Amber sighed. "Few of us are. Daddy was—probably still is—manipulative and controlling. The center of the universe. Everything had to be his way, and his almighty reputation had to be protected at all costs. And Uncle Jack did whatever Daddy asked him to do. As usual."

"How do you feel when you think about them?"

"Furious, mostly." Amber bit her lip and shrugged. "For a long time I tried not to think about the two of them at all—the emotions were too overwhelming, and I was afraid I wouldn't survive them. But now—"

"Now?" Susan prompted.

"Now the anger I've been suppressing all these years has surfaced again. I guess I knew it would, but this time it feels different. While I was doing this sculpture, I let it come out, as you advised me to do. I threw a few old pots against the barn wall. Then I started to work on this piece, night and day, until my eyes were so bleary I couldn't see straight and my shoulders were tied up in knots. And even though I exhausted myself doing it, I felt good afterward—really good. Like I was taking something of myself back."

A jolt of adrenaline shot through Susan's veins. They were getting close; she could feel it. "What were you taking back?"

For a minute or two Amber didn't answer. She seemed far away, as if she had momentarily slipped into another place, another time. Then she looked up, her face animated. "Something that hasn't been mine for years," she said. "The power to control my own life."

19

Murder of the Soul

Amber sat on the high bank above the Hood Canal and watched as the afternoon sun melted across the Olympic peaks and spilled rivulets of pink and purple and orange down the jagged slopes into the water below. If she lived here for the rest of her life, she would never tire of the ever-changing colors of the sunset. A lone eagle, silhouetted black against the sky, made a swooping pass at the water but came up with empty talons.

Empty. That's how Amber felt, too, and she couldn't explain it. When she had sat in Susan's office and talked about taking her life back, the very act of uttering the words had made her feel invincible. And now, a few hours later, her heart seemed drained and heavy. Even the beauty of the sunset couldn't offset the creeping darkness in her soul.

Eventually, she would have to tell Susan the truth—all of it. She dreaded the day and the pain it would bring, but her only other choice, she now knew, was to be forever bound by the fear and questions and condemnation that gnawed at her. She would never find out whether she could be forgiven, or whether she could forgive herself. As long as she kept even part of the truth about herself hidden, she would never be sure that anyone—even the God Susan talked about—could love her as she was. Unless she told, she would never truly be free.

But she had never told anyone. Not once. Not her therapist in Raleigh, not even Meg.

When the first star came out, Amber zipped up her jacket against the chill that permeated the evening air. A shudder coursed through her, and almost without thinking, she began to whisper the little chant that had been her ritual throughout childhood: "Star light, star bright, first star I see tonight, wish I may, wish I might . . ."

What did she wish?

She wished it had never happened. She wished she had been stronger. She wished . . . she wished . . .

She wished he would go away. She shut her eyes and huddled under the blankets, her heart thudding against her rib cage as the footsteps drew closer on the bare marble floors of the hallway. She knew what was coming, but she didn't dare make a sound. If she stayed still enough, wished hard enough, maybe—

The door creaked open, admitting a beam of bright light from the hall. She felt the light sizzle red against her closed eyelids, heard music drifting in from the big parlor on the other side of the house where Mama and Daddy and Uncle Jack and the rest of their friends were having a party. She hated this house; it was so huge and everything was so far away. Even if she had yelled at the top of her lungs, no one would have heard her.

But she didn't yell. She didn't even whimper. She just lay there waiting, wishing, praying, holding her breath. The door closed again, smothering her in inky darkness as the sickly sweet odor of liquor drew closer and closer. The star-wish didn't work. God didn't answer. Nobody came to save her.

It was her fault, he said, for growing up into such a beautiful young lady. So sweet and innocent, so pure and undefiled. So perfect, exactly like her mama. She was nearly thirteen, nearly a woman, he said. This is what women do when they're all grown up.

He put a hand around her throat and stroked her neck, his thumb putting a little extra pressure on the vein that throbbed right below her ear. "Never, never tell a soul," he whispered, just before he kissed her on the forehead and went back to the party. "This is our secret, remember. You know what happens to little girls who tell."

She knew. She believed him. And so she didn't cry out, not this time or any of the times before.

20

The Plan

TwoJoe stepped onto the porch and let the screen door slam behind him. He had been working on the books since sunup, had gone over the figures a dozen times or more, and the result was always the same. They were in trouble.

He ran a hand through his hair. When he had peered in the mirror this morning, he had seen new streaks of gray at the temples. And it was getting long, down over his collar and past his ears. Maybe he should just let it grow, wear it in a thick braid down his back the way Grandpa Joe had done, weave a feather into it. It would save the price of haircuts.

Meg followed him onto the porch and handed him a mug of coffee. "Breakfast will be ready in a few minutes. Where's Amber?"

TwoJoe shrugged. "In the barn, probably. She's been spending twelve hours a day in that studio. I hope she's about ready to sell some of that stuff."

Meg tilted her head to one side but said nothing.

TwoJoe leaned back against the porch rail and looked at his sister. She wasn't a child any longer, but he still thought of her that way some-times—as the bright, sunny little girl who always laughed and smiled and made everyone around her feel like laughing, too. She had the bluest eyes—Grandma Simi's eyes—and her face was flawless, except for the narrow white line that puckered her left eyebrow.

His eyes focused on the scar—a grim reminder of the time Bart Walker hit her in the face with a beer bottle. It was a good thing Bart was all the way across the country, or he would have to answer to TwoJoe for that one. Any man who took out his anger on a woman deserved whatever he got in return.

TwoJoe hadn't been around to protect his sister back then, but when he had returned to Kitsap County, he had promised himself that he would never let anything—or anyone—hurt her again. And now he was about to break that promise.

"TwoJoe?" she said, gazing up at him with a guileless expression. "Is anything wrong?"

He ran his fingers through his hair and set his coffee mug on the rail-ing. "I've been going over the books, Meg. It doesn't look good. We're in debt, and the truck needs a new transmission. Lloser isn't earning his keep. Taxes went up again, and we're already four months behind."

"Is it that bad?"

TwoJoe frowned. "The influx of rich people building big houses on the canal has made the land more valuable, but that doesn't help us un-less we sell the place. In the meantime, property taxes are going sky-high. We're being taxed at the same rate as the developers, even though we're not developing."

Meg thought about this for a minute. "We own this place outright. Couldn't we get a loan?"

"No one will give us a loan, Meg. We have too much debt, and our credit rating is, well, not good. Not unless we're willing to mortgage the property, and Grandpa Joe absolutely forbade that in his will."

"Yes, but Grandpa Joe didn't envision the kinds of difficulties we're up against now."

"Doesn't matter. The will is very clear on the issue."

"All right, then what about subdividing and selling off a few acres, just enough to cover the taxes?"

"There's a land covenant in effect. We can't sell any of it in parcels less than ten acres. Besides, what the developers really want is this piece, right here." He pointed toward the porch floor. "The prime canal frontage. Our home. If we give up that, we might as well sell the whole thing and go live in some yuppie condo on Mercer Island."

His sister shook her head. "Impossible. They'd never let Lloser and Llittle Bit move in."

In spite of himself, TwoJoe laughed. He could just see himself taking his llamas for walks around the cobbled streets of Seattle. Somehow he suspected Llittle Bit would get a lot of attention with her head hanging out a streetcar window.

Meg was silent for a minute. "Well, I've got a supply of new rugs ready for consignment, and Amber's just received orders from several of the shops in town, as well as a couple in Seattle. In a month or two the tourists will start coming, and people will need packers for trips into the mountains. Don't you think we can hang on until then?"

TwoJoe shook his head. "I don't know, Meg. You and Amber are doing all you can, but I just don't think it's going to be enough."

"It's been enough so far. We've managed. We'll manage again."

"You've got more faith in me than I have."

She chuckled softly. "No offense, big brother, but it's not faith in *you*. I think it's time you realized that Amber and I aren't children. We're all in this together, the three of us, and the financial responsibility falls on all of us. You're not carrying the burden alone."

Something tightened in TwoJoe's throat. "Sometimes it feels that way." Meg got up and came over to stand beside Joe. She took his hand and held it, squeezing his fingers as she spoke. "We'll come up with a plan. Amber and I can get some things together to sell. Beyond that, we'll just have to trust God."

He put an arm around her shoulder. "I don't get it," he murmured.

"You've been through so much hell in your life. How can you keep on believing when things look so rotten?"

"Maybe you have to go through hell to know what's important," Meg answered. "Maybe once you've been through hell, you know what heaven looks like." She turned and leaned on the porch rail, gazing out over the magnificent vista of Hood Canal and the Olympic peaks. "This is heaven, TwoJoe. This is where we belong. This place is God's gift of grace and peace and healing—for me, for Amber, even for you. We're not going to lose it."

I wish I were as sure as you are, he thought. But he didn't say so.

Halfway through breakfast, Sam Houston appeared on the porch and peered in through the screen door. "Oh, you're still eating." He ducked his head. "I was coming to help TwoJoe with the chores. I'll just wait out here."

"Don't be ridiculous." Meg motioned him inside and set a place for him. "How about some bacon and eggs, Sam? We've got plenty." She passed the platter in his direction, and he eyed it cautiously.

"No thanks, I've already had breakfast."

Meg smiled at him. He was such a well-mannered little boy, so courteous and polite. And intelligent, too. He was fascinated by the llamas, wanted to learn everything about them. He adored TwoJoe, and apparently the feeling was mutual.

Meg had watched them together, the little tow-headed cowboy and her dark-skinned brother. Thick as thieves, the two of them.

"Go ahead, Sam," she urged. "I know a growing boy like you is always hungry."

He grinned up at her. "Well, maybe just a little." He piled his plate with the remaining scrambled eggs, slathered two pieces of toast with strawberry jam, and sandwiched three slices of bacon in between. "Grandma gives me bran flakes at home. She says it's good for me, but—" He screwed up his little face in an expression of disgust. "Yuck."

Out of the corner of her eye, Meg slanted a glance at Amber. She was looking down at her plate, biting her lower lip. She hadn't uttered a word since Sam arrived. After a minute or two she muttered, "I'd better get to work," filled a thermos of coffee, and headed out the door.

TwoJoe frowned in Meg's direction as if to ask, *What was that all about?* Meg shrugged, but said nothing. TwoJoe thought she was just being rude, but Meg suspected there was more to it than that. The expression on Amber's face whenever Sam came around was not one of disapproval, but of pain . . .

❧

A light knock sounded on the screen door, and TwoJoe looked up to see a man in a dark suit. "Excuse me," he said when TwoJoe opened the door, "is this the Elkhorn place?"

"That's right." TwoJoe went onto the porch and shut the screen behind him. "I'm TwoJoe Elkhorn."

"Just the man I was looking for." The stranger pumped TwoJoe's hand enthusiastically. "You got a few minutes?"

TwoJoe glanced back inside the house, where Meg was clearing the table and Sam sat staring curiously at the stranger. "Yeah, just give me a second." He stuck his head back inside. "Sam, come on out here." Sam scrambled down from his chair and banged out the door, clutching his bacon and jelly sandwich in one hand. "How about if you go on down to the pasture and start feeding the stock? Get the small pitchfork and wheelbarrow from the barn. You can put out fresh hay and fill the watering trough. I'll be down there in a little while."

Obviously delighted to be trusted with such an important job, Sam gave TwoJoe a one-handed hug around the waist, let out a whoop, and took off on a run. "Make sure you latch the gate behind you!" TwoJoe called to his retreating back.

"Nice looking kid," the stranger commented, peering past TwoJoe into the kitchen, where Meg was running soapy dishwater in the sink and wiping down the breakfast table.

TwoJoe motioned to the Adirondack chairs on the porch. "Have a seat, Mr.—"

The man hesitated. "Shivers," he said. "William Shivers."

"I'll get us some coffee. Sugar or cream?"

"Just black, thanks."

TwoJoe went back into the kitchen. "What does he want?" Meg asked in a whisper.

"I have no idea, but I'll let you know when I find out."

"Okay. I'm going down to the barn. I'll finish these later." Meg gestured at the sink full of dishes.

When Meg was gone, TwoJoe went out onto the porch with the coffee. He settled himself in the chair opposite the stranger, handing him a mug. "What can I do for you, Mr., ah, Shivers?"

The man's name certainly fit. With those broad shoulders and meaty hands, he put TwoJoe in mind of guys with names like Scarpetti or Mangione or Capone. He had olive skin and dark eyes, and wore a black T-shirt under a gray silk suit, impeccably cut—the kind of suit even Reggie the Snob, the Microsoft Golden Boy, would find acceptable. His tasseled leather loafers were damp from the dew.

"I'll get right to the point," William Shivers began with a smile. "I represent, well, certain parties, let's call 'em, who might be able to help you with your current financial setbacks."

TwoJoe bristled. "What do you know about my finances?"

Shivers took a drink of his coffee, grimaced, and set the cup down. "You folks out here sure like it strong, don't you?" He raised both hands, palm up, in a gesture of conciliation. "Some things are a matter of public record, you know. Back taxes, land appraisals, that sort of thing."

"Are you some kind of lawyer? A loan shark? What?"

Shivers laughed. "Lawyer? Not a chance. And I'm sure not here to offer you a loan. You could call me—" He paused. "A kind of broker. A go-between."

TwoJoe glared at him but said nothing.

"Here's the deal," Shivers continued as if they were carrying on a friendly business discussion. "My people have authorized me to offer you half again the appraised value of your property here, cash. You get foreclosed on, my people will get it anyway. You're going to lose this place eventually, so you might as well take the money and run." He lifted one eyebrow and grinned. "It's a good offer, Elkhorn. The best you're likely to see. Take it, and be thankful. You'll be a rich man."

"And what if I don't care about the money?"

"Everybody cares about money. Especially when they don't have it. Especially when—"

"Look, Mr. Shivers," TwoJoe interrupted. "In the past few years I've had every realty company on both sides of the Sound after me to sell my land. I said no then, and I'm saying no now. This place has been in my family for generations, and that's where it's going to stay." He rose to his feet and stood towering over the stranger. "Give my regrets to your *people*, whoever they are. And now if you'll excuse me, I've got work to do."

"That's your last word?"

"The very last."

Shivers got to his feet and went to the porch rail, looking out at the canal and the rugged mountains beyond. "You're making a mistake," he said quietly. "A big mistake."

TwoJoe watched as the man retreated down the porch steps, his muscular shoulders straining against the silk jacket. At the small of his back, right at the waistline, TwoJoe could make out an irregular bulge. The blood drained from his head, and he felt a twisting knot form in the pit of his stomach. And he wondered, for the first time in his life, if the price of holding onto this land and this life might be more than he'd be willing to pay.

❦

"It's gone?" Amber stared at Meg, incredulous. "My Two Sisters sculpture? It's gone?"

"Well, don't say it like that," Meg protested. "It's not like it was stolen, for heaven's sake. Mr. Jorgensen was quite taken with it. He thinks it will bring a very good price in his gallery."

"Tell me again what happened."

"I told you three times already," Meg sighed. "He came in to pick up that consignment of stoneware he ordered. Usually his gofer Robbie comes out, but Mr. Jorgensen was in Bremerton scouting some of the smaller shops, and he decided just to swing by here and see if his order was ready. I knew you were finished with it, so I brought him in here while I packed it up for him."

"And where was I when all this was happening?"

"At the church, I think. Talking to Susan."

"And so he saw the sculpture—"

"Yes, he saw it on the shelf. He couldn't take his eyes off it. Said it would bring several hundred dollars, he was certain. Maybe as much as a thousand—minus his 20 percent."

"And you just let him take it."

"Of course I did. He's honest and reliable; he won't cheat you."

"I'm not worried about being cheated," Amber shot back. "When I first noticed it was gone, I assumed you just moved it somewhere else. I can't believe you'd hand it over to some gallery owner without my even knowing about it."

"I meant to tell you; honestly I did." Meg furrowed her brow. "Amber, am I missing something? Isn't this what you wanted—to have your work shown, to become known as the wonderful artist you are, not just some hippie woman who throws pots in a barn?"

"But why not that one?" Amber pointed to the dark statue of the man with the little girl in his lap. "The Two Sisters was special."

"I know it's special. Jorgensen knew it, too—that's why he wanted it. And he wants others—he said so. Besides, it's not like it's lost forever. You've got the cast; you can make copies, in bronze, if you want. People are going to love it, Amber. It captures something wonderful and magical about being a child."

"Right," muttered Amber dully. "The magic of childhood."

"I can call him and get it back before he sells it," Meg offered. "But Amber, before I do, there's something you have to know."

Amber looked up. "What?"

"I had a talk with TwoJoe this morning. We're in financial trouble, and it will be a couple of months yet before the tourist trade picks up. That money might make the difference between keeping the farm and losing it."

Amber looked into Meg's eyes. She told herself that Meg was doing what was right, what was best for all of them. Meg was her closest friend; she would never deliberately do anything to hurt Amber. Without Meg and TwoJoe, Amber would never have had the chance to start over, to make a place for herself. And Meg was right; this might be the break she had worked for, longed for. The opportunity to be known as not just a potter, but also an artist.

It was just a statue, after all. One sculpture.

One sculpture probably wouldn't save the farm, but it was a beginning. It was a long shot, but if Jorgensen could sell it, it might mean the launching of a whole new career for her.

After all, one small course correction could change a life forever.

⁓

Jackson Underwood finished his conversation, hung up the phone, and immediately picked up the call that was waiting on his private line. "Underwood."

"It's me, Mr. Underwood. Shiv. I found them."

"Diedre and that friend of hers—Carlene what's her name?"

"No, sir, not them." He paused. "Well, yeah, come to think of it, I got them, too. The friend's name is Donovan. They're headed out I-90 on their way toward Seattle. They've been using the Donovan girl's credit cards."

"Go on," Jack said.

"Well, once we got the Donovan woman's last name, the credit card trace was a piece of cake. Led me to some small burg in Minnesota. Woman at the motel there said they were headed for Seattle and told me if I was joining them, to make sure to stop at some place called the Corn Palace along the way." He laughed. "They're taking it pretty easy, looks like. I'll keep tabs on them once they get to Seattle."

"Good man, Shiv. Now, what else?"

"This is the interesting part. I found the other one, too. She's living on a llama farm, can you believe that? Doing some kind of artwork in the barn. Looks like a real low-budget operation."

"Sounds like something you can handle, then?"

"Well, yes and no. The place is owned by an Indian by the name of Elkhorn. I went out there and met the guy. He's got a pretty little blonde wife and a kid who looks just like her. He's in deep financially. Debts up the wazoo."

"Great. Buy him out. Get him off that land. More important, get the woman out of sight. I want her lost again, so lost she'll never be found."

"I tried, Mr. Underwood, but he's not budging. Says he'll never sell."

Jack snorted. "Everybody's got a price. Find out what his is. Money is no object."

"That's the problem. The guy doesn't seem to care about money. He just wants to keep his family farm under him. He won't listen."

"Make him listen."

"You want me to—"

"I want you to do whatever is necessary. But listen to me. I want her lost, not dead. You hurt her, you'll have to answer to me. Got it?"

Jack heard a low chuckle on the other end of the line. "Yes sir, I got it. No tough stuff. Just intimidation."

"That's right." He paused. "One more thing, Shiv. You're not using your real name out there, are you?"

The voice on the other end of the line hesitated. "Of course not. Do you think I'm stupid?"

Jack hung up the phone. Yes, he thought the man was stupid. But he was good at his craft. He would do the job, ask no questions, leave no trail. Being stupid was just a bonus.

He punched a number on his speed dial and waited while the phone rang. When the line picked up, he didn't even bother identifying himself.

"We've nailed them," he said. "It won't be long now."

Part 3

❦

Secrets and Lies

Because our hearts are unprepared for truth,
we cling to the deception
as a shipwreck victim on a storm-tossed sea
will grab at anything that floats.
But the splintered rubble of our broken trust—
those temporary buoys of our shattered dreams—
betray us,
gouging rough gashes into our souls,
drawing our blood and leaving us to sink.
Only the truth can bear our weight
and bring us safely home.

21

Holding On

Amber was having trouble keeping her mind on her work. Her eyes kept wandering to the gaping space on the shelf where her Two Sisters sculpture had sat.

She tried to identify the emotions that were churning inside her: loss and emptiness, confusion and disbelief. Like the time she found out, quite by accident, that her best friend from junior high had died. She was seventeen at the time, living in Charlotte with Aunt Edith—she hadn't yet gone to the hospital in Raleigh. Mama had sent her a copy of the Heartspring *Gazette* that contained a front-page spread about her father's new summer parks program for underprivileged youth. Amber had seethed over the article, which canonized in glowing terms a man who could give attention to other people's children when he had betrayed and discarded his own. She was just about to toss the paper in the trash when she caught a glimpse of a small article on the back page:

LOCAL TEEN'S MEMORY HONORED
AT HEARTSPRING HIGH

Melinda Suzanne Tucker, who died in a single-car accident in May of last year at the age of seventeen, was commemorated in a brief ceremony on Tuesday as a plaque in her honor was placed in the main hallway of the high school. Tucker, who would have been a senior this year, had been an honor student and a member of the student council . . .

Melinda—Lindy—had been Amber's closest friend since elementary school. The two of them had been inseparable, at least until Amber had been sent away. But even though time and distance had come between them, Amber had thought of her often. She imagined Lindy leading the cheering squad at football games, playing softball on the girls' league in the summer, maybe attending the prom with some handsome quarter-back in tow.

Not trapped in a totaled car on a mountain road in the middle of the night. Not gone forever.

The stark words of the news article had hit her like a body blow: Lindy was dead. Dead and buried. Everybody else had mourned her loss and moved on. But she had continued to live and laugh and grow in Amber's mind long after her last breath had been crushed out of her. And Amber couldn't even cry, because it didn't seem real. How do you mourn someone whose passing is already ancient history?

And that was the way she felt about the loss of the Two Sisters. As if something had been ripped out of her without warning. As if two people she loved had been killed and buried, and no one had told her to stop thinking about them as alive.

She was overreacting, and she knew it. It was just a sculpture, for heaven's sake. A slab of clay. A product of her imagination, not a living, breathing person. And maybe—if Meg's account of Jorgensen's reac-tion was accurate—a catalyst for new directions in the future. Some real money coming in. The chance to leap the chasm between artisan and artist.

A clattering behind her jerked Amber back to reality, her heart pumping and every nerve in her body standing on end. When had she become so jumpy? She whirled around and saw little Sam Houston facing the far wall of the barn, reaching over his head with a pitchfork.

"*What are you doing?*" The words came out louder and more harshly than she had intended. Sam dropped the pitchfork and whirled in her direction.

"I'm sorry, Amber. I was just—" He pointed toward the hook, well over his head, where the pitchfork was supposed to hang. "TwoJoe made me promise to put the tools back where they belong, and—"

He tried again, but he had to hold it by the tines to get the handle high enough to reach the hook, and the weight was too much for him. It dropped into the wheelbarrow with a bone-jarring clang. The boy turned again to Amber, a sheepish expression on his face. "It was easier to get down."

Amber got to her feet, walked over and took the pitchfork, and lifted it into its place. "Better?"

"Yeah, thanks."

She went back to her sculpting table, and much to her dismay, Sam followed like a devoted puppy. He stood there for a minute, his eyes following her every move as she wet down a lump of clay and began kneading it.

"You want something, Sam?"

"No ma'am."

Amber went on working, but the unrelenting gaze of this pint-sized supervisor rattled her. Finally she turned to him again. "What is it, Sam?"

"Oh, nothin'. I was just wondering—"

Her nerves were on edge, and her patience—if she'd had any to begin with—was totally depleted. She tried hard to keep her voice even. "Wondering what?"

"What happened to the statue of the little girls playing?"

Amber narrowed her eyes at him. "How do you know about that?"

Sam shrugged. "TwoJoe showed me. He told me I could come in here to get tools and stuff, but never to touch your things. He let me look at the statue of the two girls, and told me that you're a—" He groped for the words. "A talented artist."

"TwoJoe said that?"

"Yep. And I think so, too. I loved that statue. It was wonderful, the little girls smiling and laughing like that." His pale blue eyes shone with admiration. "I tried to make a horse out of Play-Doh one time, but it looked more like an elephant. Could you show me how?"

Amber gazed at him, suddenly overcome with a desire to sweep him into her arms, to hug him, to stroke his tousled haystack of hair. She pushed the impulse aside as quickly as it came and turned away from him. "I'm busy, Sam. This is grown-up work, and it's got to get done."

"OK." He took a step away from her. "I'm sorry you're so sad, Amber."

All the breath went out of Amber's lungs. "What makes you think I'm sad?"

"Just a feeling," he answered quietly. "The girl in that statue—was she your little sister?"

Amber hesitated. "Yes."

"And she went away?"

She could barely get the words out. "Actually, I went away."

"But she's not dead."

Amber peered at him. What could a child like this know of death? "No, she's not dead."

He drew close again and patted her on the arm. "That's good. I bet she misses you. I bet she loves you a lot."

"I don't know, Sam. People change. They forget."

"I'll never forget my sister if I live to be a hundred," he declared solemnly.

Amber peered into his face. "What about your sister?"

"Her name was Beth. She was older'n me, but she always treated me like a real person, not like a baby. Then she got sick and stayed sick for a long time. She died in the hospital. That's why I'm staying with my grandparents. My mom is real sad, too."

"I thought you told TwoJoe that your teachers were on strike."

"I did. They were. But that's not the real reason I'm here. I'm here because Beth died."

"I'm sure Beth was a wonderful person."

"Yeah."

Amber went back to the clay. It had begun to dry, and she applied more water and pummeled it mercilessly. Still Sam didn't move. At last he said, "Amber, can I ask you a question?"

"You just did."

He stared at her without comprehension.

"Sure," she sighed. "Go ahead."

"Is it because of your sister that you don't like kids? Or is it just me?"

Amber closed her eyes as a stab of pain knifed through her heart. "I never said I don't like you, Sam."

"You don't have to say it. You're always busy, and you never look at me or talk to me the way Meg and TwoJoe do. But it's okay, Amber." He smiled at her. "I think it's just because you miss your own little sister, and other kids remind you of her." Amber sat like a stone as Sam put his arms around her and gave her a clumsy, self-conscious hug. "I'm going to go now."

"Where are you going?"

Sam pointed toward the wooden ladder that led up to the hayloft. "TwoJoe said I could go up and see the new kittens. I'll be real quiet, I promise."

"Are you sure you should? It's a long way up there." Amber followed Sam to the ladder and looked up. The loft in the big old barn was as high as the top of a two-story house, a dizzying distance, and the ladder seemed rickety and unstable. She felt vertigo setting in just from looking up there. "I'm afraid of heights," she admitted.

"I'm not." He scrambled up the ladder until his boots were on a level with the top of her head. "Besides, it's the only way to see the kitties until they're old enough to come down."

"Be careful, Sam."

"I will." He took a few more steps up and looked down at her. "It'll be okay, Amber. About your sister, I mean. I hope you'll see her again someday. You never really let go of somebody you love, and they never let go of you. My dad told me so."

He climbed until he was out of sight, and Amber went back to her work, wondering how a child that small could be so wise.

She had mud up to her elbows, but she wasn't getting much accomplished. She just kept kneading the clay like an enormous lump of bread dough, pounding it, twisting it as her mind twisted and pounded around the events of her life.

Even though the Two Sisters sculpture was gone, the image still existed as vivid as ever in Amber's mind. She could see the way the little girl's hair blew back in the wind, the way she lifted her face to the sky as she started to take flight. She could recall with startling clarity the expression of exuberant joy her own hand had sculpted into the clay, could remember as well the pain and horror she had felt after that same hand had severed the connection between them.

There was something mystical and mysterious, Amber thought, about the process of creativity. Sometimes it was sheer drudgery, like the way she watered the clay and softened it, working it with her fingers until her forearms and shoulders ached and knotted with the effort. But when it was prepared and pliable, ready to take on the form that lay dormant in her mind—ah! that was magic. Sometimes she almost felt as if she stood outside herself watching the shape emerge, observing as her own fingers molded and carved it into something new, something incredibly beautiful and inspiring and alive.

Susan Quentin called it "the angel touch" and attributed it to the work of the Divine Spirit flowing through Amber. Amber wasn't quite ready to agree that some Power other than herself was moving in her— such an idea made her feel a little like a puppet whose strings were being pulled by an invisible manipulator. But she had to admit that on occasion it seemed truly miraculous, this business of turning mud into life. The joining of herself with the clay produced something greater than either of them.

Every now and then, Amber caught a glimpse—for just a fleeting moment—of what God must have felt when the form of Adam inhaled that first breath, stood upright, and became a living being. She wasn't sure she bought the whole package as literally true, God kneeling in the dirt and making people out of mud pies. But the image was compelling; she found herself drawn to the story. It made her feel as if Susan might be right, that there just might be a flicker of that creative fire in all of us.

God breathing holy air into human nostrils. Michelangelo's Creator hanging off the ceiling of the Sistine Chapel to pass the divine spark into the flesh-and-blood creature. The Good Shepherd stretching over a cliff to rescue a lamb from the thicket. God reaching out. Holding on.

"You never let go of someone you love," Sam had said.

But she had let go. And she could not forgive herself.

Distracted by footsteps overhead—small boots clumping against the wooden floor—Amber cast a smile toward the hayloft. Maybe someday she would do a sculpture of a scruffy little boy in jeans and cowboy boots, sitting on a bale of hay with a lapful of kittens.

She could hear Sam calling—quietly, so as not to disturb her work. "Here, kitty, kitty. That's a good kitty." The footsteps moved faster, and Amber could imagine Sam with hay stuck in his hair, scrambling after a little gray tabby—

Suddenly an earsplitting creak filled the barn. Swallows, startled from their nests, swooped down from the rafters. There was a bang. A slam. A scream.

Amber jumped to her feet and looked up. The air was filled with dust and hay, asphyxiating her and making her eyes water. And then she saw it—high above her, a gaping open space. The trapdoor, which opened from the loft to dump hay down onto the barn floor, had sprung open. A tiny figure hung from the door, flailing its legs, scrabbling for a toe-hold. But there was none.

Amber ran to the barn door and screamed for TwoJoe, but got no response. If he was in the pasture with the llamas, he might hear her, but if he was down on the beach gathering clams or inside the house, he would never get here in time.

"Help!" Sam called—a pitiful, choked cry.

"I'm coming, Sam. Hang on!" She craned her neck to look up. It was so high. She could never catch him. He would drop like a sack of bricks; they could both be killed.

"Help. Please!"

Amber could tell he was trying not to cry. "Hold on!" she yelled again. "Hold on!"

She dashed to the ladder and started up, but her hands were slippery with wet clay, and twice she almost fell. *Don't look down*, she told herself over and over. *Don't look down. Just keep climbing.* At last she reached the top and swung off the ladder into the loft. Her knees were trembling violently and every muscle in her body felt like Jell-O, but she kept moving. "Sam, I'm coming. I see you!"

The truth was, Amber didn't see him. She only saw the yawning open square where the trapdoor had been. For a moment her nerve failed her. "God, no," she muttered under her breath. The wooden floor was slick with hay—she could slip and fall as easily as he had. She got down on all fours and crawled toward the opening.

The flap of the trapdoor hung like a broken wing into the open space below the hayloft floor. And clinging to the hinged side of the door, his little fingers wedged into the tiniest of spaces, Sam Houston was still hanging on.

Amber slid on her stomach toward the hole. She was at an awkward angle, reaching down to try to grab him, but the trapdoor opening was too wide for her to reach him from the other side. There was no other way to get to him.

"Sam, look up," she commanded. "I'm right here. Can you see my hand?" She couldn't see much of him, but she could feel his rigid fingers under her touch.

"Yes," he choked out.

"All right. I want you to let go with one hand and grab on."

"I'm scared."

"I know you are, Sam. I am, too. But that's not going to stop us. On three, now: one, two, *three!*"

His hand shot out into thin air, and Amber grasped at it for all she was worth. She gripped him around the wrist, but as small as he was, he was solidly packed and heavier than she had counted on. His weight pulled her farther out over the opening. She could see his face now, taut and white with fear, his eyes wide. He let go with the other hand and gripped her right arm with both fists.

She slid a little farther.

"I'm slipping!" he screamed. "Don't let go!"

Amber's free hand found an angled rafter, and she held on for dear life. She could see beyond him, down, down, down into the barn below. Her head started to reel.

"Don't . . . let . . . go!" Sam yelled.

The words came from very far away, an echo on a distant wind. Everything around her lurched, as if she had been spinning in circles for hours.

"Don't . . . let . . . go!"

"I won't!" Amber shouted. "I won't let go!"

She felt a tightening around her waist, as if an arm had gone around her, pulling her back, steadying her. She took in one deep breath and abandoned the rafter, her only anchor, to lunge for the child. Her free hand touched flesh—his thin little arm—and she fell backward into the strength that held her, hauling Sam Houston with her.

He was in her arms, burrowing into her, crying, shaking.

"It's all right," Amber gasped, holding him close and stroking his hair with a trembling hand. "I've got you."

"You didn't let go," he sobbed. "I was afraid you'd let go."

Amber's own tears mixed with his. "Never," she said fiercely. "I would have died myself before I'd let you go again."

She heard shouting and running and the clattering of feet on the ladder. Completely drained, she turned to see TwoJoe vaulting into the loft. He fell to his knees and put his arms around both of them. "I heard yelling. I came as fast as I could. Thank God you're all right."

Amber stared at him dazed. Wasn't he there, just a moment ago? Holding her, helping her, pulling her back from the edge?

It didn't matter. He was here now.

Still clutching Sam in a tight embrace, she sagged against TwoJoe's comforting warmth and wept with exhaustion and relief.

22

The Colonel

A cold rain had set in, and after dinner, TwoJoe had built a fire in the big stone fireplace and made popcorn over the open flames. The bowl sat untouched on the coffee table. Meg slouched in the overstuffed chair with a book on her lap; she hadn't turned a single page in the past hour. Amber lay on the couch, staring vacantly into the flickering light. A gray tabby kitten, whom Sam had claimed and named Pocahontas, was curled into a tight ball on the arm of the sofa behind Amber's head, sound asleep. The only one among them who seemed at peace tonight.

Strange, he thought, how quickly the weather could change. Most of the month of April had been unseasonably mild and clear—warm sunny days and moonlit nights fresh as chilled white grapes. But in a heartbeat the wind had shifted and the spring storms had come again.

The pounding monotony of rain on the roof suited TwoJoe's mood. For a while after the ordeal with Sam in the hayloft, everyone had walked around in a kind of adrenaline-induced euphoria. But now the elation of triumph had dissipated, and the dismal drizzle of everyday life had reasserted itself. Nobody felt like talking, so they all sat together in the quiet room, insulated by their private thoughts.

TwoJoe's mind inevitably came around, once again, to his dilemma about the farm. He wouldn't let go of the place, that much was certain, not even for the enormous amount Mr. William Shivers's "people" had offered. He supposed he could sell most of the llamas and find an accounting job in the city. There had to be some opportunities for a CPA, and at least it would pay the bills . . .

A knot formed in his stomach when he envisioned himself in that role. A three-piece suit, a cell phone, a reliable mid-sized car, an office cubicle in some high-rise. Between driving to Bainbridge and taking the ferry, a total of two hours or more every day in the commuting maze with all the other rats. Leaving before dawn and coming home after dark. It would kill his spirit by degrees. He could feel the light in his soul dimming just from thinking about it.

The old Seth Thomas on the mantel—his Grandma Simi's pride and joy—ticked loudly in the silence. Finding a job might take weeks. Creditors were already breathing down his neck; the farm could be history before he ever got around to punching a time clock.

TwoJoe closed his eyes. The light from the fire penetrated his eyelids, creating red-hued patterns across the network of veins in the thin skin—an ever-changing road map with no signs to point him in the right direction. *Trust*, Meg had told him a hundred times or more. *We're not going to lose this place.*

Joe believed it—at least theoretically. He had felt so strongly that coming home to Kitsap County was the right thing to do, had even said that God had led him in the decision. The physical labor exhilarated him; the natural beauty nurtured and sustained his soul. Giving up a lucrative career hadn't seemed like much of a sacrifice at the time. God cared about the inner self, not the outward trappings of success. It didn't matter how anyone else would assess his choices—TwoJoe Elkhorn had found his place in the center of God's will.

He had been obedient. He had said yes when God called. Why, then, had heaven slammed shut like a steel door, unresponsive to his cries for help, his need for affirmation? Why wasn't God answering him? Was the Almighty not so almighty, after all? TwoJoe believed in a God of grace and mercy, a God who loved people and intervened on their behalf. But if God truly knew about his troubles and shared his worries, why had his prayers been met with silence?

TwoJoe could only think of two reasons, neither of which was very satisfying: either God didn't care, or God cared but was incapable of intervening. An indifferent Deity or an impotent one, take your pick. Neither one was the kind of God that inspired TwoJoe Elkhorn to love and worship.

Maybe in the whole scheme of things, TwoJoe's prayers just weren't that important. No one was dying of some slow and painful disease, after all; the world wasn't coming to an end. All that was at stake was an old log farmhouse, forty acres of land, a few llamas. He could take Shivers's cash tomorrow, walk away, and live off the interest the rest of his days.

Poor old Judas only got thirty pieces of silver in exchange for a life— and a very special life, at that. TwoJoe had a much bigger offer on the table. But was it enough? Could it ever be enough?

What was the current market value, he wondered, on three ordinary souls?

Amber jerked awake and tried to sit up. Somewhere, someone was running a jackhammer—or maybe it was just the pounding in her skull. She couldn't move. Her legs were paralyzed. But no, they couldn't be— she could feel needles of pain going up and down her calves.

She propped up on her elbows and looked toward the end of the sofa. Pocahontas, the kitten Sam had claimed as his own, was stretched across her feet, and her legs had gone to sleep. That boy better talk his grandparents into letting Pokie come to live with them soon, or—

The sound registered in her brain. Someone was knocking on the front door. She nudged the cat, who arose leisurely and gave her an irritated look, digging her tiny, needle-sharp claws into Amber's shins before stalking away. By the time Amber got her feet to the floor, TwoJoe had already gotten up to open the door.

Sam came running into the room and flung himself on her, squeezing the breath out of her with an enormous hug, then flopped down beside her on the couch and picked up the kitten. His jacket was soaking wet; Pocahontas squirmed away from him, went to the hearth, and sat down to groom.

Amber felt in need of a grooming herself. She felt dazed and stuporous from sleeping at the wrong time, and her mouth tasted fuzzy and disgusting. What time was it? She squinted at the clock on the mantel—eight forty five. At night, she assumed astutely, since it was dark outside. But what was Sam Houston doing here at this hour?

She didn't have to wait long to find out. TwoJoe was standing over her, and behind him hovered a towering tree of a man. Beneath the rim of what must have been a twenty-gallon hat, she could see a wild mane of snow-white hair and a complexion like tanned cowhide.

"So this is the little lady who saved my grandson!" the man thundered.

Amber struggled to her feet while TwoJoe made the introductions. "Amber, this is Colonel Houston, Sam's grandfather."

"Vernon," the man corrected. "Or just plain old Vern."

Plain old Vern, Amber noted as he pumped her hand enthusiastically, was neither plain nor particularly old. He might have been anywhere between fifty and sixty, with a handsome weathered face and a broad grin—a robust western type who still fit quite neatly into a pair of low-slung jeans. Amber was not a small woman—not petite like Susan or Meg, anyway—but Vernon Houston dwarfed her. She estimated his height at six foot five, at least, and his hand enveloped hers like a massive bear's paw.

"Sorry to come so late, and on such a foul night, but Sam insisted. The missus is down with a cold; she sends her apologies and says she'll be over in a day or two."

Meg was on her feet, ready to play hostess at a moment's notice. "Sit down, please, Colonel Houston. Let me take your coats. And how about if I brew up a pot of coffee?"

"Make mine black," little Sam piped up.

Meg leveled a gaze on him and pointed a finger. "You'll get milk, young man. Now, how about if you come and help me? I've got some of that chocolate cake you love."

Sam jumped up to follow her, and the two of them left the room amid Meg's admonitions for him to wash his hands after playing with the kitten.

"My grandson has really taken to y'all," Vernon was saying. "I want you to know how much I appreciate it; it's helped him a lot, dealing with losing his sister like he has."

"We admire him a great deal." TwoJoe smiled. "He's quite a boy."

"Well, he sure loves them llamas," Vernon chuckled. "He's after me to start raising 'em on my ranch back in Texas."

"They're wonderful animals. I'd sell you a great packing stud."

"Lloser?" the Colonel burst out laughing. "I bet you would, wouldn't you now?" He clapped TwoJoe on the shoulder. "My grandson's already told me all about Lloser, so don't you go trying to pawn him off on an old man like me. I may not know llamas, but I been around the back forty a few times, and you can't pull the wool over my eyes." He winked at Amber. "No pun intended."

By the time the coffee was ready, Colonel Vernon Houston had made himself comfortably at home. Amber had to keep reminding herself that he was a multimillionaire, that he was king among the Texas oil barons, that his Fortune 500 company could buy and sell half of Kitsap County before breakfast on any given morning. He was so real, so relaxed . . . so ordinary.

"Great place you've got here, son," he said to TwoJoe as they adjourned to the kitchen for coffee and cake. He motioned to the ancient post-and-beam construction of the living room. "The little woman wanted a fancy place on the water, so I built it for her. But tell the truth, I'd be a whole lot more at home in a log cabin like this one."

"This place has been in our family for a hundred years," TwoJoe explained. "Our ancestors were Norwegian loggers."

Vern pulled out a chair and sat down heavily. "Norwegian?" He laughed again, a great booming sound that reminded Amber of thunder or kettle drums. "Somehow I'd a never guessed Norwegian, not in a million years." He grinned and inclined his massive head in Meg's direction. "Now her, I'd guess as Norwegian."

"We're half Suquamish," Meg said. "TwoJoe got the dark genes; I got the blonde ones."

Vernon polished off two huge wedges of chocolate layer cake before he leaned back in his chair and fixed his attention on Amber.

"Sam told me what happened in the barn. That was a mighty brave thing you did, little lady, and I'll always be indebted to you." He took Amber's hand in his and planted a kiss on her knuckles, then unsnapped the breast pocket of his shirt and drew out a folded piece of paper. "There's no way to thank you properly, but maybe this'll serve as a little token of my appreciation for taking such good care of my grandson."

She could see it was a check. He laid it on the table and pushed it in her direction.

"Colonel Houston, no—," she began.

"We can't take it," TwoJoe stated flatly. "Absolutely not."

"Was I talkin' to you?" He fixed TwoJoe with a glare that would melt rubber.

"He's right," Amber said softly. "It's a very nice gesture, Colonel, but you don't take money for something you did for love."

Vern scratched his head and blinked. His eyes watered, crinkling at the corners, bright with unshed tears. "I already lost my granddaughter. It ain't right, outliving your kids or grandkids. I couldn't have stood it to lose my grandson, too."

"I understand that," Amber whispered. "But I don't need a reward." She glanced over at Sam, who sat gazing at her with wide eyes, a little smudge of chocolate icing on his freckled nose. "Your grandson has given us much more than we could ever ask for, just by being here, by being himself. We love him. I think he loves us. I didn't do anything particularly brave in that barn, Colonel Houston. Maybe I even saved him out of cowardice and selfishness, because I was afraid to lose him. Whatever the case, he's saved me just as much as I've saved him."

A tear spilled over onto his leathery cheek, and the Colonel reached up to wipe it away. "I don't reckon I understand quite what you mean, little lady, but I'll take your word for it. Sam's right—y'all are special people. Just the kind of folks I'd want my grandson to know."

He got up and motioned to Sam. "We'd better get on home, son, before your grandma sends the Cavalry out lookin' for us. Thanks for your hospitality. If you don't mind, we'll go out the back door. Real friends don't use the front, and I'm hopin' after tonight you'll count me as a friend."

He shrugged into the jacket Meg held out for him and clamped the Stetson down on his head. "Oh, and by the way, Emmaline—that's my wife—will give you a call tomorrow or the next day. She said she'd like to have you all over for a real Texas-style barbecue."

Amber pushed back her chair and retrieved the check from the table. "We'd love to come. And don't forget this—" She extended the check in his direction.

He frowned, but took it, shaking his head. "Get that kitten, Sam—your grandma finally gave in and said it was OK."

Sam went over to the hearth, scooped up Pocahontas, and tucked her inside his shirt. "I'll take good care of her," he promised.

Amber smiled. "I know you will, Sam. Bring her back to visit her brothers and sisters anytime. We'll come and see her, too."

"Tell you what," the Colonel said, fingering the check and then slipping it into his shirt pocket. "I ain't in the habit of treading on other folks' pride, so I won't fight with you about this business of the money. But if you ever need anything—anything at all—you come to me first. You promise?"

Amber nodded. "Promise." She squeezed his callused hand. "Come back soon."

Then he was gone, herding Sam and Pokie out the door and into the rain-soaked night.

Amber sat down at the kitchen table and put her head in her hands.

"You did the right thing," TwoJoe said. "Not taking the reward, I mean."

"I wonder. That money would have solved a lot of our problems."

TwoJoe laughed. "It would take a lot more than a little reward money to get us out of this hole, and—" He stopped suddenly when he saw the look on Amber's face. "You saw how much the check was, didn't you?"

Amber nodded. "Five zeros," she whispered. "Five. That check was made out for one hundred thousand dollars."

23

Plan B

Amber had spent three days second-guessing her rejection of Vernon Houston's generous reward. TwoJoe and Meg both concurred that she had made the right decision; no Elkhorn had ever taken charity, not once in all the lean and difficult years. They had always "stood proud in their own moccasins," as Grandpa Joe often reminded them when they were children, had always managed to get through whatever hard times came their way.

Well, family honor was all well and good, but what use would it be if they lost the land and were forced to move? Amber hadn't said so, but privately she thought it had been stupid and shortsighted of Grandpa Joe to forbid taking a mortgage on the farm. Still, he had been an old man, accustomed to the old ways. He couldn't have foreseen what was happening to them now. And TwoJoe was probably right: even if they could take a mortgage and pay off the taxes and their other bills, what about the next tax bill, and the one after that? Mortgage companies didn't care what happened to a small-time llama farmer and his forty acres of land.

What they needed was another source of income, something that couldn't be snatched out from under them at a moment's notice. Maybe TwoJoe wouldn't feel it was charity if they took a *loan* from Vernon Houston . . .

But Amber knew better. The Colonel might be a great fellow, but even if he did have so much money that writing out a check for a hundred thousand would be like giving up pocket change, TwoJoe would never go for it. Vernon wasn't family. And although Meg and TwoJoe had shirttail relatives scattered here and there throughout Kitsap County, nobody who *was* family had any money to speak of. Certainly not enough to float a loan large enough to bail them out of this situation.

Her mind cast about for other possibilities while she put the finishing touches on a set of forest green stoneware—a large order, for one of Mr. Jorgensen's clients in Seattle. Jorgensen had called yesterday to check on the order and tell her that although he hadn't yet sold the Two Sisters piece, it was getting a good deal of attention and he would welcome the opportunity to display other sculptures when she had them ready. If they only had more time, Amber might be able to come up with enough money to hold the wolves at bay.

But they didn't have time.

TwoJoe had begun talking about selling the llamas and looking for an accounting job in the city. He tried to keep a cheerful attitude, but Amber could see in his eyes that the prospect was destroying him. The corporate world was his worst nightmare come to life, and yet he was willing to give up everything he had worked for, everything he loved, for Amber and for Meg and for the farm.

An idea crept into the corner of Amber's mind and lurked there until she began to pay attention to it. There was someone else who had money. A lot of money. Not as much as Vernon Houston, but enough.

Daddy.

No. It was impossible, unthinkable. Amber was not about to go crawling back to her father after all this time begging for help. He had betrayed her trust, turned his back on her, and she had made a life without him. A good life, though not a wealthy one. The very idea of contacting him now turned her stomach. And besides, she couldn't take the chance of letting him know where she was, of becoming vulnerable to him again.

There had to be another way.

Mama would help; Amber was sure of it. Maybe Mama could find a way to get money to her without Daddy finding out about it. She hated going to Mama, too, but not as much as she hated the idea of TwoJoe giving up all his dreams for her.

Amber glanced at her watch. It was just past 9 A.M.—that would make it noon in North Carolina. Her father would probably be at the office, or meeting with the city council, or having lunch with some of his cronies. The chances of his being at home this time of day were pretty slim. If she were going to do this, she ought to do it now, before she lost her nerve.

On a square wooden post next to her sculpting table, TwoJoe had installed an extension phone and a buzzer that ran from the house to the barn. They only had one telephone line, so she couldn't call the house with it, but if she received a call, someone could buzz her and she could pick up down here without having to stop in the middle of her work. She rarely used it unless a dealer called during the day.

She put one hand on the receiver and stared at the telephone. It had once been white, but was now overlaid with a film of dried clay, splotches of different-colored glazes, and a fine coat of grit from the hay that sifted down from the loft. Cleaning it didn't help, so she had given up long ago.

Just as she had given up on a lot of other things . . .

Amber raised the receiver to her ear and listened for the dial tone. She racked her brain but couldn't remember the number. And before she had a chance to punch in the number for Information, her eyes lit on the sculpture she had taken in to show to Susan Quentin. The man in the armchair with the little girl on his lap. It sat on the shelf next to her sculpting table, side by side with the plaster cast of the Two Sisters. They could have been called Captivity and Liberty.

Amber felt a strange sensation rise up from her midsection. *"I'm taking back something that hasn't been mine for years,"* she had told Susan that day. *"The power to control my own life."*

In a moment, with a single telephone call, all the progress she had made would be undone. It wouldn't simply be a step backward, but a long slide into the darkness, a surrender, a capitulation of every shred of mental and emotional health she had managed to gather over the years. It would be the most blatant kind of prostitution—an exchange of her life, her very *self*, for money.

But what other choice did she have?

Father Susan had once told her that as long as there was life, there were choices. Options you never saw until it seemed as if every door had slammed and locked in your face. With God, she said, nothing was impossible.

Amber had no idea what other options might present themselves, but in that moment she knew for certain that only one choice lay before her now: captivity or liberty.

"All right, God, if you're out there," she muttered with clenched teeth. "I'm going to try to trust you on this—or at least to trust in Susan's trust. I choose liberty."

Exhaling a deep breath, she replaced the receiver on the hook and turned back to her work.

After he had finished the evening feeding, TwoJoe sat on a ten-gallon bucket under the overhang of one of the llama shelters and gazed absently across Clear Creek Road to where the late afternoon sun reflected on the lush rolling hills beyond. Earlier this morning, he had spent an hour after breakfast on the back porch, just staring out over the Hood Canal and Olympic Mountains. He wasn't sure quite what he was doing—maybe getting his fill of the views that nurtured and sustained his soul. Chances were, he wouldn't be seeing much of them from here on out—except through the windshield of a car.

Meg and Amber would have resisted him had they known, but he had gone ahead and put out some feelers for jobs in the city, calling in a few favors and placing calls to old acquaintances from Berkeley who now headed up CPA firms in Seattle. He even had two interviews lined up next week, but he would no doubt be competing against twenty-five-year-olds fresh out of graduate school and just starting their careers. Although part of him hoped that someone would take pity on a middle-aged man and give him a break, he had to admit that the idea of groveling for an entry-level position didn't do much for his pride.

Pride. It had been one of Grandpa Joe's favorite words. TwoJoe had grown up as a boy at the old man's knee, hearing stories of tribal honor and family dignity. And he had never once in his life thought of pride in negative terms. Ethnic sensibility compelled him to be proud of his heritage, his race, even his accomplishments. For a beleaguered minority, pride was synonymous with self-respect and courage, not vanity or arrogance.

But TwoJoe was beginning to wonder where the line was, that nearly invisible demarcation between strength of character and personal ego. Was he just being bullheaded not to take Vernon Houston up on his offer of help? Was it stubbornness rather than integrity that made him consider selling the farm—or worse, selling his soul to corporate America—rather than take what he condescendingly called charity?

For the past few days, he and Meg and Amber had talked of nothing else. Clearly, neither of them wanted to give up this land and their home. Amber, especially, needed this place for the healing of her soul and the nurturing of her creativity. He had seen the look on her face and knew that, no matter what it cost him, he could not let this land go. Even if the price was everything he had to give.

But when he had brought up the idea of taking a job in the city, her expression of worry and anxiety had changed to a look of near-despair.

Pain—for him, for what such a decision would do to him. And he had dared to hope that maybe, in the deep recesses of her heart, there burned a spark of love. A spark that might, in time, be fanned to a flame.

Still, TwoJoe was sensible enough to know that whatever sacrifice he made could not be the motivation for Amber to love him. He didn't want her come to him out of obligation or pity or admiration or need or any of the other pathetic imitations that sometimes masqueraded as love.

And if he did this—if he transformed himself into something else for the sake of saving his land and his world and his chance at love—how would she feel about the person he would become? TwoJoe couldn't imagine liking himself as a corporate accountant; how could a woman like Amber possibly love that man?

It was all so complicated. Every option he could think of seemed to be at odds with what he really wanted out of life, with the man he believed himself to be. If he sold the place, he would be selling every dream he ever held dear. But he could keep the dream only by giving up his most cherished vision of who he was created to be.

TwoJoe shut his eyes, put a hand over his face, and sighed. The real issue, he supposed, had to do with what God was asking of him, but he didn't know the answer to that question, either. In the past he would pray and come away with at least a general sense of where God was leading—a gut feeling, an impression, a glimpse of possibility. But these days his prayers weren't being answered, not with any clarity he could discern, anyway.

He felt a tickling sensation on his fingers and opened his eyes to find Llittle Bit nuzzling her whiskers against his hand. In spite of himself, he laughed and stroked her wooly neck. He would miss these wonderful creatures when they were gone.

A shadow fell over him, and he looked up into the piercing gaze of the man who called himself William Shivers.

"Thought I'd stop by once more and see if you changed your mind about selling," Shivers said without preamble. "Figured by now you might have seen the light."

TwoJoe stood up and faced him. Something in the man's countenance—a contemptuousness, a haughty certainty—made TwoJoe dislike him intensely. "I don't know what light you're talking about, Mr. Shivers, but here's a little illumination for your benefit: I'm not selling. Not now, not ever." His voice held more conviction than his heart, but as he spoke the words, TwoJoe felt a little courage and hope come to life within him.

The man grinned—not a nice expression on him in the least. "My people really don't like to take no for an answer."

"Sorry," TwoJoe repeated. "That's the only answer I have to give them."

Shivers scrutinized TwoJoe for a minute. His hands clenched into fists, and his eyes narrowed. But then his grip relaxed, and he extended an outstretched hand in TwoJoe's direction. "Well, you can't blame a guy for trying. Just doing my job. No hard feelings?"

"Of course not." TwoJoe shook hands with the man and breathed just a little easier.

"So, what are you going to do?" Shivers asked, clapping TwoJoe on the shoulder as if they were a couple of old cronies. "About this place, I mean. Not going to sell it to somebody else, I hope. Because if that's your intent, I can beat any offer you'll get."

"I'm not going to sell it to anybody." TwoJoe kept a wary eye on the man's face. "I've got some—some options."

"Options. Right. Well, good luck to you. See you around." He rubbed Llittle Bit's ears and turned toward the gate.

Halfway between the pasture and the big barn, Shiv ducked out of sight into a copse of trees and sat down on a fallen log. He had to think. Underwood wasn't going to like this, not a bit. And if Underwood wasn't happy, Shiv didn't get paid.

To tell the truth, he hadn't expected Elkhorn to cave. The man had backbone, that much was sure. But he had to give it one last shot. Now it was time for Plan B—whatever that was.

He pulled a cell phone from his pocket and punched in a speed-dial number. It rang twice, but before anyone answered, Shiv shut down the call. What was the use of calling just to say he hadn't succeeded? He'd take care of things, and *then* he'd let Underwood know the job was done.

He crammed the phone back into his pocket and swore under his breath. The truth was, he didn't have the faintest idea how he was going to take care of it. There was no Plan B. But he'd better come up with one. Fast.

If he only knew what kind of "options" Elkhorn had up his sleeve.

The path back to the house and his car took him directly past the barn door. It was open, and he hung back for a moment, looking in. He could see someone sitting on a stool in front of a big table, but from this angle he couldn't tell who it was. Might be the wife. Might be the woman Underwood wanted lost.

He took a couple of steps inside, then heard a telephone ringing and flattened himself against the wall into the shadows. The woman had dark hair, and she was bigger than Elkhorn's little blonde wife. It was the artist, the target, the one who called herself Amber.

"Hello, Mr. Jorgensen," she said. "Meg told me you really liked it; I'm so glad." A pause. "You sold it? That's wonderful! How much?"

Shiv heard a gasp. "Yes, Meg said you were interested in other pieces. I'm working on a couple of ideas right now. A commissioned sculpture? Of course I'd be interested! Tell me what you have in mind."

She alternated listening and talking for a minute or two—something Shiv didn't understand in the least, about composition and castings and bronze. At last she went on: "I've never done anything of that magnitude before, Mr. Jorgensen, but I certainly think I could handle it." Then she dropped the receiver and scrambled to recover it. "Sorry, Mr. Jorgensen. Did you say ten thousand dollars in advance? And another ten at delivery?" She choked a little. "Yes, that would buy me plenty of time to work on it. I'll start right away. And I'll anticipate the check and the customer's sketch. Good-bye, Mr. Jorgensen—and thank you!"

She hung up the phone and threw her hands into the air with a whoop. "Thank you, thank you, *thank you!*" she yelled into the rafters.

She was still doing a little victory dance when Shiv slipped out the door and made for his car.

A ten-thousand dollar advance. So that was the "option" Elkhorn was talking about. Some kind of art stuff this Amber woman was working on. From the information he had been given about Elkhorn's financial situation, that amount wouldn't nearly cover all the debts, but it would take care of the taxes and allow them some breathing room, some time to get their act together. And if the woman was any good, there would likely be more where that came from.

But not if Shiv could prevent it.

Plan B was already formulating itself in his mind. It would work. He was sure of it.

He slipped into the car and started the engine. It was nearly dark, and just as he turned his lights on, he caught a glimpse of Elkhorn coming up the path toward the house. He lowered the window and gave a friendly little wave.

Elkhorn came over to the car, frowning a little. "I figured you'd be gone by now."

"I'm heading out. Just couldn't help watching the sunset over the water." Shiv laughed. "Beautiful place you've got here. Well, good night—and good luck."

He swung the car around and eased onto the long gravel driveway that led to the main road. The property was shielded on three sides by trees—big ones, close together. He could park at that vacant cabin up the road and walk in without anybody ever seeing him.

Once he turned onto Clear Creek Road, he flipped open his cell phone again.

"Mr. Underwood? Just wanted to let you know you got nothin' to worry about. One more day. Two at the most."

24

Occidental Discovery

"You've been behind the camera this whole trip," Carlene said as she herded Diedre into position. "This may be the last time we ever get to Seattle, and I want at least one picture with you in it. Now, smile!"

Diedre lifted a hand and waved as Carlene snapped the shutter on the camera. She felt a tug on the leash and looked down to see Sugarbear lapping water from a moss-covered fountain in the square.

Carlene chuckled. "I could use something to drink, too, although I'm not sure I'd want what's coming out of that fountain." She motioned toward a small open-air cafe. "Let's sit for a while and get a sandwich and some coffee."

Diedre was only too happy to comply; she felt as if they had been walking for weeks. She sank gratefully into a wrought-iron chair and waited with Sugarbear while Carlene went inside to order.

The place, she learned from her visitor's map, was called Occidental Park, in the center of Pioneer Square. Under other circumstances, Diedre would have been delighted with it—and everything else about Seattle. Occidental Street was a kind of pedestrian park, paved with cobblestones and surrounded by shade trees. Several totem poles and statues watched over the perimeter of the square—most notably, the tourist guide said, the "welcoming spirit of Kwakiutl." In the pergola across the way, a small jazz trio was performing for donations from passersby.

Welcoming spirit, Diedre mused. In many ways Seattle had been welcoming. Although the past few days had been overcast, it had only rained significantly one morning—the day they had spent in the Department of Records, trying to find some lead to the whereabouts of Diedre's sister. Every search for "McAlister" proved to be futile, and although they knew she had probably changed her name, they had very little to go on. They left the department without a single scrap of useful information.

This was a fool's errand. They weren't going to find Sissy—not this week, not ever. Diedre would never know what became of her big sister, or who her real father was. She would just have to adjust to the frustration of living with the unknown.

Disappointed and discouraged, Diedre had been ready to pack the car and go home three days ago. But Carlene had insisted that they take advantage of the opportunity, and so they had armed themselves with maps and brochures, cameras, and trolley passes and set out to see a few of the sights.

It was only the second week in May, and the summer tourists had not yet descended upon Seattle, but even so the city was a noisy, bustling, active place. Yesterday Carlene and Diedre had taken in the Pike Place Market, with its enthusiastic vendors throwing fish high into the air, and the Waterfront, where they had a fabulous dinner of fresh salmon and Dabob Bay oysters on a pier overlooking the Sound. This morning they had spent three hours in the Elliott Bay Bookstore and cruising some of the art shops in Pioneer Square, and Carlene had come away with a host of ideas for things she wanted to do with Mountain Arts once they got back home again.

The sun came out, dappling the cobblestones of the square with mottled light. Music from the jazz trio mingled with the clacking of wheels and the clanging of a bell as a trolley pulled into the small covered station across the street. Diedre closed her eyes and raised her face to the warmth. A gentle breeze caressed her face. If she hadn't come all the way across the country on a mission that had failed so miserably, she might have considered this a perfect day.

She heard a chair scrape across the cobblestones and opened her eyes to see a flash of blue and purple as Carlene sat down beside her. On the table between them lay two thick sandwiches wrapped in plastic, two large Styrofoam cups brimming with a dark, fragrant coffee, and a waxy paper bag with "Grand Central Bakery" stamped on the outside.

"They've got the most marvelous selection of cookies in there," Carlene said, unwrapping one of the sandwiches. "And all the bread is fresh-baked—just get a whiff of that." She held the sandwich up to Diedre's nose.

The sandwich did, indeed, smell heavenly and looked even better. Thick slices of a crusty French roll with assorted cold cuts, two kinds of cheese, lettuce, and sprouts, all spread with a delicate garlic dressing.

Carlene bit into her sandwich with relish. "Nice music," she said in between bites. "This is a great place, isn't it?"

"Yes, it is," Diedre agreed. "Except—"

"Except that we haven't found what we came for."

"No, we haven't. And I don't know what to do next. Maybe we should just go home. I don't want to give up, but—"

Carlene wasn't listening. Her eyes were fixed on a point across the cobbled square, a bench next to a totem depicting a man riding the tail of a whale. "There he is again," she said.

"Who?" Diedre looked.

"That same guy, the one we saw the other day in the lobby at the Claremont. He was in the Pike Place Market yesterday, too, and on the sidewalk in front of the restaurant at the Waterfront. Do you think he's tailing us?"

"You've got to quit watching *Law & Order*," Diedre muttered. "Why would anyone follow *us?*" Still, a tingle ran up her back. The man in the dark suit did look a little familiar. He sat on the park bench like any tourist, his face turned in the direction of the jazz band. But he was wearing sunglasses; his eyes could be looking anywhere.

Carlene finished her sandwich and fished in the bag for a cookie. "Probably just a coincidence," she agreed. She was silent for a moment, then reached out and laid her hand over Diedre's. "Look, Diedre. I know this is painful for you—and discouraging. I can only imagine how I'd feel if I were in your position. And I'm not trying to make light of the situation, really I'm not."

"I know," Diedre sighed. "You've been wonderful, Carlene. I'd never have made it this far without you, either physically or emotionally. I'm so thankful you're in this with me."

"So what do you think we ought to do?"

"I don't know." Diedre sipped her coffee. "A few days ago, when I asked what you believed about God's guidance, you told me all I needed to do was follow my heart and be open to direction. I'm trying to do that, but I seem to keep hitting up against a brick wall. My heart tells me that I need to find my sister, and that if I do find her, all my questions—well, maybe not all my questions, but at least *some* of them—will be answered. I've even tried to pray, Carlene, honestly I have. But I don't seem to be getting much response."

"Maybe the response is to wait."

"How long can we wait? Every day we stay here, we're running up more bills than I can keep track of—and it's all going on your tab. I've been assuming that once I get home, I can come up with the money to pay you back, but even that I'm not sure about. If Daddy cut off my credit cards—"

"We'll face that problem when we get home." Carlene patted Diedre's arm. "Tell you what—let's go back and check out of the hotel. I know it's convenient to be so close to everything, but the Claremont is pretty expensive, and we can find something cheaper. That way we can stay a few more days."

"And what will that accomplish, when we don't have the faintest idea where to go next?" Diedre pulled a piece of turkey out of the remains of her sandwich and held it down to her side for Sugarbear. "Come on, girl, take it."

She looked down. The end of Sugarbear's leash was still wrapped around the leg of the table, but her collar lay empty on the cobblestones a few feet behind Diedre's chair.

Panicked, Diedre jumped up and looked around the square. The dog was nowhere in sight. "She slipped her collar. She's gone! Carlene, come on!"

A sinking sensation washed over her as she frantically scanned the park for any sign of the little dog. Mama was dead. Daddy wasn't her father. Vesta was a thousand miles away. She had been unsuccessful in the search for Sissy. And now Sugarbear—faithful, loving Sugarbear—had disappeared. Diedre couldn't bear the thought of losing her, too.

Murmuring a frantic plea for divine help under her breath, Diedre took off running with Carlene at her heels.

Fifteen minutes later, Diedre had made the circuit of the two blocks around Occidental Park, looking into every alleyway and behind every dumpster, and was back where she started. Carlene had gone down the hill to First Street to scan the area around Elliott Bay Books.

Diedre sat down on the pergola steps, exhausted and alarmed. In fifteen minutes Sugarbear could have gone anywhere. She could be down at the wharf chasing sea gulls, or up on Capitol Hill in the middle of traffic. For all Diedre knew, she could be on a ferry halfway across the Sound by now.

A minute or two later, Carlene came huffing up. "No luck," she panted. "Where could she have gone?"

"I don't know." Trembling, still holding the empty leash, Diedre put her face in her hands and began to cry.

A gentle hand touched her shoulder. "Excuse me?"

Diedre looked up into the clear, hazel eyes of a stout middle-aged woman with hair graying around the temples.

"Were you looking for a dog—a little one, blonde, about so high?"

"Yes!" Diedre grabbed the woman by the hand. "Have you seen her?"

"She crossed the trolley tracks and went the other way on Occidental, down toward Jackson Street. About five minutes ago, I think."

Infused with fresh adrenaline, Diedre jumped to her feet, thanked the woman profusely, and headed in the direction the woman had indicated. She could hear Carlene straggling along behind, gasping, "Go on . . . I'll . . . catch up."

The other end of Occidental Street, away from the park, proved to be a wide, shaded walking boulevard with lush trees in the center and buildings of dark red brick on either side. Like the square, it was paved with cobblestones, and the uneven terrain made running difficult. Diedre peered down the length of the street, calling, "Here, Sugarbear. Come on, girl."

As she slowed a bit to catch her breath, Carlene caught up and fell into step beside her. "I can't lose her," Diedre said miserably. "I just can't."

"We'll find her; let's keep looking."

Just as Diedre was peering into a dark crevice behind a set of low brick stairs, the door above her opened and a man stepped out onto the stoop. He was tall and thin, with salt-and-pepper hair and a neatly groomed gray beard, and wore immaculately pressed khaki slacks, a starched denim shirt, and a tan and blue necktie. At his side stood a massive golden retriever. "Is this who you're searching for?"

In his arms he held a small bundle of blonde fur.

Once Diedre had determined that Sugarbear was all right, none the worse for her little adventure, all the adrenaline drained out of her and she felt as if she could no longer stand up.

"Please come in," the man said, opening the door and motioning them inside. "You look as if you need to sit down."

"I was just so worried," Diedre murmured. "Sugarbear, how could you?"

The man laid a hand on the golden's broad head. "Meet Casey. He's the bad influence, I'm afraid. He sneaked out a while ago—a bad habit, although he usually doesn't go very far—and your little Sugarbear followed him down here." He ushered Diedre and Carlene through several large rooms into a small parlor and invited them to sit. "Don't be too hard on her, now; I think she's in love with my handsome guy."

Diedre sank into a cushioned chair. "Thank you so much for rescuing her. We're just visiting, and she doesn't know her way around. I was afraid—"

"I know. They're like family, aren't they?" The man came over beside Diedre and fondled Sugarbear's ears. "Allow me to introduce myself. I'm Andrew Jorgensen. This is my home, and out there—," he motioned to the rooms they had passed through on their way to the parlor, "is my gallery."

Diedre had been so upset over Sugarbear's disappearance that she hadn't noticed much of her surroundings. Now she saw she was in a tastefully decorated sitting room with an exquisite marble fireplace as its centerpiece. The lamp on the table at her elbow had to be a Tiffany, and she was pretty certain that every piece in the room was authentic; not a reproduction in sight.

"I'm Diedre—Diedre McAlister," she stammered. "This is my friend Carlene Donovan. And of course you've met Sugarbear."

"If you'll excuse me for a moment, I was just making tea. You'll join me, of course?"

"That's very generous of you, but we don't want to take up any more of your time, Mr. Jorgensen." Diedre began rummaging in her pockets for Sugarbear's collar and leash.

"Nonsense. Just stay put. It won't take a moment."

"This is some place," Carlene said when he was gone. "I wish I had some of these pieces for Mountain Arts." She got up and began wandering toward the doorway.

Diedre remained in the chair with Sugarbear firmly on her lap. She craned her neck to see what Carlene was doing. "Don't go snooping."

"I'm not snooping. This is an art gallery; he said so. I just want to take a look around."

The golden retriever, Casey, came to stand beside Diedre and laid his long nose over the arm of the chair, gazing at her with liquid brown eyes. "You're a sweet boy," she said, stroking his silky head. "Thanks for taking care of my baby." Casey licked her hand and nuzzled at Sugarbear, who quivered all over.

Carlene's voice drifted in from the next room. "Diedre, come here a minute. You've got to see this."

"Carlene, I don't think we should—"

"Come in here—*now*."

Diedre set Sugarbear on the floor next to Casey. "Be good," she commanded. "You've had all the trouble you're allowed for one day." She went into the next room and found Carlene staring at a display of small tabletop sculptures on glass shelves.

"What do you make of this?"

Diedre drew closer and looked. At the center of the display, crafted in oatmeal-colored clay and rendered with breathtaking detail, sat a likeness of a teenage girl clasping hands with a very young child. The little girl's feet were just about to lift off from the ground in flight, and her face bore an expression of absolute ecstasy.

Diedre felt all the blood rush out of her head, and she clutched at Carlene's arm for support. Her eyes blurred with tears, so that she could barely make out the writing on the tag: *Two Sisters. Original by local artist. SOLD.*

⤫

"It's magnificent, isn't it?"

Diedre turned to see Andrew Jorgensen hovering behind them.

"This is the very first piece of hers, to my knowledge, to come on the market, to be displayed and sold," Jorgensen explained. "She's a local artist. A fine eye, don't you think?" He grinned. "I rather like to think of myself as the one who discovered her."

"I have to have it," Diedre blurted out.

"Oh, I'm sorry, that's quite impossible. As you can see, it's already sold. A gentleman saw it in the shop just yesterday and purchased it on the spot. But he had other business to attend to and said he'd be coming in next week to pick it up. Quite a tidy sum for a small sculpture, I might add." His brow furrowed into a frown when he saw Diedre's expression. "I have a number of other pieces by that same artist—stoneware, mostly. Vases and such."

She shook her head.

"Let's have tea, shall we?" Jorgensen directed them back toward the sitting room.

Diedre's head was beginning to clear, and the tea helped. She nibbled on a sugar cookie and tried to catch her breath. Carlene sat next to her on the sofa, her eyes fixed on Diedre's face, saying nothing.

At last Diedre found her voice. "About that artist—I need her name and address."

Andrew Jorgensen busied himself with rearranging the tea tray. "I'm sorry, Miss McAlister, but that's quite impossible. I can't give out the home addresses of the artists whose work I carry. I have a responsibility to protect their privacy. You and your friend seem like nice young women, and Casey here is a very good judge of character—" He paused, stroking the golden retriever under the chin. "But it's a firm policy of mine, and of every other reputable dealer in town, not to disseminate such personal information. Just yesterday a man came into my shop asking questions about this very same artist—"

Carlene jerked to attention. "A big muscular guy, in a dark suit and T-shirt?"

Jorgensen stared at her. "Exactly. Do you know him?"

"I think he's been following us."

"Following you? A most reprehensible-looking fellow. I did not, as you might expect, entrust him with any pertinent information whatsoever."

"That's a relief."

"Forget about him!" Diedre blurted out, more suddenly than she had intended. She turned a pleading gaze in Jorgensen's direction. "Can you at least give me her name—the artist who created that sculpture?"

"Of course. Her name is Chaney. Amber Chaney."

Diedre's eyes stung, and her face went cold and clammy. Carlene was gripping her hand so tightly that she couldn't feel her fingers. "Chaney. Of course."

Andrew Jorgensen stared at her with an expression of concern. "Are you quite all right, Miss McAlister?"

"It makes sense," Diedre murmured, half to herself and half to Carlene. "If I were going to change my name, I'd pick something that connected me to someone I loved." She shook her head. "I should have thought of it. I should have known that—"

"Excuse me," Andrew Jorgensen interrupted. "Not that it's any of my business, but would someone care to fill me in on what's going on here?"

Diedre swiped aside a tear that had streaked down her cheek. "Amber Chaney is my sister."

"We've come to Seattle looking for her," Carlene added. "It's—well, a little complicated. Diedre hasn't seen her sister in over twenty years."

"Then how do you know—?"

Carlene left the room and came back in a minute bearing the Two Sisters sculpture. She pushed the tea tray to one side and set the statue down on the coffee table. "Look at Diedre's face, and then look at the face of the older girl."

Andrew looked. "My stars," he breathed at last. "I believe there *is* a resemblance."

"Chaney was our mother's maiden name." Diedre dug in her bag and came up with her driver's license. "It's my middle name, as you can see."

"Yes, but—"

"My sister disappeared from my life when I was very small—three or four years old, maybe. And that statue is a representation of the only memory I have of her." Diedre turned toward Carlene. "It wasn't just a dream. It really happened. She's alive. She's here. And she remembers."

 ❧

Andrew warmed up the tea, and the young woman named Diedre McAlister told him the whole story—about what she called the Spinning Dream, the discovery that her sister was still alive, the letters and post-card, the trip to Seattle to try to find her. All during her narrative, his eyes darted back and forth from the Two Sisters to the young woman's face. This was turning into quite an adventure—a mystery, dropped square into his lap.

By the time Diedre was finished, he was wiping his eyes with a paper napkin. "And so," she concluded, "I've come to see her, to try to re-connect with her. To get some answers. Will you help us?"

"Of course, of course."

"What can you tell us about her?" the friend, Carlene, asked.

"Well, she's a very promising artist. She lives on a farm out in Kitsap County, across the Sound. With a couple of friends—a brother and sis-ter. She has a good life, I think. Although she does seem to be a rather quiet person—almost sad. Rather withdrawn and self-protective. I can't say I know her well."

"So you don't really know how she might respond to the idea of see-ing me," Diedre said.

"There's only one way of finding out." Andrew excused himself, went to his office, and came back with a Rolodex card. "Here's her address and telephone number." He watched while Diedre copied the informa-tion onto a napkin. "Shall we call her?"

The young woman cast a panicked look at her friend. "I—uh—"

Carlene jumped in. "I think it might be better to do this in person, don't you, Diedre?"

Diedre agreed, and Andrew stifled a rush of disappointment. He did so hate to be left out of things. But he gathered himself together and determined to be gracious. "I probably should call her for permission, but in this case—well, what a wonderful surprise it will be for her—I'll give you directions. It's a bit complicated, getting there, so let me explain it a bit. You have a car, is that right? Then take the ferry to Bainbridge Island, and—"

Diedre barely heard Andrew Jorgensen's instructions, but Carlene was writing everything down and nodding as if she understood, so she didn't concern herself with the details. All she could think about was the fact that her sister was alive, and little more than an hour away from where they sat this very minute.

Her eyes lingered on the statue, tracing the fluid lines of windblown hair and clasped hands and little feet about to take off from the ground. Objectively speaking, it was a beautiful piece, but Diedre couldn't be certain of her objectivity. She looked at the faces and saw . . . .

Home. Belonging.

"First thing tomorrow morning," Carlene was saying as she stood and accepted Andrew Jorgensen's business card. "And yes, we'll let you know how it turns out."

25

Soul Aflame

Amber sat on the back porch and watched as the moon slid lazily over the Olympic Mountains and hovered at the peak of Mount Constance. The night was cool and quiet; she could almost hear the wind under the eagle's wings as he glided like a dark shadow over the glimmering waters of Hood Canal.

Meg and TwoJoe had gone to bed hours ago, but Amber couldn't sleep. She was still too full of amazement and wonder at what this day had brought. In one brief moment, in the blink of an eye, everything had changed. Everything.

Amber had work—real work, bringing in real money. TwoJoe wouldn't have to sell the llamas . . . or the farm . . . or his soul. They could all stay together, right here, where they belonged.

Maybe Susan was right—maybe God did answer prayers. Just not in the way we expected. *And without a moment to spare*, Amber admitted wryly. But no one seemed inclined to quibble over the timing.

They had all gone out to dinner to celebrate. Amber and TwoJoe and Meg, Vernon and Emmaline Houston and little Sam—even the Reverend Doctor Susan Quentin—had piled into two cars and driven into Port Ludlow to have seafood at a restaurant overlooking Paradise Bay.

For two hours they had laughed and joked and hammered crabs and thrown shells at each other. Sam had circled the table gathering a box full of scraps to take home to Pocahontas. Meg and Susan marveled over the Miracle, as they called Amber's commission. TwoJoe sat beside her, gazing at her, his expression filled with pride and wonder. The anxiety of the past few weeks was gone, replaced with joy and tranquillity. And at the head and foot of the restaurant table, Vernon and Emmaline Houston beamed over all of them like the proud parents of a slightly rowdy brood.

As Amber recalled the scene in her mind, a creeping awareness trickled through her veins and into her heart. For the first time in years, she had trusted—or at least she had tried to trust. And a response had come. But the wonder of it was that the answer turned out to be a gift much more valuable than simply the money they needed to save the farm.

A phrase floated to the surface of her mind, a verse Susan had quoted to her a couple times, something like "Lord, I believe, help my unbelief." She had looked it up later, that Bible story, and it seemed that Jesus had honored that honest prayer—just as Amber's feeble attempts had been honored. But as usual, God had done something different—and deeper—than anyone had expected. God had reached into the hidden places of Amber Chaney's soul and answered a need even she had not been able—or willing—to articulate.

God had given her back a family. Not kindred of blood, but of spirit. A protecting father. A doting mother. A sister who loved her. A mentor who challenged her to grow. A little brother who made her laugh and swelled her heart with delight. A big brother who—

Her heart accelerated as she recalled the look on TwoJoe's face, his brown eyes dancing with candlelight. A look of pride. Of tenderness. Of . . . love.

He had been willing to sacrifice everything—the land, the llamas, his dreams—for Meg, and, somehow in a deeper way, for her.

For her.

God loved her. TwoJoe loved her. And with a clarity that startled her, Amber realized that nothing inside her, no buried secret, no insecurity, would be terrible enough to undermine that love.

Almost physically, she could feel the change. At the epicenter of her spirit, in a place she had never been able to reach, that cold dark something, that lump of black ice, began to melt. As if the sun had started to reappear after a total eclipse, her bones began to warm from the inside out, her lungs exhaled a pent-up breath she had held for years.

Amber Chaney surrendered. And the cleansing tears came.

Heavy clouds had shrouded the moon, and the night had grown cold and damp. An owl hooted in the distance.

Amber didn't know how long she had sat there weeping. She only knew that she didn't feel depleted and exhausted, the way she usually did when she cried, but somehow filled and rested and energized—as if she had just arisen from a perfect night's sleep. Her heart overflowed, and her mind raced with ideas. She wanted to wake TwoJoe, but it was late; she would talk to him in the morning. But since she was awake—perhaps more awake than she had ever been—she would go to her studio in the barn and do some preliminary sketches, to get some of these ideas down in more concrete form.

A small boy and a llama, Andrew Jorgensen had said. That's what the customer—probably one of those rich estate owners who kept llamas as pets—wanted. A life-sized sculpture, cast in bronze.

Life-sized. When Amber had first heard the request, her heart had quailed with fear, even though she knew she had to accept the commission. They needed the money. It was their way out.

Now, barely twelve hours later, she had a different perspective on the job. It was her way *in*. Into her own soul, into a place of joy, into an expression of everything that now filled her heart.

Amber could see it all, like a photograph burned into her brain, just the way she would sculpt it. She would use Lloser and Sam as her models— the enormous packer and the adoring little boy. Lloser lying with his feet folded under him, his long neck stretched upward, his gentle face looking down at the innocent child who slept with his head on the llama's thick woolen coat. She would capture the expression of love on the llama's guileless countenance, the implicit trust in the relaxed form of the boy, warm and protected, smiling in his sleep. She would call it the Guardian.

By the time she got to the barn, Amber could feel the creative impulse flowing through her veins like wine. She didn't bother with the overhead lights, but went directly to her sculpting table, turned on the big lamp over her work area, and pulled out a sketch pad from the bin underneath.

Then she smelled something—a strong, pungent odor. Recognizable. What was that stench? It was almost like . . . gasoline.

Amber rose from her stool, intending to find the source of the odor, but before she had a chance to follow it, she eyed something in the corner and stopped. In the farthest corner of the enormous old barn, where she should have been able to see nothing but blackness, her eyes discerned a faint, flickering light. A spreading light. A distant crackling noise came to her ears. Another smell—

Smoke.

The barn was on fire!

Panicked, Amber looked around. There was a fire extinguisher hanging in here somewhere, but where? On the front wall, maybe. The lamp over her sculpting table cast a little light in that direction, but not nearly enough to help her find it. She ran to the wall and groped around, knocking down a rake and a pitchfork before her hands grasped the cylinder and pulled it from its bracket.

There was no time to go for help. The barn was old, and the dry walls were like tinder. Hay was scattered about over most of the floor. By the time she would get back to the house, it would be too late.

Pulling the nozzle out and extending the hose as she ran, Amber dashed toward the back corner of the barn where the flames were already as high as her head, and spreading quickly. She pointed the hose at the base of the fire and felt a rush of relief as foam poured out and smothered the blaze.

But her relief was short-lived.

When Amber turned, she saw a line of fire snaking across the floor, flaring up against the south wall, slithering toward the door.

And a few yards from the doorway stood a dark figure holding something bulky in one hand.

Spraying foam as she went, Amber lunged in his direction. The fire blazed up around her, and just before she hit him, she caught a glimpse of a face and a big red gasoline can.

The heavy cylinder found its mark, striking the man in the head and sending him reeling. But Amber was trapped now, with the fire behind her and the man between her and the door. He regained his feet and staggered in her direction, blood rushing from a crescent-shaped cut above his right eye. If she could just get past him—

She hesitated a fraction of a second too long.

As she tried to make a run for it, the metal gas can came crashing into the back of her skull. Amber felt herself falling, falling, into a bottomless pit. The stench of gasoline overpowered her. An eternity away, she heard bumping noises, like feet running.

And then the darkness closed in.

Under the dark, heavy clouds, in the dense trees at the edge of the property Shiv hunkered down, watching. He could see flames coming out of the door of the hayloft and up through one portion of the roof.

He cursed under his breath. If it hadn't been for the woman, this job would have gone perfectly.

Blood trickled down from the cut on his head, and he touched it gingerly with one finger. He hadn't had time to set the fire properly, hadn't spread nearly enough gasoline around. If only the woman hadn't surprised him. Now she was in there, and if he hadn't killed her with the gas can, the fire would most likely get her. It was too late to go back.

He swore again, clenching his fist and banging it against one knee. Underwood told him the woman should be lost, should disappear. He had made it very clear that killing her was not an option. Now everything was going wrong.

Shiv hadn't signed on for murder. He wasn't going back upstate for the rest of his life on somebody else's ticket. And if the woman was dead, prison would be the least of his worries.

She shouldn't have been out there in the middle of the night, anyway. He couldn't have known she would show up. It was an accident, that's all.

He heard a rustling sound above him. It was beginning to rain—that slow, steady kind of drizzle that could go on all night. Blast! Well, he'd just have to sit tight and see it through. It might be a long night, but he wasn't going anywhere until the job was over and done with.

What he needed was a drink to steady his nerves. He reached into his jacket and retrieved a small flask. He took a long pull, relaxing as the burning liquid slid down his throat and warmed his belly. Then a second one, just a little one for good measure.

That was better. He felt calmer now, more in control. He shook a cigarette out of a mashed pack and reached for his lighter. It was his favorite—a sleek, silver one with his initials engraved on one side. Where was it? He knew he had it. He had used it just a little while ago . . .

In the barn.

Frantically he stood up patting down all his pockets—his jacket, his pants, even his shirt.

But the lighter wasn't there.

26

The Guardian

Dark. Everything was dark.

Something was tickling her face. Tiny little gnats, maybe, or feathers floating on the wind. She raised one hand to brush them away and felt two sensations at once: something moving, velvety, on her cheek, and a searing pain up her fingers and through her arm.

If she could just go back to sleep for a little while . . .

But some kind of noise kept blaring in her ears, wailing like a banshee. An alarm clock? She moved to shut if off, but the pain came again—in her hands, her arms, her neck, her back, inside her head. Her skull felt as if it might explode; white-hot lightning forked through her brain in agonizing throbs.

All right, all right, I'm getting up, she thought, but when she went to say the words aloud, she found her tongue swollen and stuck to the roof of her mouth. She couldn't swallow. Couldn't get her eyelids to open.

She flung out one arm, searching for the clock, groping for the snooze button. Still the alarm went on, howling high above her. Her hand reached out, gripped something. But it wasn't a clock. It was alive. And it moved.

With great effort Amber pried one eye open to see what looked like a slender tree trunk, covered in shaggy, chamois-colored wool. Her mind wrapped groggily around the image. It was a foot. Attached to a leg. An enormous llama foot.

She gasped in a lung full of air and began coughing. Smoke stung her eyes and made everything swim, but she raised her head to see Lloser standing over her, his neck stretched to full length, caterwauling madly.

Then she remembered. The barn. The man silhouetted in the doorway. The smell of gasoline. *The fire*.

She attempted to get up, but her head reeled. For a moment she thought she was going to be sick. Then her mind cleared, aided by small splashes of cold water dripping on her face. She peered upward into a yawning chasm above her. Part of the barn roof had fallen in and lodged in the rafters overhead. Rain was pouring in.

Holding onto Lloser for support, Amber struggled to her feet and looked around. Some of the flames, apparently, had been doused by the rain, but on the far side of the barn, fire still licked up the posts and consumed whatever dry wood it found. It had reached her sculpting table. She watched as it curled upward, dancing around the broad wooden legs, up over the top, further up toward the shelves that stretched between the posts, toward the sculpture of the man in the chair, toward the plaster cast of . . .

The Two Sisters.

Amber's breath caught in her throat. Jorgensen had already sold the sculpture; she had to get that cast.

Before her, the flames seemed to be gathering strength, leaping higher toward the shelf. At her back, Lloser was still screaming. She staggered forward a couple of steps.

She turned and looked over her shoulder, past the llama, past the

rain-soaked circle where she had lain. The barn door stood open, beck-
oning her away from the fire, into the night, into the rain, into a place
of safety.

It only took a split second to make up her mind.

⁓

TwoJoe sat bolt upright in bed and strained his ears. His heart pounded
as if he'd been running. There had been a noise, something.

Sometime during the night, rain had begun to fall, but that wasn't it.
It was more like a shriek, an ear-piercing call. He stared at the silent telephone, then at the clock on his bedside table. The luminous dial indicated that it was a little after two. The house was quiet. He must have
been dreaming.

TwoJoe punched his pillow into a ball and started to lie back down
when the noise came again. A strident bellow. But this time he was wide
awake. He had heard the sound before, a year or two ago, when three
wild dogs had gotten into the pasture. It was the alarm call of a male
llama.

He thrust his legs into his jeans, grabbed his boots and jacket, and
slammed open the door that led from his small apartment into the main
part of the house. By the time he got to the front door, Meg was downstairs in her pajamas.

"What is it?"

"It's Lloser, I think. An alarm call. Something's in the pasture."

TwoJoe pulled on his boots and jacket and flung open the door. Amid
the misty rain, a pall of thin, gray smoke hung over the front yard. The
acrid scent stung his nostrils and made his eyes water. "Call the fire
department!"

Meg went for the phone. TwoJoe grabbed the flashlight that hung on
a hook next to the door and set out on a dead run toward the pasture.
The bawling continued, growing louder by the minute. When he finally
came around a bend in the path, he flashed his light around to see the

cause of the disturbance. The barn door yawned like an open maw, and above, from the hayloft, black smoke billowed into the dark night. Beyond the barn, he caught a glimpse of the gate standing open. That earsplitting shriek came not from the pasture, but from inside the barn.

TwoJoe covered his eyes with his arm and fought his way into the barn.

The doorway was so thick with smoke that his flashlight could barely penetrate three feet ahead of him. Then suddenly the smoke cleared; he saw light . . . and movement.

He took it all in with a single glance: the blackened barn, the hole in the roof, the huge llama standing with his feet planted on the floor, sounding the alarm. The flames racing across Amber's sculpting table, consuming the studio corner of the structure. And the silhouette of someone headed directly toward the fire, lurching unsteadily, falling to her knees, then reaching upward.

"NOOOOOO!" The scream came up from somewhere deep inside of TwoJoe, louder than Lloser's bellowing. He lunged after Amber, pulling her back, dragging her roughly over the charred floor.

She fought him, clawing at his sleeve with hands that looked like burnt steak. "Let me go! Let me—I have to—" Then, just as he got her to the door, she lapsed into unconsciousness.

He laid her on the wet grass outside the barn and knelt down beside her. Lloser, apparently satisfied that his job was done, had followed them out and stood quietly gazing down at her.

"Stay with me, Amber," TwoJoe urged. "Breathe!" His face was wet from the rain, maybe, or from his own tears. He did a few CPR compressions, then placed his mouth over hers and exhaled into her. In the distance he could hear sirens drawing closer and he muttered a fierce prayer under his breath that they would get there in time.

27

First Contact

Diedre hung over the rail on the observation deck of the ferry and stared into the dark waters of Puget Sound. She ought to be enjoying the scenery, but she could not quell the churning of her stomach.

"Need something to eat?" Carlene pointed back toward the passageway that led to the cafe area. "A donut or something? I think you can even get a full breakfast if you want it."

Diedre groaned. "I couldn't eat anything if my life depended on it."

"Butterflies?"

She slanted a glance toward Carlene, who stood holding Sugarbear's leash. "More like fire-breathing dragons."

"Try not to think about it." Carlene lifted Sugarbear up to the rail and waved her paws in the air. "Look, Mommy!" she said in a high squeaky voice, as if she were a ventriloquist throwing her voice into the dog. "Look, I see dolphins!"

Diedre looked. Sure enough, a small pod of dolphins ran beside the ferry, arching their fins out of the water and zipping ahead toward the massive prow. As if everyone on board had heard, a group of passengers surged to the left side of the ferry. But none of them paid any attention to the dolphins. Instead, they all raised their eyes outward, toward the horizon.

"What is everybody staring at?"

The young man next to her turned and grinned. He appeared to be a college student, wearing a flannel shirt and faded jeans and carrying a backpack over one shoulder. "The mountain is out."

"Which one?"

He laughed as if she had just said something exceedingly funny, but Diedre couldn't see the humor. Weren't they surrounded by mountains on all sides? The student shrugged and shook his head. "When locals say, 'The mountain is out,' they're only referring to one." He pointed. "The big one. Mount Rainier."

Diedre followed his gesture, and her breath caught in her throat. There it was in the distance—the massive, snowcapped peak of Mount Rainier, rising like a vision out of nowhere.

"It's probably fifty or sixty miles away," he went on. "But even from this distance, it's pretty stupendous."

It was a magnificent sight, huge and lonely, with its base hidden in mist and its high slopes lit by the morning sun. Nothing at all like the lush layers of green and purple and indigo that made up the Blue Ridge back in North Carolina. She wished she had her camera, but it was locked in the trunk of the Lexus three decks below. For a fraction of a second Diedre forgot her apprehension and let her soul fill with the beauty of this natural wonder.

But it didn't last long. The ferry veered around a wooded point, and Mount Rainier vanished from sight. More quickly than she expected, the ferry dock at Bainbridge Island slid into view, and everyone scattered into the depths of the great iron monster that carried them.

"We'd better get back to the car," Carlene said. "Come on; I think the elevator is this way."

By the time they had driven off the ferry and found Route 305 heading through a place called Suquamish, Diedre's jitters had turned into major anxiety. Her mind had difficulty getting around the truth, but her nerves clearly understood the reality of the situation: for the first time in more than twenty years, Diedre McAlister was about to stand face to face with the sister she remembered only in her dreams.

∽

"It looks deserted," Carlene said. "Are you sure this is the right place?"

"The sign on the fence said *Elkhorn*. We passed the llama pasture on Clear Creek Road, just like Mr. Jorgensen said. This has to be it."

They sat for a moment, peering through the windshield at the log house that stood in a clearing surrounded by fir trees so tall they seemed to stretch to heaven itself. The main part of the house, rectangular in shape, had a narrow front porch and dormer windows peering from the second-story roof like curious eyes. On one side, a single-level addition stuck out like an afterthought.

"Look at those logs," Diedre hedged, trying desperately to buy a little more time. "They have to be two feet in diameter."

"There's a light on. Let's go knock."

Diedre grabbed Carlene's arm and held her back. "I don't know. Maybe we should just—"

"Just what? Just leave, after coming all this way? I don't think so." Carlene got out from behind the wheel and stood hanging on the open car door, glaring in at Diedre. "If you want to sit out here until you're fifty, that's fine with me. I'm going in." She slammed the door.

"Oh, all right," Diedre muttered. She leaned over the seat and patted Sugarbear on the head. "You stay here, girl. We won't be long." Then with an exasperated sigh, she heaved herself out of the car and reluctantly followed Carlene up to the porch.

"Hello? Is anyone home?" Carlene called. No answer. She peered through the frosted glass of the front door. "I can see light. It almost looks like you can see straight through the house to the back." She raised a hand to knock on the door, and it gave a little under the pressure. "It's open!"

Diedre took a step back. "Carlene, you are not going in there."

"Of course I am. Didn't you notice *anything* on the way here? We're in the country." She opened the door a little wider and stepped inside, calling, "Hello? Anybody home?" as she went.

Trembling, Diedre followed. She could just imagine the headlines: LOCALS CAPTURE FEMALE TRESPASSERS: TAR AND FEATHERING AT ELEVEN.

The front door opened into a small foyer, where a wide set of rough-hewn steps went up on the left. Carlene had been right about the light: straight ahead of them, daylight streamed into the house, and when they had gone a bit farther, Diedre could see why. The foyer opened up into a sizable kitchen, dining room, and huge post-and-beam living room with a vaulted ceiling and stone fireplace. On the back side, away from the road, tall windows with a couple of doors opened onto a wide covered porch.

The old house was impressive, but what stunned Diedre most was the view—a vista more magnificent than any she could possibly have imagined. They were sitting on a high bluff, and trees had been cut away to reveal a wide canal flanked on the other side by low rolling hills, and beyond that, a jagged mountain range that seemed to go on forever. It looked like photographs she had seen of the Norwegian fjords, a rugged landscape carved by glaciers a million years ago.

"Can you believe that?" Carlene whispered. "It's incredible."

Diedre opened her mouth to answer, but before a sound could come out, she heard a noise behind them, a definitive click.

Then a voice spoke—a low, angry drawl. "I wouldn't make any sudden moves if I was you. Now turn around—nice and slow."

Diedre turned, her heart pumping madly, and what she saw made her feel as if she had suddenly been transported into a grade-B western.

A double-barreled shotgun was pointed directly at her head. And holding it, with his finger on both triggers, stood a man as tall as a tree with a hide like old leather. A shock of white hair fell across his brow as he motioned toward the sofa with his head. "Sit down, both of you," he commanded. "Sam, call 911 and tell 'em to send the sheriff."

A movement at the big man's side drew Diedre's attention. It was a small boy, no more than six or seven, with wide blue eyes and shaggy blond hair. He was staring at her, transfixed.

"Sam, now!" the man repeated.

"Grandpa, no. Look at her. She looks just like Amber!"

Between the excited interruptions of the little boy and the information provided by the grandfather, Diedre had finally begun to get the gist of things. At least the old man had put the gun down and wasn't threatening to shoot their heads off. She and Carlene had introduced themselves, apologized for coming into the house uninvited, and retrieved Sugarbear from the car. Sam was now sitting on the hearth rug with her, obviously enthralled. He had taken off one boot and made a ball from his sock, and the two of them were playing a rambunctious game of fetch.

Yes, they were in the right place, Houston said. This was the Elkhorn property, and Amber Chaney did live here. Joseph Elkhorn, whom little Sam called TwoJoe, was not here at the moment, nor were his sister Meg or Amber. Something about a fire and an injury and going to the hospital in the middle of the night.

"TwoJoe oughta be home real soon," the grandfather, who had introduced himself as Colonel Vernon Houston, repeated. "With the fire and all, I figured we'd better keep an eye on the place. Whoever done it might still be lurking around."

Did he actually think this fire—it destroyed part of the barn, Diedre gathered—was deliberately set? "Surely you don't think the fire was the work of an arsonist?"

"Can't rightly see how it could be otherwise," Vernon Houston drawled. "Don't know much in the way of details yet, though. Reckon TwoJoe'll call when he's got some news on Amber."

Diedre stared at him. "Wait a minute. *Amber* was the one hurt in the fire?" She felt her face go clammy, and Carlene, on the couch beside her, gripped her hand and gave her a worried glance.

Houston eyed her warily. "What did you say your connection with Amber was, Miss McAlister?"

Diedre hesitated. She hadn't said anything, not really. Just that she had come to see Amber, and that it was personal. There was no point in telling everybody her business, after all.

Sam, however, heard his grandfather's question and stopped his game with Sugarbear. He stood up and limped over to stand in front of her with one foot bare and the other encased in a cowboy boot. "I told you, Grandpa," he said quietly, without ever taking his gaze off Diedre's face. "She's the one in the statue. The sister." He tilted his head curiously. "She missed you," he whispered. "She got really sad without you."

"I was sad without her, too, Sam."

"I know. I told her so."

A lump formed in Diedre's throat, and she reached out to take the boy's hand. "What else did you tell her?"

He smiled. "I told her you never really let go of somebody you love."

28

Family Matters

Amber's eyes slit open to see the wavering, indistinct shape of a tall, dark man looming above her. A warning bell went off in her mind somewhere, and she shrank away from him. Then her vision cleared. It was TwoJoe, with Meg at his side gripping his arm. TwoJoe was filthy, his face smudged with black, his eyes rimmed in red. Meg looked exhausted—and worried.

"Where am I?" The words sounded strange in her ears, the utterings of a strangled frog. Her throat ached, and when she swallowed, it felt like liquid fire going down. She looked at her hands, both of which were swathed in bandages.

TwoJoe blinked. "You're in the hospital. You have a concussion and some burns, and you took in some smoke. But the doctor says you'll be all right, thank God."

"There was a fire?" Amber tried to sit up, but her head spun, and she sank back down on the pillow.

"Don't you remember? The barn was on fire. Lloser sounded the alarm."

"I can't—I don't—" Amber shook her head, a movement that made the throbbing at the base of her skull worse. "The barn burned?" she repeated.

"Part of it. It's salvageable, with some work. But let's not worry about that right now. What's important is getting you well." TwoJoe reached to take her hand, then drew back, his eyes fixed on the bandages.

Amber knew there was some reason she should be concerned about the barn burning, but she couldn't quite locate it. Something about a job she had to do, about saving the farm, about her future with TwoJoe. *Did* she have a future with TwoJoe? She couldn't remember. Everything was all mixed up. She vaguely recalled feeling *something* about him—last night or last week or—when was it? What was it? And she had a nebulous image of him looking down on her from above, kissing her. Had he done that? Had she imagined it? Or maybe it was the llama, standing over her. She couldn't make her mind put it all together. It was like fragments of a dream that should have meant something important, if she could just get it back . . .

"We're going to go now. You need to rest. We'll be back later." He leaned over her and carefully pressed his lips to her forehead. Meg came and stroked her hair back from her eyes, murmuring something Amber couldn't hear. She closed her eyes, and the darkness rolled over her, pressing her into oblivion.

TwoJoe didn't speak during the entire drive back to the farm. His heart lay in his chest like a lump of lead. He ought to be relieved; the doctor, after all, had assured them that Amber would heal just fine, although the concussion might cause her some disorientation for a while. Still, he couldn't stop the selfish feelings that assailed him. Twenty-four hours ago, they had been celebrating the miracle. Amber had had work. They had all had hope. And from the way she had looked at him in the candlelight at the restaurant, he had dared to let himself believe that she might be opening up to the idea of loving him. Now everything was gone, burned to ashes. Couldn't God, just once, give him a break? Meg sat in the passenger seat of the truck, staring out the window. He suspected his sister was praying—for Amber, and probably for him. Meg always knew what he was thinking, but her instincts were balanced with an innate discretion that kept her from prying into his soul at a time like this. She loved him enough to allow him his privacy, and she had enough discernment to know when to keep her insights to herself. It was a gift for which TwoJoe was deeply grateful.

Not until they turned off Clear Creek Road into the long gravel drive that led up to the farmhouse did Meg speak. She laid a hand gently on his arm, looked into his eyes, and said, "It'll work out, TwoJoe."

That was all. But her confidence and trust were enough to bolster his flagging faith.

She had introduced herself as *Diedre Chaney McAlister*. TwoJoe couldn't keep from staring at her—she was a younger version of Amber, with the same dark hair and eyes, the same chin, even the same dimple on the left side of her mouth when she smiled. He had no doubt that the girl was telling the truth, that she was indeed the sister Amber had not seen for more than twenty years. As soon as he had laid eyes on her, he had known.

TwoJoe and Meg had come home from the hospital to find a champagne-colored Lexus in the driveway and Sam and Vernon entertaining two young women and a small dog in the living room of the farmhouse. TwoJoe had excused himself to take a quick shower, and when he returned, Meg was talking with the two of them as if they were long-lost friends.

The Colonel was obviously taken with both girls, but especially with

Diedre's exuberant friend Carlene. He laughed uproariously at her sto-ries of driving the Tackyville Highway and collecting hideous memora-bilia along the way. At the moment the two of them were speculating about how many tacky places they could find in Texas to add to the list.

Little Sam apparently regarded Diedre as his own personal discovery. He sat at her feet with the dog in his lap, gazing adoringly at her and insisting that he knew right away that Diedre and Amber were sisters. "I was just about to tell Diedre how Amber saved my life when I fell through the trapdoor in the barn," Sam told TwoJoe excitedly. "And then I was gonna take her down to the pasture to meet Lloser and Llittle Bit."

"Maybe that should wait for just a while," Meg intervened. "Why don't you come out to the kitchen with me, Sam, and help me put together some lunch for all of us?"

"Do I *have* to?"

Meg smiled. "I think so."

"But that's women's work!" The boy puffed out his chest to demon-strate his manliness.

"Not so," she countered, raising a warning finger in his direction. "Many of the great chefs of the world are men. And besides, in this house we don't have women's work and men's work."

"You do so," Sam argued. "TwoJoe takes care of the llamas, and you do the cooking."

"That's because he likes working with the llamas, and I like to cook. And if you had ever tasted his cooking, you'd realize that it was a very sensible arrangement."

TwoJoe reached down and lifted Sam up until his boots dangled in midair. "We'll go see the llamas later, sport," he said. "Right now you need to give me a chance to talk to Diedre, all right?"

"Okay. I guess." Dragging his feet, Sam followed Meg toward the kitchen, giving Diedre a soulful glance over his shoulder as he went.

"He's a great kid," Diedre said as TwoJoe turned his attention back to her.

"Yes, he is. He's become a member of the family, and we're crazy about him. Vernon and Emmaline, too. They're good people."

"So I gather." Diedre's smile faded, and a shadow filled her eyes. "The Colonel told us what happened last night. Is Sis—ah, my sister—going to be all right?"

"She received second-degree burns on her hands and arms, some lung irritation from smoke inhalation, and a fairly serious concussion. It could have been a lot worse. She'll need to be in the hospital for another day or two, and according to the doctor, she may have a little residual disorientation, but she'll be just fine."

"That's a relief."

Diedre cocked her head and regarded him with a curious expression, as if she were evaluating him. TwoJoe felt a slow flush creep up his neck. "Is something wrong?"

"No." She paused. "It's just—well, forgive me for saying so, but you seem very articulate for a—a farmer."

He burst out laughing and shook his head. "That's *exactly* the kind of thing Amber might have said. You are more like your sister than you realize."

"I trust that's a compliment."

"It is. It certainly is." For a split second TwoJoe drifted, distracted by his thoughts of Amber and a wave of longing for the intimacy he might never have with her. Then he recovered himself and continued. "To answer your question, in my former life I was a CPA from Berkeley. The corporate world didn't agree with me. When our mother died, I came home to settle the estate and decided to stay."

If Diedre McAlister caught a glimpse of his feelings for Amber, she didn't reveal it in her expression. She said, simply, "It seems that my sister has found a good life here, with a loving family to support her."

"Your sister is an extremely talented artist and a wonderful woman." TwoJoe looked away, in case his own face might give him away. "She and Meg have been close friends for a long time, ever since—" He stopped abruptly, uncomfortable with where the sentence was leading him.

"Ever since the hospital?" Diedre gazed at him intently. "Yes, I'm aware of that—well, not the details, but I know she spent a long time there." She closed her eyes for a moment. "I guess I have a lot of questions."

"I'm sure Amber will, too," TwoJoe responded gently. "And in case you're wondering, I don't think you have anything to worry about in coming here to find her. She'll be thrilled. Do you want me to take you to the hospital to see her?"

Diedre shook her head. "Thanks for the encouragement, but I don't think that would be a wise idea. My coming here is bound to be something of a shock to her, even if she is glad to see me. It might be better all the way around if I waited until she's released and is feeling better. If you can give me a recommendation of a place nearby that allows pets, Carlene and I will take Sugarbear and check into a hotel for a few days."

"There's the Viking Motel out on the highway, but you'd be welcome to stay here with us," TwoJoe offered. "It's not much—"

She interrupted him with a wave of her hand. "It's beautiful—especially the view."

"The house was built by my ancestors a hundred years ago, and added onto here and there over the years. It could do with a little maintenance, I suppose, but—" Joe clamped his mouth shut. Diedre McAlister might be Amber's long-lost sister, but she was a virtual stranger to them. And Elkhorns didn't burden strangers with their financial difficulties.

Suddenly the truth closed in on TwoJoe like a suffocating blanket. They had been counting on Amber's new sculpture to get them out of the hole. He hadn't had a chance yet to assess all the fire damage, but he was pretty sure there wasn't much left of her studio except a pile of ashes. Amber's hands were badly burned. Her workspace was gone, her kiln in ruins. She couldn't possibly finish the project in time. He wasn't sure that even someone who appreciated her work enough to commission a large project like this would wait forever, especially with a ten-thousand dollar advance in limbo.

"I don't think you need the distraction of two strangers in the house," Diedre was saying. "The Colonel invited us to come and stay with them, but I don't want to burden anyone."

TwoJoe dragged himself back to focus on the conversation. "I'm sure Vernon and Emmaline would enjoy your company," he managed. "He and your friend Carlene seem to be getting on like two cows in clover, and it's clear that Sam adores you just like he does your sister."

She chuckled. "Carlene has never met a stranger. It seems she and the Colonel are cut from the same cloth."

"Well then, the choice is pretty clear."

"It's a very generous gesture," Diedre hedged. "And I'm tempted to accept, just for the sake of being close by. But two extra people and a dog can fill up a house in a hurry. Do you think they would have enough room?"

TwoJoe thought about what Vernon Houston called "Emmaline's summer house," with its six huge bedroom suites, multilevel decks overlooking the canal and mountains, and separate two-bedroom guest cottage adjacent to the pool. He chuckled to himself as he imagined the look on Diedre's face when she got her first glimpse of the place.

"Might be a bit cramped," he said with a grave nod. "But I expect they'd be disappointed if you didn't accept."

Diedre hadn't realized how hungry she was until she sat down at the kitchen table to a lunch of smoked salmon, cheese, fresh fruit, and sourdough bread. All the apprehensions associated with this trip had diminished her appetite, but the inviting presence of Meg and TwoJoe Elkhorn and their friends—and their assurance that her sister would, indeed, be delighted with the unexpected reunion—caused that knot of tension in her stomach to relax. She ate ravenously.

Earlier in the morning, before TwoJoe and Meg had arrived, she had put off the Colonel's questions, claiming she'd rather wait until everyone got home so that she'd only have to recount the story once. The truth was, Diedre was uncertain how much she really wanted to reveal. At first she had intended to leave certain parts out—Mama's death and the mind-bending revelation that Daddy was not her real father. But they were all so warm and accepting that once she got into the account, she felt safe enough to tell it all.

Everyone listened intently as she related events from her early years—the lifelong obsession with the sister she had never known; the recurrent dream in which she saw herself as a tiny child, spinning in the sunlight and laughing with an older girl.

"Like the statue!" little Sam interjected, his face lighting up. "The statue of the Two Sisters! You both remembered it."

"Yes, we both had the same memory, Sam." Diedre smiled at him. "Only I didn't know it was a real memory. I thought it was just a dream—until I saw the sculpture at Mr. Jorgensen's gallery."

"And Sugarbear led you right to it," Sam went on, picking the dog up and setting her on his lap. "You're a real hero, Sugarbear."

"Yes, she is," Meg agreed. "She is, however, a dog, and dogs should not be at the table. Please put her down."

Reluctantly Sam obeyed, but sneaked a bit of smoked salmon to Sugarbear when he thought no one was looking.

Diedre continued with her tale, explaining how she had been led to believe that her sister was dead, and didn't know otherwise until after Mama's funeral, when she discovered the letters and birth certificate in the cigar box.

"Sugarbear found those, too!" Sam interrupted, but fell silent again when the Colonel gave him a hard look.

"I'm so sorry to hear about your mother's death," Meg said quietly. "Amber doesn't talk much about her family, but I know she loved her mother a great deal. And I knew about you, of course—at least in sketchy terms. It seems she has a lot of pain associated with her thoughts of home."

"I'm sure she does," Diedre agreed, fighting back the lump that rose in her throat. "My father—that is, *her* father—I guess he didn't feel like they could handle her anymore. He had her placed in a hospital—" She stopped suddenly and slanted a glance in Sam's direction. "Well, you know."

A somberness settled over the table, and Diedre went on. "Anyway, when I found the birth certificate and realized that my father wasn't who I had always believed him to be, it explained a lot."

She produced the browned photograph of her sister sitting on her father's lap in the big armchair. "You can see from the picture how much he adored her. He never felt that way about me."

TwoJoe and Meg exchanged a significant glance.

"Is something wrong?"

Meg stared at the picture, and TwoJoe averted his eyes. "Amber created a sculpture similar to this, except with—" she hesitated for a moment until TwoJoe nodded in her direction, "some subtle differences."

"What kind of differences?"

Meg bit her lip. "I think I'd rather leave that story for Amber to tell. Please, go on."

Ruffled, Diedre gathered her thoughts and continued. "Once all this came out after Mama's funeral, I knew I had to find my sister and learn the truth. But I also needed some time to think about what was happening in my life, the confusion I was facing surrounding my identity." She looked around the table and forced a smile. "Everything happened so fast—losing Mama, discovering the reality about Daddy and—," she stumbled over the unfamiliar name— "and Amber. I suddenly had no idea who I was. That's one reason I drove here rather than flying—to give myself time and space to sort everything out."

Meg reached across the table and laid a hand on Diedre's arm. "I can imagine how all this would make you feel—grief over your mother's death; excitement and anticipation, probably mixed with a fair amount of fear, at the realization that Amber was still alive. Not to mention anger at the man you had called your father, and anxiety over the possibility of finding out who your real father is. If there's anything we can do to help—"

Diedre stared at Meg. How could she identify so succinctly what Diedre was feeling? Despite the fact that she had to be close to her sister's age, she looked so young and innocent. "Are you a counselor?" she blurted out.

Meg laughed. "No. Why do you ask?"

"Because you've nailed me so accurately. TwoJoe said earlier that you and my sister met in . . . in Raleigh. I thought maybe—"

"I have a good deal of experience with therapy—if that's what you're asking," Meg answered quietly. "I was a patient. Just like Amber."

Diedre felt all the blood drain from her face. "I—I'm sorry. I didn't mean to pry." But the truth was, she *did* want to pry. She wanted answers to a hundred questions, questions she wasn't sure she'd be able to ask once she was face to face with Sissy. Still, she couldn't expect Meg to—

"Go ahead," Meg said, as if she'd read Diedre's mind. "What do you need to know?"

Diedre exhaled heavily. "When I asked Daddy about all this, he told me she was—well, unbalanced, *not right*."

"Is she crazy, you mean?"

The blunt words shocked Diedre as if an icy hand had gripped her heart, but she nodded. The question hung in the air between them, and silence descended as Meg held Diedre's gaze. "Amber has endured a lot of pain in her life," Meg said at last. "Some of it I know; some I can only guess at. But I can tell you this: Amber Chaney is one of the most *right* people I know. You'll see for yourself, soon enough."

The cold fingers of dread released in Diedre's chest, replaced by a warmth almost as comforting as Meg Elkhorn's compassionate touch.

"I've waited twenty years," she whispered. "Nothing short of yesterday is soon enough for me."

29

Counting the Cost

Drifting back from that nebulous place between wakefulness and slumber, Amber heard footsteps approaching the door of her hospital room. Probably the nurses coming to check on her—which they seemed to do every hour. It was hard getting a good night's sleep in a hospital. If she kept her eyes shut and pretended to be asleep, maybe they wouldn't disturb her.

The door opened, and a crack of light streamed in from the hall. The bright beam settled across her closed eyelids, sending an impression of moving red shapes to her brain. Then the door swung shut again, and all was dark and quiet.

Good. The nurse or whoever it was had gone away, leaving her to the healing power of sleep. Her whole body cried out for rest, for relief from the fire that still burned in her arms and hands, for the blessed oblivion that came when darkness eased the pain at the base of her skull. She turned her face away from the door and let out a deep, relaxing sigh.

Then she heard it: the sound of someone breathing. Her eyes snapped open, and she came fully awake. Although she didn't move, every nerve in her body jumped to attention. She strained her ears, but the pounding of her own heart was so loud she could hear nothing else. She could feel the blood pulsing in her temples, feel the rush of adrenaline surging through her veins.

Someone was in the room with her.

She heard one step. A pause. Another step. The inky blackness of the hospital room closed in upon her.

No, no, NO! her mind screamed. But the steps drew closer, bringing with them a sickly sweet smell, something vaguely familiar. She had felt it before—this terror in the darkness. Heard the heavy, hesitating footsteps, smelled the same rancid, nauseating odor.

The breathing was louder now, nearer, carrying a stench of liquor and stale tobacco. The presence hovered over her.

Amber turned her head just in time to see the black outline of a hand above her. It clamped roughly over her mouth. She squinted, trying to make out the face, but all she could discern was a shadowed bulk and a slash of white against the blackness, white as the bandages that swathed her own hands.

"I'm watching you," a slurred voice whispered in the darkness. "I know every move you make. What happened to you was an accident, you understand? You're going to leave this place, disappear so that no one will ever be able to find you—if you don't do it for yourself, I'm going to do it for you. And don't tell a soul. You got it?"

Amber nodded.

The huge hand slid down to her throat, and a powerful thumb clamped down on the vein that throbbed just below her right ear. "I found you once; I can find you again. Besides, I know where your friends live. The next time an accident happens, it might be one of them. You breathe a word of this to anyone and—" The fingers tightened around her neck. "You know what will happen, don't you?"

She nodded again.

"Good," the voice rasped. "We understand each other."

The hand released her, and Amber lay trembling, her eyes clenched tightly, until the footsteps retreated and the door closed softly behind them.

Shiv slipped out the door and made his way down three flights of stairs into the chilly night. No one had seen him. Even in the dark room, he could tell the woman was terrified. She wouldn't talk, not in a million years.

Underwood ought to pay him double for all the extra trouble this job had cost him. From now on, he'd stick to the simple stuff—bugging phones, snapping pictures of guys with their mistresses, calling in overdue loans. The money wasn't nearly as good, but the risks were easier to stomach. Breaking a few kneecaps wouldn't send him back to prison, and nobody in the loan shark business ever prosecuted, anyway. This business of going after a woman made him want to puke.

When he reached his rental car, stowed away on the lower level of the deserted parking garage, he sank into the driver's seat, lit a cigarette with the car lighter, and pulled a flask from his pocket. He was almost finished. Just one more little detail to take care of, and he'd be home free.

Amber tossed restlessly until the gray light of dawn crept through the blinds. When she came to, groggy and exhausted, the clock on the wall opposite her bed read 6:35.

Her throat ached, and she was thirsty. The ice in the jug on the table had melted in the night, and the water was lukewarm, but she drank it anyway. It hurt terribly going down. She put a hand to her neck, and the memory came flooding back.

It hadn't been a bad dream. Someone had been here, in her room in the middle of the night, threatening her.

Gradually, like a picture coming into focus, she remembered everything she hadn't been able to recall yesterday. A man had been there, in the barn, pouring gasoline. He had struck her with the gas can and left her to die in the fire. But not before she had hit him in the head—

Of course! The white patch she saw in the darkness—it was a bandage, over the cut she had inflicted with the fire extinguisher. Whoever had set the fire had come back. Not to finish her off, apparently—he could have done that last night—but to warn her to disappear, and never to say a word, or someone *would* get killed.

There was something else, too, a vague, misplaced image that had to do with TwoJoe hovering over her as she lay on the ground outside the barn. Something about . . . a kiss.

The memory returned on a warm, gentle tide. Just before she had gone to the barn to sketch out her ideas for the new sculpture, she had felt something—a calming presence, freeing her, reassuring her. She and TwoJoe were meant to be together. He would accept her. It would be all right. She could let herself trust him and . . . and love him.

No, you can't, a voice inside her head objected. The man had not only threatened Amber, he had threatened the people she loved. Meg. TwoJoe. Maybe even Sam. He knew where they lived. The next time an "accident" happened, someone would be dead.

Panic overwhelmed Amber so that she could barely breathe. She had no choice but to do what he demanded: tell no one, and disappear from this place as fast as she could.

She had to run, to hide. She had to get away. She could still hear his footsteps in the dark, feel his hand around her throat, smell the liquor on his breath. It all seemed so sickeningly, eerily familiar. And his words: *You know what will happen if you tell . . .*

But *why?* Why would anyone want to hurt her?

Unbidden, an answer rose to the surface of her mind: *Because you've grown up into such a beautiful young lady . . . sweet and innocent, pure and undefiled. Just like your mama. This is what women do when they're all grown up . . .*

Amber shook her head to rid herself of the intrusive memory. She was getting confused. The situations were similar, but—*but her reaction was the same*. Fear. Abject terror. Silence.

The truth descended upon her in a rush. When she was a girl, she had no other choice but to submit. A child couldn't fight back. But now she was an adult, and something had happened, was happening, deep within her soul.

She didn't have to give in. She could have faith. She could speak the truth and trust God for the outcome.

She was no longer powerless.

Even as the idea formed in Amber's mind, the knot in her stomach released. Her mind cleared, and the fear began to dissipate, replaced by a white-hot flame of rage. If this was how righteous anger felt, Amber liked the sensation. Her soul swelled with it, and resolution rose up on the crest of the wave.

"No," she muttered under her breath. "Not this time. I'm through with being intimidated." Then, louder, exultantly, although her seared throat burned with the effort, she shouted to the empty room, "I WILL NOT GIVE IN!"

The door flew open, and a white-clad nurse stood in the doorway, framed by the opening and backlit by the bright lights from the corridor. "Are you all right? I thought I heard yelling."

Amber laughed out loud. "I'm fine. Really."

The nurse stood back to admit a petite figure in dark gray slacks and a black clerical shirt.

"For somebody who's been through hell and back," Father Susan said dryly, "you don't look so bad."

Susan entered the room and regarded Amber Chaney with a measuring gaze. Was it just two nights ago they had celebrated Amber's success, what Meg called "the miracle commission"? At the restaurant, they had all been relaxed and happy, confident that God had answered their prayers and—at least for the time being—given them a reprieve from the worries that had plagued them.

And now this. The fire. Amber in the hospital with burns and a concussion. Her studio in ruins. The commission, in TwoJoe's opinion, a hopeless impossibility.

Susan closed her eyes and sent up a brief prayer for wisdom. What on earth was she going to say to this woman whose tender faith was already dangling by a thread? That God has a purpose in everything? That struggles make you stronger? Cold comfort to someone whose future has already gone up in flames.

She pulled a chair over next to the bed and sat down, eying Amber warily. The woman didn't appear to be disturbed or depressed or worried. Given her physical condition, she actually seemed in good spirits. A simple case of denial, perhaps?

"How did you get in here?" Amber pointed toward the clock. "It's not even eight."

Susan grinned. "This collar is like a skeleton key—it'll get you in almost anywhere. Even hospital regulations defer to the authority of the clergy."

"Well, your timing is perfect. I assume Meg called you?"

"TwoJoe, actually. I would have come last night, but I had a vestry meeting and didn't get the message until after ten. I phoned the hospital, and they said you were on drugs and sleeping comfortably, so I decided to wait until this morning."

"I wouldn't exactly say I slept comfortably." Amber pressed a button on the side of the bed and raised the head until she was sitting upright. "I was about to call you anyway. There are some things I need to talk to you about."

"All right." Susan settled back in the chair and waited.

"I had a visitor last night," Amber began. "Or maybe early this morning—I'm not sure of the time."

Susan listened as Amber related the events from last night and worked backward, telling about the intruder and his threats, about the fire in the barn and how Amber clubbed him with the fire extinguisher.

"And you're certain it was the same man?"

"Positive. I couldn't see his face, but he had a bandage above his eye, which would have been where I hit him. He warned me to keep quiet about what I knew, told me to disappear."

Susan's anxiety level kept escalating throughout the story, and at last she interrupted. "Amber, we've got to call the sheriff. We've got to get you some protection, get an investigator out to TwoJoe's place. We've got to—"

"We'll do all that," Amber said. "But first let me finish. I've got to get this out before I lose my nerve."

Susan sat back down and tried to focus. "Go on."

It didn't take long for Amber to have Susan's full attention. "When he came in, the room was dark. I was terrified. I could hear him breathing, hear his footsteps drawing closer, smell the liquor on his breath. It was exactly like—" She hesitated. "Before."

"Before?"

"I was a girl—eleven, maybe twelve—the first time it happened."

Susan felt her heartbeat quicken. She had been waiting for this moment since the first day Amber Chaney had come to her office for counseling. The moment of truth, the key revelation that would open the door to freedom and wholeness. "What happened?"

Amber looked at her without blinking. "He would come to my room at night—usually when there was a party, a meeting, some kind of distraction. Sometimes I would hear music coming from another room. It would always be dark, like it was last night. He would open the door and come in, smelling of liquor. Afterward he would threaten me, warning me of what the penalty would be if I ever told anyone. And so I kept the secret."

"Until now."

Amber nodded. Up to this moment, she had been calm and in control of her emotions. She had told the story of her midnight attacker without flinching. Now, before Susan's eyes, the wall broke down, and Amber's tears overflowed.

Susan resisted the impulse to comfort this woman who sat before her in so much pain. This was the most difficult challenge a counselor ever faced—to allow a client she truly cared about and respected to endure the agony, to go through it to the other side. But she dared not short-circuit the process now. A medical doctor's job was to put pressure on the severed artery, to stanch the flow of blood, to stitch the patient up as quickly as possible. Her job was to let the bleeding continue as long as necessary. And so she waited, and as she waited, she prayed—not for a quick end to the pain, but for the truth to come out, a truth that would probably hurt more than the denial ever had.

"I didn't tell," she said in a whisper when the tears had subsided. "I couldn't, even after I left home."

Susan clenched her fists in her lap and closed her eyes. Her instincts had been right, and she felt her own anger and pain rise and merge with Amber's. "What were you afraid of?" she whispered through gritted teeth. "You can tell me, Amber. You *need* to tell me."

The response, when it came, was a low moan, laced with shame. "I was afraid he would do to her what he did to me."

"To her? To your little sister, you mean? That was why you tried to take her away?"

Amber nodded.

"You were protecting her."

"Yes." The word came out as a hoarse whisper, and Amber shifted against the pillows.

"By your silence."

"I believed I was. But I understood for the first time this morning that silence doesn't protect anyone except the perpetrator."

Susan shuddered, but she didn't hold back. "And what did he do?"

"He raped me." The words came out cold, clipped. For a moment neither of them said a word, but let the silence hang between them like a moment of reverence for one who has died.

Then Amber spoke again. "I've carried this secret for a very long time. I was ashamed. I felt guilty. I didn't believe anyone could love me or accept me if they knew."

"You do understand that this wasn't your fault?" Susan spoke quickly, earnestly. "That you're not responsible for what someone else did to you?"

Amber nodded, and her eyes held that bleak, haunted look Susan had seen so often before. "In my mind, yes, I know that. It's been difficult to convince my heart, though. For a long time I blamed myself for not doing something to stop him. And even now, all these years later, the memory of it still makes me feel dirty, defiled—as if I need to get in the shower and scrub my skin off. But the other night, when we were celebrating at the restaurant, I looked around at all those people who loved me, and I suddenly realized that God loved me, too. Even knowing all of this, God still loved me."

Susan took a deep breath. She couldn't help being amazed at Amber Chaney's courage, and even her faith. She hadn't asked why God hadn't protected her when she was a helpless child, why God had let it happen in the first place. No doubt that question would come later, the age-old theodicy debate, the unanswerable dilemma of good versus evil. But for now, she had made an enormous step toward freedom.

"When I was attacked last night, there were so many similarities," Amber was saying. "The darkness, the footsteps, the smell, the hand at my throat. All the old fears came flooding back, and when I tried to sort it out, my mind got the two events confused. That's when I understood. As a girl, I had no power, no options. All I had was silence. But things are different now. *I'm* different."

"How are you different?" Susan asked gently.

Amber laid a hand over her heart. "I let go, Susan. Right before the fire. I gave in—not to fear, but to love. I've lived in fear for years, believing that something bad would happen if I told the truth. But the cost of not telling is much, much greater."

Susan reached out and gently took one of the bandaged hands. "Who was it, Amber? Who did this horrible thing to you?"

Amber bit her lip for a moment, and when she spoke the truth, a hundred missing pieces fell into place in Susan's mind.

⤳

As the long morning hours stretched out toward noon, Amber replayed the conversation with Susan in her mind. In contrast to her bruised and battered body, her soul had found new strength, had discovered a courage and power she never knew she had. The power of the truth. But there was something wrong, something her attacker said that didn't quite . . . fit.

She had assumed all along that the fire in the barn was intended to force TwoJoe into selling the place. He had told her about a disreputable-looking man named Shivers who had come around several times trying to strong-arm him into a sale. A mediator for some real estate tycoon, no doubt. Maybe a mob connection, who could tell? There were a lot of people in this world who wouldn't think twice about resorting to criminal activity in order to get what they wanted.

Amber had been so fixated on the emotional issues raised by the incident that she hadn't given much thought to the details. But the fourth or fifth time she went over it, she realized that the midnight attacker hadn't said a single word about TwoJoe or the farm. He had told *her* to disappear, had said, *I found you once, I can find you again.* It all seemed very . . . personal.

But who would do such a thing? And why?

The words echoed in her mind: *I found you . . . found you . . . found you. Never tell a soul . . . never breathe a word.*

With a sickening lurch and a crash, her mind ran headlong into the answer. This wasn't about real estate or about TwoJoe's farm or about money. It was about silence. Her silence.

There was only one person on earth who could possibly be threatened by anything Amber had to say.

Only one.

But why now? For years he had left her alone. She *had* disappeared—she had relocated far away, taken a new name, built a new life. Why would he possibly think she could be a danger to him now, after all this time?

She didn't know why. But she knew *who*.

And he knew where she was.

30

Plan C

"There's a call for you, Jackie," Pamela Langley's sultry voice came over the intercom. "Someone named Shiv Willis, on Line 2." Jackson Underwood snatched up the receiver and snapped off the intercom, cutting Pamela off just as she said, "If you're free tonight—"

He stared at the blinking light on the telephone and cursed under his breath. Shiv was never supposed to call on his office line, only on the private number. And he had given his name? His real name? Was he a complete idiot?

This whole affair was turning into the fiasco of the century. Shiv, the fool, had tried to burn the barn down, but had failed miserably, and only succeeded in landing the girl, who now called herself Amber, in the hospital. It was only a matter of time before the whole thing led back to him quicker than a fuse on a truckload of dynamite. It was time to take Shiv out of the picture.

Jack wondered, not for the first time, how he had gotten into a mess like this. Two decades ago, it had seemed so simple: get the girl out of the way, and everything would run smoothly from there on in. He hadn't taken into account how lies and deceptions could complicate themselves over time, and twenty years was a long time for trouble to be brewing unattended. Now there was nothing he could do but see it through and hope that the whole thing didn't come crashing down on his head.

He punched the lighted button on the telephone and snarled, "Underwood."

"Mr. Underwood?" Shiv's voice sounded garbled, as if his cell phone battery was low, or he was in a tunnel somewhere. "Just wanted . . . check in . . . ever-thing . . . fine . . . just some last-minute . . ."

"Where are you?" he barked.

". . . arking garage . . ."

"Can you hear me, Shiv? Get in your car and drive out of the garage, then call me back—ON THE PRIVATE NUMBER!" He slammed the phone down and sank back into his chair.

The door to his office opened, and Pamela slid in through the crack and shut the door behind her. "Is everything all right, Jackie?" She lowered her eyes and sidled over to the desk. "You sounded a little . . . upset. I bet I know what could make you unupset . . ." She leaned against his shoulder and twirled one finger in the hair at the base of his neck. "C'mon, Jackie, let Pammie kiss it and make it better."

"Leave me alone, Pamela."

"You don't mean that, now do you?" Her sultry voice dropped half an octave. "Whatever's bothering you, I've got the cure."

Jack stared at her, incredulous. How could he ever have found himself attracted to a woman like this? She didn't seem so bad in a dark bar or candlelit bedroom, but in the harsh light of day, when he was sober— well, he must have been out of his mind to hire her, not to mention the other things he had done with her.

"Pamela," he said with forced patience, "I have some things to take care of, and I don't want to be disturbed—by *anyone*."

"Jackie, Jackie," she cooed. "All this worrying is giving you a frown line." She reached a manicured hand to smooth away the line between his brows, and he grasped her wrist with more force than he had intended. "Ouch! You're hurting me!"

"Out, Pamela," he repeated pointedly. "Now." He paused for a moment, his eyes drifting over the low-cut blouse, the makeup, the three-inch heels; then he sat down, grabbed his checkbook from the top drawer of the desk, and scribbled out a check in the amount of two weeks' pay, plus a sizable bonus. "Pack your desk," he said, handing the check to her. "This is your severance; I want you out of the office within the hour."

A confused look came over Pamela's face. "You're firing me? You can't do that!"

"Sure I can. I need a *real* secretary—"

"Legal assistant," she corrected.

"All right, I need a *real* legal assistant. All you've done since you came to work for me is answer the phone and do your nails."

"I've done a lot more than that, and you know it." Her eyes narrowed. "I know a thing or two about sexual harassment. I've got half a mind to lodge a complaint—"

"Half a mind is all you've ever had," Jack countered. "Take your check and go."

She flounced out of the room and slammed the door so hard it rattled the windows behind Jack's desk. He rubbed his aching temples and sighed. Why couldn't he find a *real* woman, one he didn't have to hire, one who had a brain as well as a body, one like—

Like Cecilia McAlister.

Jack could still see her the way she had been before the cancer drained the life out of her—vital and beautiful, witty and creative and smart. The best dancer he had ever held in his arms. The woman who had made all others—including his three ex-wives—pale in comparison.

All his life Jack had envied his best friend, not for his wealth or his status or his power, but for the wife who had graced his arm at social functions and served as hostess for his campaign parties. Cecilia had deserved better—so much better—than Duncan McAlister.

Ironic, that the only woman Jack had ever loved was the one he couldn't have, at least not in the way he wanted to have her, not permanently, not as *his*. And so in the end he had settled for protecting her—shielding her from the knowledge of who her husband really was, from an awareness of what a sham her marriage had become.

And he would go on with the deception, even now after her death. He would guard her memory, even though the price included covering for Duncan as well.

His private line rang once, and he picked up the receiver. "Underwood."

"It's me, Mr. Underwood. Sorry about the delay."

Jack let out an exasperated sigh and propped his feet up on the desk. With any luck at all, this might be the last call he ever had to take from Shiv Willis.

Shiv tried to keep his voice calm as he talked to Jackson Underwood, but it wasn't easy. He wouldn't tell him the truth—that after slipping in and out of the hospital in the middle of the night, he had emptied his pocket flask and slept for five hours in the car. It was just dumb luck nobody had spotted him—once he got outside the parking garage, he found the place swarming with black-and-whites. He had managed to evade them and found a deserted alley to park in while he called Underwood back, but his stomach was churning like a cement mixer.

They were onto him. Despite his intimidation of the woman—which he thought had been pretty convincing—apparently she had talked. If she could identify him, he was dead meat.

"Yes sir, everything is just fine," he lied, swallowing down the vile taste of his own stomach acids. "Got it all taken care of."

Shiv listened with half an ear while Underwood droned on; his mind raced to come up with a plan. The best thing for him to do was vanish, with or without the money owed him. Just cut his losses and get out while the getting was good. One thing was certain—he was not taking the fall for a couple of suits.

"I don't want to have to come out there myself," Underwood was saying in a threatening tone. Shiv laughed under his breath. The man would never get this close to his own dirty work. He'd stay right where he was, safe in his high-rent office, and hope the trail never led back to his door. In the meantime, Shiv could make his getaway.

He reassured the man one more time that everything was under control, hung up, and let out a pent-up breath. It was time to tie up loose ends and ditch this rotten job once and for all.

31

Gifts from the Ashes

Amber sat up in the hospital bed and sipped orange juice through a straw as she watched News at Noon. The third story was about the fire, her injuries, and the ongoing arson investigation. "We know the fire was deliberately set," the burly Kitsap County sheriff was saying as he looked into the camera. "The arsonist got away, leaving a woman to die in the burning barn. We'll get him, and when we do, the charges will be much more serious than arson. Assault, at the very least—possibly attempted murder."

"As yet, the authorities have no suspects, and no one has been apprehended," the female reporter went on in a low, consciously moderated voice. "On the scene we have Ted Tanner. Ted?"

A Robert Redford look-alike appeared on the screen, fiddling with his earpiece and looking properly somber. "Thank you, Heather. We're here at the Elkhorn farm with proprietor Joseph Elkhorn. Mr. Elkhorn, what can you tell us about the night this incident occurred?"

He thrust the mike in TwoJoe's direction, and Amber fixed her gaze intently on TwoJoe's handsome face. "It happened about two in the morning," TwoJoe said. "My sister and I were both asleep. I heard a ruckus and woke up to hear the alarm call of one of my male llamas."

The reporter looked confused. "Do you mean that a *llama* alerted you to the danger?"

TwoJoe nodded. "They're really very good guard animals. This one's name is Lloser—"

As if on cue, Lloser poked his enormous head over TwoJoe's shoulder and began wrapping his huge, flexible lips around the microphone. Amber laughed out loud.

Ted Tanner, for all his training in television journalism, was clearly at a loss. He tried to pull the microphone away, but the llama wouldn't let go. After a brief tussle, Lloser gave in, but by then the microphone was slimed with llama spittle, and the reporter held it at arm's length as if it were contaminated with some deadly virus. He patted the curious beast awkwardly on the neck and turned back to TwoJoe.

"We're just thankful that no one was badly hurt or killed," TwoJoe was saying.

"I understand the woman who was injured was your fiancée?" Ted continued with a sly smile.

TwoJoe blushed furiously, but his eyes grew soft and liquid as he considered the question. "Not yet," he said at last. "She's a friend. A very, very good friend."

"Not *yet?*" Tanner said flippantly. "Sounds like a marriage proposal might come out of this incident, after all. Now, if you can just get your llama to pop the question." He turned toward the camera and grinned. "For News at Noon, this is Ted Tanner. Back to you, Heather."

Amber pushed the remote control, and the screen faded to black. Poor TwoJoe. He must be absolutely humiliated.

But come to think of it, he didn't *look* humiliated. With his hair graying at the temples, long and brushed back from his forehead, he looked proud and strong, like an ancient warrior. A chief. A man who knew his own heart. A soul at peace with himself, even in the face of prying and insolent questions.

And he hadn't said, "No." He had said, "Not yet."

She lay back against the pillow, finished her orange juice, and smiled.

⁓

At three o'clock in the afternoon, the door opened and Vernon Houston came into the room, followed by Sam, who was gripping a paper grocery bag to his chest.

"We got special permission for Sam to come visit," the Colonel said in a whisper, "but we can only stay a few minutes. How you doing?"

"I'm all right." She motioned for Sam to come sit beside her, and he clambered up onto the bed and set his bag down. "I don't seem to have any lasting effects from the concussion; it'll just take some time for the burns to heal."

"Guess you won't be able to work for a while."

"Probably not." Amber shook her head. "Besides, even if my hands were all right, I don't have a studio to go back to."

Sam gazed at her with wide, blue eyes. "But you *are* going to be okay, aren't you, Amber?"

"I'm going to be just fine. I'm coming home tomorrow."

"That's good," Sam said with a grin. "'Cause we've got a BIG surprise for you."

Amber shot a quizzical look at the Colonel, who raised his eyebrows. "Don't ask me; I'm not telling."

"Well, then, I guess I'll just have to wait." Amber pointed toward the paper bag. "Does my surprise have anything to do with what's in there?"

Sam nodded. "Kinda." He glanced at his grandfather. "I brought you something, Amber. It got a little messed up in the fire, but—" He pushed the paper bag in her direction.

She held up her bandaged hands. "You'll have to open it for me, Sam. I don't have the use of my fingers right now."

"Okay." He reached into the bag and came up with something blackened and charred, and laid it on the top of the blanket that covered Amber's lap. "I went in the barn and got it myself," he said proudly. "I know how much it means to you."

Tears blurred Amber's eyes as she looked at it. It was the cast of the Two Sisters, irreparably mutilated by the fire.

"You told me that long as you had this, you could make the statue again," Sam was saying excitedly. "And I knew you'd want to, 'cause—" He stopped suddenly, clapping a hand over his mouth.

For a minute or two, she couldn't speak. Then she drew the boy into an enormous hug and held him there, blinking back the tears as she gazed over his head into the Colonel's seamed and weathered countenance. "Thank you," she whispered.

"It was the best gift I could think of," Sam said, his voice muffled as he pressed his face against her. "I love you, Amber."

"I love—," she choked out. "I love you, too."

The Colonel shifted from one foot to the other and cleared his throat. "I think we'd better be going now."

Sam gave Amber one last squeeze and climbed down from the bed.

"Meg and TwoJoe have invited us for dinner tomorrow, if you think you're up to it," the Colonel said as he held out a hand for Sam.

"Of course. I'd be disappointed if you didn't come."

"We'll see you tomorrow evening, then."

When the door shut behind them, Amber just sat there staring at the plaster cast of the Two Sisters. Soot-covered and disfigured, it reminded her of grisly images she had seen in newsreels—a charred corpse, nearly unrecognizable as anything that ever held life or vitality or joy.

Poor Sam. She could just see him in the barn, his angelic little face covered with sweat and grime, searching through the rubble and letting out a whoop of joy when he found the cast. He thought he was recovering something precious for her, but his gift only served to remind Amber of how much she had lost.

Almost as quickly as it had appeared, the miracle had vanished. Gone were her studio, her plans, her kiln, the Two Sisters—even, for the time being, her hands. She had no idea how long it would be before she could mold clay or hold a sculpting knife. And what about the commission? She couldn't possibly complete it now. All their hopes and dreams had hinged upon that project. Without it, she couldn't buy a new kiln, reestablish a place to work, rebuild the barn. Without it, there wouldn't even *be* a barn—or a farm, for that matter. Or even a life.

It all had come crashing down in one brief moment, dissolved to nothing in a flash of gasoline and fire.

"Lord, I believe," she murmured through her tears, remembering the lines that Susan had quoted to her. "Help my unbelief."

A knock on the door brought Amber to herself. She blotted her eyes with the bandages and swiped her hair back from her face. "Come in."

The door opened a crack, and Vernon Houston's face reappeared. "Sam's waiting in the lobby. Can I have a minute alone with you?"

"Sure."

He entered the hospital room and sat down on the chair next to her bed, his long legs stretched out in front of him. "I reckon that's pretty much useless." He pointed to the ruined plaster cast.

Amber nodded. "I'm afraid so."

"Couldn't convince him otherwise. Nothing coulda stopped him going into that barn to retrieve it for you. It coulda still been on fire, and he woulda gone in after that thing."

"It was very sweet."

"He said you'd want it more'n anything else in there."

"He was right." Amber smiled. "Your grandson is a wonderful boy, Colonel. I hope he keeps that sensitivity as he gets older."

"Yeah, me, too. Wouldn't want him to grow up into a nasty old buzzard like his grandpa."

"He could do worse."

The Colonel flushed red under his tan and grinned sheepishly, then sobered and straightened in his chair. "I need to talk serious for a minute." Amber nodded, and he went on. "Seems to me like you and TwoJoe and Meg are gonna have to do a little regrouping."

"You mean because of my injuries?" She nodded. "I've been thinking about that. The commission for that big project was a godsend, but—"

"But you don't think it's gonna happen."

"I doubt it." Her throat felt tight, and she strove to keep her voice from breaking. "The barn has to be repaired; even if the insurance covers it, there's still the deductible to think about. And who knows how long it might take to get a settlement? I don't know, Colonel. We're back to square one, I'm afraid. Or maybe even farther back than that."

"Not quite." He reached into his pocket. "I've got something for you—"

"Colonel, we can't take that," she protested automatically.

"Hang on there, missy. You don't even know what it is yet."

"You're a very generous man, Colonel, but you know how TwoJoe feels about charity."

"This ain't charity." He handed it to her.

Amber gasped. It was a check for ten thousand four hundred dollars, made out to Amber Chaney, from Andrew Jorgensen's business account drawn on a Seattle bank. "What is this?"

"I thought you said that concussion hadn't done any major damage." Houston chuckled. "It's a check. The down payment on the sculpture, plus the money for the Two Sisters, minus Mr. Jorgenson's 20 percent. It came in the mail yesterday, and since TwoJoe's tied up with stuff at the farm and won't get here until later this afternoon, he gave it to me to give to you. Jorgensen called to make sure it arrived OK and said that the fella who commissioned the sculpture ain't in no big hurry. Said he'd wait long as it takes."

Amber peered at the seamed, weather-beaten face. The Colonel's eyes were bright with mirth. He was hiding something. She could sense it. A sudden thought struck her, and she shook the check in his face.

"It was you, wasn't it?"

He frowned. "What do you mean?"

"You know perfectly well what I mean." She fixed him with her most intense stare. "*You're* the one who commissioned the statue. A little boy and a llama—I should have guessed before."

"I'm gonna go get the doctor. He needs to take another look at your head." The Colonel got to his feet.

"You stay right where you are, Vernon Houston. You did it, didn't you? And unless I miss my guess, you're the one who bought the Two Sisters, too."

His eyes slid off to one side and he twirled his hat nervously in his hands.

"Look at me, Colonel. And tell me the truth."

He let out an explosive sigh and swung back in her direction. "Dang it all, woman! You're just like my Emmaline. Never could put anything past her, not in a whole lifetime of lovin' her."

Amber sank back against the pillows. "You can't do this, Colonel."

"Why not?"

"You know why not."

He peered at her intently. "You and TwoJoe are just alike, Amber. Stubborn as a brace of old mules. This is business. I want that statue of my boy and the llama. And I want you to sculpt it, no matter how long I have to wait for it. Yeah, I also bought the Two Sisters. Sam loved it, and I figured it might just help him get through the grief of losing his own sister. Every time he looked at it, he'd be reminded of what he said to you—that you never really lose somebody you love."

"But, Colonel," she protested, "a ten-thousand-dollar advance? And another ten when the project is completed? How am I supposed to see that as anything but a handout?"

He set his hat on the floor and leaned over, taking both her bandaged hands gently in his. "It's about time you took a hard look at yourself, Amber Chaney. You're an artist. A good one. In time, maybe a great one. Twenty thousand is chicken feed for a fine sculpture. Once your name gets known, it'll double in value."

Amber shook her head. "Pardon me for asking, Colonel, but since when are you an expert?" The words came out harsh, and she instantly regretted them. "I'm sorry," she murmured. "You're only trying to help. I shouldn't have said that."

He stared at her for a minute, then let out a great booming laugh. "I own three Remingtons, Amber. And a Picasso—a small one. A Grant Wood and a couple of Andrew Wyeths. It's a mistake to underestimate me just 'cause I got a little dirt under my fingernails. I know a bit about art." He paused and grinned widely at her. "And yeah, maybe I *am* trying to help—trying to help a new artist get her feet under her. What the blazes is so awful about that?"

She lowered her eyes. "Nothing."

"Tell you what, Amber, I'll make a deal with you. You keep the ten thousand as an advance on the project. Get the barn fixed, replace your kiln, whatever else you need to do. When you're able to work again, you do the sculpture, and I'll pay the other ten thousand. All through Jorgensen's gallery, minus his commission, nice and businesslike. In ten years, if your sculpture isn't worth forty thousand, you can pay me back the twenty thousand at 5 percent interest."

"And what about the Two Sisters?"

"I only paid three thousand for it. I'm keeping it. But you can borrow it to make a new cast."

Amber closed her eyes for a brief moment. "Thank you," she whispered.

"You're mighty welcome," Houston answered, then gazed at her oddly. "Something tells me you weren't talking to me."

"No, I wasn't," Amber chuckled. "But thank you, too. I never knew angels came dressed in jeans and cowboy boots."

The Colonel shook his head. "I don't reckon the Good Lord needs help from an old fool like me," he muttered. "And don't go thinking this is some kind of philanthropy. It's selfishness, pure and simple. I'm gonna be known as the brilliant fella who bought his very first Chaney *before* her name became a household word."

He gathered up his hat, kissed her on the forehead, and headed for the door. "See you tomorrow. And take care of them hands. You're gonna need 'em."

"Colonel?" Amber called after him. "If I ever *do* get really famous—"

He turned. "You will, mark my words."

"Then you can expect me to charge you a whole lot more than twenty thousand for the next one."

Vernon Houston tipped his hat and winked. "I'll count on it, little lady. And it'll be my pleasure to pay every last dime."

32

Homecoming

"You sure you don't want to go to the hospital with me to pick her up?" TwoJoe said to Meg's back as she stood at the drainboard pouring her special marinade onto the salmon fillets.

"No, you go on." She turned and smiled at him. "I've got a lot of preparations ahead of me if everybody's coming to dinner at six." She covered the salmon and slid the dish into the refrigerator. "Besides, it'll be good for you and Amber to have a little time to yourselves."

TwoJoe leaned against the counter and frowned at his sister. "A little time to ourselves? What does *that* mean?"

Meg shrugged. "I don't know. Maybe you two have some things to discuss—" She grinned and tilted her head. "Unless you're planning to let Lloser do the talking for you." She dissolved into fits of laughter and doubled over, wiping her streaming eyes on her apron.

"Very funny."

"Where's your sense of humor, big brother?" Meg straightened up, trying in vain to put on a serious expression. "You're going to ruin this whole evening if you don't take that look off your face. This is a *celebration*, for heaven's sake!" She peered into his eyes. "You're not worried about Amber's reaction to Diedre, are you?"

"I don't know. Maybe we should have told her right away—you know, given her a chance to get used to the idea instead of just springing it on her."

"We're not exactly springing it on her," Meg countered. "We'll sit down and talk to her before dinner, before Diedre and Carlene and the Houstons show up, just like we planned. She's had a lot to deal with, TwoJoe—the attack and the fire and the concussion and all. Give her a chance to get home and relax a little." She went back to the marinade. "What time is it?"

TwoJoe craned his neck to look at the clock on the stove. "A little after two."

"Then you'd better get going. The doctor said he'd be there at three to sign the release."

"All right." TwoJoe picked up his keys from the kitchen table. "We should be back by four." He started for the front door, only to turn around and come back to the kitchen when he heard Meg calling his name. "What now?"

"Stop by the grocery on your way home, will you? I don't have enough Romaine lettuce for the salad."

"Romaine. Got it." He turned to go.

"And a bottle of that Vidalia onion dressing."

"OK."

"The one with the purple label."

"Purple label?" he repeated.

"Yes, purple. Don't get the one with the green label—it's too strong."

"Anything else?" he asked through gritted teeth.

"We could use some vanilla ice cream to go with the cake."

TwoJoe rolled his eyes. "Should I make a list?"

"Maybe you should just call me before you leave the hospital to double-check."

"I'm leaving now." He bolted for the door.

"Call me!" she yelled to his retreating back.

"I'll call, I'll call," he muttered. He shut the front door behind him and stood on the porch for a minute, enjoying the silence, then heaved a long-suffering sigh. Sometimes he felt exactly like a husband, and he didn't even have a wife yet.

Amber had only been in the hospital for three days, but it might as well have been three months—or three years. Everything seemed different. Even though she was perfectly capable of walking on her own two legs, TwoJoe had insisted on taking her down to the front entrance of the building in a wheelchair, holding two huge flower arrangements on her lap. He even made her wait while he retrieved his truck from the parking garage.

She barely recognized the pickup when it arrived; apparently just for this occasion, TwoJoe had washed it and cleaned out the interior. The poor old beat-up Dodge looked naked and vulnerable, with all its scars and rust spots uncovered for the whole world to see. Inside, the familiar rich scents of hay and llama feed and manure were overpowered by the pungent odor of Armor All, and the slick shine simply emphasized the cracks and gouges on the dashboard.

Amber's mind flashed back to her childhood, when at the age of five she had been forced to attend her grandmother's funeral. Gramma Chaney, a sweet-faced, wise old woman, had the most wonderful skin—soft and puckered, like old flannel. Amber could still remember stroking Gramma's face and marveling at the wrinkles that fanned out from her cheeks all the way to her ears. But at the funeral home, someone had taken the liberty of making a few improvements and had plastered that dear face with makeup—bright pink rouge, blue eye shadow, and garish red lipstick. She had taken one glance and started howling, protesting that this wasn't her Gramma, and had to be carried out kicking and screaming.

Amber felt the same way about the modifications TwoJoe had made to his truck, about being pushed in a wheelchair, about not being allowed to walk to the parking garage with him. Why did people insist upon changing things, upon acting differently toward her, when all she wanted was for her life to hurry up and get back to normal?

"Old gal looks pretty good, doesn't she?" he asked, patting the oily dashboard with pride.

And Amber forced a smile and said yes, even though she didn't mean it.

It took exactly six and a half minutes for the two of them to exhaust all possible topics of conversation, including her health, his health, Sam's kitten, and the weather. Amber raised a question or two about the fire and what it might cost to repair the barn, but TwoJoe didn't seem to want to talk about that. They rode in silence for a while.

He was acting so odd, and Amber was pretty sure she knew why. The television interview. Undoubtedly he was feeling self-conscious about what he'd said on camera about her not being his fiancée—not yet, anyway. Well, they might as well get it out of the way so they could go back to being . . . whatever they were. Friends, at the very least. Very good friends.

Amber opened her mouth to speak and a strange tingling sensation filled her stomach, the fluttering of an unexpected anxiety. She wasn't accustomed to feeling uncomfortable in TwoJoe's presence, and she didn't like the sensation very much. Summoning all her willpower, she said, "In case you're wondering, I did see the interview on television, TwoJoe."

He inhaled sharply and gripped the steering wheel so hard that his knuckles went white, but he kept his eyes focused on the road beyond the cracked windshield. "Yeah, well about that—," he began.

Amber laid a bandaged hand on his arm. "I thought you did a wonderful job," she said quietly. "You seemed so strong and in control. I was very proud of you."

His head snapped around. "You were?"

"Of course I was. And I nearly fell out of the hospital bed when Lloser tried to steal the microphone and slimed that reporter."

TwoJoe began to chuckle, and as Amber's laughter mingled with his, the cold wall of formality between them dissolved. At last he turned and looked at her. "About the other part of that interview, Amber—"

"You mean the part where the reporter asked if we were engaged?"

"Yeah. That part." He bit his lip and exhaled heavily. "That question just came out of the blue, and I didn't have the faintest idea how to handle it."

"I thought you handled it just fine."

"I didn't mean to put any pressure on you, or to assume anything. What I said about not being engaged yet just sort of popped out. I apologize if it hurt you or offended you."

"I wasn't offended," Amber murmured. "To tell the truth, I was honored." She hadn't meant to say that—it came out spontaneously, but as soon as the words had been uttered, she realized that they were true.

"Anyway," he went on, barreling ahead as if she hadn't spoken, "I just want you to know that I don't expect anything from you, and—"

They had just turned into the long driveway that led up to the farmhouse, and he braked hard, stopping the truck so suddenly that Amber had to brace her hands against the dashboard to keep from hitting the windshield. She winced in pain.

"Sorry." He raked a hand through his hair. "I wasn't thinking." He stared at her. "What did you say—a minute ago, before?"

"I said, I wasn't offended," she repeated, smiling at him. "I said I was honored."

"You mean—you might—if I—we could—," he stammered.

"Maybe you *would* be better off letting Lloser do your talking for you." His ears turned a bright red, and she went on. "A lot of things have happened in a very short time, TwoJoe—some things you don't know about yet. We'll need to talk about them eventually, but—" she pointed toward the house, where Meg stood on the front porch with one hand shading her eyes. "It'll probably have to wait."

He raked his hair back and gazed at her, his eyes shining. "I've waited a long time, Amber. I can wait awhile longer."

"I'm not making any promises, you understand," she warned. "But I do want to talk about it." She edged closer to him, and he rested his arm lightly around her shoulders. A rush of warmth went through her at his touch, and every nerve in her body seemed to relax. "There is one thing I should tell you now, though—"

"What?"

"The night of the fire—outside the barn. I vaguely remember someone kissing me. Was that you, or Lloser?"

His hand tightened on her shoulder, and he grinned sheepishly. "It was me. But it wasn't a kiss. It was a resuscitation."

"Ah." She chuckled. "Well that's good to know, because if it *was* a kiss, you're going to have to do better than that."

Amber followed TwoJoe's gaze as he peered through the windshield down the long gravel driveway. The porch was empty; Meg had gone back into the house.

He turned to her and bent forward. "I'm a little out of practice. Maybe you should show me how it's done."

Their lips touched—briefly, gently at first, then with fervor. Amber leaned into him, her mind spinning. So many things still lay unspoken between them, but she felt no fear, no agitation. Only safety and longing . . . and love.

Meg settled Amber at the dining room table and sent TwoJoe back to the store. He had forgotten to call her from the hospital, as he had promised—even forgotten, apparently, that he was supposed to pick anything up in the first place. When she asked him where the groceries were, he stared at her blankly as if she were speaking a foreign language.

Something was going on, and although Meg didn't know what it was, she had her suspicions. TwoJoe's countenance bore a dazed, wistful expression. His eyes tracked Amber's every move, and he seemed reluctant to leave her side, even for a few minutes. Amber didn't seem much more coherent.

"Are you OK?" Meg asked as she placed the smaller of the two floral arrangements on the table as a centerpiece.

"I'm fine." Amber reached out and touched the petals of a rose with a hand swathed in bandages. "I'm wonderful, in fact." She sighed deeply. "It's good to be home."

"How's your head? Are you in pain?"

Amber looked up. "Quit fussing, Meg. I'm all right." She got up from the table and followed Meg into the kitchen. "What can I do?"

"Nothing. It's all done. When TwoJoe gets back from the grocery store, I'll make the salad. Just sit."

"I'm tired of sitting. I've been in bed for three solid days."

"Yes, and you have a concussion. You're not to exert yourself—the doctor said so."

"What do doctors know?" Amber wandered to the window and gazed dreamily out over the Hood Canal and Olympic Mountains. "It's so beautiful here."

Meg started to ask what was up with Amber and TwoJoe, but she thought better of it and clamped her mouth shut. Amber was her closest friend; when there was something to tell, she would let Meg in on it. In the meantime, if the two of them were finally beginning to discover each other, Meg didn't want to get in the way by meddling.

She glanced at the clock—it was nearly five. If TwoJoe didn't get back soon, they wouldn't have time to prepare Amber for Diedre's appearance.

Amber's voice cut into Meg's thoughts. "What are we having for dinner?"

"Salmon. The potatoes are already baking, and the fish will take about half an hour. I thought I'd make my famous garlic and cheese biscuits—I know you like them." She opened the refrigerator. "Do you want a snack? I've got grapes and cheese and crackers, if you need something to tide you over."

Amber shook her head. "I don't want to spoil my appetite. Everything sounds wonderful, especially after hospital food." She walked around Meg and peered into the oven, where ten large potatoes coated with butter and rock salt were baking. "Good grief, Meg, it looks like you're cooking for an army."

Meg hesitated, pretending to concentrate on her biscuit dough. "The Houstons are coming, and I invited Susan. And a couple of other . . . friends."

"What friends?" Amber slit her eyes at Meg.

"Just a couple of young women who are staying with the Colonel and Emmaline for a few days," Meg hedged. She heard the front door slam. "That must be TwoJoe—thank goodness he's back!"

She wiped her floury hands on her apron and, leaving Amber standing in the kitchen, made a run for the front door.

Amber frowned at Meg's back as she watched her friend bolt for the door. Had they all been dropped into the twilight zone? Everybody looked the same, but no one was acting normally.

She could hear Meg hissing at TwoJoe in the hallway and caught snatches of their conversation: "Do you know what time it is? Everybody . . . in forty-five minutes, and we haven't had the chance to talk to Amber about . . ."

TwoJoe's voice came through a little clearer. "All right, all right. Calm down, will you? The grocery store was packed, and I had to wait in line forever—"

Meg's tone went up several decibels: "If you'd remembered to go in the first place, you wouldn't have had to wait in line!"

The two of them came back into the kitchen, Meg carrying the grocery bag and TwoJoe jangling his keys nervously. "There's something we wanted to talk to you about before all our guests arrive," TwoJoe said, not meeting her eyes. "But I don't quite know how to begin."

Amber sank down at the dining room table and waited while all her earlier euphoria vanished like an early morning dream. Clearly, this wasn't something TwoJoe wanted to tell her. Maybe the authorities had given up on finding the man who attacked her. Maybe the insurance company wasn't going to pay to have the barn repaired. Maybe they were going to lose the farm after all . . .

"It's OK, TwoJoe," she assured him with more confidence than she felt. "As long as—" She was going to say, *As long as we're together, we can handle anything*, but she stopped herself. Such a sentiment was premature at best, and she couldn't even be certain it was true, at least not until she heard what he had to say.

Out of the corner of her eye, Amber watched as Meg finished the biscuit dough and put the salad together. All the while, TwoJoe tried to get his momentum going, but he didn't seem to be getting anywhere. After she pulled out the potatoes and slid the salmon into the oven, Meg sat down next to Amber at the table and fiddled with the flower arrangement.

"Just tell me, all right?" Amber demanded after a minute or two. "What is going on?"

TwoJoe clenched his hands together. "I guess we'd better start at the beginning. We didn't want to tell you about this while you were in the hospital, Amber—we thought it would be easier for you to absorb once you were in familiar surroundings."

Amber's heart constricted. "If it's bad news, I wish you'd spit it out and get it over with."

"No," TwoJoe answered slowly. "It's not bad news—it's good news, really. Kind of a gift . . . for all of us."

Amber stared at him. If it really was good news, why was he having such a hard time getting it out? "In the hospital the other day, Sam let it slip that you had a big surprise waiting for me when I got home. Is that what you're talking about?"

Meg cut a worried glance at the clock on the kitchen stove. It was quarter to six.

"In a way." TwoJoe nodded. "The morning after the fire, when Meg and I came home from the hospital, we found someone waiting for us—someone sent here by Andrew Jorgensen."

"Another commission—or a sale? That's wonderful!" Amber's mind latched onto the idea with enthusiasm. "My hands will heal before long, and as soon as we get my studio up and running again, I can get back to work. The Colonel's statue has to come first, of course—I assume he told you about that—but I can—"

"Hold on, Amber!" TwoJoe protested. "It wasn't another buyer." He turned toward Meg. "Help me out here."

"I wouldn't dream of interfering," she muttered. "Not while you're on such a roll." She got up and went to the china cabinet. "Keep going. I have to set the table."

TwoJoe sent a murderous glance in his sister's direction, then turned back to Amber. "Anyway—"

But before he could say another word, Amber heard the front door burst open. Sam Houston careened into the dining room with a small, blonde dog close on his heels. He threw himself at Amber and gave her an enormous hug. "I'm so glad you're home, Amber!" he panted. "I've been waiting and waiting. I brought you your surprise."

Amber reached down and gingerly picked up the little dog, who snuggled into her lap and gave her a wet kiss on the cheek. "This is my surprise? She's wonderful!"

"No, no!" Sam protested. "Shut your eyes."

Amber obeyed and felt a small hand on her arm, just above the bandages, as Sam helped her to her feet and steered her in the direction of the living room. "Keep them closed," he ordered. "A few more steps. Now, your surprise is right in front of you."

"Amber, wait—" TwoJoe's voice came from behind her. "They're early. I wanted to tell you first—"

But Sam was saying, "Open your eyes, Amber."

Amber opened them, blinked, and tried to take in what she saw. In the living room were four people—the Colonel and Emmaline, sitting on the sofa, and two women in their mid to late twenties, standing by the fireplace. One was large and vivacious, with a pixie haircut and rosy cheeks, wearing a flowing pants outfit of bright aqua. The other, much smaller, had dark, curly hair and brown eyes that pierced into her own. She stared at Amber for a moment, then gave a tentative smile, revealing a dimple at the corner of her mouth.

The breath went out of Amber as if she had been kicked in the stomach. She felt her knees buckle, and she sank into a chair.

She had no doubt who she was looking at. It could have been herself, fifteen years ago. It could have been Mama, two decades before that.

But it wasn't. It was Diedre. Not a baby anymore, not the tiny child she had spun with under the trees. She was a grown woman now—and by the looks of her, a grown woman on the verge of breaking into tears.

"Perhaps I shouldn't have come," she said in a voice shaking with emotion. "I—I hoped—" The tears overflowed, and she began to sob. "Oh, Sissy—"

Sissy. The name she hadn't heard in more than twenty years pierced Amber's heart like a flaming arrow. Finding her legs, she rose from the chair and walked unsteadily across the room. She put her bandaged hands to Diedre's face and began wiping away the tears. "No, you shouldn't have come," she whispered. "I should have come to you—a long, long time ago."

Then she put her arms around Diedre's shoulders, drew her close, and held her.

33

Too Many Questions

Diedre breathed a sigh of relief when TwoJoe shut the door behind the Colonel, Emmaline, and Sam.

Even though it had only been three days since she and Carlene had arrived—the day Vernon Houston had held a shotgun on them in TwoJoe's living room—Diedre had become increasingly attached to the Elkhorn family and their friends. The Colonel doted on both her and Carlene; little Sam was a wonderful, sensitive, loving child; and Emmaline was an earth mother who embraced everyone who came within reach. Meg and TwoJoe could have been her own big sister and brother, the way they had treated her. Still, despite her growing love for all of them, Diedre had shifted restlessly in her chair throughout dinner, wishing they would all just disappear.

She needed to talk with her sister. And there was much she couldn't—or wouldn't—say during dinner with everyone present. She had simply listened as everyone had discussed the fire, speculating on who could have done such a thing, and why.

TwoJoe was clearly in love with Amber. He had sat next to her all evening with his arm across the back of her chair, gazing at her as if he couldn't take his eyes off her. Amber could have been watching a tennis match, the way her attention bounced between his face and Diedre's. Whenever she looked at Diedre, an expression passed over her countenance that seemed to be a mixture of love and pain. Diedre forced herself to focus on the love and tried to rationalize the pain, but she couldn't help feeling as if her presence made Amber edgy.

Well, what did she expect? It had been more than twenty years, and if she was honest, Diedre herself had to admit to a little anxiety of her own. But there were too many questions yet unanswered. She was not about to let a little nervousness get in the way of the reunion for which she had waited so long.

Once the Houstons were gone, Meg excused herself to clean up the kitchen. The priest, whom Amber jokingly called "Father Susan," joined her. TwoJoe made an excuse about checking on the llamas, and Carlene retrieved her jacket and Sugarbear's leash and took the dog for a walk.

The moment she had longed for had finally come. But when Diedre finally faced her sister, the two of them alone in the living room, reticence overtook her and she found herself tongue-tied.

She bit her lip and stared at the hooked rug on the hardwood floor. "Ah, if you need to rest, I'll understand. This can wait—"

"This has waited long enough."

Diedre looked up at her sister's serious face, surrounded by dark hair and punctuated by those large, brown eyes—a face so like her mother's, years ago before the cancer took its toll. So like her own would be in another fifteen years. "Sis—ah, Amber—," she began, struggling over the name. "Sorry. It'll take me a while to get used to calling you that."

"It's all right. You were so young—I don't suppose you ever knew that Amber was my middle name."

Diedre shook her head. "No. I didn't know. But I understood imme-diately why you had taken Mama's maiden name as your own."

Amber let out a sigh. "I still miss her. It's so odd, thinking that some-one you love is still alive after they're gone. It was breast cancer, you said?"

"Yes. We all thought she had beaten the cancer, but when it came back, she refused further treatment. She took drugs for the pain and died peacefully. Her last gift to me was what brought me to you." Diedre closed her eyes for a moment and fought against the emotions that assailed her. "I thought you were dead, Amber. If I'd known you were alive, I would have found you sooner."

"I expect Daddy wanted you to think I was dead."

Diedre raised her head and stared at Amber, startled by the anger and raw pain that filled her sister's face. Then Amber's expression cleared, and she waved a bandaged hand. "Please, go on. Tell me the whole story, from the start."

"From the time I was very young—four or five years old," Diedre began, "I couldn't get you out of my mind. I had this recurring vision— I called it the Spinning Dream—" She paused and smiled. "The dream that was re-created in your sculpture of the Two Sisters. Until I saw the statue, I didn't know it was an actual memory, not just something my imagination had conjured up. But it always seemed so *real*. And when-ever I would try to get anyone to talk about you, Mama would dissolve into tears, and Daddy would shut me up."

"That figures," Amber muttered.

Diedre shot her a puzzled glance and continued. "Anyway, on my twenty-fifth birthday, Mama gave me this." She reached into her bag and drew out the battered cigar box. "I'm pretty sure she knew she was dying and couldn't bear to go into the next world with all this on her conscience."

She retrieved the old photograph from the box and extended it in Amber's direction. Amber reached for it, but with her bandaged hands she couldn't grip it properly, and it slid to the floor. Both of them leaned forward to grab it, and their arms touched. Diedre felt a gentle shock, like static electricity, flow through her veins.

She sat back, breathless. "This picture raised a lot of questions for me. It's so obvious how much Daddy adored you. Although he provided for me and tried to love me, he was never able to—"

She stopped suddenly as one side of Amber's mouth turned up in an odd twist. "Is something wrong?"

"No. I just—" The bandaged hand that held the picture shook a little. "I want to hear the rest."

"All right." Diedre cast around for her train of thought. "As I was saying, Daddy never loved me like that—" She pointed at the photograph. "And I never knew why. I assumed, when I thought about it, that losing you was so painful and difficult that he simply never recovered enough to be able to be vulnerable again. But then I found these, hidden in the bottom of the box—" She held up the birth certificate and letters.

"In the letters of yours that Mama saved, you implied you knew the real circumstances of my birth. Even apart from that, I would have come to find you anyway, once I knew you were alive. But since nobody else could tell me, I knew you were also my only hope for finding out the truth. When I realized that Daddy wasn't—" She hesitated. "Wasn't my real father—"

Amber's head snapped up. "What did you say?"

"The birth certificate," Diedre repeated. "It lists my mother as Cecilia McAlister, and my father as 'unknown.'"

"Jack," Amber muttered, shutting her eyes tightly.

A thrill shot through Diedre as her sister uttered the name. "That was my guess," she whispered. "He always doted on Mama so . . ."

But Amber wasn't listening. Without warning, she leaped to her feet. "Diedre, you—you have to excuse me," she stammered and fled the room.

Diedre sat there, stunned, as she watched Amber's back retreating through the doorway that led through the dining room to the kitchen. She didn't know what to do—or what to think.

Was it possible she could have offended her sister by suggesting that Mama had an affair with Uncle Jack? But the letters were pretty clear: Amber knew the circumstances of Diedre's birth and understood—or at least did not condemn—her mother.

Maybe Amber was angry that Diedre had come in the first place, dredging up old unpleasant memories that were best forgotten. But *Amber* hadn't forgotten—she had created the sculpture of the Two Sisters from her memory of Diedre as a child. And unless the statue lied, it was a happy memory, a welcome one.

Against her will, tears sprang to Diedre's eyes. *Maybe*—

Her thoughts were interrupted by the sound of the front door opening. She heard the clicking of Sugarbear's toenails across the hardwood floor, and the dog barreled into the room and leaped onto the sofa. Within seconds Carlene followed, shrugging off her jacket and tossing Sugarbear's leash onto an empty chair.

"It's absolutely beautiful here!" she said, her face flushed pink by the night air. "You should see the moon over the canal. What a view—"

Then she caught sight of the expression on Diedre's face. "What happened?" Her eyes flitted around the room. "Where's your sister?"

"She left." Diedre could only manage the two words before her throat clogged with tears. She swallowed hard. "I said something wrong—I don't know—"

Carlene sat down beside her and put an arm around her shoulders. "What did you say?"

"I was just telling her about the stuff Mama gave me before she died—you know, the birth certificate and letters." Diedre gulped and fought for air. "When I said I knew Daddy wasn't my real father, she just jumped up and ran out of the room."

"Did she say anything—anything at all—before she left?"

Diedre nodded. "She said, 'Jack.'"

Carlene leaned against the back of the sofa and let out an exaggerated sigh. "Whew. Well, that answers one question."

"Yes." Diedre regained control of herself now and cleared her throat. "I guess I always suspected it was Uncle Jack. Now I know—but I don't have the faintest idea what to do with the information."

"Go home, throw yourself into his arms, and yell, 'Daddy!'?"

"I don't think so." Diedre managed a halfhearted smile. "But thanks for the laugh."

"So what do we do now? Do you want me to go get her?"

Diedre shook her head. "I don't want to push her if she's not ready to talk. I'm sure this is painful for her, as well. I've had some time to prepare, but my appearing out of the blue must be a real shock to her."

"Maybe we should just go back to the Houstons, get a good night's sleep, and try again tomorrow."

"That sounds like a sensible plan." Diedre shut her eyes tightly and buried her face in her hands. "I don't know what else to do."

Carlene snapped the leash onto Sugarbear's collar, held out a hand to Diedre, and pulled her up from the couch. "Come on."

"You're not leaving, are you?"

Diedre looked up to see TwoJoe standing in the doorway. He stared around the room and frowned. "Where's Amber?"

Diedre pointed toward the kitchen. "I must have said something that upset her, but I'm not quite sure what it was. Carlene and I—well, I think we should go for now. Thank Meg for the dinner, will you? And tell my sister we'll be at the Houstons' at least until tomorrow. If she wants to see me—"

TwoJoe took two strides across the room and laid a hand on her arm. "Please, stay for a minute." He cut a worried glance toward the dining room. "I'll be right back."

"So, should we stay or should we go?" Carlene asked when he had left the room.

Diedre sank back down on the couch. "Let's stay, at least for a few more minutes." She leaned over and retrieved the photograph from the floor, where it had fallen when Amber had made her escape. For a few seconds she looked at it longingly—the loving picture of father and daughter, an image trapped in time. "What's a few more minutes when I've waited twenty years?"

34

The Brutal Truth

Amber rushed into the kitchen and whirled Susan around to face her. "I know who's after me—and why. At least I think I do."

Susan whirled around to face Amber. "What are you talking about?"

"It's her—Diedre," Amber said, her words coming in staccato bursts. "He knows she's here, knows she's found me. He probably had her followed. The man who set the fire—the one who attacked me in the hospital. He hired him, don't you see? He's got too much to lose. But now she's found me. And if I tell her the truth—"

"If you don't get back in there, you won't be telling her anything," TwoJoe said, coming in on the tail end of the conversation. "She thinks she's upset you, and she's going home."

Amber whirled on him. "Maybe I should let her go. Maybe it's for the best."

Susan frowned and shook her head. "Amber, think. You've come so far, and you've waited so long—"

"Don't you understand? I have to protect her! I have to—" Her breath came in gasps, and she couldn't continue.

Susan drew Amber into one of the chairs at the kitchen table, caught her gaze, and held it. "Amber, what are you feeling—*right now?*"

The question took Amber off guard, but she didn't have to delve very deep to know the answer. "Fear," she responded truthfully. "But it's not irrational fear, Susan. I know what he could do to her."

"What did you tell me the other day in the hospital?" Susan asked quietly. "About giving in?"

A wrench in her gut told Amber that Susan had struck a nerve. "I told you that I had given in not to fear, but to love." She closed her eyes and winced against the pain. "That no fear is worth the loss of my soul. And that silence doesn't protect anyone but the perpetrator."

"Does somebody want to tell me what's going on?" TwoJoe interrupted.

Amber looked up at him and felt an amazing rush of love and strength. The terror was still there—fear of Diedre's reaction, fear of what might happen if she told the truth, fear that TwoJoe might not love her enough after all. But for the first time in her life, the love was stronger.

She stood up and, summoning all her courage, laid a hand gently on his cheek. "Yes," she said softly. "I do want to tell you. I want to tell all of you."

Diedre and Carlene were just about to slip out the front door when Amber returned to the living room.

"Please," she said, "sit down. I'm sorry I ran out on you like that." She slanted a glance at Susan, who smiled encouragingly. "It's not the first time, but I hope it will be the last."

She perched on the edge of a high-backed chair and waited while everyone settled. Diedre, Carlene, and Sugarbear took the couch; Susan and Meg claimed the two chairs next to the fireplace; and TwoJoe sat on the floor facing her.

Her pulse was pounding like a sledgehammer, but Amber tried her best to ignore it. "There are some things that I—well, that I've been afraid to say for a very long time. But you all deserve the truth. Especially you, Diedre." She gazed at Diedre, who stared back with a pensive expression on her face. A few unshed tears glistened on the girl's lashes.

"If you don't mind, I'd like to tell this from start to finish. It may hurt, but it's important that we all get the whole truth. Is that all right?"

"The truth can't possibly hurt more than the lies Daddy told me," Diedre murmured. "I want to know everything."

"You may not feel that way when you've heard it," she said, "but I'll have to take that chance. You know that for a long time I was in a hospital—a mental institution. I was there for five years."

Diedre nodded. "Because you tried to kidnap me. That's what Daddy said."

"That's true. I did try to take you away with me, but it wasn't because I was crazy or unbalanced. But that was why he had me committed, and then when I was finally released from the hospital, I came out here, at Meg's invitation. I was running from a lot of things—not the least of which was my own fear. But of course it didn't work." She lifted an eyebrow in Susan's direction. "Everything I was running from followed me."

"Except me," Diedre put in.

A stab of pain pierced Amber's heart. "I was never running from you," she said. "I loved you. I've always loved you. I just—well, I didn't know *how* to love you." She shifted her gaze to TwoJoe. "I didn't know how to love anybody."

She caught a glimpse of a smile passing between Meg and Susan.

"The night of the fire, we had been celebrating my commission of the new sculpture, and I couldn't sleep. I was out on the deck, and something happened. It's hard to explain, but for the first time in my life, I knew that some power greater than myself was at work in my life. Prayers had been answered. Miracles had happened—or at least I perceived them as miracles. The family I had left behind so long ago had been restored in all of you—" she waved a hand toward Meg and Susan and TwoJoe, "and in the Colonel and Sam and Emmaline."

Amber took a deep breath and looked around. Everybody was listening, waiting for her to continue. "I gave in that night—as I told Susan, not to fear, but to love. I gave in to God. I surrendered. And somehow I knew that no matter what happened, I would be strong enough to handle it, as long as God's presence was with me."

"But then everything fell apart," TwoJoe interjected. "The fire, your injuries. It didn't look much like God was with us then."

"No, it didn't. But I believe now that it was all part of the process—for me, at least. The fire wasn't a random act, TwoJoe. It wasn't set to drive you to sell the farm so that some real estate tycoon could get his hands on this land. I was the target."

An expression of anger and loathing filled TwoJoe's eyes. "You think the guy was after you? But why?"

"Because I know something that could destroy some very influential people." She turned in Diedre's direction. "I'm not sure I can prove it, but I'm certain that the man who set that fire—the same one who came after me in the hospital and warned me to keep quiet—was hired by Uncle Jack."

All the color drained out of Diedre's face. "I don't understand."

"I know you don't, honey. But bear with me—you will. Years ago, back in North Carolina—" A lump rose to her throat and she couldn't go on.

"You can do this," Susan whispered. "You can."

"I know I can. I have to." Resolutely, Amber squared her shoulders and took a deep breath. "From the time I was eleven or so until the time I left home at fifteen, I was sexually abused, Diedre. Daddy and Uncle Jack had it all hushed up, because if anybody had known, it could have destroyed both their careers."

Amber had avoided looking in TwoJoe's direction while she spoke the words, but now she couldn't help herself. Her eyes went to his face as if drawn by a magnetic force. "I was afraid to tell you, TwoJoe. I didn't even tell Meg. I think, deep down, I knew all along that I loved you, but I was pretty fragile emotionally, and if you hadn't been able to handle this, it might have been the last straw." She broke his gaze and looked away. "Besides, I had to come to grips with it myself before I could deal with your reaction."

His hands were shaking, and his face contorted in a mask of fury. For a minute Amber thought his anger might be directed at her, and her heart quailed. Then he growled, "I'll kill him, I swear. I'll—"

Before TwoJoe could finish, Diedre interrupted. "*Uncle Jack?* How could he do such a thing?"

Amber held a hand up for silence and looked frantically toward Susan for help.

"Let her finish, please," Susan interjected.

When the room had quieted again, Amber turned back toward Diedre. "It wasn't Jack," she said.

Diedre blinked. "What did you say?"

"I said, it wasn't Jack."

A silence filled the room, so profound that it seemed as if no one was breathing.

"It wasn't Jack," she repeated. "It was Daddy."

At first Diedre was certain she had heard wrong. *Daddy?* It couldn't be. Daddy loved her sister, doted on her. It was all there, in the picture.

Then Amber was speaking again. "When Jack found out about it, he should have turned Daddy in. But he didn't. He had too much invested in Daddy's career. I suspect, too, that there were too many secrets between the two of them—unethical business deals, bribes, things like that. Jack had to protect his own interests, and that meant protecting Daddy. They had to get rid of me, and aside from killing me, the only way to keep me quiet was to have me committed."

Diedre stared at her sister. This was all too incredible. But in an odd way, it made sense. No wonder Mama and Uncle Jack found each other—

"My guess is, Mama didn't know about it, or had her suspicions but couldn't confirm them," Amber went on. "And I expect that part of the deal was the agreement that Daddy would keep his distance from you, Diedre."

Yes, Diedre thought. *Daddy kept his distance, all right.* But there were other reasons for that . . .

"Then when Mama let you know I was still alive and you came looking for me, Daddy and Uncle Jack knew they could lose everything. I had kept silent for years, but they couldn't be sure that once I saw you again, I wouldn't tell you the truth." She smiled grimly. "And they were right."

"So you think your Uncle Jack sent someone out here to follow Diedre and Carlene and keep them from finding you?" TwoJoe asked.

"Yes, and failing that, to do something—whatever was necessary—to ensure that I disappeared again. And it almost worked. When he came to the hospital, he threatened to hurt you or Meg next time. I was almost convinced that my only option was to run."

"There's one thing I don't understand," TwoJoe said. "It's been years since this happened. Why would your father still be afraid of the repercussions? Wouldn't the statute of limitations keep him from being prosecuted by now?"

Amber shrugged. "Probably. I don't know what the statute is on child rape."

The word *rape* sliced over Diedre's nerves like a razor.

"But it wouldn't matter," Amber continued. "If the slightest hint of an accusation got out about what he did, his reputation would be ruined whether he was prosecuted or not. His career would be history—and for Daddy, that was too big a risk. He had too much to lose."

Diedre had kept quiet for just about as long as she could stand. "I thought he loved you so much!" she raged. "I was even jealous of the way he loved you!" A sudden thought struck her, and she went silent. "That's why you did it," she whispered. "That's why you tried to kidnap me. You were trying to protect me . . . from *him*." The reality washed over her like cold water, and she shivered.

"Yes," Amber said softly. "At least partly."

❧

Amber watched as a caravan of emotions paraded across Diedre's face—horror and disbelief, fear and despair, confusion, and at last, comprehension tinged with utter rage. Her soul swelled with pride and admiration. She marveled at the courage the girl demonstrated—certainly more strength than she had possessed at that age.

Part of her still wished to spare Diedre from this pain. But Diedre was no longer a child depending upon Amber not to let her fall. She was a grown woman, capable of handling whatever curves life threw at her. And Amber was learning the hard way that true freedom only comes by speaking the truth.

She had been silent long enough.

Amber glanced over toward Susan, who sat in front of the fireplace with her hands in her lap. She could read the look of affirmation and confidence in Susan's eyes, almost feel the urging in her soul. *Keep going*, the expression said. *You're almost done.*

"Diedre," Amber said, "may I see that birth certificate?"

Diedre handed it over. "You can have it. It just reminds me of what Daddy did—of all his deception—and Uncle Jack's. I don't suppose Uncle Jack's any better, if he helped Daddy cover all this up and send you away, but anyone who would do such a thing to a little girl is not a man—he's a monster! I'm *glad* Duncan McAlister is not my father!"

Amber heaved a deep sigh. "Unfortunately, he *is* your father."

❧

Diedre's heart sank like lead.

"He can't be! This is my real birth certificate. The one I had early on—the one that has both his and Mama's names on it—*that* was the fake!"

"Yes, the one you have is the real one—although it doesn't have all the pertinent information on it."

Diedre furrowed her brow into a frown and held out her hand for the document. "It says *Mother: Cecilia McAlister. Father: Unknown.*"

"Yes, so it does."

"So that means that Mama had an affair with Uncle Jack, and—"

Amber shook her head. "Diedre, what was Mama's name?"

"Cecilia McAlister," Diedre answered.

"Cecilia Marie Chaney McAlister," Amber corrected. "How does the birth certificate read?"

"Cecilia . . ." Diedre squinted at the paper. "Cecilia A. McAlister."

"And what did you call me when you were little?"

"Sissy. I always called you Sissy. So did Mama and Daddy."

"No, they didn't. They called me CeCe."

Sissy. CeCe. As a little child it would be easy enough for her to get it wrong, to distort the name into something she recognized more readily. But what did it mean?

Then she looked again. *Mother: Cecilia A. McAlister.* When the truth descended upon Diedre, it came not as light, but as a blinding darkness, a shadow on the sun, a sudden, terrifying eclipse at midday.

Her sister's middle name was Amber.

"That's why you were so intent on protecting me?" Diedre whispered.

Amber nodded.

"And that's why he was so determined to keep you from talking?"

"Yes."

Diedre's eyes swam. "Because—because—"

"Because Duncan McAlister is your father," Amber whispered. "And I am your mother."

Part 4

New Beginnings

Every end brings new beginnings,
every path leads forward,
every dangerous crook in the road
hides glorious surprises.
Around the bend, beyond what we can see,
destiny lures us onward,
into cool shadows
and blinding lights
and lives we never dreamed of.

35

The Sacrifice

TwoJoe turned up his collar against the misty night rain and kept on walking. He was getting soaked but couldn't seem to convince himself to bother about it. Twice he swiveled on his heel in the wet grass and looked back toward the house. All the lights were out, except for one dim lamp burning in the window of an upstairs bedroom.

Amber's room.

It was nearly 2 A.M., and TwoJoe didn't have a hope of sleeping tonight. A little after midnight, Susan had left, and Carlene had taken Sugarbear and walked back to the Houstons' guesthouse alone. Diedre was up there with Amber; they would probably keep on talking until daybreak.

The revelation that Amber was Diedre's mother had imploded in TwoJoe's soul like a ton of well-placed dynamite. Now everything was crashing inward, collapsing, and he had no idea what to do about it—or why he even felt the way he did.

He should have known—from the minute he laid eyes on Diedre, he should have guessed. Now his mind lurched backward, searching desperately for the clues that ought to have led him to the truth long before this night. Yet the only image his mind could conjure up was the vision of that young girl, so vulnerable, so innocent, being abused and violated by a man who should have been protecting her.

The image tortured him, but he couldn't rid himself of it. He slammed his fist into the trunk of an enormous fir tree and heard the knuckles crunch, felt the blood seeping to the surface. But there was no pain. Only blind rage and bitter disappointment.

TwoJoe could imagine himself standing in front of that smug, perverted maniac and pinning him up against the wall, gripping him by the throat. But there would be no mercy for one who had shown no mercy. Not even from TwoJoe Elkhorn, who had never committed a violent act in his entire life.

Maybe he should ask forgiveness for even entertaining such a thought, but TwoJoe searched his heart and couldn't find a shred of remorse hiding anywhere. Oh, yes, he could do it. He could kill Amber's father. He could throttle Duncan McAlister with his bare hands until the man's eyes bulged and his windpipe crushed under the pressure. And he wouldn't be sorry.

The mindless fury he understood. What he couldn't fathom was the disappointment that lay like a gray cloud at the bottom of his soul. He should be happy for Amber, reuniting with Diedre. He should be able to rejoice with them. Instead, he felt as if all his hopes for a life with Amber—hopes that in the past few days had taken on a new and vibrant life—had been dashed once again. Someone else had usurped his place in her heart. Amber Chaney had a daughter.

And he was . . . *jealous.*

Impossible, TwoJoe thought. How could he conceivably be jealous of Diedre? And yet he knew it was true; the green-eyed monster was gnawing a hole in his gut, and he couldn't do anything to stop it. He wanted Amber to himself, wanted to be first in her life. Diedre was a distraction that lured her attention away from him.

It was a reprehensible thought, and Joe cursed himself for it. How could he be so selfish?

He walked on a ways until he stood on the high bank that overlooked Hood Canal. A pale, diluted moon shone through the mist, and scattered lights glimmered on the Toandos Peninsula, just the other side of the canal. Beyond them, the Olympic Mountains rose like protective sentinels, dark battlements against a barely lighter sky.

Even at night, even in the rain, this was the most beautiful place TwoJoe had ever known. He wanted to stay here forever, to live out his days in the majestic view of these mountains, to gather clams and oysters on his own beach, to watch the hawks and eagles fishing in these waters. He wanted to be buried here, when his time came, alongside his ancestors.

But he also wanted Amber Chaney at his side.

And what if he couldn't have both? What if Amber decided to return with Diedre to North Carolina, to face her father and force his hand? A few weeks ago TwoJoe couldn't have imagined such a turn of events, but then he couldn't imagine, either, that Amber might have a daughter. Or that she would have the kind of faith and courage she had demonstrated tonight, when she told the truth about herself and her past.

He knew the answer, even as his mind grappled with the question. If he couldn't have both, he would choose . . . the woman he loved.

Casting one final, longing glance over the canal, TwoJoe turned and started back toward the house. With any luck, she would still be awake. Maybe he could talk to her now, before he lost his nerve.

With every step, his will grew stronger, his heart more certain. As a single man responsible solely for himself, he would never voluntarily *choose* to leave the farm. But he was no longer alone, and whatever was good for Amber would be good for him, too. If she needed to go back to North Carolina to be near Diedre, he would do it, no questions asked. It would be all right. They could make it work, as long as they had each other . . .

As he drew even with the barn, TwoJoe could see in the distance through the trees that the light still burned in her window. She was still awake. He could go to her now, profess his love for her. He could ask her to marry him, extract a promise from her, make sure—

He stopped and collapsed against a tree trunk, breathing hard. No. He couldn't.

He couldn't ask her. Not now. Not under these circumstances. Amber had endured too many changes, too many emotional conflicts lately. Asking her for that kind of commitment now would simply put more stress on her, more pressure. And as much as he wanted to hear her say yes, to solidify things, to secure their future, it was selfish of him to obligate her to such a pledge. He needed to give her room to breathe, to find her own way. In her own time.

Longingly, he gazed at the distant square of light, a beacon in his darkness. God willing, his time with Amber would come. But for now, again, he would wait and—

A brief shimmer at the corner of his eye distracted him, and he turned. The barn door stood open a foot or two. Again he saw a narrow beam flicker across the opening and disappear. His heart constricted, and his breath caught in his throat.

A flashlight.

Someone was in the barn.

Shiv Willis had stumbled through the rain-soaked woods for fifteen minutes before he finally came to the Elkhorns' barn and let himself in. The odor of wet charcoal hung heavily in the air.

Water dripped on his head from the hole in the roof, although it didn't matter much since he was already wet all the way down to his boxers. He slicked his hair back from his forehead and focused the long, heavy flashlight on his wrist watch. It was nearly three.

Starting at the door, he began a systematic search of the barn. It was nasty work; black residue from the burned debris mixed with the rain to create a kind of sticky paste, and it was hard to see anything. There was probably a rake in here somewhere, but he couldn't take the risk of making too much noise. He'd just have to comb through the mess with his hands.

Down on all fours, he filtered through the rubble, backing across the floor from one corner to the other on his hands and knees like a crab. His back ached, and he cursed under his breath.

Surely if the cops had found it, he would have heard about it on the news. The last report he heard, they were giving up, assuming he had left the state. That's probably what he should have done, now that he thought about it. But he couldn't just walk away and leave his lighter here for somebody else to find. The trail might be cold now, but it would heat up pretty fast if the wrong people got their hands on that lighter.

Shiv slid on his knees toward the big desk where the woman had worked; it was charred black, but still standing. He leaned down, groping on the floor. Then, as he pushed back a pile of burned rubbish, his flashlight passed over something silvery.

"Gotcha!" He chuckled under his breath as his fist closed around it. He lifted his prize to the light and grinned. Now he could get out of here, and no one would ever be the wiser.

"Find what you're looking for?"

Shiv's throat went dry, and he raised his head so fast that he cracked it on the underside of the desk. Slowly he turned and focused the beam of his flashlight upward. Elkhorn stood there towering over him, holding a pitchfork in one hand.

"Oh, I—no, I—" Shiv stammered.

The smile faded, and Elkhorn motioned with his head. "Get up."

Shiv obeyed, scrambling to his feet. "This isn't what it looks like," he lied frantically. "I was just—"

"Save it for the sheriff," Elkhorn snapped, pointing the pitchfork directly at Shiv's chest. "I'm sure he'll be very interested in whatever story you have to tell."

An icy finger of panic ran up Shiv's spine, and he looked around desperately for a way of escape. But the only exit was behind Elkhorn.

"Hand over the flashlight," Elkhorn was saying, "then turn around and put your hands flat on the desk."

Shiv paused. He only had one chance at this, and he didn't want to screw it up. He smiled. "All right. Take it easy, now—" He extended the flashlight in Elkhorn's direction, then quick as a snake, heaved it with all his might at the man's head and ran for the door.

Instinctively, TwoJoe ducked, and the flashlight, still sending out a focused beam, grazed his shoulder and bounced a few feet away. Shivers was making a run for it, but he wasn't about to get away a second time, not if TwoJoe had anything to say about it.

TwoJoe had two things going for him: anger, which flooded him with adrenaline and made him both quick and strong, and an intimate knowledge of the barn. He dashed after the intruder.

Shivers was heading for the door, but in the darkness he couldn't see the collapsed rafter and other debris that had fallen when part of the roof had caved in. TwoJoe heard the footsteps, the trip, the heavy thud as Shivers went down. The man let out a roar of pain.

TwoJoe scooped up the flashlight and followed the sound. The focused, watery beam revealed a filthy, soot-covered Shivers lying on his back on a pile of rubble, one ankle twisted at an unnatural angle.

TwoJoe looked at him, lying there in a heap, and the fury he had felt earlier came rushing back. His face went hot, and he felt his jaw clench. This man—this pathetic excuse for a human being—represented everything horrible that had been done to Amber. The fire, the injuries, the threats . . .

Even, indirectly, the sexual assaults.

An image swam to the surface of his consciousness—Amber as a little child, lying rigid and terrified in the darkness, crying out for help, begging her assailant to stop. TwoJoe's fingers closed around the handle of the pitchfork in a death grip, and all his rage at what had been done to her focused into one white-hot flame, directed at the man who lay on the ground in front of him. He could say that Shivers had attacked him, that it was self-defense. No one would ever know the difference, and probably wouldn't care much, anyway. This hired thug, this animal, deserved to die like the rabid dog he was. TwoJoe raised the pitchfork and, holding it aloft like a spear, aimed it directly at Shivers's throat. It was a simple matter of—of justice . . .

Do justice . . . love mercy . . . walk humbly with your God . . .

The words formed unbidden in TwoJoe's mind. He clenched his teeth and felt a muscle in his jaw twitch. Yes, justice. That's what this was about.

Again he took aim.

I desire mercy, and not sacrifice . . .

He gripped the pitchfork harder. But what about Amber's sacrifice? Where was the mercy when she was being abused? His eyes watered, and he expelled a pent-up breath. He had been so certain that he was capable of murdering Duncan McAlister and everyone else responsible for causing her pain. Now he had his chance, and he couldn't make himself do it.

All the adrenaline drained out of him, and TwoJoe's arm began to shake. A rancid bitterness filled his mouth, and for a minute he thought he was going to be sick. If this was the taste of revenge, it wasn't sweet at all.

He let the pitchfork drop, and it fell with a clatter against the barn floor.

36

Out of the Depths

When Diedre followed Amber upstairs to the rustic bedroom, she felt as if she were entering a sanctuary, a holy place. Her sister's room. Her *mother's* room.

It was a simple space, its outer walls made from the huge logs that formed the shell of the house. An enameled iron bed in verdigris. A hand-quilted comforter of purple and green and blue pinwheels. A small stained-glass lamp burning on a table beside the bed. On one wall, a framed print of Van Gogh's *Starry Night*. And overlooking the canal and the mountains, a wide window seat with a cushion and pillows that matched the quilt.

Amber excused herself to go to the bathroom, and while she was gone Diedre began to make a circuit of the room, touching her mother's few possessions as if they might impart some supernatural wisdom to help her deal with what she had learned tonight. She trailed her fingers over the stitching in the quilt, rested her hand on a pillow, fingered the iron bedstead with its small grape-leaf design. Then she came to the dresser, and stopped.

The wide, old bureau was crafted of oak, with curved legs and a beveled, shield-shaped mirror. But unlike most dressers, which usually collected odd bits of their owners' lives—spare change, car keys, notes or receipts emptied from a pocket or purse—Amber's was neat and tidy, bearing only a single photograph and a vase of flowers.

The stoneware vase Diedre recognized as one of Amber's own creations—she had seen one almost exactly like it in Andrew Jorgensen's shop. A graceful, fluted design narrowing upward from a wide base, with a glaze of purples and blues and just a touch of green. Peaceful colors that echoed the hues of the deep blue-purple irises the vase contained.

But it was the photograph that caught Diedre's attention and held it. A black-and-white photo, softened to brown tones with age, captured in a simple frame. A young girl, perhaps four or five, being spun around by an older teenager.

Diedre's breath caught in her throat, and she picked up the photo and held it to the dim light. Tears pricked the corners of her eyes. With one finger she traced the flowing lines of the older girl's dark, windblown hair.

"Mama took that picture."

Startled, Diedre whirled around. "I—I wasn't snooping."

Amber smiled. "I didn't think that." She had changed into soft flannel pajamas, and she came over and put an arm around Diedre's shoulders. "My hair was longer then."

"This was—this was—"

"Just before I was sent away?" Amber nodded. "She sent it to me when I was at the hospital. Whenever I got to believing that life was just too hard, I'd get it out and look at it. It reminded me that I had something to live for."

"And Mama never knew about the—" She hesitated. "What Daddy did to you?"

Amber bit her lip and looked away. "No. She thought I'd been with some teenage boy. She was devastated."

"Why didn't you tell her?" Amber recoiled visibly from the outburst, and Diedre instantly regretted her accusatory tone. She lowered her voice. "Why didn't you tell *someone?*"

"I was fifteen when you were born. The abuse had been going on since I was eleven or twelve. Every time it happened, Daddy would threaten me if I told. I believed him. I knew what he was capable of." She held up her bandaged hands. "What he's still capable of."

She turned back the quilt and lay down across the bed, flinging one arm over her eyes. "Do you mind if I rest for a while?"

A little shock of self-reproach stung at Diedre's mind. Amber had been released from the hospital less than twelve hours ago. "I should go."

"Please, stay. I just need a little nap, and I want you here."

"All right." She replaced the photograph on the dresser and gently covered Amber's shoulders with the quilt.

"That picture is a copy—I had it enlarged," Amber mumbled. "If you'd like, I'll give you the original."

"Yes, I'd love to have it," Diedre began. But Amber had already drifted off to sleep.

She went to the dresser and picked up the photo again.

Amazing, how a simple snapshot could be such a perfectly composed work of art. The lighting, the shadows, the fluid sense of motion. Maybe that's where she got her own gift—from her mother.

Diedre felt a jolt in her stomach. No. Not her mother . . . her *grandmother.*

Her hands shaking, she replaced the photograph on the dresser and stood staring into the mirror. Behind her she could see the reflected image of the window seat, and beyond that, the glittering waters of the canal and the mountains that rose above. The rain had stopped, and a weak, yellow moon hung over the jagged peaks and illuminated the snow that still clung to the highest ridges.

It was a beautiful scene, almost like a painting. But it was only a reflection. She was looking in the wrong direction to see the real thing.

Just as all her life she had been looking in the wrong direction. It had all been a sham, a carefully constructed lie, nothing but smoke and mirrors. And now she had fallen through the mirror to the other side.

⁓

From the window seat, Diedre stared vacantly out over the mountains. Two hours had passed, and the setting moon now balanced at the top of one of the Olympic peaks, as if preparing for the long slide down the slope. Behind her, she could hear shallow breathing.

She turned and looked at Amber's face, relaxed in sleep and illuminated by the soft lamp that still burned at the bedside. The light accentuated the curve of cheek and brow. A perfect portrait. Her sister. Her mother.

Diedre was exhausted, too, but the revelations of this night still swirled in her head, murky as an ocean wave stirred by an invisible undertow. The questions that had brought her here had all been answered, but the answers simply raised other dilemmas, deeper ones. It would have been challenging enough to begin a new relationship with a sister she had never really known. But a *mother?* How was she supposed to relate to a mother who was only fifteen years older than Diedre herself? How could she let go of the memory of Mama, who had raised her and loved her all her life, and transfer that unique devotion to a stranger?

And how could she ever think about herself in the same way again?

Even given the idea that Mama had been unfaithful to Daddy and borne a child out of that passion, Diedre could still regard herself as the product of tenderness and desire. Now she had to face the horrible truth that her conception was the result not of love but of *rape*—perhaps the ugliest, vilest, most brutal four-letter word in the English language.

A tremor went through her. She tried to push the terrifying image out of her mind, but it wouldn't leave. Her eyes swam, and she groped for the cigar box, which lay next to her on the window seat. Rummaging inside, she finally came up with the photograph of Daddy and the child Amber.

She couldn't see it clearly in the dim light, but the image was so impressed upon her brain that it re-created itself in her mind: the huge, overstuffed armchair, the little girl on the man's lap, the man's arms wrapped around her, the smile, the look of adoration on his face—

God, she groaned inwardly, *dear God, no.* From the depths of Diedre's soul the plea came—a wordless, agonized cry for help, for understanding. Her whole body shook, and a wave of nausea swept over her, leaving her breathless and clammy. She wanted to run away, to scream, to throw things, to beat on something—or someone. "No!" she whispered—this time aloud. "No, no! God, no!"

Her hands clenched into fists, and she began pummeling the pillow in the window seat. With every blow, her emotions grew wilder and fiercer, until she had fallen to her knees on the floor, bashing the stuffing out of the pillow, screaming, "I hate you! I HATE you, Daddy! I HATE YOU!"

When she paused for breath, Diedre felt a weight leaning against her back and arms embracing her. Tears fell on her shoulder, and Amber's voice whispered in her ear, "It's all right, honey. I've got you. I'm here. Get it out. Get it all out."

As the rage subsided, Diedre turned and collapsed into Amber's arms, sobbing. For a long time the two of them sat there on the floor, propped against the window seat, while Diedre wept. Then, finally, when she could catch her breath enough to speak, she wiped her eyes with the back of her hand and looked at Amber. "I'm sorry. I wanted you to sleep. You need to rest."

"I had a nap. I'm fine. Talk to me. Tell me what's going on, what you're feeling."

"I don't *know* what I'm feeling," Diedre murmured. "Except that I hate him. I'm so ANGRY at what he did to you. And . . ." She paused.

"And what?"

"I don't know how you stand it. How do you deal with it, every single day?"

Amber touched Diedre's cheek. The bandages, rough against her skin, reminded Diedre once again of all that her sister . . . her mother . . . had been through in the past few weeks.

"I've had twenty-five years of experience dealing with it," Amber said quietly. "I've been in therapy. I've learned—well, I'm still learning—to redirect my anger. I've learned containment when the memories threaten to derail me. It takes time. It's taken me years—and I'm just now beginning to feel whole again."

"I hate him," Diedre repeated. "I hate him for what he did to you. And I hate myself, too."

"I understand why you'd hate *him*," Amber whispered. "But why on earth would you hate *yourself?*"

Diedre touched one of Amber's bandaged hands very gently. "Because all this is my fault."

Amber gazed at her intently. "Diedre, you had no way of knowing that he would have you followed when you came out here to find me. You did what you needed to do, to get your questions answered and—"

She stopped short as Diedre shook her head. "That's not what I mean." Diedre took in a breath and let it out again, summoning her courage and putting her thoughts in order. "If it hadn't been for me, you would never have been sent to the mental hospital. You wouldn't have had to endure this for all these years. From now on, every time I look in the mirror, I'll see *him*. What he did to you. What you had to go through on account of me. It's as if I'm covered with filth that can never be washed away. And I know that's what you'll see, too, whenever you look at me. You'll see it. And you'll hate me."

Amber closed her eyes and battled for breath as a fist closed around her heart. "Hate you? I could never hate you, Diedre. I love you!"

"But how could you? How can you even be in the same room with me without being reminded of—of *him?* Of the horrible things he did to you? Of all the pain, the fear, the isolation, the loneliness. I'm the walking, flesh-and-blood image of that abuse, the—"

"No, Diedre, you're not," Amber interrupted. "I knew it the moment I saw you, just after you were born, when I held you for the first time. I knew it years ago, when I came back and tried to take you away with me. And again tonight. Don't you see? *You are the blessing brought out of the curse.*"

Diedre stared at her, slack-jawed. "No, I don't see."

Amber smiled. "It's taken me a long time to understand it, too. It's a concept Susan likes to talk about—a verse in Deuteronomy, I think. Something like, 'God turned the curse into a blessing for you, because the Lord your God loved you.'"

She paused for a minute, amazed that she could even think such a thing. How had she come to the place of being able to find something positive in the midst of life's challenges and heartbreaks? But Amber knew the answer. She had changed—or rather, she had *been* changed. She had found something in the life of faith—a blessing—that was innately true.

Diedre frowned and let out a grunt of disapproval. "How can you talk about God, Amber? Where was God when all this happened—when you were being raped, when I was being conceived, when you were being committed to a mental hospital?"

It was a question Amber had been mulling over for weeks, and still she hadn't come to any satisfying conclusions. She thought for a minute, and then admitted, "I don't know, Diedre. This is one of those spiritual dilemmas that has a lot of bad answers but not very many good ones."

"What do you mean, bad answers?"

Amber let out a sigh. "Listen, Diedre, I'm pretty new at this faith stuff, but I know when what I hear doesn't make sense. I've heard some people talk as if everything that happens is God's will—as if it was God's will for Daddy to molest me. In my book that's a bad answer. Other people say that God doesn't *will* bad things, but still *allows* them, so that we can learn some kind of lesson from them. I can't buy that, either." She watched Diedre's face closely. "I guess my beliefs about God are fairly practical—I can't imagine a loving God who would use sexual abuse to generate trust in a twelve-year-old. That kind of logic just has too many holes."

Diedre leaned against the window seat and swiped a hand across her tear-stained face. "I couldn't accept that either. But I don't see how you can accept *any* notion of a loving God, given what you've been through."

Amber nodded. "It's amazing, I'll have to admit. Until recently, I hadn't given God more than a passing thought—and a pretty negative thought, at that—for more than twenty years. But then I looked around—at TwoJoe and at Meg and at Father Susan. I started trusting in their love for me and their acceptance of me. That's where my faith comes from— seeing God in them. And that faith is starting to take hold not *because* of what happened, but *in spite of* it."

Diedre's eyes held a shadowed, suspicious look. "I always thought I believed in God. Now I think I've lost my faith completely."

"It'll come back," Amber murmured. "Grace is pretty irresistible, once you've had a taste of it. A very wise person once said that faith can't be lost—it's just buried. And buried seeds will sprout again in their time."

"I'm not going to hold my breath," Diedre said curtly. "But go on. You've told me about the bad answers to why things like this happen. Are there any *good* answers?"

"Sometimes I don't think there are any answers at all," Amber replied. "Your conclusions will probably be different, and that's OK. I think that God doesn't cause terrible things to happen, but when they do, God can turn them around. Like the 'curse into a blessing' concept." She looked intently into Diedre's eyes. "Evil exists, honey, and bad things happen. Terrible things, sometimes. But something good did come out of this horrible mess, Diedre. You. You are the blessing in all of this."

When Amber had started into this discussion, she had felt as if she had been set down in a high hedge maze, groping this way and that for an exit. Suddenly, miraculously, she came to the end. The truths hadn't originated with her, but they had become hers. And she knew in the deepest places of her soul that what she had told Diedre was right. The young woman who sat before her now was, indeed, the blessing that had come out of the curse. Her sister . . . her daughter . . . her friend.

❧

Diedre tried to assimilate what Amber had said, to believe it, to hold onto it the way a drowning person grabs onto anything that floats. And yet something in her heart told her that it would be a very long time before her own resolution came. The best she could do right now was try to see herself through Amber's eyes.

"Give yourself time to learn how to deal with this," Amber was saying. "It's not easy, although it does get better. I suppose the question now is, what do you need? What can we do to help get you on the road to healing?"

Diedre didn't have to think twice to come up with an answer. "Confront him. Make him pay. If possible, get his can thrown in jail."

Amber threw back her head and laughed. "Where on earth did you get so much fortitude, girl?"

"I don't know," Diedre said slowly, gazing into Amber's eyes. "Maybe I really am my mother's daughter."

❧

Amber was still sitting on the floor beside Diedre when a faint knock sounded on the door.

"Come in."

The door opened a crack, and TwoJoe's head appeared around the doorpost. "I didn't want to wake you two if you were sleeping, but since you're up, would you mind coming downstairs?" He waited while they got to their feet.

"What time is it?"

TwoJoe looked at his watch. "Quarter to five. Jake Nordstrom's here, and Meg is making coffee."

"The sheriff? What does he want?"

TwoJoe shrugged and gave a sheepish grin. "I suppose he wants to take our prisoner into custody."

"Prisoner? The guy who attacked me and burned the barn? You caught him?"

"I did. But he's got a few things to say before Jake hauls him away, and I expect both of you are going to want to hear it."

The two of them—Amber in flannel pajamas, and Diedre still dressed in her jeans from the night before—followed TwoJoe down the stairs into the living room, where Meg held out a mug of coffee in Amber's direction and handed a second one to Diedre. Sheriff Nordstrom stood with his back to the fireplace, dangling his handcuffs from one meaty finger. Vernon Houston, his hair a wild mane of white, slouched against the living room wall.

In front of Vern, on the sofa, sat a wet, bedraggled man in a dark green jacket, his hands bound with silver duct tape and his right leg splinted with a couple of mismatched boards and more of the silver tape. A livid, crescent-shaped cut above his right eye stood out against his pale skin. Amber immediately recognized her attacker.

Diedre let out a gasp when she saw him. "Carlene was right—you *were* following us!"

Amber turned to TwoJoe. "He's hurt—shouldn't we call an ambulance?"

"His ankle's broken," the sheriff said. "The EMTs are on their way. We'll make a stop at the hospital to get it set, and then he'll get booked and spend the night in jail." Nordstrom cut his eyes at the interloper. "You ready to talk now?"

The man nodded.

"His name is Shiv Willis," TwoJoe told Amber. "Jake's got the warrant for his arrest, and he's been read his rights. Meg and I both witnessed it. He's decided to come clean."

"Decided to roll, is more like it," the sheriff growled. "You've been down this road a few times before, haven't you, Willis?" When the man did not reply, the sheriff turned toward Amber. "I checked him out. Rap sheet as long as your arm. He'll cut a deal with the D.A. for a reduced sentence, and most likely be extradited back to North Carolina." He turned a cold eye back on Willis. "All right, we're listening. What you got to say for yourself?"

Shiv Willis fixed his gaze on Amber's hands. "I started the fire in the barn. I'm sorry about that . . . and hitting you with the gas can . . . and coming to the hospital and . . . everything." He shook his head. "It was a job—just a job. But I didn't mean for anybody to get hurt. I don't—well, I don't hold with going after women. It's against my principles."

"Yeah, we know, you're a regular boy scout," the Colonel interrupted. "Get on with it."

"I was hired by a lawyer named Underwood—," Willis began.

"Uncle Jack," Diedre muttered.

"Yeah, that's right. Jack Underwood. He sent me out here to follow you and your girlfriend—" he looked at Diedre, "and to make sure you didn't hook up with *her*—" He motioned with his head in Amber's direction. "I didn't know why—in my business, we don't ask too many questions. Underwood just told me to do whatever was necessary to keep the lid on, that his client's daughter—the older one—had information that could cause problems for everybody."

"And the client was—?" Houston prompted.

Shiv Willis quailed visibly at the Colonel's daunting presence. "Guy by the name of McAlister. I don't think Underwood intended for me to know that, but he let it slip once. I got the impression McAlister was some bigwig politician or something—somebody important."

"And the two of them hired you to make sure Amber kept her mouth shut?" Colonel Houston asked.

"That's right. Underwood put me onto the real estate angle. Thought if I made it impossible for Elkhorn to keep this place, the woman—

Amber—would have to disappear again." He licked his lips. "Can I have some water?"

"When you're done," the sheriff said.

"Okay, well, anyway—" Willis shifted, wincing as his injured leg took some of the weight. He sagged back against a towel someone had thrown over the back of the sofa to protect the fabric. "Anyway, I figured burning the barn down would be like an intimidation thing—that Elkhorn here would cave in, sell the place, and—" He shook his head. "Guess it didn't work."

"About as well as the scheme of that guy who ordered a pizza to his own address and then robbed the delivery boy." The Colonel gave a short bark of a laugh.

"It *would* have worked if I hadn't lost my lighter," Willis protested, swearing under his breath. "But I didn't know she—," he nodded in Amber's direction, "was going to be in the barn that night."

"But she *was* in the barn," Jake Nordstrom interjected. "That makes it a felony—attempted murder."

"I didn't attempt to murder anybody. Especially not a woman."

"But your employers did, didn't they?" The Colonel fixed his gaze on Amber. "Sounds like conspiracy to me. Attempted murder, arson—"

"Not to mention some other charges that are even worse," TwoJoe put in. When the Colonel raised his eyebrows, TwoJoe said, "We'll tell you about that later."

The sheriff went over to the sofa and ripped the duct tape off Willis's wrists, replacing it with the handcuffs. "I assume you're going to cooperate with the D.A. and testify real nice and neat, just like you've done here tonight."

Shiv Willis nodded. "Long as I get my deal."

"Don't worry. You'll get your reduced sentence as long as you deliver your bosses." He turned to TwoJoe and Amber. "You can press charges here on the arson and assault, but if you want to get the lawyer and the father—"

TwoJoe put his arm around Amber and looked into her eyes. She smiled grimly up at him, then caught Diedre's gaze and nodded. "We'll be making a call to North Carolina first thing."

A flashing red light flickered through the glass of the front door and streaked down the entryway into the living room. "That must be the paramedics," the sheriff said. He hoisted Shiv Willis up and, supporting him under one arm, ushered him out.

When they were gone, Amber let out a sigh and sank into the cushioned back of the big armchair. "I can't believe it."

"Can't believe I caught the guy, or can't believe he's going to talk?"

"Can't believe it's over."

TwoJoe laid a hand on her shoulder, and she rested her cheek against it. "It's not over yet," he said quietly. "It won't be over until we see that animal who calls himself your father behind bars." He sighed. "Justice may be a long time coming."

Amber closed her eyes. TwoJoe was right—they still had a difficult road ahead of them. But a heavy weight in her spirit had lifted, and for the first time in nearly thirty years, Amber Chaney felt almost free.

37

If It Takes Forever

On the deck overlooking Hood Canal, TwoJoe sat in the moonlight, holding Amber's bandaged hand gently in his own. It was a clear, cool evening; silence stretched between them as they gazed out over the mountains. He wished the burns were healed, wished he could stroke her skin and feel it soft and pliable beneath his fingertips. He wanted to hold her hand so tightly that she could never get away from him, never leave his side.

But she *was* leaving.

Tomorrow morning, she would put her suitcase in the trunk of her dead mother's car and head east with Diedre and Carlene. Back to North Carolina, to confront the man who had molested her.

TwoJoe wanted to go with her, to be there to support her, but Amber had refused his offer. "I have to do this myself," she had said. "It's important to my recovery—and to Diedre's."

After Shiv Willis had been taken into custody, she and TwoJoe had sat down and explained to Vernon Houston the parts of the story he had not yet heard. Once he got past his initial anger, the Colonel had shifted into his problem-solving mode: he had a friend in the D.A.'s office in North Carolina, he said, and she would take care of everything.

He had been right. The assistant district attorney, a bright young woman named Elise Glass, had taken Amber's statement over the phone and talked with the Kitsap County sheriff's office in order to arrange the extradition of Shiv Willis as a primary witness in the case. According to Glass, they would likely be able to build a strong case on three major charges: conspiracy to commit arson, attempted murder, and conspiracy to conceal a crime. The older charge, aggravated child molestation, was questionable because of the statute of limitations, but Glass said the judge had some leeway to determine how that statute was interpreted. If they could make an argument for the crime not being *known* until now, the limitation might be applied from the time of the knowledge of the crime, not the actual molestation. The tactic was iffy, Glass admitted, but at least it would get the accusation on the table and the truth would come out.

Amber had requested, much to TwoJoe's surprise, that they hold off on the actual arrests until she and Diedre could get back to North Carolina. "We want to be there," she told Glass firmly. "We want him to have to look us in the eye when he tries to deny what he's done."

And so, first thing tomorrow, Amber, Diedre, Carlene, and Sugarbear would begin the long drive home. "Diedre and I have a lot to talk about, a lot to work through," she said. "Right now, we just need time together."

TwoJoe understood. At least his mind comprehended what Amber was saying, even though his heart had difficulty accepting her departure. He and Meg and the Colonel would fly down for the actual trial, but in the meantime, her absence would leave a gaping hole in his soul.

"I'll miss you," he whispered into the night.

"Oh, I'll miss you, too," she responded fervently. "But you know why I have to go."

"Yes, I know." He longed to ask her to marry him, right here and now.

The question burned in his gut like a pure, blue flame, but he swallowed it down. She had enough on her mind without having to consider something else that would change her life forever. Sooner or later their time would come. He hoped it would be sooner.

Amber held her breath, waiting. For a moment she had thought he was going to say something else, and suddenly the silence felt awkward and strained. When he didn't continue, she exhaled slowly and choked back the lump in her throat. She had been hoping to hear *I love you*, or *Come back to me*, or *Marry me*. The idea had been hanging in limbo between them ever since the day she had come home from the hospital. But if he couldn't say the words, how could she?

She wanted him to haul her into his arms and kiss her again, to tell her that he'd wait forever, as long as it took, until she could return to him. She desperately longed for a promise, something she could lean on, something to remember. But TwoJoe was too wise, too steady, to ask her for a commitment when the future lay before them as vast and unknown as an uncharted ocean. Maybe the old seafarers had been right; maybe there was some point at the end of the world where ships sailed over the edge into oblivion.

In some ways, Amber felt as if she were moving rapidly toward that precipice. The idea of returning to North Carolina and facing her father after all these years terrified her. And yet she had to do it. Although she didn't know all the reasons why, she felt certain that it was a kind of calling, a destiny that she could not evade or deny. Something that had to do with justice, and with liberty.

For more than twenty years she had tried to outrun her past. She had fled from it with every ounce of strength and determination she possessed. And now she was going back to it, with equal strength and determination. She was taking her life back—hers and the life of the child she had carried.

Diedre's face materialized in her mind, and Amber felt herself almost overcome with a rush of love and regret. She could never recapture the years she had lost. She could never go back and see her little girl's first step, hear the word "Mommy" for the first time, revel in the little details that made up a life and formed a character. But she could stand by her daughter as she found her own way to peace, to the resolution of a pain no child should ever have to bear.

Dawn broke much too early for Amber's liking. She had rested little, and when sleep did come, she had dreamed of TwoJoe vanishing into a heavy mist and not being able to find him again.

But when she lugged her suitcase downstairs and went to the kitchen to make coffee, there he was, draining bacon and scrambling eggs. The first rays of the sun had illuminated the highest peaks of the Olympic Mountains, and a golden light streamed in the window and caught in his eyes.

Her heart lodged in her throat, and it took her a minute to regain her composure. "Don't tell me you're cooking?"

He grinned. "I know; Meg's going to have a fit. But almost nobody can mess up bacon and eggs." He handed her a steaming cup of coffee. "How'd you sleep?"

"Like a baby," she said. "Up every two hours."

"Yeah, me, too." He motioned to a seat at the kitchen table and set the platter of bacon and eggs in front of her. "Toast?"

"Sure, why not?" Amber struggled to keep her voice light as she watched him spread on butter and strawberry jam for her. "I can do that."

TwoJoe cut the toast into two triangles, the way she liked it. "You don't want to get your bandages all messy. Take a bite and tell me if it's edible." He held the toast to her mouth and watched as she chewed.

"It's delicious."

He drew closer. "Okay, let's try the bacon," he said in a husky voice. He broke a piece in half and fed it to her.

"Wonderful. Nice and crisp."

"Want another slice?" When she nodded, he put the bacon between his teeth and held it there.

Amber chuckled. "Have you been watching *Lady and the Tramp* again?"

"Worked for him," TwoJoe mumbled, putting an arm around her and drawing her closer.

Trying not to laugh, she nibbled at the end of the bacon until she reached his lips, then dissolved into hysterics. "Wait, wait! I can't kiss you with my mouth full of bacon!"

He gazed into her eyes, his expression serious and thoughtful. "I'll wait," he murmured. "I'll wait however long it takes."

Amber could barely swallow around the lump in her throat, but she managed to get the bacon down and came to him with a slow, smoky-flavored kiss. When their lips parted, he drew her into his arms and rested his chin on her shoulder. "Please, take care of yourself," he whispered into her ear.

Her eyes stung, and she blinked the tears away. In the moment before he released her, she mouthed the words, *I love you, TwoJoe.* But somehow she couldn't bring herself to say them out loud.

It had been twelve hours since the Lexus with North Carolina plates had pulled out of the driveway, taking away the woman TwoJoe loved. For most of the day he had wandered around the farm, just staring out over the water or talking to the llamas, who didn't have much to say in return. He and Meg had just finished a silent dinner of leftovers, and Meg had moved into the living room to read. But TwoJoe couldn't stand the thought of sitting in that big room, now emptied of Amber's presence. He excused himself and, claiming he had to go over the books, secluded himself in his two-room apartment.

The clock on his desk said seven-fifteen. The llamas were fed and settled for the night. What was he going to do with himself for the next three hours? He didn't really need to work and couldn't have concentrated on anything if he'd tried. Usually he didn't watch much television, but maybe tonight that was just the distraction he needed.

TwoJoe went into the darkened bedroom, kicked off his boots, and flopped across the bed. He always kept the remote control in the drawer of the bedside table, and without even looking, he opened the drawer and felt around for it. Instead, his hand closed on something else. Something stiff and rectangular.

He sat up and turned on the light. It was an envelope, pale yellow, the kind that held a greeting card. On the front, in an awkward, unsure hand, the word: *TwoJoe.*

For a moment or two, TwoJoe couldn't move. He just sat there, cross-legged on the bed, running his thumb over the letters of his own name. Then he peeled up the flap and removed the card.

On the front was a photograph of two llamas, facing each other, their foreheads touching. The arched curve of their long necks created a kind of heart shape in the space in between.

Inside Amber had written, *Don't give up on us. I love you.*

"I love you, too," he whispered. "And I'll never give up."

38

The Mayor's Memorial

Heartspring, North Carolina
Late May

Duncan McAlister leaned on the window sill and gazed out at the crowd that had begun to gather on the square around the courthouse. "Appears we're going to have a good turnout, doesn't it?" He turned and looked back over his shoulder. Jackson Underwood sat slouched in a chair, his eyes glazed and fixed on some middle distance. "Jack?"

"What?" Underwood sat up and stared at Duncan. "Did you say something?"

"Come on, Jack. It's a beautiful day. The sun is shining, the birds are singing, and—" he waved a hand toward the window, "my faithful followers are waiting to honor me. What could be better?"

"It could be better if I had heard from Willis."

"Would you quit worrying about Willis? He's probably holed up somewhere drinking himself into a stupor."

"He's dropped completely out of sight, Duncan. I haven't heard from him in over a week."

"And he's probably celebrating right now," Duncan interrupted. "Just like we ought to be doing." He reached into the bottom drawer of his desk and came up with a bottle of scotch and two glasses. "What do you say? A little toast?"

"For pity's sake, Duncan, it's ten-thirty in the morning!"

Duncan poured himself a glass and raised it in Jack's direction. "Since when have you become so fastidious?" Downing the scotch in a single gulp, he motioned to Underwood. "On your feet, man. It's time."

"Aren't you the least bit worried?"

"About what? Let it go, Jack. Your man in Seattle took care of things. She's not going to make any trouble—and even if she tried, who would believe her?" He went back to the window, smiled, and waved to the crowd below. "Look at them. They love me!"

"Yeah?" Jack snorted. "Well, be careful. The mob that shouts 'Hosanna' today yells 'Crucify' tomorrow."

On the steps of the courthouse, where a makeshift stage had been set up, Duncan's devoted yes-man Oliver Ferrell was making the most of his fifteen minutes of fame. A gaggle of newspaper reporters stood bunched up near the podium, and behind them, beside a huge, white van with a satellite dish on top, a remote crew from one of the Asheville TV stations focused enormous lenses on Ferrell. Duncan sat in a folding chair and grinned surreptitiously at Jack as Ollie began his speech.

"I have been given the very, very great honor," he said, his words echoing into the microphone, "of introducing the man, the one man, the one and only man, who is responsible for making Heartspring into the lovely, lovely little village it is today. Now the whole world knows what a wonderful, wonderful town this is, for just yesterday, *Carolina Magazine* revealed its choice of Heartspring, North Carolina, as the Most Desirable Small City in the Carolinas."

The crowd applauded, and Ollie Ferrell gave a little bow, as if the honor were his alone. When the noise diminished, he went on.

"Visitors to Heartspring can readily see the physical beauty of our little town, with its green, green parks, its beautiful, beautiful flowers, its serene, peaceful, tranquil, and bucolic way of life—" Ollie hesitated at the word *bucolic*, scanning the faces in the crowd to make sure his listeners understood the meaning of the term. When a few of them nodded, he went on. "But only those of us who enjoy the great, great pleasure of living here—every hour, every day, every week, every year—can truly appreciate the hard work of our wonderful, wonderful mayor, Mr. Duncan McAlister, and our Town Council—" here he paused and gave a self-deprecating nod, "in transforming Heartspring, in maintaining, nurturing, cultivating, and developing the kind of life we want for ourselves, our children, our great-grandchildren, and all the future generations of Heartspringians—ah, Heartspringonians—"

"Yeah, yeah, get on with it," Duncan muttered under his breath.

"Before I introduce our esteemed, honored, acclaimed, and praiseworthy mayor, however," Ollie continued, raising his voice a little to carry over the smattering of laughter, "I'd like to talk for a moment about the deeper, more significant, more portentous aspects of our life together in Heartspring."

People began to murmur among themselves, to scratch their heads and glance at their watches. "I'd say he's being just a little *portentous* himself," Duncan whispered in Jack's ear.

"Heartspring," Ollie was saying, "is not just a charming little town. Its beauty, its loveliness, its desirability extend beyond the external, into the heart, the soul, the spirit of who we are as a people. This is a town, I am very, very proud to say, whose values go far beyond the surface to its very core. Values such as honor, truth, courage, safety, self-sacrifice, love for one another. We are a family, a family joined together in a common purpose for the common good. And the person who best represents those values is Mayor Duncan McAlister—"

The crowd applauded, and Duncan rose to step forward. But Ollie

Ferrell wasn't done. He grinned and waved, then went on, as if gathering steam. "Here in Heartspring," he shouted over the throng, "we know the meaning of true family values! And today, we dedicate this plaque to the man who has made life as we know it in Heartspring a possibility." He reached behind the podium, and with some effort lifted up a huge, bronze plaque bearing the likeness of Duncan McAlister in bas-relief. "I'd like to read the inscription on this plaque, which will be installed at the door of the courthouse for everyone to see: *In honor of Duncan McAlister, Mayor of Heartspring, North Carolina, with the grateful thanks of the citizens of Heartspring for his tireless efforts in making our city—*"

Duncan came up behind Ollie and nudged him, nearly causing him to lose his grip on the plaque. "Thank you very, very, very much," he intoned into the microphone in a rather good imitation of Ferrell. "We are so, so grateful for this wonderful, wonderful honor." The crowd laughed uproariously and burst into spontaneous applause.

Ollie, who clearly didn't get the joke and had no idea he was the one being made fun of, inclined his head magnanimously and grinned as flashbulbs went off and the television cameras zoomed in for a closeup. He put an arm around Duncan and smiled again, as if expecting more adulation from both the crowd and the reporters.

Duncan eased Ferrell off the platform and posed with his bronze likeness. It would make a great picture, him smiling at himself. He let the cheering go on awhile, and then, in that split second before everybody grew uncomfortable, he set the plaque down on the platform and motioned for silence.

Timing. It was all about timing. Any good politician knew that you came off better if you had to ask for quiet, rather than allowing applause to dwindle on its own. Half a second could mean the difference between coming across as a hero and looking like a buffoon.

"Thank you, thank you." He swept his gaze out across the crowd, making eye contact here and there and calling out the names of some of the little people, who would be flattered by being singled out. "Ralph!

Good to see you! And Amy! How's that new baby? Marcus! Glad you're up and around again. That broken leg healing up all right?" When the man grinned and lifted a crutch in salute, Duncan laughed. "Catch me afterward, and I'll sign your cast for you!"

Then his eyes lit on someone on the very outskirts of the crowd, and he shaded his brow with one hand. "Ladies and gentlemen," he called out, "I see a very special person out there. She's been out of town for a little while, and I had no idea she'd be home for this occasion. But of course she'd be here to see her Daddy honored. Come on up here, honey! My beautiful daughter, Diedre!"

When he called her name, Diedre flinched, and for a minute she couldn't move. She had already had plenty of second thoughts about this public confrontation, and now they all came back in a rush. But Elise Glass had made it clear to Diedre and Amber that the molestation charge might not stick; this could be the nearest thing to closure they were likely to get. And, Elise said, it was also a kind of poetic justice— taking control away from the controller.

Diedre didn't for one moment believe that her father would cave when confronted publicly with the charges against him. But it was important to do this, anyway—to stand up and tell the truth. To break the silence.

Diedre felt a hand swathed in bandages squeeze her own, and when she looked to one side, Amber was nodding.

"Go on," Amber whispered. "It's now or never."

Diedre threaded her way through the crowd, followed by Amber, Assistant District Attorney Elise Glass, Heartspring Sheriff Jim Barstow, whom Diedre had known all her life, and Barstow's deputy, Kirby Austin.

Daddy apparently didn't recognize Amber and didn't have a clue that this day of celebration was about to go horribly wrong. As she approached the platform, he resumed speaking.

"You all know, of course, that my beloved wife, Cecilia, succumbed to cancer recently. I wish she could be here to share this day with me, but I firmly believe that this morning she is looking down from heaven and smiling on all of us. Our daughter, Diedre, was the light of her mother's life, and I'm pleased to have her stand with me to accept this honor, and to thank you all for the support and love you have given to our family." He extended a hand in Diedre's direction. "Come on up here, sweetheart."

She stopped just short of the podium, out of his reach, and her eyes drifted to the platform behind him. Uncle Jack sat there, frozen, his gaze fixed not on her, but on someone just behind her. He had seen Amber. He knew.

Sheriff Barstow approached Duncan and motioned to him. "Mr. Mayor, I need to speak to you."

"Not now, Jim," he hissed. Then he turned and grinned at the audience. "How about a round of applause for our sheriff, Jim Barstow?" The crowd clapped politely and began whispering to one another.

Jack was on his feet. "We'd better cut this short, Duncan."

Barstow stepped in front of Diedre and reluctantly ascended the platform. "I'm sorry, Mr. Mayor, but I got no choice."

Duncan stared at him, a look of confusion on his face. "Just a minute, folks," he said with a forced laugh. "It seems our sheriff has some urgent business with me."

Barstow pulled a sheet of paper out of his pocket and frowned at it. "Duncan McAlister and Jackson Underwood, I have warrants for your arrest on the charges of conspiracy to cover up a crime, conspiracy to commit arson, attempted murder, and, in your case, Mr. McAlister, aggravated child molestation." He tried to speak quietly, but the words caught in the microphone and floated clearly out across the square. For a minute no one moved; no one even breathed. Then, as if on cue, cameras began clicking and the television crew started running, shouldering through the crowd for a better vantage point.

Diedre watched as her father's face went white as paper. "Is this some kind of joke?" he spluttered. "It's all a mistake—it's some kind of stupid mistake."

Barstow stuffed the paper back into his pocket and retrieved two pair of handcuffs from his belt, one of which he tossed in the direction of his deputy, who stood beside Jack with one hand gripping his upper arm.

"I'm sorry, sir, it's no mistake." He pulled Duncan's hands behind him and secured the cuffs. "You have the right to remain silent. If you give up that right, anything you say can and will be used against you in a court of law. You have the right to an attorney. If you cannot afford an attorney, one will be appointed—"

"I know my rights, you fool!" Duncan yelled, the veins in his neck bulging out like knotted ropes. "I got you that badge! You never would have been elected without my support, and I demand—"

He stopped suddenly, and the only sound to be heard was the whirring of video cameras and the popping of flashbulbs. His eyes locked on Amber, who now stood beside Diedre with an arm around her shoulder.

"You!" His voice, when it came, was a choked, strangled sound.

Diedre turned her head and looked at Amber. The expression on her face was not one of satisfaction, as Diedre might have expected, but one of unutterable sorrow. "Yes, Daddy," she whispered, her voice barely audible. "Me."

"Why?" he croaked. "Why are you doing this?"

"Because it's time," she said resolutely. "Time for the truth."

The reporters had honed in like heat-seeking missiles, and now crowded around Diedre and Amber. "What truth is that?" a reporter from the Asheville television station asked, thrusting a microphone toward Amber. "And what is your connection with the mayor of Heartspring?"

Amber's eyes followed the two handcuffed men as the sheriff led them off to the waiting patrol cars. "Duncan McAlister was my father," she said quietly. "Once, a long, long time ago."

39

The People's Court

Duncan McAlister paced back and forth across Jack Underwood's living room, glancing at the headlines of the local newspapers scattered about and watching the evening news with a sinking feeling in his gut. He might be out on bail, but being confined to this house wasn't much better than being behind bars. Still, he wasn't about to show his face in public.

Because of the high-profile nature of the case, the indictment had come speedily, and the trial was set to begin exactly five weeks later in Superior Court in Asheville. Meanwhile, the court of public opinion had already rendered its decision. The case was tried on the six o'clock news every night, and reprised at eleven. Newspapers were swept up in the feeding frenzy—even one of the national tabloids had a small story on him, calling them "Mayor Duncan Molester and his attorney Jack Underbelly." Still photos and ten-second film loops showed the Mayor of Heartspring being carted away in handcuffs.

Long before the first gavel fell, Duncan McAlister and Jackson Underwood were declared guilty on all counts.

It was just the kind of story that roused people's passions and incited their righteous indignation: an honored public figure with his entrails exposed. Hiring a thug to go after his own daughter. Conspiring with his lawyer to conceal a crime. Abuse of power. Betraying the people's trust.

And the charge that raised the loudest outcry was the one that had been thrown out in the initial indictment: aggravated child molestation.

The judge—much to Duncan's dismay, a woman—didn't seem to have much doubt that he had, indeed, molested his older daughter, and that his younger daughter, Diedre, was the fruit of that abominable act. But the statute of limitations had expired, and she had to adhere to the letter of the law. The rape charge was thrown out; on the other charges he and Jack were going to trial.

In the end, it didn't matter much whether or not Duncan was brought to trial on the rape. The damage had been done—the truth had already gotten out. Less than thirty-six hours after his arrest, Oliver Ferrell called for a vote at a hastily convened Town Council meeting, and McAlister's position as mayor of Heartspring was abruptly terminated.

So much for being innocent until proven guilty, Duncan thought.

Even after they had made bail, Duncan stayed sequestered in Jack's house. On the rare occasions when he did go out, no one in town would speak to him, except for a few who muttered insults whenever he got within earshot. Former supporters turned away without a word; women clutched their children protectively when he walked by. The bas-relief plaque that was supposed to have been installed at the courthouse door had mysteriously disappeared, and his office—what was left of it after the authorities had taken his computers and files—had been vandalized.

Duncan began to panic.

Jack continued to tell him that he had to remain calm, to exude an attitude of innocence, to stay above it all. But Jack's office had been taken apart piece by piece as well, and there was enough information in those files to send them both to jail for the rest of their lives.

Their attorney was an old pal of Jack's from law school, now practicing in L.A. Brash, tenacious, and notorious for winning acquittals for guilty clients, T. J. O'Malley had been a middleweight Golden Gloves champion in his youth and had been dubbed by the media as "Boxer." O'Malley liked the nickname; he claimed it was a tribute to his ability to deliver a one-two punch on cross-examination. In truth, it was a reference to his annoying habit of uttering Muhammad Ali–type predictions about the outcome of his trials. Ali might have been O'Malley's hero, but instead of "Float like a butterfly, sting like a bee," O'Malley came up with lines like, "Any shadow of doubt, and my client gets out."

According to Jack, Boxer O'Malley also had a ruthless taste for bloodletting and a reputation for fancy courtroom footwork. But Duncan feared that even "the greatest" couldn't dance around the evidence forever.

Diedre sat on Carlene's couch, wedged in on both sides by the cats, Calvin and Hobbes. Hobbes, the gray one, should have been called Harley—he weighed about twenty pounds, and his constant purr mimicked the rumble of a large motorcycle. Sugarbear, jealous of the cats' proximity to her human, kept bringing a tug toy for Diedre to throw for her and pawed impatiently at Diedre's legs when she didn't pay enough attention.

"Carlene," Diedre asked for the third time when her friend passed through the room, "are you sure you're okay with us staying here? Amber and I could get a hotel; it's a terrible imposition."

"Nonsense." Carlene shook her head. "The guest room would just sit here empty, and besides, I like having the company. Now, if you start demanding that I get up and cook waffles and eggs every morning—"

Diedre raised one eyebrow. "I know, this is a *B no B*—Bed, no Breakfast."

"You got it." She glanced at the clock on the VCR. "Want to go out for dinner tonight?"

"Amber's taking a nap. I'll check with her when she gets up, but probably yes. As soon as the news is over. It's nearly six."

Diedre picked up the remote and clicked on the local news. It barely mattered what channel she chose; everybody was carrying the story. The whole world, it seemed, now knew that her father was a rapist—albeit an unconvicted one—and that she was the product of that abuse. The list of his other crimes, the ones he had actually been indicted for, took a backseat to sensationalism when the mayor of the Most Desirable Small City in the Carolinas was confronted with his long-lost elder daughter and accused of forcibly fathering the younger one.

Watching the news was rather like witnessing a head-on collision—she knew she shouldn't look, but she couldn't seem to help herself. And there she was again, standing with Amber, watching as the sheriff led their father away in handcuffs.

Diedre couldn't blame the reporters. It was news, and by television standards it was a ratings gold mine. Still, every time she saw it, her stomach clenched into knots and a black hole opened up inside her, threatening to swallow what was left of her soul.

She and Amber talked about it incessantly, late into the night as they lay sleepless in Carlene's guest room. The judge had cleared the court calendar and set a quick trial date, but the trial itself could go on for months. Every day Diedre felt more drained, more depressed. Amber insisted it was all part of the process, coming to grips with a terrible truth such as this one, but her assurances didn't help much.

Elise Glass had told them that the prosecution's chances of winning were good. In exchange for a reduced sentence, Shiv Willis would testify. So would Amber. And even though the rape charge was not on the table and any testimony about it would be excluded, jury members would nevertheless look at Amber and know what had been done to her. They would think of their own preteen daughters and grand-daughters. They would hear how Duncan McAlister and his lawyer had conspired to terrorize Amber—how they had falsified documents and taken her newborn child from her. How they had committed her to a mental hospital and threatened her if she ever talked. How she had almost been killed in the fire that was designed to ensure her silence.

It would all come out as part of the public record. But even if her father were eventually convicted and sent to jail, even if she had that closure, it wouldn't be over. Not for Diedre.

She had gone looking for the truth—about her sister, her father, herself. And she had found it.

But how in God's name could she ever learn to live with it?

40

A Question of Guilt

The conference room, located a few doors down the hall from the D.A.'s office, seemed stiflingly hot. The ceiling fan overhead wasn't moving; somewhere above him, Duncan could hear the droning buzz of a fly bouncing off the wall.

The place obviously doubled as a library; except for an open rectangle to accommodate the single door, all four walls, from floor to ceiling, were lined with shelves holding ponderous legal tomes. But the rectangular, windowless room—Duncan estimated it at twelve-by-fourteen feet, tops—wasn't nearly large enough. There was barely enough space to pull out a chair and sit at the table without bumping into the bookshelves behind. Every time he moved the slightest bit, he knocked into something. He was beginning to feel as if the walls were closing in on him.

"Where *is* she?" Duncan ground his teeth and drummed his fingers on the scarred wooden tabletop.

The "she" in question was the assistant D.A., a woman named Elise Glass, who was obviously trying to make it in a man's world because she couldn't *get* a man. A homely, flat-faced woman with dishwater hair and, in Duncan's estimation, barely above average intelligence, Glass had telephoned Boxer O'Malley yesterday afternoon and proposed a meeting, the subject of which she had refused to reveal. O'Malley was pretty sure she wanted to cut a deal, since she obviously—in O'Malley's words—"didn't have squat" in the way of evidence.

But if Elise Glass were running scared, her actions this morning certainly didn't indicate it. "She called this meeting, and so far she's kept us waiting—" he glanced at his gold wrist watch, "twenty-five minutes. Doesn't she know that I'm—"

Duncan was about to say, *that I'm an important elected official with a town to run*, but he stopped himself. The fact was, he no longer held public office, no longer had urgent business demanding his attention, no longer could claim anything, in fact, of what had once been his life.

Jack put a hand on his arm. "Take it easy, pal. Calm down. You know the drill. She calls us here, keeps us on ice, tries to psych us out. It's a power play."

Duncan stared at Jack. Since when had his attorney started talking like a B-grade private detective in the movies?

"Don't tell me to take it easy!" Duncan shot back. "Don't tell me to calm down!" He rolled his chair back from the table and hit the bookcase so hard that the volumes above him shifted and threatened to come down on his head. He jerked at his collar, dislodging the top button, and loosened his tie. "It's sweltering in here."

Jack dragged a sweating pitcher of water from the center of the table and poured a glass full. "Look, Duncan," he said, cutting a glance at O'Malley, who sat at the far end of the table, "this is exactly what they want. They want us to be nervous, to get rattled. But we've got nothing to be rattled about. The only proof they have hinges on CeCe's testimony about the molestation. And that charge has already been thrown out." He pushed the water in Duncan's direction. "Take a deep breath, now, and when the D.A. gets here, try to keep your mouth shut and let Boxer do the talking."

Duncan nodded, drained the glass, and poured another. "Okay. I'm—I'm all right." He took a few short, shallow breaths. But he wasn't all right. He felt as if a million tiny spiders were running up and down along his nerve endings. The room was getting smaller by the minute. And then, just as he feared he might start climbing the walls, the door opened.

Duncan looked up. Elise Glass entered, carrying a cardboard file box and wearing an ill-fitting navy pantsuit. Two other figures followed close on her heels and seated themselves on the opposite side of the table. Diedre and . . .

Her.

Duncan felt his insides lurch. He had seen her in the square, on the morning of his arrest, but except for that brief glimpse, he hadn't laid eyes on his elder daughter for more than twenty years.

He remembered it as if it were yesterday—the wild, disbelieving look she gave him, the fear in her eyes, the way her dark, wavy hair tumbled around her face. She had been—what? Fifteen, sixteen? Barely grown, still with that gangly, coltish appearance.

But old enough. Old enough to give him what he needed. Old enough to bear a child. Old enough to know to keep her mouth shut.

He glanced in her direction again. She wasn't a child any longer. She was a woman, older than Cecilia had been when it first happened. She could have *been* Cecilia, for that matter, sitting there with her hands folded in her lap, avoiding his gaze. The wife who had withdrawn from him, despised him. The wife who told him she hated what he had become.

It was her fault. Everything was her fault . . .

⁓ℰ⁓

Amber hadn't been in a room with her father for more than two decades, and seeing him now, up close, shook her to the core. What would he do? What would he say?

She could feel his eyes on her, scrutinizing her; she reached to straighten her collar. But her hands, still bandaged, moved clumsily, and she dropped them back into her lap.

She ventured a glance at him out of the corner of her eyes. He was older, beefier, his face red, his eyes bloodshot. A thin sheen of sweat shone on his upper lip, and his tie had been loosened and lay crookedly below his Adam's apple. Not the man she remembered as being a meticulous dresser, scrupulous about his appearance.

With Daddy, it had always been about appearances. Keeping up a good front, making other people believe you were smarter or richer or more savvy than you really were. He had always been smooth; she'd give him that much. He had pulled himself out of that swamp of poverty and disgrace into which he had been born by sheer force of personality and an iron will. Even his marriage to her mother, Amber believed, had been a calculated act designed to improve his image.

And it had worked. He had made it—until now.

Diedre, Amber noticed, had not so much as glanced at him since they entered the room. Now she nudged Amber and whispered, "Look at him. He looks awful."

"I thought so, too. But I haven't seen him in twenty years."

Diedre shook her head. "Something in his eyes. He was always so composed, so in control. Now he looks like he's coming apart at the seams."

The defense attorney had begun speaking, and they fell silent. "Well, Ms. Glass," he said, emphasizing the *Ms.*, "we're all assembled, as requested. This is your meeting. I'm listening."

Elise Glass reached into her box and removed several thick file folders, clapping them down on the table. "These are records from the office of your client, Mr. Underwood. After a thorough investigation, aided by a former legal assistant of Mr. Underwood's, we have uncovered a trail of evidence that points to your clients' collusion in falsifying legal documents—namely, the birth certificate of Diedre Chaney McAlister. We also have information on a cash payment made to one Silas B. Willis, a convicted felon known as Shiv, for various criminal acts."

"Pamela Langley?" Jack burst out. "Pamela helped you? I'll kill her, I swear—"

"If I were you, Mr. O'Malley, I would advise my client not to further incriminate himself."

"Shut up, Jack," O'Malley growled.

But Jack wouldn't shut up. "It's a bluff, Boxer," he insisted. "I fired Pamela Langley, so she'll say whatever they want her to say. They can't prove a thing without Shiv's testimony, and they can't find him."

"Mr. Willis is in custody even as we speak," Elise corrected smoothly. "He has agreed to testify, and he'll say enough to put your clients away for, oh, at least seven to ten. *On each count.*" She smiled briefly. "An aggravated child molestation conviction would have gotten Mr. McAlister thirty, but by the time we're done, it'll add up to about the same."

Amber watched as her father's face went an odd shade of gray. He tugged at the knot of his tie and exhaled heavily.

"If you're so certain of your case," O'Malley said, "why are we here?"

Elise's gaze flitted to Amber and Diedre, then back to the defense attorney. "Mr. McAlister's daughters have endured a great deal of suffering at his hands—particularly Amber Chaney, the elder daughter. They need closure and resolution. They don't need to be further abused by the trauma of a trial. Let's save the state the cost—"

"Enough of the bleeding-heart speech," O'Malley interrupted. "What are you offering?"

As if through a fog, Duncan heard the woman's words.

"They plead guilty and serve the minimum time on each count. Seven years for each charge—a total of twenty-one. With any luck, they'll be out in fifteen."

"Ridiculous," Boxer O'Malley shot back. "Absolutely absurd. What have you got? An ex-con who's agreed to roll for a reduced sentence and an indignant bimbo who lost her job and has a beef with her employer.

Not exactly unimpeachable or objective witnesses. Unless you can give me one good reason why I should even consider this offer, we'll take our chances at trial."

"Restitution," the woman said quietly.

"What do you mean, restitution?"

"Your clients have caused Miss Chaney and Miss McAlister immeasurable harm. They called him—" she pointed at Underwood, "*Uncle Jack*. Did you know that? He was like a member of the family. They trusted him. And him—" her accusatory finger swung around and aimed like a pistol at Duncan's chest, "they called Daddy. He raped his older daughter, stole her child, had her committed to a mental institution, lied to the younger one, and together he and his attorney conspired to cover up the crimes. They hired Shiv Willis to do their dirty work, and if Willis hadn't bungled the job, they probably would have succeeded in killing Miss Chaney." She paused and leveled her gaze on Boxer. "Neither of your clients has ever once taken any responsibility for the ruin they brought to these two young women's lives. Plead them out, O'Malley. Let them stand in open court and say, 'Guilty.'"

All during her speech, Duncan had struggled to keep a firm grip on his resolution to stay quiet. But the tiny conference room was as close as a coffin; it had begun to shift, just slightly, and he felt his head reeling. He couldn't breathe. The assistant D.A.'s litany of his sins ground into his brain like salt on a gaping wound, and the final word, *guilty*, pierced like a red-hot knife into his skull. An invisible jackhammer slammed into his temple, pounding . . . pounding . . .

"No!" he yelled, jumping to his feet so quickly that his chair flung itself against the bookcase behind him and bounced back to clip him in the knees. "*She's* the one who's guilty!"

He watched as his arm stretched out and his finger, shaking violently, pointed at the woman sitting across from him. His daughter. Or was it his wife? He couldn't tell, couldn't quite remember. For a moment he felt as if he had been lifted from his own body and was watching the scene from high above—from the ceiling fan, or the top of one of the tall bookcases. Maybe he had become that fly which had been buzzing around all morning. Maybe he was dead . . .

His voice came again, sounding oddly strained and foreign to his ears. "She got what was coming to her! It was my right; she had a duty to me! She *wanted* it!"

"Shut up, Duncan. Shut up NOW!"

He heard Boxer's strangled plea, but paid it no mind. "We worked it all out, you and I, didn't we, Jack? It was brilliant. A mental institution—that would keep her quiet, and even if she told, who'd believe her? She was crazy! She could have ruined everything, but we took care of it."

The hammering in his head grew louder, and his daughter's face swam before his eyes, as if she were submerged in shallow water. "Nobody knew, did they? Nobody knew the secret. We kept it from them all, didn't we, Jack? Even Cecilia didn't know. Then why did she stop loving me? Why did she turn away and say those terrible things to me?"

O'Malley was yelling now, trying to get control of the situation. But Duncan had the floor, and he wasn't about to relinquish it. They were going to hear him out, and then they'd understand. "We fooled them all, didn't we, Jack?" he shouted. "I made it. I was respectable, honored. Everybody loved me. They even put a bronze plaque of me on the courthouse . . ."

Both of his hands were stretched out now, shaking uncontrollably, as if they had suddenly developed Parkinson's disease. He watched them with detached curiosity as they reached in her direction. "I loved you. I always loved you. Just like your mama, so pure and beautiful and undefiled. But you couldn't keep quiet, could you? You had to talk, had to tell—," one hand wavered in Diedre's direction, "had to tell *her*."

Jack reached for him, trying to pull him back down into the chair. "Get off me!" he screamed. "You know this is her fault! If she had just kept her mouth shut—if she had only stayed away. And now it's gone . . . gone. Everything's gone, all because of her. She's the one. SHE'S THE GUILTY ONE . . ."

Amber sat frozen in her seat as her father disintegrated into a quivering heap. She felt Diedre next to her, holding onto her, sobbing against her shoulder, but she couldn't move.

Jack stood behind Daddy with both forearms clenched around his chest as if to keep him from jumping up again. But there was no danger of that. The man who had once been her father had no place left to go.

"We'll take the deal," the defense attorney was saying in a subdued voice. "Notify the judge and tell her we're changing the plea."

41

Strange Justice

Diedre stood on the front steps of the stone mansion and hesitated. "Should we ring the bell, do you think?" she asked Amber. "I doubt that Vesta's still here, but I've got a key." She rummaged in her bag, then stopped when she felt Amber's eyes on her.

"This feels so eerie," Amber murmured. "Like I'm stepping back in time. I always hated this house—it held so many terrible memories. But there were good ones, too." She drew in a deep breath and sighed it out again. "Until now, it hasn't seemed real that Mama's gone."

Diedre's eyes stung. "*Everything's* gone," she murmured.

"Not everything." Amber's dark gaze met and held Diedre's, and for just a moment, Diedre felt as if she were looking into Mama's eyes. "We've got each other."

Each other. The words should have comforted Diedre, but she felt nothing. She was dead inside, wasted and empty as a vast desert. Even the memory of seeing Daddy and Uncle Jack standing before the judge pleading guilty, and the knowledge that they were now both in prison, hadn't brought the closure and resolution she had longed for.

She wasn't sorry justice had been served, but it gave her no satisfaction. The hatred she had felt when she'd first learned what Daddy had done to Amber had metamorphosed into aching sorrow, and just a little pity. But oddly, she missed the anger. It had brought her strength, and now that it had dissipated, she felt drained and hollow. The final verdict had come, but it had turned out to be an anticlimax.

Diedre nudged Amber's elbow and pointed toward the glider and chairs that stood on the far side of the wide front verandah. "Let's sit out here for a few minutes."

They settled into the chairs and sat gazing across the expanse of lawn to where the yard fell away into a magnificent view of the Blue Ridge Mountains. The morning was warm and clear, and a faint breeze blew off the ridge and stirred the rhododendrons that surrounded the house. Diedre unhooked Sugarbear's leash, and the dog took off at a run, sniffing every bush and blade of grass and bounding like a puppy with the joy of being back on her home turf.

"Well, it's over," Diedre sighed. "How do you feel?"

Amber stared down at her bandaged hands and shook her head. "I'm not quite sure. I'm glad we didn't have to go through a long, drawn-out trial. But I have to admit that I was pretty shaken by Daddy's meltdown. And I wish—" She stopped suddenly and shook her head.

"Wish Daddy had taken responsibility for his actions?" Diedre supplied. "Wish he had at least said, 'I'm sorry'?"

Amber nodded. "Because the molestation charge was thrown out, I'm afraid I'm left feeling, well, not quite vindicated."

"Me, too," Diedre admitted. "But what do we do about that?"

"There's nothing we can do, except go on with our lives."

"I'm not sure I have much of a life to go on with."

Amber cocked her head and gazed at Diedre curiously. "What do you mean? You're twenty-five years old, honey—you have your whole life ahead of you."

"But you're going back to Washington. And I certainly can't live here—" she waved a hand at the gray stone facade.

"If you need me to stay, I will."

The words fell on Diedre's soul like water on dry ground, but she shook her head. "I can't ask that of you. You belong with TwoJoe. He loves you. You love him."

"Yes, I do. But I love you, too." Amber leaned forward and smiled earnestly. "You are my daughter. I want to be with you, to get to know you better, to be part of your life. If I need to stay in North Carolina in order for that to happen, that's what I'll do."

A rush of gratefulness welled up in Diedre's heart. "I have a better idea. Carlene and I already talked about it—she doesn't really need me to set up the shop, and as we both know, I have some emotional work to do, work that's going to require the help of a counselor."

Amber raised one eyebrow. "And?"

"And I was thinking—well, maybe I should come back to Washington with you for a while. Your priest friend Susan is a good therapist, isn't she? I could find a place to rent, do some freelance photography, maybe even sell some of my photos through Andrew Jorgensen's gallery. It would give us time together—and a chance for me to get my life in order. A change of scenery might be good for me."

For a minute or two Amber didn't say a word, and Diedre wondered if perhaps her brilliant idea wasn't so brilliant after all. Maybe Amber wouldn't want her hanging around all the time, getting in the way of her relationship with TwoJoe. Maybe—

"Let's go in," Amber said, getting to her feet. "We've got things to do."

"Like what?"

"Well, for one thing, I need to call Meg and TwoJoe. And then we'll need to make a run to the store."

"To the store? Why?"

She leaned down and kissed Diedre lightly on the cheek. "Boxes," she said. "If you're going to pack, we'll need lots and lots of boxes."

❦

Duncan McAlister could barely remember his outburst in the D.A.'s office, or standing before the judge entering a guilty plea. It was all a blur, like a vague dream that vanishes in that split second between hearing the alarm clock and waking to consciousness. He knew it had happened; it just didn't seem real.

But his incarceration was real enough, and it was no dream. They had not, as both Jack Underwood and Boxer O'Malley had promised, been sentenced to a minimum security white-collar "country-club" prison. This was the real thing, with clanging iron bars and armed guards and tiny, high windows that barely let any sunlight into the cells. The noise level—shouting, cursing, banging at all hours of the day and night—was enough to drive a man mad. And the smells! Stale sweat, disinfectant, urine, mildew—the combined stench seeped from the cinder block walls like ooze from an open sore.

Even worse than what *was*, however, was the fear of what *might* be. Since the moment he had been led into this place and shoved roughly into his cell, anxiety had gripped Duncan like a bad case of dysentery. His cellmate, Rufus Kiley—a tattoo-covered Neanderthal who went by the nickname Blade—had sized him up with narrowed eyes and a guttural warning to keep out of his way. Duncan took the man seriously and had not spoken a word to him since.

Breakfast was over. Somewhere in the cellblock a bell rang, and the bars slid sideways with a clank. Duncan got to his feet and stood two steps behind Blade, whose bulk completely filled the open cell door.

A guard came down the corridor with a clipboard in his hands and paused outside the cell. "Kiley, McAlister—laundry," he muttered. "Get moving."

Duncan's heart sank. Laundry duty was the nastiest, smelliest, sweatiest job imaginable. Jack had been assigned there on his first day, and at dinner last night, had been complaining about how awful it was. If there was any hope of surviving in here, Duncan would have to get on the warden's good side—and fast. If he could just get himself out of this brain fog, show the man how adept he was at administrative duties—

Blade craned his neck and gave him a leering grin, revealing a crooked row of tobacco-stained teeth. He jerked his head and set off down the hall, with Duncan following behind like a cowed dog.

If Duncan thought the chaos in the cellblock was bad, it was nothing compared to what he encountered in the laundry room. The yelling, the noise of the machines, the steam, and the humid, stifling heat convinced him that his initial evaluation of this place was accurate: he had been sentenced not to prison, but to hell itself.

A tall, skinny black man—apparently the prison trusty who ran the laundry—pointed toward a bank of washing machines. "In the back on the right!" he shouted in Duncan's ear. "You'll work with Kiley!"

Duncan looked. Blade Kiley, who obviously had been here before and knew the ropes, stood between two bins of dirty laundry, grinning and motioning to him. The trusty nudged him from behind. "Go on."

Duncan made his way down the row between the machines, feeling as if he were negotiating a narrow city street. Along both sides, and higher than his head, the huge machines thumped and whined. It was like walking through a nightmarish mechanical maze. When he got to the back of the room, he took a right in the direction Blade had indicated, and—

"Augghhh!" The air rushed out of him as something solid as iron collided with his midsection. Stunned, Duncan doubled over, grasping the nearest laundry bin for support. He looked up to see Blade standing over him, pounding one fist into the other open palm. Around Kiley in a jagged semicircle stood eight or nine other inmates, all glaring at him. Blade grabbed the front of his jumpsuit and jerked him forward, and the circle closed in around the two of them.

Duncan tried to scream, but no sound would come, and even if he had been able to yell, no one would have heard him above the noise of the laundry. Frantically he looked around; there was not a single guard in sight.

Blade hit him again, a blow to the jaw that drove Duncan's lower teeth all the way through his tongue. Something warm and liquid filled his mouth. He gasped for air and spit out a mouthful of blood.

His heart was pounding a wild, erratic beat, and his head spun.

Kiley drew him up by the collar, so close Duncan could smell the man's foul breath. "Think you're such a big man?" he spat out. "A big important man? We know about you." He let fly a string of curses directly in Duncan's face, and the circle of inmates closed in tighter.

Someone snaked a leg out, catching Duncan around the ankles, and he felt his knees crack when they hit the concrete floor. Blade grabbed a fistful of hair and lifted Duncan's face upward. "We know what you did to your little girl, you piece of garbage. It's time you learned exactly what happens in a place like this to a slime ball like you."

Diedre pulled open the bottom desk drawer and began loading its contents into a cardboard box. Amber sat on the bed watching, and Vesta, who hadn't been able to stop smiling in the past two hours, hovered about like a protective angel.

They hadn't been able to see Vesta at all since they had returned to North Carolina—neither Diedre nor Amber had been willing to take the chance of running into Daddy. After the aborted trial and sentencing, Vesta could have simply left the house and gone back to the little cottage she had inherited when her parents died, but she hadn't. She had stayed alone in the big, old mansion, braving its memories, its ghosts. Waiting. Waiting for her girls to come home.

The reunion between Amber and Vesta was a joy to behold. Vesta kept stroking her, touching her, calling her "my baby," and fussing over her burned hands. In a private moment, Amber had confessed to Diedre that she hadn't expected Vesta to seem quite so . . . so *old*. It had been more than twenty years since Amber had seen Vesta, of course, but Diedre had to admit that Vesta had aged noticeably just in the past few weeks. She seemed frail and nervous. Her spotted, brown hands shook, and she had a worried, exhausted look around her eyes.

It was no wonder, given what she had been through. First Mama's illness and death, then Diedre's absence, Daddy's arrest and imprisonment, and now Amber's return and the revelation that she was Diedre's mother.

But once she had heard the entire story and gone through the cycle of tears, laughter, and more tears, Vesta seemed remarkably able to adapt. "I reckon it's about time for this old woman to retire anyway," she said. "I'll just take my old self home, prop my feets up, and watch *Murder, She Wrote* reruns until the Good Lord takes me on to glory."

"I'll pay you what Daddy owes you," Diedre promised, although she had no idea how she would come up with the money. She had nothing of her own, and all Daddy's assets were frozen. Now that she thought about it, she was, in fact, destitute. Nearly everything she owned would fit in a few small boxes.

"What about this house?" Amber asked as Diedre went on packing. "Is there a mortgage on it?"

Diedre shook her head. "It was paid off five or six years ago. But I have no idea what will happen to it now. I guess it'll just sit here empty until it falls in on itself."

Amber let out a cynical laugh. "An appropriate monument to Duncan McAlister's life, I'd say. But it is a shame to let it go to ruin."

"I wouldn't live in it. Would *you?*"

Amber shook her head. "Heavens, no. This house represents my worst memories and my most vivid nightmares. Still, it seems like a waste."

Continuing to sort through items from her desk drawer, Diedre pulled out two green slips of paper and grinned to herself. "Vesta," she said over her shoulder, "do you still have a driver's license?"

"Course I do, child. I ain't decrepit, and I got eyes like a hawk." She chuckled. "A real old hawk, maybe."

"You want a brand new Lexus with a CD player and power everything?"

Vesta gave Diedre a puzzled frown. "Most anything'd be better than that beat-up old Ford I got. Spends most of its time in my nephew's shop."

Diedre flipped the title over, signed it, and handed it to Vesta. "Mama willed it to me when she died. Now it's yours. I'll keep my Camry. It's only got twenty-two thousand miles on it; for a Toyota, that's barely broken in. Except for the tires. Driving in the mountains is murder on tires. Do you think your nephew could get me a deal on new ones?"

"Honey, you ain't gonna give me your mama's car!"

"Nope. I'm going to sell it to you, if you want it. One dollar, and that's my final offer." She winked in Amber's direction. "Metallic champagne with matching leather interior. You'll look great in it, Vesta. Call it an installment on what I owe you."

Vesta fished a wrinkled dollar bill out of her pocket, pressed it into Diedre's hand, and smothered her with a hug. "You don't owe me nothin', baby," she said in choked voice.

"I owe you more than that," Diedre responded. "Much more."

Amber shifted on the bed and tucked her legs under her. "Does this mean we're taking the Camry back to Washington?"

Diedre nodded. "I hate to make that long drive back again, but I'll need a car when I get there, and we have to haul all this—" She gestured to the boxes scattered around the bedroom and grinned in Amber's direction. "Besides, I felt a little pretentious in the Lexus, and I prefer Midnight Blue to Metallic Champagne."

The telephone on the bedside table rang, and Diedre jumped, her heart thudding in her chest. "Should I answer it?"

Amber cut a glance at Vesta, who nodded. "Why not? If it's for Daddy, it has to be somebody who's been hiding under a rock or abducted by aliens. Tell them he's temporarily indisposed . . . for the next twenty years or so."

Diedre picked up the receiver and answered formally: "McAlister residence."

She strained to listen as the unfamiliar voice on the other end of the line spoke in subdued tones. Amber and Vesta went on talking about

Washington, about TwoJoe and Meg and the llamas and little Sam Houston, about how long it would take for Amber and Diedre to make the trip—

"H-hang on a second, will you?" Diedre put the receiver to her chest and fought for breath. She turned in Amber's direction. "I'm afraid we won't be going anywhere—at least not for a while."

"What?" Amber swung her legs over the side of the bed and stared at Diedre. "What are you talking about? Who's on the phone?"

"It's the warden at the prison. He called Elise Glass, who called Carlene's house. She told them we were here."

"Well, what does he want?"

"He wants us to go to the county morgue and claim the body. Daddy's dead."

42

A Sure and Certain Hope

A small cluster of black-clad mourners huddled beneath dripping umbrellas at the graveside: apart from Diedre, only Amber, TwoJoe, Meg, Colonel Houston, Carlene, and Vesta Shelby. Susan Quentin, dressed in clerical garb, stood beside the local Presbyterian minister—a man Diedre had only seen once or twice in passing—and uttered the words, "Ashes to ashes, dust to dust . . ."

She didn't add the traditional line, "in the sure and certain hope of redemption," and Diedre silently blessed her for that moment of candor. The truth was, no one in this circle was very certain of anything.

Duncan McAlister's death certificate read: *Cause of Death—Myocardial Infarction*. He had suffered a massive heart attack and dropped dead on the floor of the prison laundry room. The warden and the prison physician had attempted to evade their questions, thinking to spare the feelings of the bereaved family, but in the end the truth came out: a group of prisoners, including his own cellmate, had assaulted him.

"Gave him a taste of his own medicine," was the way the warden put it. Apparently it was a matter of honor among hardened convicts to punish child molesters. Even murderers and armed robbers, Diedre supposed, had their standards.

It might have been a twisted kind of poetic justice, but still, it was painful to think about. Amber couldn't talk about it, except to say that she wouldn't have wished it on anyone.

As Susan went on with the graveside service, Diedre let her eyes rest on each of the faces in turn. Amber looked stunned and disbelieving. TwoJoe stood at her side, stoic and silent, his face an unexpressive mask. Meg bit her lip and gazed anxiously in Amber's direction. There was no mourning here. Only shock and emptiness and a grim kind of acceptance.

"Let us pray," Susan was saying. Diedre bowed her head, gripped Carlene's hand, and waited.

"Gracious God—" The words hung on the chilled air for a moment before Susan's voice continued. "This group of family and friends gathered here today must, above all things, depend upon your grace. We have so many unanswered questions, and so many unresolved conflicts, and we can do nothing except commend to your wisdom and justice the soul of Duncan McAlister. We ask that you reach down into our hearts and heal our wounded places, that you would be with us and among us to comfort and strengthen us. There has been far too much loss among us in recent days, and we pray for your guidance through our grief, and your light for a new beginning . . ."

Diedre's heart clenched with longing and with pain. This was no formulaic prayer, no attempt to gloss over the horrible realities of Daddy's life and death. The honesty of Susan Quentin's prayer pierced to the depths of her soul, and she felt tears rise into her throat—not sorrow for her father's passing, but grief for her own losses, and a desperate desire that Susan's words might be true, that God really might be present with her to comfort and to heal.

"Give us courage to face the future," Susan continued, "and empower us to speak the truth, for only the truth will set us free. May we come to you with our brokenness, and may your Spirit lead us in finding new ways to redeem this moment and bring resurrection out of death. May you be for all of us—especially for Amber and Diedre—the mother who always embraces and nurtures, and the father who always loves and protects. In the name of the One who created us, redeemed us, and continues to sustain us. Amen."

Diedre lifted her head and looked at Amber. Two shiny tracks ran down her cheeks, but whether they were from rain or tears, she couldn't tell.

"It will take a couple of months for the will to get through the probate system," the lawyer said, "but as there are no other relatives involved, it should be a fairly straightforward process."

Diedre watched the thin, intense face of Clifton Rivers as he shuffled the papers in front of him. Rivers, an attorney who had attended law school with Elise Glass, had come highly recommended. He was a little stuffy and a bit obsessive, but extremely thorough and meticulous.

He unfolded the will and scrutinized it. "In accordance with Duncan McAlister's wishes, as expressed in this last will and testament, signed and notarized shortly after the death of Cecilia McAlister, the entire estate will pass to Diedre Chaney McAlister." He cast an anxious glance in Amber's direction. "Unless you intend to contest, Miss Chaney? You do have that right."

"No." Amber shook her head. "I won't contest it."

"She doesn't need to contest it," Diedre said. "Half of it will be hers anyway."

The lawyer nodded. "As you wish. It is yours to do with as you please." He handed a certified check to Diedre.

"What's this? I thought you said it would take a couple of months."

"That check represents the proceeds from your father's life insurance policy. Life insurance payments do not go through probate, nor are they subject to any inheritance taxes. Since your mother predeceased your father, you are the secondary beneficiary."

Diedre stared at the check. "Two million dollars, tax free?"

"The exposed tip of the iceberg," the attorney said. "The entire estate, including stocks, bonds, cash value of your father's IRA, and the estimated value of the house and personal property, comes to—" He flipped pages in his leather-covered notebook. "Just under ten million."

"Ten million dollars?"

"Actually, the precise figure is nine million, eight-hundred fifty-six thousand—"

Diedre held up a hand. "I get the idea."

"That's not counting the two million you hold in your hand. Also, you can sue the state prison system for negligence in your father's death."

Diedre sent a sidelong glance in Amber's direction. Amber was shaking her head and frowning slightly. "I don't think so."

"I believe you might have a good case," Rivers persisted. "I am not a litigator, but there is a gentleman in my firm who—"

"Absolutely not," Diedre said firmly. "I can safely say that we've both had our fill of the legal system for quite some time to come." She pushed an index card across the table. "We can be reached at this address and telephone number. When the will has cleared probate, let us know, and meanwhile we'll make some decisions about what we're going to do with the inheritance."

"Decisions? What's to decide? Travel around the world; buy the Biltmore Estate." The attorney, clearly attempting to inject a lighter note into the proceedings, forced out a barking kind of chuckle, as if completely unfamiliar with the sound. "With ten million dollars, you can have everything you ever wanted—"

He caught a glimpse of Diedre's expression and, properly chastened, clamped his mouth shut.

"Not everything," Diedre corrected. "All the money in the world can't buy back the past."

While Meg and Diedre went to get new tires installed on the Camry, Amber and TwoJoe sat in the porch glider and gazed out over the Blue Ridge. Susan Quentin and Vernon Houston had already flown back to Seattle, and Meg and TwoJoe were booked on the last Delta flight out of Asheville, with connections in Atlanta. Amid all the chaos of her father's death and funeral, Amber had had little time alone with TwoJoe, and she wanted to make the most of these few stolen moments.

"You were right—it is beautiful here," he sighed, stretching his long legs out in front of him.

"It's beautiful at home, too." She touched a hand to his arm.

"I wish you were flying back with me. I'd love to make the drive with you and Diedre, but I just can't—"

"I know, you can't spend too much time away from the llamas." Amber laughed. "How is Lloser, anyway?"

TwoJoe grinned. "To tell the truth, he's getting a little out of hand. He takes all the credit for rescuing you from the fire, and now that he knows you're going to use him for a model for your next sculpture, he's demanding a private dressing room and a thirty percent raise in his feed allotment." He dropped his voice to a whisper. "He even wants a legal name change—he wants to be called *Winner*."

"Did you agree to his terms?"

"Not yet. We're still in negotiations."

"Sounds like he needs a good agent."

TwoJoe put an arm around Amber's neck and pulled her close. "Whose side are you on, anyway?"

"Your side," she said and lifted her face for a kiss. "I'm always on your side."

When he released her, Amber leaned against his shoulder. "I want to show you something." She removed the gauze bandages from one hand and held it out to him, flexing her fingers, which were still covered with dark scabs. "Look. They don't crack when I move them." She unwrapped the other hand and set the gauze aside. "I think I can do without the bandages now, but they're still pretty ugly. I wonder if—"

"Nothing about you could ever be ugly." He captured her hands gently and pressed them to his lips.

"They'll always be scarred, but they're getting better all the time. I think I should be able to get back to work again soon."

TwoJoe threw back his head and laughed. "What's the matter? Is half of twelve million dollars not enough for you?"

Amber poked him playfully in the ribs. "It's not about the money, and you know it. If I had all the money in the world, I'd still sculpt. It's therapy. It's my creative outlet. I love it." She kissed him on the nose. "So get used to it, buster. You've got yourself a woman with dirt under her nails."

He pulled back and looked into her eyes. "Do I?"

Amber felt her stomach quiver. "If you want me, you do."

TwoJoe closed his eyes for a moment and took a deep breath. "Amber, I—"

"Wait." She put her fingers to his lips. "Let me say something first."

"All right. Go ahead."

She exhaled heavily and tried to collect her thoughts. "You are the finest man I've ever met in my entire life, TwoJoe. You're honest and sensitive and loving. You make me laugh. You accept me as I am. I feel safe with you—and you know I have a lot of reasons not to feel safe."

"You'll always be safe with me."

"I believe that. But I've spent a lot of years trying to find a way to re-appropriate the power that was taken from me when I was very young. I've had a hard time allowing myself to open up to love, and—"

"You're saying you won't marry me." His voice was distant, strained, and his jaw tightened.

"I'm saying I don't want you to *ask* me to marry you."

He averted his eyes and stared off over the multilayered peaks of the Blue Ridge. "All right. If that's what you want."

"TwoJoe, please look at me." He turned his head back in her direction, and she felt a rush of love and tenderness welling up in her and flowing out toward him. "I need to make my own choices, to determine the course of my own life," she said. "I want to act, to be decisive, not simply to respond." She smiled at his look of confusion and put a hand to his cheek. It was the first time since the night of the barn fire that her fingers had felt the touch of his skin, and a tingle went up her arm. "I love you, TwoJoe. I've loved you for a long time, even when I couldn't admit it to myself. I want to spend the rest of my life with you." She looked deep into his eyes. "TwoJoe Elkhorn, will you marry me?"

"Huh?"

Amber laughed so hard that tears filled her eyes. "I said, will you marry me? There are only two possible responses: yes or no. Not 'huh?' It's not a difficult question."

The truth of what she was saying finally registered on him, and his eyes widened. "You want to get married? You and me? The two of us?"

"Of course I do, you big dolt. And yes, I do think it would be preferable if it were just the two of us. I tend to be a little rigid on the monogamy issue. Yes or no?"

"Yes!" he shouted. He jumped up and lifted her off her feet, swinging her around in an enormous hug. "Yes! Yes! YES!"

"TwoJoe, put me down," she gasped. "I'm getting dizzy."

"Sorry." He set her on her feet again, then drew her close in a lingering kiss. "I told you I'd wait forever for you," he murmured into her hair. "Thanks for not taking me up on the offer."

43

Holy Saturday

Kitsap County, Washington
March 1996

Diedre sat at her desk and stared through the rain-streaked window at the shrouded mountains and the gray waters of Hood Canal. She could hardly believe she had been here nine months—in this snug little cabin half a mile down the road from Amber and TwoJoe and Meg.

It was a small place, only one bedroom, but it had a nice big living room with a fireplace and was surrounded by woods and faced out over the water. It couldn't have been more perfect.

For years the owner, like TwoJoe, had been badgered to sell, but he had resisted, and for much the same reason. When TwoJoe had contacted him, offering to rent the empty cabin, he had jumped at the chance. With a little fixing up, it had become an ideal situation for Diedre—close enough to be part of the family, far enough away to give her some privacy.

She took out her journal and rummaged in the desk drawer, looking for a pen. But instead, her hand closed over a stiff, white card, and she pulled it from the drawer and held it to the light.

With great joy and eternal gratitude to God,

Amber Chaney
and
Joseph Elkhorn II

request the honor of your presence
as they respond to God's calling
and celebrate their vows of lifelong love

Saturday, April 20, 1996
4:00 P.M.

All Saints' Episcopal Church
Viking Junction, Washington

Buffet and Barn Dance to follow at the Elkhorn Farm
6:30 P.M.

Diedre smiled at the invitation and ran her fingers over the raised lettering. In just a little over three weeks, Amber and TwoJoe would be married. The barn had been restored—razed to the ground and rebuilt, actually, with a wonderful new studio for Amber. Her hands, although scarred, had completely healed, the sculpture of Sam and Lloser was finished, and she had commissions that would keep her busy for at least the rest of this year.

Everything seemed to be working out. Everyone seemed to be moving on with their lives. Everyone except Diedre.

She had certainly made progress in her therapy—she couldn't deny that. She had come to grips with the recurring anger at her father and her frustration that he had died before ever acknowledging his culpability. She had finally quit blaming God for what had happened and accepted the inevitability of evil in the world. She had even been able to embrace her faith again—not the blind trust of her childhood, but a deeper, more reality-based, more thoughtful faith. She just hadn't been able to get over that last hurdle—that invisible, unnamed barrier that stood between her and a sense of her own worth. In Susan's words, she hadn't yet crossed the great divide between *victim* and *survivor*. She hadn't found her own place of rest and acceptance and peace.

Diedre opened the journal and, following Susan's suggestions, began to try to write about what she was feeling. But the words wouldn't come. Nothing would come. She had been spinning her wheels for weeks now, bogged down in an emotional quagmire all the way up to her psychological axles.

Something is missing, she wrote. *Something I can't seem to get my mind around. I've spent hours with Susan, and even more hours writing in this blasted journal, and although part of me thinks I'm coming to grips with what has happened, there's still an enormous hole in my heart. I keep coming back to a phrase Susan used in her prayer at Daddy's funeral, something about "finding new ways to redeem this moment," but I'm not at all sure what that means. I feel as if I'm waiting for something, waiting in the darkness . . .*

Diedre laid the journal entry down in front of Susan Quentin and flopped into the leather chair across from her desk. "I'm stuck," she sighed.

"Stuck?" Susan gave her a curious look. "Why do you say that?"

"Just read it, will you?" Diedre's tone came out cross and demanding, and she shook her head. "I'm sorry. I didn't mean to be irritable with you. It's simply that—well, I don't know where to go from here."

Susan gazed down at the journal. "Waiting in the darkness, huh?" She tilted her head. "Ah, yes. Holy Saturday. I remember it well."

"Saturday?" Diedre tried unsuccessfully to restrain the sarcasm in her tone. "Last time I looked, it was Tuesday."

"Chronologically, it is Tuesday," Susan chuckled. "But spiritually, it's Saturday."

"What do you mean by that?"

"Well, next week is Passion Week—for the Christian church, the most important celebration of the year. But too often, when we remember Christ's passion, we tend to make this quantum leap from Good Friday to Easter Sunday. Straight from the crucifixion to the resurrection. It's human nature, I guess. We have to acknowledge the bad stuff, but we want to rush ahead to the good stuff as quickly as possible. So we skip over Holy Saturday altogether."

"And Holy Saturday implies—" Diedre prompted.

"The waiting place, the tomb of in-between. The place of darkness, of death. We may have faith that resurrection is coming, but we still have to wait. Wait for the night to pass. Wait for the stone to be rolled away, and for the morning light to come in. Wait for the redemption that is to be."

Deep in Diedre's inner being, something quivered—the twang of a bowstring, the vibration of a tuning fork. In these months of counseling with Susan, she had learned to listen to her spirit, had begun to discern when some idea struck a nerve. This one reverberated in her soul like an entire handbell choir, and she leaned forward.

"All right," she said. "Let's talk about this idea of redemption. During the graveside service at Daddy's funeral, you said something about finding new ways to redeem the moment. Do you remember?"

"I remember." Susan nodded, raising both eyebrows. "I'm just shocked that *you* remember. Most people forget what my *sermon* was about between the final benediction and the time they get out the door—never mind anything I say in the prayers." She grinned and leaned back in her chair.

"Well, this prayer must have been important, because I do remember it," Diedre said. "And I think we need to talk about it. I assume you weren't talking about *eternal* redemption—like, being saved."

"No. I was referring to discovering the blessing in the midst of the curse."

"Amber talked to me about that once. She said I was the blessing that had come out of the curse of her abuse."

"And do you believe that?"

"I don't know. I still have questions about it."

"She means it. You've been an essential factor in her healing—you've helped her redeem that experience and find a way to wholeness." She paused and gazed into Diedre's eyes. "It seems to me that the challenge before you now is to find your own catalyst, your own path to justice and healing."

"But I wasn't abused—not directly, anyway," Diedre objected. "Daddy never did to me what he did to Amber."

"Still, you're affected by it—very deeply affected. And the results are the same. Your father may not have molested you, but he did abuse you. He betrayed your trust. He violated you. He withheld his love from you. He took something very important away from you—your mother. And your identity."

Diedre sighed. She knew all this. They had been through it a hundred times. "I've accepted that. I've confronted the truth, faced the pain. So what's missing? How come I'm not making more progress?"

Susan shook her head. "Diedre, I know you're eager to have this over and done with, to get on with your life. I want that for you, too. But you have to realize that healing takes time. Sometimes years—even decades."

"You're saying I just have to sit on my hands and wait for some kind of miraculous intervention?" Diedre snapped. "That's not very encouraging."

"Maybe not, but it's reality." Susan paused. "In counseling women who have been abused, therapists have identified a number of factors that make healing possible. Do you remember our discussion of them?"

"Yes, I did some journaling about them." Diedre retrieved her journal from Susan's desk, flipped pages, and read through the list: "Truth-telling, Acknowledgment of the Story, Compassion, Protection for

Others, Accountability for the Perpetrator, Restitution, Vindication."

"Anything there you want to talk about?"

Diedre shrugged. "The first three are pretty much covered, I think. I've addressed the truth about what Daddy did, and everyone in my life has given me affirmation and understanding about what I'm going through. As to protection, Daddy's dead now, so he can't hurt anyone else. And his inheritance provided a kind of restitution for me and Amber, although he didn't do it voluntarily." She paused. "But the accountability one still bothers me a lot."

"Because your father never admitted his culpability?"

"Yes. Amber and I have talked about it. We both wish he had said something—anything—to indicate that he took some kind of responsibility for the abuse, for all the pain and suffering he caused. But we're never going to have that."

"No, you won't," Susan agreed. "This list is a paradigm, an accounting of what survivors of abuse ideally need to come to healing. Most of us live with less than the ideal."

Diedre looked up, startled. "Sometimes I forget you are a survivor of domestic abuse."

"That's a compliment, I think. But you need to know, Diedre—I *never* forget. And neither will you."

"But aren't you *required* to forget? As a Christian, I mean. Doesn't the Bible say we're supposed to 'forgive and forget'?"

"That's not from the Bible. It's from *King Lear,* if I recall correctly," Susan chuckled. "A lot of what people attribute to the Bible is actually Shakespeare—or *Poor Richard's Almanac.* Not the kind of sources I'd choose to formulate my theology—or my psychology either, for that matter."

"Still," Diedre persisted, "the Bible *does* talk about forgiving our enemies. But where Daddy is concerned, I just can't stomach the thought. The idea of having to forgive him makes me physically sick. I can't go there."

"Then don't."

Diedre opened her mouth to respond, but for a minute no sound came. Then she blurted out, "You're an Episcopal *priest*, Susan! Won't they excommunicate you, or something, for saying such a thing?"

Susan shrugged. "Let 'em try. Diedre, when people talk about forgiveness—especially in a situation of sexual abuse—what they're really asking you to do is short-circuit the process of healing. They're really saying, 'Hurry up and forgive him so we won't have to think about these uncomfortable issues.' But we're not dealing with a four-year-old who takes away his little sister's toy, or even an adult who inadvertently hurts someone else's feelings. This isn't something we can gloss over by saying, 'It's OK.' What your father did is *not* OK, and I'd be doing you a grave disservice if I even *suggested* that forgiveness is some kind of spiritual cure-all."

She paused and looked into Diedre's eyes. "One of these days—one of these *years*—you'll look back and think about what your father did, and it will truly be *past*. You won't forget it, but when you remember, you'll see it from a different perspective. It will still be part of your history that once caused you great pain, but it will also spur you on to justice, to help others like yourself find peace and safety and healing. I believe that's what forgiveness means—that you ultimately find yourself set free, no longer controlled by the abuse or the abuser."

She pointed toward the list Diedre held in her hands. "That brings us to the final item on that list. Vindication. To be set free, to be whole, to be justified. To be declared worthy."

"Do you think that will ever happen for me?" Diedre asked.

"Yes, I do. But you need to give it time."

"It seems to me," Diedre mused, "that what I'm really looking for is a way to unearth some justice in what Amber and I have gone through—in your words, to find a catalyst that might turn the curse into a blessing. You say that Amber's relationship with me has done that for her. But I'm still trying to find my way to the blessing." She looked up. "Let's get back to your prayer at the funeral, when you spoke of 'new ways to redeem this moment.' What, exactly, did you mean by that?"

Susan gazed at the ceiling, obviously considering the question. "Literally, the word *redeem* means to buy back, to recover ownership. And that's exactly what you're seeking to do—to get the ownership of your life back. I suppose in that prayer I was asking for the Spirit's guidance that all of us—especially you and Amber—might be able to find some creative ways to rediscover God's presence in the midst of this darkness." She put a hand to her forehead and furrowed her brow. "That's not very specific, I know, and maybe not very helpful. I just have to believe that there's a way to bring something constructive out of so much destruction."

"Maybe at least part of the answer for me lies in the money I inherited when Daddy died."

"As restitution?" Susan asked.

"Partly restitution, but more than that. When the lawyer told Amber and me about Daddy's will, he joked that such an enormous inheritance could buy anything our hearts desired. It made me angry. I told him all the money in the world couldn't buy back the past."

"And you were right," Susan affirmed. "It can't. We don't have the power to change what has happened."

"But we do have the power to change what *will* happen," Diedre mused. "Maybe that's what redeeming the moment means for me. Maybe that's where the justice lies, if I can do something to make tomorrow different—and better."

She got up from her chair, pulled open the door to Susan's office, and stood there for a moment in the doorway. "I may have to wait awhile longer for this tomb to open. But I think I see a crack of light, feel just a bit of fresh air. It gives me hope that Holy Saturday won't last forever, that Easter will eventually arrive. And maybe a little bit of hope is all I need."

44

Sacred Promises

Saturday dawned clear and cool, with a topaz-blue sky and just enough of a breeze to stir up the waters of Hood Canal. TwoJoe sat on the back porch sipping from a mug of coffee and watched as the sun tipped the high peaks of the Olympic Mountains. It was a perfect day, a day bright with promise and graced by the sweet breath of benediction.

Of course, it wouldn't have mattered one bit to him if it had been a typical drizzly spring morning with dark clouds lowering overhead. It wasn't the weather that made this April day perfect. It was the fact that this afternoon, before God, their friends, and a mighty cloud of invisible witnesses, he and Amber Chaney would take vows that would unite them as one—heart, soul, mind, and strength.

"For better or for worse," he murmured under his breath. And he meant it. But he couldn't help believing that they had already weathered the *worse*, and that from here on out their life together would be mostly *better*. Except, of course, for the fact that he was going to feel like an overstuffed penguin in that tuxedo.

TwoJoe heard a noise in the kitchen behind him and looked through the screen door to see Amber pouring herself a cup of coffee. Still in her flannel pajamas and a blue chenille bathrobe, she looked sleepy and rumpled and absolutely adorable. Since both of them were still living in the farmhouse, they had decided to forgo the wedding day tradition of the groom not seeing the bride until she walked down the aisle. He still hadn't gotten a single glimpse of her wedding dress, but he was pretty sure the sight of her in it would knock all the breath out of him. If she was this delightful in flannels, with her hair stuck up in all directions—

She came out to the porch with her coffee, kissed him, and dropped into the chair beside him. "G'morning."

"Not quite awake, I see."

"It'll get better," she mumbled. "Just give me a chance to get some caffeine into my system."

TwoJoe looked at her and began to laugh. "I love you so much!"

She glared at him over her coffee cup. "Are you making fun of me?"

"No. I mean it. I do love you. You're so—so cute."

"Well, honey, if you think I'm cute now, give me a few hours."

"I can't wait." He slid his chair closer to hers and nuzzled her neck. "Why don't we get married now—I mean *right now*, with you in your flannel jams and me in my jeans?"

"And waste the five hundred dollars I spent on that wedding dress? I don't think so."

TwoJoe sat back and chuckled. Like most of the men he knew, he didn't care much about the pomp and circumstance of a wedding. But if that's what Amber wanted, that's what she'd get. And it wasn't really a big wedding, as weddings go. They had planned a simple ceremony, with Meg and Diedre as dual maids of honor, Vernon Houston as best man, and little Sam, who had flown in from Texas two days ago, as the ring-bearer. Afterward, in place of a formal reception, they would host a dinner and dance in the barn. The figures Amber had picked out for the top of the wedding cake were a Native American chief in buckskins and a bride in homespun. Not quite a conventional wedding, but then, they weren't exactly a conventional couple.

"I assume everything's ready, that we haven't forgotten anything?"

She slanted a glance at him. "Whatever we've forgotten just won't get done. I'm trying not to obsess. We're getting married at four, and I intend to enjoy this day to the fullest."

TwoJoe reached over and squeezed her hand. The new skin was still a little puckered, but it was soft and smooth, and he relished the feel of it. The modest diamond solitaire caught the morning sunlight and flickered little dots of color around the porch. "We could afford a bigger ring," he mused.

"We could afford a lot of things," she countered. "But I don't see any reason to change our whole lifestyle just because we've got the money to do it." She shifted in her chair and looked at him. "What do we want that we don't already have?"

He grinned at her. "Not a thing. I've got you, and all this—" He waved a hand toward the mountain vista. "A new barn, and a brand-new bright red pickup truck. What else could any man desire?"

"And you're OK with staying here? Meg's got all her stuff moved down to your apartment, and I've shifted my things to the master bedroom. You don't want a new house, do you?"

"Good grief, no." TwoJoe blurted out. "I love this house. Although when we get back from our honeymoon, I would like to do some renovations on the upstairs bathroom, and—" he waggled his eyebrows at her and poked her in the ribs— "buy a new king-size bed."

She slapped his hand away playfully. "Ah. Don't want to have to be *too* close to me, huh?"

"Make that a *single* bed." He captured her hand and kissed it. "I want to be as close to you as possible."

❦

Meg and Amber were clearing the breakfast dishes from the table when TwoJoe heard footsteps on the back porch and looked up to see Sam Houston peering in through the screen. "Come on in, Sam. We've just finished breakfast, but there's some French toast left." He slammed through the door, gave hugs all around, and flopped into a chair at the table.

Amber tousled his blonde head and gave him a kiss on the cheek.

"Aw, Amber." He grimaced and swiped at his face, but the flush of pink that went up his neck told TwoJoe that he was pleased with the attention.

"How's Texas? You doing all right down there?"

"Yeah. Mom and Dad are glad to have me back, I think. But I miss Grandpa and Grandma—" He ducked his head. "And all of you."

"Well, we've missed you, too." Meg set a plate of French toast and bacon in front of him. "You're growing."

"I turned seven last month," he said with his mouth full. "And I did a report for school on llamas. Grandpa says he'll buy two of them for me when I'm ten."

"You got your tuxedo for the wedding?" Amber asked.

"Yeah. Do I really have to wear it?"

"Yes, you really have to wear it. You'll look so handsome in it—just wait, you'll see. And there's a little girl from church who's just about your age. I bet she'll think you're the best-looking fellow she's ever seen." Amber winked in TwoJoe's direction.

"Girls? Yuck!" Sam wolfed down the last of the French toast and stood up, grabbing TwoJoe's hand. "Thanks for the breakfast, Meg. You gotta come with me, TwoJoe. I got something to show you!"

"You're welcome." Meg took Sam's plate to the kitchen. "What's the rush, Sam? What do you have to show TwoJoe?"

He gave her a condescending look. "Guy stuff. It's a secret. You'll know soon enough."

"So, what is this all about?" TwoJoe said when Sam had led him by the hand down the path past the barn.

"Keep your eyes closed."

"They *are* closed. If I break my leg and have to miss my own wedding, Sam Houston—"

"We're almost there."

TwoJoe could feel the sun on his face, smell the scents of grass and hay and llama feed. They must be nearing the pasture gate. "Almost where?" He suppressed a chuckle. He had, indeed, missed Sam's presence in his life the past few months. The boy had a way of turning the most mundane event into an adventure, and—

"Okay, stop. Now, open your eyes."

TwoJoe obeyed, blinking in the bright sunlight. Just on the other side of the gate, Lloser stood tethered to the fence. Around his long wooly neck, held in place by elastic bands, he wore a black bow tie and a starched white pin-tucked shirt front with gray pearl studs. A tuxedo. A llama in a tuxedo!

TwoJoe laughed until tears streamed down his face and he couldn't breathe. "It's wonderful!" He swept Sam up in an exuberant hug and set him on the top rail of the fence. "Where did you come up with such an idea?"

"Grandpa helped." Sam grinned so broadly that TwoJoe thought his face would crack.

"Well, we've got to show Meg and Amber. They'll love it."

"No, we can't," Sam objected. "It's supposed to be a surprise."

"A surprise?"

"Yeah. I'm going to bring him with me this afternoon."

TwoJoe stared at the boy. "To the *wedding?*"

"Well, yeah, to the wedding." Sam twisted his mouth in an expression that said he thought TwoJoe was incredibly dense. "I mean, Lloser *did* save Amber from the fire, didn't he? He's practically family—"

"Sam, he's a llama. He can't come to the wedding."

The boy's face crumpled. "Why not?"

"Because—" TwoJoe groped for the right words. He hated to disappoint Sam, especially after he had gone to so much trouble, but he doubted that Amber, as much as she loved the animals, would care to have Lloser as an unexpected member of the wedding party. "Because the church is going to be very crowded, and llamas don't like enclosed spaces."

Sam thought about this for a minute. "Oh."

"You wouldn't want him to be uncomfortable, would you?"

"I—I guess not."

TwoJoe could tell that Sam was on the verge of tears and trying very hard to hide it. "Tell you what, Sam. After the wedding, tonight, we're going to have a party here, in the new barn. It's going to be much more fun than the wedding ceremony, with lots of food and a band and everything. Don't you think Lloser would enjoy that more than a stuffy old service in the church?"

"I guess so." He brightened a little. "Can he wear his tuxedo?"

"Absolutely. If we're going to have to wear ours, I guess he will, too." He patted the llama's long neck. "Sorry, old boy."

Sam reached over and unhooked the shirt front from Lloser's neck, then untied the rope that tethered the llama's halter to the fence. "I'll put it back on him in time for the party," he assured TwoJoe solemnly. He got down from the fence, holding the makeshift tuxedo in one hand. "Let's not tell Amber and Meg about this," he said. "I want them to be surprised."

TwoJoe stifled a laugh. "They'll be surprised, all right," he said as they started back toward the house. "Believe me, they'd never guess this one in a million years."

Diedre stood at the front of the church and watched as Meg made her way down the aisle to stand next to her. The strains of "Love Divine, All Loves Excelling" emanated from the pipe organ and reverberated through the rafters. All Saints' was a small church, very old, with leaded glass windows and exposed beams, and relatively unadorned except for the banks of candles entwined with flowers that now stood on either side of the altar.

She glanced over at TwoJoe, so handsome in his tux, so proud and tall, with Vernon Houston at his side as best man. He craned his neck and shifted nervously, waiting for his bride to appear. Diedre knew without looking exactly the moment Amber stepped into view, because TwoJoe 's dark eyes went wide and soft, and he bit his lip to suppress the tears that instantly sparkled in his dark eyes.

The congregation rose to its feet and turned. Amber, resplendent in an off-white dress with tiny satin rosebuds around the neckline, lifted her head and slowly advanced to take TwoJoe's outstretched hand.

She had never looked happier or more radiant. This love, Amber had confessed to Diedre, had given her a liberty she had never known before, a freedom to become the person she was created to be, to begin to let go of the past, to begin again.

Amber reached the altar, and together she and TwoJoe moved forward. On the step above them, Susan Quentin stood with an open prayer book in her hands and an enormous smile on her face. "God of second chances," she prayed in a triumphant voice that echoed throughout the sanctuary, "we have come to worship you!"

The ceremony was brief and simple: the exchange of vows, a short homily about loving God and one another, the giving and receiving of rings. But there was one unorthodox addition to the traditional marriage vows. Before the final benediction, Susan faced the congregation and said, "All of us have made sacred vows in our lives—commitments to God, to our loved ones, to our calling. In honor of the holy promises Amber and TwoJoe have taken in our presence today, let us join together to reaffirm our own commitments in a Litany of Covenant."

Diedre looked down at her program and, along with the rest of the congregation, joined in a vow to support and honor Amber and TwoJoe's marriage, a vow to pursue truth and the knowledge of God, a vow to remain faithful to the people God had placed in their lives as family. But when she came to the closing sentence of the litany, her eyes began to water and a lump formed in her throat so that she could barely choke out the words.

"Give us courage and wisdom, O God, to work for justice, wholeness, and peace in our world. May our homes be a place of sanctuary, a rest for the weary, a refuge for all who need a touch of your healing grace. Amen."

Diedre was still staring down at the page when Susan pronounced TwoJoe and Amber husband and wife. She missed the kiss, almost missed her cue to take Vernon Houston's arm and make her exit. Her mind was spinning, and something deep in her spirit said, "Yes!"

May our homes be a place of sanctuary . . .

This was it. The guidance she had been waiting for. The confirmation she had sought. The catalyst that would bring healing and freedom not only to Diedre herself, but to countless others like her.

She had never before felt so totally shaken and so completely energized all at once. Now, at last, she understood what Amber meant when she talked about inspiration—an idea that comes fully formed, totally out of the blue—so unexpected and so perfect that you knew it had to have its source in someone wiser and bigger and more creative than yourself. Her heart swelled with joy, and a warm, inescapable light penetrated the last dark place inside her soul.

Diedre McAlister had found her calling.

45

The Moment of Truth

Angel's Rest, an enormous Victorian inn situated on the strait between Port Angeles and Vancouver Island, had to be the perfect setting for a honeymoon. The two-room suite had a balcony overlooking the water, a fourposter bed the size of Rhode Island, and a marble bathroom with a tub as big as a six-person spa. A small fire burned in the grate, more for atmosphere than to ward off the chill of the evening. The flames danced, casting a warm, flickering light over the scene.

"How did you ever find such a place, TwoJoe?" Amber sighed when he led her into the room. "It's gorgeous."

"Not as gorgeous as you."

A red-vested porter brought their luggage in, then busied himself with opening the balcony door and turning down the bed while TwoJoe fished in his wallet for an appropriate tip.

"I looked at several other places," he said when the porter finally left. "But most of them were bed-and-breakfasts, and I didn't think that would give us enough privacy." He walked with her onto the balcony and stood with his chest pressed to her back and both arms around her, looking out over the moonlight-spangled water. "One of them was run by a little old lady who kept going on about how nice it would be to have *company*. I couldn't get through to her that this was our honeymoon, and we probably wouldn't be doing much socializing." He laughed and kissed her on the nape of the neck. "This is our week, and I don't intend to share you with anyone."

His right hand came up to her throat and gently caressed the sensitive spot just under her ear. His touch was achingly tender and the pressure minimal, but a chill went up Amber's spine nevertheless. This wasn't Daddy, she reminded herself resolutely, and it wasn't Shiv Willis. It was TwoJoe, the man she loved with all her soul. The man she had married. But no amount of logic could quell the shuddering of her heart, and despite her best intentions, she stiffened in his embrace.

Amber should have expected to be confronted with such apprehensions on their wedding night. Weeks ago, Susan had talked with her about the possibility that intimacy with TwoJoe might raise some old memories and fears. But Amber had dismissed the idea. Their love, she told Susan firmly, was strong enough to overcome anything from the past.

Now she wasn't so sure.

She looked down at TwoJoe's sinewy, brown arm, clasped around her waist. The watch on his wrist read 11:45. The reception had gone on for hours—for all she knew, it might still be in progress. She and TwoJoe had made their escape after the cutting of the cake, but changing clothes, saying their good-byes, and making the drive to Port Angeles took time. Now it was nearly midnight, and she was exhausted from the events of the day.

"Tired?" she asked, forcing herself to lean back against him and hoping he wouldn't discern the quaver in her voice.

"Not a bit."

"Well, I am. How about if we change clothes and relax a little?"

He kissed her again, took her hand, and led her back into the room, closing the door behind them. "Good idea. I'm starving. I didn't get much to eat at the reception. Where's that cake Emmaline sent along with us?"

"In a grocery bag next to the suitcases. I think she packed up some of the other food, too."

Amber retrieved a white negligee and her cosmetics kit from her bag and started for the bathroom. "I'll be out in a few minutes."

For just a moment he blocked her way, and as she eased around him, he fingered the satiny fabric of the gown. "Don't take too long. I can't wait to see how you look in that."

Amber closed the bathroom door and leaned against it, breathing hard. All her rationalizations failed her, and no matter how hard she tried to dismiss them, her mind kept bringing up unwelcome visions: How she had recoiled whenever Rick Knutson had gotten too close. How he had left her without a backward glance. And other images, too—memories of pain and terror and tears. Of fear in the darkness. Of footsteps drawing closer.

She tried to shake off the bitter recollections, to replace them with the image of TwoJoe's tender smile and adoring eyes. "Focus," she muttered under her breath. "What happened before had nothing to do with love, or even with sex. It was violence, power, domination. This is love. This is God's gift."

Amber pulled off the slacks and sweater she had worn for traveling. She brushed her teeth, ran a comb through her curls, and slipped into the silky, white negligee. It wasn't revealing, as negligees went, but still she felt vulnerable, exposed. The mirror showed a reflection that looked to her like a little girl trying to play grown-up. Maybe she should have just opted for her flannels.

Well, she had stalled long enough. Her husband was waiting, and no matter how understanding and compassionate he was, he probably wouldn't be pleased if she spent all night in the bathroom. Gathering together the tattered remnants of her courage, she opened the door.

TwoJoe sat on the sofa dressed in navy, satin pajamas so new they still had creases in them from the folds. His bare feet were propped on the coffee table and in one hand he held a plate piled high with smoked salmon, chicken wings, and chocolate cake with cream cheese frosting. He was just about to bite into a chicken wing when he caught sight of her. His eyes widened, and the wing hung in midair between the plate and his mouth, completely forgotten. "You," he said in a low, breathless voice, "are absolutely beautiful."

Amber sat down beside him. "I'm not. I feel stupid." She grimaced at him, then looked down at the silky gown. "This isn't me, TwoJoe. I'm flannel pajamas, not satin negligees. I feel like a phony."

He dropped the chicken wing onto the plate, set it down on the table, and turned to face her. "I don't care if you're dressed in a feed sack," he said firmly. "You are, and always will be, beautiful to me."

"I'm a middle-aged woman with a whole lot of baggage," she corrected. "Are you sure you want me?"

"I'm sure." He cut a glance over to their suitcases and grinned. "And I don't see that much baggage."

Amber cuffed him playfully on the shoulder and felt herself relax a little. "You know what I mean."

The grin faded. "I know. Do we need to talk about this?" His dark eyes caught her gaze and held it. "You do realize how much I love you."

"Yes," she whispered around the lump in her throat. "And I love you. I'm just a little—"

"Scared?" he finished.

Amber nodded. "It's ridiculous, TwoJoe. I'm not a teenager. I'm a grown woman."

"A grown woman who has had to face some terrible realities." He reached out a callused hand and touched her cheek. "What do you need from me, darling?"

"Patience."

TwoJoe smiled. "Given how long I've waited for you, I think I can do that. What else?"

"I—I need to know you won't leave me if—"

He laid his fingers across her lips. "This afternoon, I took a vow before God to love you and stand beside you as long as we both live. Grandpa Joe taught me that an Elkhorn man keeps his word. And just so you'll be sure, I'll remind you, every day for the next hundred years or so. I'm not going anywhere."

Amber stared at him, and to her horror she felt tears begin to well up in her eyes. This wasn't the way she had imagined it, wasn't the way it was supposed to be. She ought to come to him willingly, joyfully . . .

TwoJoe reached out and brushed a tear from her cheek with his thumb, then captured her hands in his and held them. "Listen to me," he said softly. "When I asked you to marry me, I knew this might be difficult for you."

"You didn't ask me." She gulped hard and tried to smile. "I asked you."

"So you did." He gave a little chuckle. "Well then, when I said yes, I knew what I was getting into. Amber, I would never knowingly cause you harm."

"I know that—," she began, but he silenced her with a look.

"This is kind of hard for me, so let me finish. I would never *deliberately* hurt you, but it's possible, even likely, that I might inadvertently do or say something that brings up disturbing or painful memories. If you feel the least bit uncomfortable with anything that happens between us, all you have to do is tell me. Be honest. We'll stop right then and there and talk about it."

Amber felt her lower lip begin to tremble. "Are you sure? You won't be upset with me?"

TwoJoe's eyes softened, and she felt as if he could see clear down to the bottom of her soul. "We've got all the time in the world, sweetheart. We have a whole lifetime together."

He opened his arms, and she leaned into him. Gently, ever so slowly, he bent forward and kissed her, a kiss that tasted of smoked salmon and chocolate. She pressed closer to him and then, as their embrace deepened in intensity, Amber forgot about the menu, forgot about the past, forgot about her fears. Her senses filled instead with an awareness of his closeness, his warmth, his passion, his selfless devotion.

All her life she had waited to be held like this. To be loved. To be safe. To be cherished. It had taken more than forty years, but in that moment, in the sweetness of that kiss, Amber Chaney found trust, and the joy and freedom that could only come with choosing to surrender.

46

Sanctuary

Asheville, North Carolina

December 1996

Diedre sat at her desk in one corner of the living room, lost in thought as thick, wet snowflakes sifted past the glass and gathered on the little, blue spruce tree beyond her window. She'd rather be outside, capturing the wonder of the first snowfall on film, but it would be dark soon, and she had promised to pick out some photos and make reprints for Amber. If they were going to get there in time for Christmas, they really should go in the mail first thing tomorrow morning.

Diedre forced her attention back to the desk and gazed at the photographs spread out before her. It was so hard to decide which ones to choose. There were, of course, the obligatory formal portraits of the wedding party, but she much preferred the casual, spontaneous shots. Colonel Houston with Sam hefted on his shoulders. Sam and Lloser standing next to the life-size bronze sculpture of the two of them. Amber and TwoJoe dancing together at their reception in the barn. Emmaline beaming over the three-tiered cake like a proud mama.

And—her favorite by far—Lloser in his starched tuxedo shirt and bow tie.

An enlargement of the huge llama in formal attire hung on display in Andrew Jorgensen's Seattle gallery, and, according to Andrew, never failed to draw a chuckle from prospective customers. He had suggested that they produce a limited edition of signed and numbered prints; he had already received a dozen requests for the picture. The copy Diedre had sent to Carlene in Asheville was now prominently situated in the front window of Mountain Arts, along with the Tackyville photo series.

Sugarbear roused herself from her bed near the fire, came to the window, and put her paws up on the sill, pushing her nose against the glass. Diedre's eyes wandered to the window again, and with a sigh and a smile, she slid the photos into a manila envelope and gave herself up to the nostalgia of the moment.

Her window. *Her* house. *Her* view of the rounded, layered peaks of the Blue Ridge that spread in a panorama to the east of Asheville. She could almost see Black Mountain from here, and on a clear day she could make out the rocky formations of Craggy Gardens high up on the Parkway.

Diedre McAlister had come home.

Well, almost. She looked around the room, where a few unpacked boxes sat stacked against the bare walls. She had signed the closing papers for this snug two-bedroom house two weeks before, and she wasn't quite moved in yet.

It was a simple, sturdy place—a one-story Arts and Crafts bungalow of brick and stone. Everything Diedre wanted in a house—a few spacious rooms, breathtaking long-range views, and a fireplace that now crackled and popped and emanated the homey scent of wood smoke throughout the house.

The telephone rang, jarring her out of her reverie.

"Hey, it's me," Carlene's voice said. "You busy?"

"Well, hi, Carlene. Not really. I should be, but I just can't seem to concentrate."

"OK if I drop by? I've got a little Christmas surprise for you."

"Absolutely. I was hoping you'd call. I'll have hot chocolate made by the time you get here, and if you're OK with leftovers, we can probably put together some dinner."

No sooner had she hung up the phone than the doorbell rang. Diedre opened the front door to see Carlene standing on the covered front porch, her head and shoulders coated thick with snowflakes. With one hand she balanced a five-foot Christmas tree. "Is that hot chocolate ready yet?"

Diedre began to laugh. "How did you—?"

Carlene held out her free hand and displayed a small cell phone. "Well, are you going to leave a girl stranded out here in the snow all night?"

"Come on in." Diedre stood to one side as Carlene struggled through the door with the tree, shedding her coat one sleeve at a time. Swathed in a bright red velour pants outfit trimmed with fake ermine, she looked for all the world like an enormous Christmas elf. Dangling from her earlobes were small gold sleigh bells, and when she moved, she made a jingling sound that reminded Diedre of one of Sugarbear's furry toys.

"I brought you a tree. I put the base on it, so it's all ready to go."

"I see that." Diedre shook her head. "Carlene, you are a wonderful, brilliant, thoughtful friend. An absolute genius. But I'm not even finished unpacking yet."

"All the more reason you should have a tree. You can't celebrate Christmas in a bare house. I've got lights and decorations in the car."

"Why does this not surprise me?" Diedre helped Carlene situate the tree in the corner next to the window, and they both sank onto the couch in front of the fire. Sugarbear jumped up between them and laid her head on Carlene's lap.

"This is so perfect," Carlene murmured as she leaned back against the sofa pillows and stroked the dog's ears. "Wish I had a fireplace, especially on an evening like this."

They sat in companionable silence for a few minutes, and then Carlene sat up straight. "Oh, I almost forgot. Your surprise!"

"Isn't the tree my surprise?"

"Oh, no, there's more—much more." Carlene shook her head vigorously, and Sugarbear jumped up and began running around the room, nosing in every corner to locate the source of that tinkling sound. "In my briefcase—I left it on the porch."

She got up and went to the door, returning with a bulging black leather case. "I ran into Cliff Rivers in town this afternoon—"

"My lawyer?"

Carlene nodded, and Sugarbear set off on round two of the hunt. "He came in the shop looking for you. Said he was going to call you tomorrow, but since I was on my way over—" She reached into the briefcase, pulled out a file folder, and extended it in Diedre's direction. "Here it is, pal—what you've been waiting for."

Diedre took the file and held it in her hands for a full minute, then slowly opened it. All the emotions of the past few months came flooding back—the pain of finding out the truth about her father, the internal struggles during counseling with Susan, the longing for some way to make sense of what had happened to her. Especially, that glorious moment during Amber's wedding when the way had opened up to her and the answer had become clear.

She felt Carlene's eyes on her as she stared at the cover page:

CHANEY HOUSE
A NOT-FOR-PROFIT MINISTRY OF
THE CECILIA CHANEY TRUST FUND
HEARTSPRING, NORTH CAROLINA

The dream was about to become a reality.

And what a dream it was—a six-million-dollar trust fund, established in Mama's maiden name, to provide refuge and support for women and children victimized by sexual or domestic abuse. A sanctuary. A place of safety and healing. A place of hope.

Cliff Rivers, the attorney who had probated Daddy's will, had done all the legal paperwork, but Chaney House was Diedre's brainchild.

Once Cliff had established the trust fund, she had signed the big house in Heartspring over to the trust. It would be months yet before the revisions were completed and Chaney House would be ready for occupancy, but the work was underway.

"You did it, Diedre." Carlene shifted on the sofa and grinned. "It's really going to happen."

Diedre took a deep breath and began flipping through the pages of the Chaney House proposal. "This is going to be wonderful, Carlene. A refuge for abused women. Psychological counseling. Educational support. Prenatal care and hospital costs for residents who are pregnant. Relocation assistance. Most of all, security. Safety. A new beginning." She paused and shut the folder. "There's only one thing missing."

"What's that?"

"A director. Where on earth are we going to find someone to oversee Chaney House? It will take somebody pretty special—she'll need administrative experience, but she'll also have to know what it means to work with abused women. This job will take more than brains and ability—it will demand a lot of heart, too, and—"

Diedre stopped midsentence as she caught a glimpse of Carlene's expression. That round, elfin face had drawn up in an enormous grin. "Let me guess—you know just the person for the job."

Carlene nodded smugly. "I do. She came in the shop this morning." She reached into the front pocket of her briefcase and came up with a crumpled paper napkin. "We had lunch together. Here's her number."

Diedre took the napkin and scrutinized it. "Sandi Ricewood. Who is she?"

"A friend. A very good friend."

"If she's such a good friend, how come I've never met her?" Diedre chuckled.

"We got to know each other while you were away at Duke. She's just moved back to Asheville from Charlotte—worked for Rape Crisis Center for years, and loved it. But she always had a different kind of dream. A dream to—are you ready for this?—" Carlene leaned forward and lowered her voice dramatically. "To establish a series of sanctuary houses for abused women."

Diedre narrowed her eyes. "Tell me you didn't lure her back here from Charlotte on the promise of this job?"

"No, she came back on her own, I promise." Carlene got up and went to the fireplace, laying on another log and stirring up the embers with a brass-handled poker. "But you do have an interview with her. Tomorrow." When the fire was blazing satisfactorily, she settled down on the sofa again and stretched her feet toward the warmth. "And mark my words you *will* hire her."

"You sound pretty sure of yourself." Diedre shut the file folder and tapped it against Carlene's knee. "What makes this Sandi Ricewood so perfect?"

Carlene turned her full-moon face in Diedre's direction and grinned broadly. "She's just like me," she chuckled. "Only better."

Diedre let her hands linger in the warm, soapy water and stared out the kitchen window. Here, on the back side of the house, the land sloped up sharply into woods. Between two trees, she could see a crescent moon tilt from the clouds to pour a wash of yellow light and dark blue shadow across the snowy ground.

Behind her, in the living room, a Christmas CD played softly on the stereo, and in counterpoint to the music, Diedre could hear the gentle tinkling of Carlene's sleigh-bell earrings as she strung lights and hung decorations on the tree. She smiled to herself.

"Hey, what about that hot chocolate?" Carlene called through the doorway.

Diedre laughed. "Kind of demanding, aren't you? You just had leftover meat loaf and leftover chicken casserole and leftover vegetable soup."

"And it was all great—my compliments to Chef Hodgepodge,"

Carlene yelled back. "But I can't decorate a tree without hot chocolate. It's against the law."

"It's coming." Diedre drained the sink, dried her hands, and retrieved two steaming mugs from the microwave. When she rounded the doorway, she stopped and stared.

The tree in the corner, transformed with tiny, white lights and silver garland and sparkling spun-glass icicles, illuminated the room with an ethereal light. Carlene, in her red velour and faux ermine, stood beside it holding Sugarbear, who was decked out in a pair of velvet reindeer antlers.

"Come look." Carlene parked Sugarbear on the floor and motioned to Diedre. "Your first Christmas tree in your new home."

Diedre set the mugs of chocolate on the coffee table and went to stand beside her friend. "It's beautiful."

"Look closer."

Diedre looked. On one branch, a little red birdhouse with WALL DRUG in block letters on the green roof. Above it and to one side, a diminutive corn-husk angel without a face. A small plastic version of the Jolly Green Giant.

And on the top, just below the angel, a miniature clay sculpture of a llama wearing a top hat and a tuxedo.

Diedre began to laugh. "Where on earth did that come from? As if I didn't know . . ."

"Amber sent it as a surprise. She wanted to be here with you—in spirit, if not in body." Carlene put an arm around Diedre and squeezed her shoulder. "Look outside. It's snowing again."

Diedre's gaze went to the window, where the tree cast a soft, golden light beyond the glass. Onto every tree and bush and blade of grass, the flakes sifted down—gently, soundlessly. At the edges of her consciousness, she heard the quiet strains of the familiar carol:

"How silently, how silently, the wondrous gift is given . . ."

Diedre smiled, and the snow continued to descend. Like a blessing. A sacrament. A benediction.

Epilogue

CHANEY HOUSE

HEARTSPRING, NORTH CAROLINA

SPRING 1998

Diedre paused on the wide stone porch of the house where she had grown up and let her eyes roam over the familiar vistas of the Blue Ridge. A fresh spring breeze blew in from the mountains—a wind that swept away the old confusing memories, a breath that brought a resurrection of spirit after the long waiting time in the tomb.

Close at her side, Vesta Shelby stood with one arm linked through hers. Behind them, Carlene talked in animated tones with Sandi Ricewood, administrator of Chaney House.

"I declares, baby," Vesta was saying, "whoever come up with this idea of retirement must be some lazy kind of so-and-so. Took 'bout two weeks 'til I'd seen every blessed murder that Jessica Fletcher ever solved. I nearbout turned into a vegetable, just sittin' around on my hind parts."

Diedre squeezed Vesta's hand and smiled. "So you like working here at Chaney House?"

"Like it? Hon, I feel like I got one foot in heaven already. Look down there. What do you see?"

Diedre's eyes swept across the vast expanse of yard, hidden from the isolated road by a high hedge and security gates. From one of the branches of the big oak tree hung a swing, and under the watchful eyes of their mothers, three small children gathered around it, taking turns pushing each other. "I see children playing."

Vesta shook her head. "Not me. I see hope." She pointed toward a young woman in blue jeans and a purple jacket. "See that gal? Name's Kathleen. Come to us straight outta the hospital—her second husband beat her near to death when she caught him doing horrible, unforgivable things to her little girl. The poor baby, Crystal—that's her on the swing—wouldn't speak a single word the whole first month she was here. Now look at her."

Diedre watched as the child squealed playfully, tussling with her friends over possession of the swing. A normal, happy little girl, unconcerned with anything except who would get the next turn. There was no sign of the dark pain she carried, or the fear. For the moment, she was safe.

"Every day, I look around me," Vesta went on, turning to gaze into Diedre's eyes, "and what I see is people gettin' a second chance at life. And not just them, neither." She waved a hand toward the residents, and a light came on in her eyes. "I'm gettin' a second chance, too— maybe what I'm doin' here can make up for all them years I missed with my CeCe."

A pretty teenage girl with long blonde hair left the cluster of women on the lawn and came toward the porch. "That there's Anna Louise," Vesta whispered. "She's fourteen. Social Services sent her to us when her uncle—"

She paused as Anna Louise approached. "How you doin', baby?"

The girl stopped to receive a hug and a kiss on the cheek from Vesta. "Doing good, Vesta. Except for a little morning sickness, real good." She pushed her hair out of her eyes and sent a brief, embarrassed smile in Diedre's direction. "Thanks," she said, ducking her head. "I'd be on the street if it wasn't for this place." She pushed past them and went into the house.

Diedre watched her go and stood in silence for a moment staring out over miles of mountains.

"How 'bout you, sweetie?" Vesta asked softly, reaching to take her hand. "You doin' all right?"

"I miss Amber," Diedre admitted, "but yes, I'm doing fine." She almost said, *I've finished my counseling and found my peace,* but something stopped her. For her, as for all these women, healing was an ongoing process, not a one-time event. At this moment, she felt more complete and whole than she ever thought possible. But she also realized that there would be other moments—loose ends to tie up, emotional left-overs to contain. Still, she had hope, and a faith that had been put through the fire and come out stronger on the other side.

They had just turned to go into the house when a commotion on the lawn caught their attention. Little Crystal stood tugging at her mother's hands, squealing, "Twirl me around, Mommy!"

Diedre stopped in her tracks. She pressed close to Vesta, and as she stood there watching, tears began streaming silently down her cheeks.

"Whirl me faster, Mommy. Faster!"

Faster they went, until Crystal's little feet lifted from the ground. She began to giggle, her hair streaming in the wind, her childish voice rising with exhilaration. "We're flying, Mommy. We're flying like birds in the sky!"

Her mother laughed, too. "Yes we are, honey."

"Don't let go!" the little girl yelled.

"I won't," her mother shouted back. "I won't let go!"

They went on circling until both of them were dizzy, then collapsed in a giddy heap on the grass. The mother drew her tiny daughter into a fierce embrace and held her there, panting.

A face materialized in Diedre's mind, so real she almost believed she could reach out and touch it. Amber's face. Her sister. Her mother. Two thousand miles away, and yet as close as her own heartbeat. She could almost read the expression in those eyes, almost hear the words that echoed in her soul: *I'll never let go. No matter how far apart we are, I'll never let go of you again.*

Diedre blinked back the tears, then gazed once more toward the laughing child on the grassy lawn. "Keep flying, little one," she whispered. "Glide on the current of your Maker's breath. Fly into freedom, and into grace. Fly, fly, and never look down."

And like a bird on a mended wing, her own heart soared, propelled by a hand she felt but could not see.

Acknowledgments

Many people have contributed their knowledge, expertise, and personal life experiences to the creation of this book.

Special appreciation goes first to the cast of extraordinary women who have shared their stories of pain and healing with me. Their honesty, anger, power, and faith have enlightened me and sensitized me both to the presence of evil in the world and God's ability to bring blessing out of brokenness. Thank you. I love and honor you all.

I also owe a debt of gratitude to the following people who aided immeasurably in my research for this novel:

Catherine, John, and Andrew Ahl, of Poulsbo, Washington, who welcomed me into their home on Hood Canal, squired me all over Kitsap County, and gave me a wealth of ideas for the portions of this novel set in Washington State

Sandi Rice, of OUR VOICE in Asheville, North Carolina, who provided invaluable information and inspiration, and whose friendship I value immensely

Nora Robillard, whose tireless research into the law made my work infinitely easier

Rev. Dr. Gary Gundersen of the Interfaith Health Project, who reminded me that buried seeds of faith will sprout again

Rev. Dr. Marie Fortune, founder of the Center for the Prevention of Sexual and Domestic Violence in Seattle, whose workshop on "Faith, Justice, and Healing" helped shape my perspectives and give me renewed hope for the future

A Word from the Author

The Amber Photograph has been a difficult and challenging novel to write. Readers have asked if this novel is autobiographical, if this is my story.

It is not my story.

It is, however, the story of countless real-life women who have faced the terror and shame of violence and abuse, and who continue to deal with the aftereffects of that abuse on a daily basis. Diedre and Amber are fictional characters, but as any good writer will tell you, fiction must be grounded in reality. And the reality of what these two characters experienced is all too familiar—in our homes, in our churches, and in society at large.

Silence, as Amber discovered, protects only the perpetrator. If you or someone you love has been sexually abused, battered, or otherwise violated, please call the number listed below. Experienced counselors are on hand twenty-four hours a day to provide confidential hot line help free of charge.

RAINN
(Rape, Abuse, and Incest National Network)
635-B Pennsylvania Avenue SE
Washington, DC 20003
1-800-656-HOPE

A portion of this book's proceeds will be donated to
OUR VOICE
(Victim Outreach, Intervention, Counseling, and Education)
Asheville, North Carolina
and
Center for the Prevention of Sexual and Domestic Violence
Seattle, Washington.

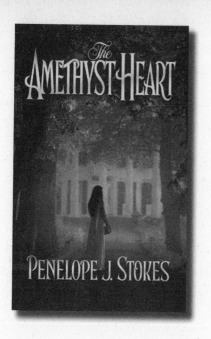

The Amethyst Heart

When she discovers her dissolute son has designs to sell her ancestral home out from under her, Miss Amethyst Noble—ninety-three years old and as sharp as ever—devises a scheme of her own. It involves an antique brooch, a difficult teenaged great-granddaughter, and a 140-year family heritage worth fighting for.

The Blue Bottle Club

Faced with the grim realities of the 1929 Depression, four young friends write their hopes and dreams on pieces of paper and stuff them into a cobalt blue bottle. Sixty-five years later, a reporter finds the dusty, forgotten bottle in an attic. Her quest to interview the now-elderly women results in some surprising revelations about their pasts and the reporter's future.

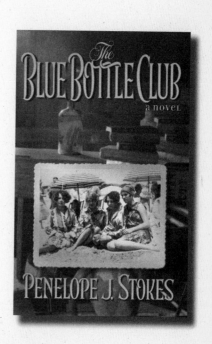

 WORD PUBLISHING
www.wordpublishing.com